In praise of

ELLEN GILCHRIST

"Gilchrist is one of the finest writers of a rare species: the happy story." — Susan Salter Reynolds, *Los Angeles Times Book Review*

"To say that Ellen Gilchrist can write is to say that Placido Domingo can sing. All you need to do is listen." — Jonathan Yardley, *Washington Post*

"Ellen Gilchrist delights in reexploring the same world again and again. . . . She is an Attila of a romantic who, as a southerner, a woman, and a poet, chooses her weapons from a well-stocked arsenal." — Julia Glass, *Chicago Tribune*

"There is such wisdom and strength and optimism in Gilchrist's writing. At her best, the prose is so clear it all but forces the reader toward clarity. . . . She has an uncanny ability to impart both the joy and the considerable brutality of romantic love and family relationships. . . . In the end, almost all of Gilchrist's stories are about hope, our ability to triumph in ways large and, mostly, small." — Julia Reed, *Vogue*

"Few writers are as adept at spinning funny, slyly insightful tales that radiate outward like tiny satellites, orbiting a fictional universe that mirrors the more unpredictable and tellingly human moments in our own." — Katherine Dieckmann, *New York Times Book Review*

NORA JANE

Date: 3/19/12

FIC GILCHRIST
Gilchrist, Ellen,
Nora Jane : a life in stories

ALSO BY ELLEN GILCHRIST

In the Land of Dreamy Dreams
The Annunciation
Victory Over Japan
Drunk with Love
Falling Through Space
The Anna Papers
Light Can Be Both Wave and Particle
I Cannot Get You Close Enough
Net of Jewels
Starcarbon
Anabasis
The Age of Miracles
Rhoda
The Courts of Love
Sarah Conley
Flights of Angels
The Cabal and Other Stories
Collected Stories
I, Rhoda Manning, Go Hunting with My Daddy
The Writing Life

NORA JANE

A LIFE IN STORIES

ELLEN GILCHRIST

BACK BAY BOOKS

Little, Brown and Company

NEW YORK   BOSTON

Back Bay Books / Little, Brown and Company
Time Warner Book Group
1271 Avenue of the Americas, New York, NY 10020
Visit our Web site at www.twbookmark.com

First Edition: August 2005

The characters and events in this book are fictitious. Any similarity to real
persons, living or dead, is coincidental and not intended by the author.

"The Panther," copyright © 1982 by Stephen Mitchell, from *The Selected Poetry of Rainer
Maria Rilke* by Rainer Maria Rilke, translated by Stephen Mitchell. Used by permission of
Random House, Inc.

Library of Congress Cataloging-in-Publication Data

Gilchrist, Ellen.
   Nora Jane : a life in stories / Ellen Gilchrist. — 1st ed.
       p. cm.
   ISBN 0-316-05838-6
       1. Harwood, Nora Jane (Fictitious character) — Fiction.   2. Women — United States —
   Fiction.   3. New Orleans (La.) — Fiction.   4. Berkeley (Calif.) — Fiction.   I. Title.

PS3557.I34258A6   2005
813'.54 — dc22   2004060773

10   9   8   7   6   5   4   3   2

Q-FF

Book design by Robert G. Lowe

Printed in the United States of America

For Molly Giles, friend, colleague, teacher

CONTENTS

NORA JANE

THE BLUE HOUSE

NORA JANE'S GRANDMOTHER lived in a blue frame house on the corner of Laurel and Webster streets. It was there that Nora Jane was happy. There was a swing on the porch and a morning glory vine growing on a trellis. In April azaleas bloomed all around the edges of the porch, white and pink and red azaleas, blue morning glories, the fragrant white Confederate jasmine, red salvia and geraniums and the mysterious elephant ears, their green veins so like the ones on Nora Jane's grandmother's hands. Nora Jane hated the veins because they meant her grandmother was old and would die. Would die like her father had died, vanish, not be there anymore, and then she would be alone with only her mother to live with seven days a week.

"Let me set the table for you," she said to her grandmother, waking beside her in the bed. "Let me cook you breakfast. I want you to eat an egg."

"Oh, honey lamb," her grandmother replied, and reached over and found her glasses and put them on, the better to see the beautiful little girl, the better to be happy with the child beside her. "We will cook it together. Then we'll see about the mirlitons. You can take them to Langenstein's today. They said they would buy all that you had."

"Then I'd better hurry." Nora Jane got out of bed. If she was going to take the mirlitons to Langenstein's she wanted to do it early so she wouldn't run into any of her friends from Sacred Heart. She was the only girl at Sacred Heart so poor she had to sell vegetables to

Langenstein's. Still, they had not always been poor. Her grandfather had been a judge. Her father had gone to West Point. Her grandmother had sung grand opera all up and down the coast and auditioned for the Met. She kissed her grandmother on the cheek and swung her long legs out of the bed and began to search for her clothes. "You cook breakfast then," she said. "I'll go pick the mirlitons before it gets too hot."

She put on her shorts and shirt and found her sandals and wandered out into the backyard to pick the mirlitons from the mirliton vines.

A neighbor was in the yard next door. Mr. Edison Angelo. He leaned over the fence. "How's everything going, Nora Jane?" he asked. "How's your grandmother?"

"She's feeling fine," Nora Jane said. "She's fine now. She's out of bed. She can do anything she likes."

Nora Jane bent over the mirliton vines. They were beautiful, sticky and fragrant, climbing their trellis of chicken wire. The rich burgundy red fruit hung on its fragile stems, fell off into Nora Jane's hands at the slightest touch. She gathered a basketful, placing them carefully on top of each other so as not to bruise them. Mirlitons are a delicacy in New Orleans. The dark red rind is half an inch thick, to protect the pulp and seeds from the swarming insects of the tropics, for mirlitons are a tropical fruit, brought to New Orleans two hundred years ago by sailors from the Caribbean. Some winters in New Orleans are too cold for mirlitons and the fruit is small and scanty. This had been a warm winter, however, and the mirliton vines were thick with fruit. Nora Jane bent over her work. Her head of curly dark black hair caught the morning sun, the sun caressed her. She was a beautiful child who looked so much like her dead father that it broke her mother's heart and made her drink. It made her grandmother glad. Nora Jane's father had been her oldest son. She thought God had given Nora Jane to her to make up for losing him. Nora Jane's grandmother was a deeply religious woman who had been given to ecstatic states when she was young. It never occurred to her to rail at God or blame him for things. She thought of God as a fallback position in times of trouble. She thought of God as solace, patience, wisdom, forgiveness, compensation.

Nora Jane's mother had a darker meaner view. She thought God and other people were to blame for everything that went wrong. She thought they had gotten together to kill her beautiful black-haired husband and she was paying them back by staying inside and drinking herself to death. Still, it wasn't her fault she was weak. Her mother had been weak before her and her mother before that. It was their habit to be weak.

Nora Jane's grandmother came from a line of women who had a habit of being strong. One of them had come to New Orleans from France as a casket girl, had sailed across the Atlantic Ocean when she was only sixteen years old, carrying all her possessions in a little casket and when she arrived had refused to marry the man to whom she was assigned. She had married a Welshman instead, a man who had been on the boat as a steward. Each generation of women was told this story in Nora Jane's grandmother's family and so they believed they were strong women with strong genes and acted accordingly. When she was about four years old Nora Jane had looked at the strong story and the weak story and decided to be strong. It was the year her father died and her grandmother sat in the swing on her porch and watched the morning glory vines open and close and the sun rise and fall and believed that God did not hate her even if he had allowed her son to die in a stupid war. Many of the men who fought with him had written her letters and she read them out loud to Nora Jane. One young man, whose name was Fraser, came and stayed for five weeks and painted the outside of the house a fresher, brighter blue and put a new floor in the kitchen of the house. Every day he sat on the porch with Nora Jane's grandmother as the sun went down and talked about the place where he lived. A place called Nebraska. When all the painting was done and the furniture put back in the kitchen, he kissed Nora Jane and her grandmother good-bye and went off to see his own family. After he was gone Nora Jane and her grandmother would talk about him. "Where's Fraser gone?" Nora Jane would ask.

"He has gone to Nebraska," her grandmother would answer. "He went to try to find his wife."

"Where's his wife?"

"He doesn't know. She got tired of waiting for him."

"She's sad, like Momma, isn't she?"

"I think so, some people get sad."

"But not us, do we?"

"Let's walk over to the park," her grandmother said, and got up from the swing. "Those Emperor geese are dying to see you. They're waiting for you to bring them some bread."

"Then do I have to go home?"

"Sometime you do. Your mother doesn't like it if you stay here all the time."

"I'll go tomorrow. In two days I'll go back over there."

"We'll see. Put on your shoes. Those geese are waiting for you by the bridge."

Of course sooner or later she would have to go back to her mother's house and watch her mother cry. Although the older she got the less she had to put up with it. Her mother's house was seven blocks from her grandmother's house. Her mother's house was in the three hundred block of Webster Street and her grandmother's house was in the five hundred block of Henry Clay. By the time she was six years old Nora Jane was allowed to walk from her grandmother's house to her mother's house anytime she wanted to as long as the sun was up. She knew every house and yard and porch and tree between the three hundred block of Webster Street and the five hundred block of Henry Clay. She knew which fences made the best sound when she ran a stick along the railings. She knew which dogs were mean. She knew which people got up early and which ones were sleepyheads. She knew who took the *Times-Picayune* and who did not. When the golden rain trees bloomed and when the magnolia blossoms opened. Hello, Nora Jane, everyone would say. How you keeping? How's everything with you?

Nora Jane carried the basket of mirlitons up the wooden steps to the kitchen. Ever since she was a small child she had sat on those steps to dream. She dreamed of elves and fairies, of ballet dresses and ballet shoes, of silk and velvet and operas and plays. There were photographs of her grandmother in operas in a book in the house. Photographs of long ago before her grandmother's face got old. In one photograph her grandmother was wearing a crown.

Nora Jane paused on the stairs, resting the basket of mirlitons on the rail. A fat yellow jacket buzzed past the door, a golden Monarch beat against a window, a blue jay flew down and sat upon a yard chair. Nora Jane walked on up the stairs and into the kitchen. It was seven o'clock in the morning. Already the sun was high. It was time to go to Langenstein's. "I'm going right now," she called to her grandmother. "I'll eat breakfast when I get back."

"Have a piece of toast then. Take it with you."

"I'm fine. I want to get these over there while they're fresh." She kissed her grandmother on the cheek and walked out through the rooms. It was a shotgun house with one room right behind the other. Her grandmother let her leave. She knew why Nora Jane wanted to get to Langenstein's so early and she approved of it. It was the same reason she swept her porch at dawn. Ladies didn't do housework. Ladies didn't sell vegetables to the grocery store.

Nora Jane proceeded down the street, down Webster to Magazine and over to Calhoun, past Prytania, Camp, Coliseum, Perrier and Pitt to

Garfield, past the Jewish cemetery and into the parking lot of Langenstein's, which is the richest grocery store in New Orleans, perhaps the richest grocery store in the world. A few ladies were already parking their cars and going in to wheel small old-fashioned carts through the narrow aisles. Past shelves of exotic imported foods and delicatessen items, past chicory coffee and avocados and artichokes and stuffed crabs and seafood gumbo and imported crackers and candy, past wine vinegar and Roquefort cheese and crème glacée and crawfish bisque and crawfish étouffée and potage tortue and lobster and shrimp ratatouille.

An old lady was being helped from her car by her chauffeur, a young woman in a tennis dress bounced by with a can of coffee in her hand, a fat white cat walked beneath a crepe myrtle tree, a mockingbird swooped down to pester it. Nora Jane ignored all that. She hurried across the parking lot and into the office and found Chef Roland at his desk. He was a man who loved the world. He loved food and God and music and all seven of his children and the idea of Food and God and Music and Children. He cooked all day and listened to his employees' troubles and then went home and listened to his wife's troubles and drank wine and talked on the telephone to his brother who was a Benedictine monk in Pennsylvania and wrote long impassioned letters to his brother who was a Jesuit in Cincinnati. Dear Alphonse, the letters would begin. Put down your apostasy and your rage. Please write to Maurice. Maurice longs to hear from you.

It concerned a religious schism that had split Chef Roland's family. For seven years his younger brothers had battled over the matter of birth control. Look at little Nora Jane, Chef Roland told himself now. No family, only one old grandmother and a mother better left unsaid. No brothers or sisters or aunts. A family which has died out. This one little blossom on the vine.

He got up from his desk and wrapped the little girl in his arms and kissed her on the top of her head. "Ah, these mirlitons," he said. "What a casserole I will make of these. Is this all? Only one basketful? You will bring me more?"

"I'll bring some more over later. If mother gets up. We wanted to bring you some early in case you needed them."

"How old are you now, Nora Jane?"

"I'm fourteen. I'll be fifteen pretty soon. This summer. You like them? You think they're beautiful?"

"Magnificent. Always your grandmother's vegetables are magnificent. I want the asparagus this year. All that she can spare." He was writing out a receipt for her to cash at the checkout stand. He knew why she was in a hurry. The Whittingtons were proud. The grandmother had sung with the opera. His father had heard her sing. He handed the receipt to her. She folded it and stuck it in the pocket of her shorts. Such a lovely child, he thought, a lovely child.

"You will come and work for me this summer?" he asked. "I will teach you to cook for me. You think it over, huh?"

"If I can," she said. "I might help the sisters with the camp at Sacred Heart. How much can you pay?"

"Four fifteen an hour and you will learn to cook. That's worth something, even for a pretty girl like you, huh?"

"I know how already. Grandmother taught me. We made a Charlotte Rousse for her birthday." Nora Jane giggled. "And we made an angel cake but it fell, because the stove is old. We need a new stove but we don't want to waste our money on it."

"I will call your grandmother and speak to her. She will tell you to come and work for me. Better than little children all day. I'll teach you a trade."

"Okay," Nora Jane said politely. "I'll think it over. I have to go now," she added. "Is there someone up front to cash this?"

"Yes, they're open. Run along then. But let me know."

"I will." She left the office and went into the store, down between the aisles of imported foods to the checkout stand. She collected three dollars and seventeen cents and put it in her pocket, then she started home, up the street of crushed-up oyster shells, past a line of azalea bushes that grew out onto the sidewalk. A black and white cat moved lazily along beside her, then disappeared into the open door of the Prytania Street Liquor Store. I better go by Momma's and get some clothes, Nora Jane decided. If I go now she won't start calling Grandmother's all day and driving us crazy.

Chef Roland stared down at his desk. Poor little girl, he was thinking. Of course she doesn't want to come work in the deli, but it's all I have to offer her. Poor baby, poor little thing.

The phone was ringing. Chef Roland pushed a button and answered it. It was his brother Maurice calling from Pennsylvania.

"So you're back from Rome," Chef Roland began. "Well, did you tell them what I told you to tell them? Did you, Maurice? Did you or not? Answer my question."

"I want to come visit you when I get through here," Maurice said. "Can I come down for a few days? I want to talk with you, Roland, bury the hatchet, smoke the peace pipe."

"What did you tell them, Maurice? Did you tell him what I said or not?"

"What's wrong, Roland, how are you in such a bad mood so early in the day? Is Betty all right? Are the children okay?"

"I just had a visit from the daughter of Leland Whittington, your old schoolmate that died fighting for the pope in 'Nam, Maurice. It broke my heart so early in the morning. Poor little fatherless thing. Poor little girl."

"No one with Leland's heart and will could be an object of pity. God, he was a beautiful man."

"Leland is dead, Maurice, and I want to know if you told the pope what I told you to tell him. It's the modern world. We have to move with it or be responsible for all this sadness. It's our fault, it's on our shoulders. The edict was preposterous."

"I'll be there this afternoon. Is that all right?"

"Of course it's all right. I'll tell everyone you're coming."

"I have to go now. We have prayers."

"Pray for sanity," Chef Roland said. "Pray to have some goddamn common sense."

Nora Jane crossed Prytania and walked down Camp to Magazine, then turned and went down Webster Street into the Irish Channel. The sun was higher now, people were coming out onto their porches, opening their Saturday newspapers, people jogged by in jogging suits, rode by on bicycles headed for the park. Maybe she won't be up yet, Nora Jane thought. And I can just grab some clothes and leave a note. She's getting worse. She really is. She's worse than she was at Mardi Gras or on their anniversary. Well, forget that. It doesn't matter. It isn't my fault. Remember Sister Katherine said never to think it's my fault. It's not my fault. It's not my fault.

Nora Jane passed her godmother Leanie's house, hurried by so she wouldn't get stopped and have to talk. She hurried on down the street and turned into the yard of her mother's white frame house. It wasn't a bad house. Only Francine never cleaned it up right and it smelled like furniture polish and cigarettes. It smells like a bar, Nora Jane decided. That's what it smells like.

"Nora Jane, is that you?" Her mother was up, walking around in a bathrobe, her hair tied back with a string. "Oh, honey, I just called your grandmother and no one answered. I was so lonely. I had bad dreams all night. Oh, I'm so glad you're home. Look, could you go down to the corner and get me a package of cigarettes?"

"I just came by to get some clothes. I have to go to school today. They have a special day."

"No one told me about it."

"I'm in a hurry. Didn't Grandmother tell you? Why didn't she answer the phone? Well, I guess she was in the yard." Nora Jane swept past her mother and went into her room and began to fill the basket with clothes, socks and underwear and cotton shirts and a dress for Sunday. She threw the things into the empty basket. Her mother stood in the door watching her.

"You won't go get me some cigarettes?"

"I don't have time. I have to hurry."

"I want you back here tonight. I can't stay here at night by myself."

"I'll come back if I can." Nora Jane threw one last pair of underpants into the jumble of clothes and turned to face her mother. "I have to go now. I haven't had any breakfast. I went to sell the mirlitons at Langenstein's. I'm going. I'm starving."

"You could eat here. I'll fix things for you."

"Like what? Some rotten oranges, like last time. I'm not eating out of that kitchen until you get someone to kill the roaches. I told you that. And I'm not sleeping here. I don't want to listen to you cry." Nora Jane passed her mother in the bedroom doorway. Her mother reached for her, almost had her in her arms. "Let go of me," Nora Jane said. "Don't hold me. I have to go." She pushed her mother away and walked back through the house and out onto the porch and down the steps. Her mother followed her.

Nora Jane stopped to inspect her broken bike. "I thought you were going to get my bike fixed," she said.

"I couldn't do it, honey. There wasn't any money."

"Okay, well, I'm off." She switched the basket to the other arm, opened the gate and struck off in the direction of the park. She had decided to walk back through the park to see what was going on. There was always something happening in Audubon Park on Saturday morning. Besides, there was a grove of birch trees Nora Jane liked to walk through for luck. Her grandmother had told her it was a copy of a sacred grove of trees in Greece where the philosophers had lived.

Nora Jane entered the park at Prytania and walked through the lucky grove of trees and over to the flower clock. A race was forming. Forty or fifty people in their running clothes were milling around the fountain and the clock. A young man was doing T'ai Chi beside the fountain. Kids rode by on bikes. Suddenly, Nora Jane was embarrassed to be there carrying a basketful of clothes. She hurried out of the park and back toward her grandmother's house. I'm so hungry, she told herself. I shouldn't have waited so long to eat.

She felt bad now. She was hungry and it made her cold. She hurried back down Henry Clay and turned into her grandmother's yard. A radio was playing, much too loudly. It was WTUL, Leontyne Price singing *Tosca*. "Vissi d'arte" from *Tosca*. That was wrong. Her grandmother never played music loudly enough to be heard in the yard. Of course, sometimes she might sing along with an aria and then her voice might reach the street, but never for long, never long enough to bother other people.

This radio was too loud. It made no sense. Nora Jane dropped the basket on the porch and went on in. There was no one in the living room. In the dining room where the radio sat upon a shelf, a dust cloth was lying on the floor. That was also wrong. Her grandmother did not leave dust cloths lying on the floor. "Grandmother," Nora Jane called. Then she looked into the bedroom. Her grandmother was lying on the floor, crumpled up on the rug beside the bed. The beautiful voice of Leontyne Price continued with the aria. Nora Jane moved like water into the bedroom and knelt down upon the floor. She covered her grandmother's body with her own and began to weep.

★ ★ ★

A neighbor found them. She had heard the music and begun to worry. April is the cruellest month, the neighbor said to herself, for she was an English teacher. Breeding lilacs out of the dead land.

"Oh, honey," the neighbor said, holding the weeping child. "I'm so sorry. So very sorry."

"I can't live with my mother," Nora Jane said. "I can't do it. Where will I live?"

"Maybe you can," the neighbor said. "We all have to do things we don't want to do." She tried to lift the child, to make her stand up.

Nora Jane lay back down upon her grandmother's body. The sirens were making their way down Henry Clay. The noise of the sirens filled the air.

Later that afternoon they came to take the body away. Two men in a station wagon wrapped the grandmother's body in a sheet of canvas and carried her out of the living room and down the stairs and put her into the back of a wood-paneled Oldsmobile station wagon and drove off down Henry Clay as if they were going to a ball game. So that's it, Nora Jane thought, pulling a morning glory pod off the vine and tearing it to pieces with her fingers. That's all there is to it, just like I knew it would be. She's gone and this will be gone too.

She tore some more buds off the vine and squeezed them in her hand and wouldn't let anyone talk to her and went out into the backyard and stood by the mirliton arbor wondering what part of the opera was playing when her grandmother died. I could go in there and find the record and put it on but they probably wouldn't let me, she thought. She climbed the stile that led over her grandmother's back fence into Mr. Edison Angelo's yard and went out that way and over to the Loyola University library and checked out the phonograph record and went into a booth to play it for herself. It was a very old and scratchy record from the collection of Mr. Irvine Isaacs, Junior. Leontyne Price with the Rome Opera House Orchestra under the direction of Oliviero Fabritiis, the same recording Nora Jane had learned to sing the opera from. She sat in the booth and sang the opera with Miss Price and cried as she sang. Nora Jane had inherited her grandmother's voice. People acted so funny when they heard her voice that Nora Jane had decided long ago to keep it to herself. It was a promise she managed to keep most of her life. For almost all of her life she only sang to people she loved or people she wanted to solace or amuse. For nearly all the years of her life she managed to keep her voice to herself.

II

OF COURSE, NOW EVERYTHING had to change. After the funeral, after the grievers and the mourners were gone, after the sisters left and her mother was still sober, had been sober for four days, had sworn to Sister Katherine to stop drinking if she wanted Nora Jane to stay. Had settled for a bottle of pills instead, had agreed to put away the bottle if she could have the pills and was in her bedroom now, like a zombie against her pillows with the radio on low, playing jazz. After all of that Nora Jane looked around the house to see what she could do. I could clean it up, she decided. I could call that damn Francine and make her get over here. Nora Jane searched in her mother's address book, found the number and got Francine on the phone.

"I'm sorry about your grandmother," Francine began. "The Lord gives and the Lord taketh away."

"Forget that, Francine. I need you to come and help me clean this place up. I can't live in this mess. Bring your husband's truck. We're going to throw some things away."

"Right now?"

"Right now. I will pay you three dollars an hour if you bring the truck. Can you come? I'll get somebody else if you won't." Nora Jane sniffed, waited, began to get mad. If there was anybody who made her madder than her mother, it was Francine. "I don't care if you do or not. Say if you will."

"I'll be there. Soon as I can get on a uniform."

"Bring the truck."

"If I can get hold of Norris."

By the time Francine got there Nora Jane had emptied the kitchen cabinets of rotten potatoes and empty bottles and half damp grocery sacks. She had filled the grocery sacks with broken cups and half-used boxes of cereal. She had reamed out the kitchen of her mother's house. And called the Orkin man. "I have money to pay you with," she told him. "If you come right now and spray us with everything you've got."

By the time her mother woke up the dining room rug was on the truck and a broken chair and stacks of magazines. The living room rug was rolled up on the porch to go to the cleaners and Francine was mopping the wooden floors with Spic and Span. "What's going on?" her mother asked, coming out into the living room, still wearing the dress she had worn to the funeral. "What's going on? My God, Francine, what are you doing?"

"We're cleaning up this house," Nora Jane said. "Go back to sleep. I won't live in a pigpen. The Orkin people are coming in a minute."

"Where's the rug?"

"We're throwing the dining-room rug away. I won't live in a house with a rug like that. And this one's going to the cleaners. Francine's going to take it on the truck."

Nora Jane's mother sat down in a chair. Her little navy blue and white print dress hung in waves around her legs, her collar was awry. The Valium was in charge. She was powerless in the face of Nora Jane's rage. Powerless in the face of anything. She pulled her legs up onto the chair. "Am I in the way?" she asked. "Do you mind if I sit here?"

Later, in the late afternoon, after Nora Jane had paid Francine her wages and the kitchen and dining room and Nora Jane's bedroom had been cleaned to her satisfaction and the Orkin man had come and sprayed so much Diazinon and Maxforce and Orthene around the house that even with the windows open it was hard to breathe, Nora Jane and her mother dressed in cotton dresses and walked down the street to eat oyster loaves for supper at Narcisse Marsoudet. "It looks wonderful," her mother said. "I can't believe you did all that in one day. I can't believe she's gone. Now you are the only one, Nora Jane. The last of the Whittingtons."

"Don't talk about it," Nora Jane said. "I don't want to think about it anymore."

"I'm not going to drink, my darling honey. I'm going tomorrow to the meetings that they have. I won't ever drink again, you can depend on that."

"I want to get an air conditioner," Nora Jane said. "Mr. Biggs said there would be enough money when they sold her house. They said I could have enough for anything I'd need. And a new refrigerator. I can't stand to have that old thing anymore." They passed Perlis' Department Store and turned down Magazine to the café.

"I won't drink anymore, honey. You can depend on that." Her mother caught sight of herself in the store window. How pale she seemed, how slight beside her striding daughter. It seemed impossible, the day, the world, the store window and its terrible reflection. The huge old live-oak tree beside them and its roots. Her terrible mean teenage daughter, the death of Lydia and the sisters saying terrible things to her, the gaping hole in the earth and Lydia lowered into it, only six, seven, eight hours before, her dining room rug from Persia thrown away and nothing to take its place, poison everywhere.

"You might not," Nora Jane said, continuing to look straight ahead. "I'll believe it when I see it."

No sooner were they in the restaurant than it began. A white-coated waiter with a towel over his arm came to take their orders. "I'd like a Seven-Up," Nora Jane said. "And a glass of water."

"A glass of white wine," her mother added. "A Chablis. But anything will do. Your house wine will be fine."

"Just a glass. One little glass." She looked at Nora Jane. "One little glass with dinner."

"No, you don't," Nora Jane said. "Don't do this to me."

"Would you like a little while?" the waiter asked. He stepped back. He'd been through this plenty of times before and he wasn't in the mood to go through it again. My God, between a mother and a child. This girl doing it to her mother. What little beasts they were. The waiter knew he would never do that to himself. Load himself down with parasites, little beasts and bitches like this frowning child. Jesus, the waiter thought. I can't believe people do that to themselves.

"Just bring our drinks," the mother said. "We'll order later."

"I won't order," Nora Jane said. "I won't stay here and watch you get drunk. I'm leaving."

"It's only one drink. Only a glass of wine."

"No. I won't stay." Nora Jane got up, pushed her chair back into the table. The waiter backed up further. Nora Jane picked up a handful of crackers from the table and put them in her pocket. She was furious and she was starving. She had been so busy cleaning up the house she had forgotten to eat. She took a second handful of crackers and turned to leave.

"Don't you do this," her mother said, and rose to her feet. "If you do this you will be sorry. I won't put up with this." The waiter came back with a tray, took the glass of wine and set it before her. Put the Seven-Up at Nora Jane's empty place. Nora Jane picked it up, drank it greedily, put the glass back down.

"Sit down," her mother said. "I order you to sit back down." Nora Jane turned and walked out of the restaurant.

"Have your wine?" the waiter said. "I don't know where they come from, these modern kids. I mean, who do they think they are, anyway? Drink your wine and I'll get a menu. You go on and enjoy your dinner and don't worry about her."

He had noticed the nice diamonds on Mrs. Whittington's hands, the nice legs, the scared gentle face. Probably a lonely divorcée. He might end up with a really big tip if he played his cards right. He leaned over the mother and straightened her silverware. "I'll get you more crackers," he said. "Don't worry about the kid. They all act like that nowadays."

Six blocks away Chef Roland was making crawfish étouffée. His brother Maurice was coming. Maurice who had given his life to God. "He knows nothing of the real world," Chef Roland said. His wife, Betty, was listening, leaning against the sink drinking coffee and watching her husband cook. She loved to watch him cook, loved to be in bed with him on top of her, she loved him. Anything he believed she tried to believe, anything he said she agreed with. They had a happy marriage. No one believed it, but it was true. Roland and Betty Dupre had a happy marriage and had always had. At night they got into the bed and touched each other from head to toe and cuddled up like bears. In the daytime they worried about their children and cooked and ate. It was a good life, a happy life and neither of them were ever sick.

"Martin's gone to his baseball game," Betty said. "I hope they win."

"They'll win, or they will not. Life is hard, Betty, don't let them forget that."

"If you say so."

"Maurice doesn't know it. How could he. He never pays taxes. He doesn't have to watch the world going to pot around him, he doesn't see the wholesale prices I'm paying for fish this week. What does Maurice know? He doesn't know the real world. He's lost touch with reality."

"When does he get here?"

"His plane gets in at seven-forty. We'll take the twins and go."

"What about Martin?"

"Leave the food on the stove. He'll get home."

"Can I taste it?"

"Sure you can. Come over here." She put the coffee cup down and went to stand beside him at the stove. He held out a spoon, blew on it to cool it down. Waited. She raised her lips to the spoon, tasted, almost swooned. It was perfect. Anything Roland did was perfect. He was a perfect man, the best chef in all New Orleans and he still found time to cook a meal for his family. "Oh, oh," Betty said. "Oh, oh, oh."

Chef Roland pushed the pot to the back of the stove, turned off the burner, and took his wife in his arms, ran his hands up and down her back, caressed her. He was still caressing her when the twins came in, two boys as alike as blossoms on a stem, Matthew and Mark, they were eleven years old, awkward and gangly and tall for their age, very funny, very skinny, very crazy and brave. They rode trick bicycles around the neighborhood, put the seats of the bikes on stilts, built ramps and ran the bicycles off of them. They were always getting cuts, breaking bones, having to be hurried to the emergency room. Roland and Betty adored them, thought they were wonderful.

"It's time to go to the airport," the twins said, coming in and beginning to eat homemade cake, cutting slices and eating it with their fingers as their parents embraced. "We better go or we'll be late. Martin's not going is he? He's at a game."

"Come along then." Chef Roland released his wife and removed his apron. He doted a moment upon his identical gangly sons. Largess, the great bounty of the earth which had supplied him with a life of adventure and good work and a gentle wife and three daughters and four sons. "Get a fork," he said. "What will people think if they see you eating with your fingers?"

"There's no one here," the twins said, and laughed their secret identical laugh.

"You're right." Chef Roland gathered his family and began to march out through the rooms of his huge Victorian house, past the dining room with its beautiful unbleached domestic drapes his wife had made to save him money, down the hall past the polished stairs, into the parlor and out of the double doors with the broken lock.

Nora Jane was coming up the sidewalk, tears running down her face and her fists clenched in rage. "Can I stay with you?" she asked. "Momma's drinking wine. She's at the restaurant drinking wine so I left. I'm never going back."

The family curled around her. Chef Roland took her into his arms, the twins patted her. She was their baby-sitter when their sister was away at school.

"Don't cry," they all said. "You can stay. Come on, we're going to the airport to get Father Maurice. You want to go with us to the airport? There's room. There's lots of room."

"Don't cry," Chef Roland said. "Come get in the car. We're going out to Moissant to get my brother."

Maurice was no more in the car than the argument began. Nora Jane was sitting in the back of the station wagon with the twins. Betty and Chef Roland and Maurice were in the front.

"Well, your buddies have certainly done it down in South America," Chef Roland began. "I guess you're proud of that?"

"In what way?"

"You know goddamn well what way. In the birth control way. No solving it now. Let 'em starve. Right, Maurice?"

"You think you can solve the problems of South America by killing babies."

"Killing babies! Jesus, Maurice, you sound like a born-again Baptist. Killing babies, I'm hearing killing babies. Jesus, Betty, did you hear that?"

"I didn't see you killing any of yours," Maurice said.

"Yeah, but I stopped having them."

"I stopped having them," Betty put in.

"We stopped having them. I didn't kill my wife. I didn't have a bunch of kids I couldn't feed or house. They're all born addicted now in Peru. Half of them are born addicted to cocaine. You call that Christianity, Maurice? You think that's what He wanted you to do?"

"Oh, Roland, don't do this to me. I've looked forward to this so much. I can't tell you how I've missed all of you."

"You don't miss shit, Maurice. You guys sit up there and lay down edicts. You went to Rome last month, didn't you? Weren't you the personal envoy of the bishop? And what did you do? Did you speak up or did you get drunk and kiss ass?"

"Watch out," Betty said. "You almost hit that car."

"It's his brother?" Nora Jane asked the nearest twin.

"Yeah." The twins giggled. "Isn't it wonderful?"

"Right here in New Orleans," Chef Roland went on. "We got kids being born to thirteen-, fourteen-year-old girls. We got poor little girls with no homes having babies. You want me to kill you, Maurice? I'm thinking of killing people if it doesn't stop. The Church has to join the modern world. The Church has to help, not this anti–birth control crap. I've had it. I don't go anymore. We don't go, do we, Betty? We don't send the kids."

"I'm so sorry," Maurice said. "I can't tell you how that saddens me."

"Are you going to spend the night?" Matthew asked Nora Jane. "Are you going to live with us now? You can have our room. We'll let her stay in our room, won't we, Mark?"

"Her grandmother just died," Chef Roland explained to his brother. "She's got a bad situation at home."

"It isn't bad," Nora Jane spoke up. "My mother drinks because my dad died. It's not too bad. I just don't like it when she drinks. She quit for six weeks."

"I'll go over there tonight," Chef Roland said. "We'll get it straightened out. Meanwhile, you stay with us. There's plenty of room. You can have a room with Margaret Anne. You don't have to stay with them." He swerved to avoid a city bus, turned onto Webster Street and resumed his argument. "Life is short, Maurice, the life of the planet may be short. We can't let people suffer. People suffer because of your bullshit. You're too smart to keep on buying all that crap. I'm ashamed of you. You had a good mind before the Jesuits got hold of you."

"Oh, Roland, we need to have a long talk. I can't believe I find you so full of venom. Sadness and venom. What do you have to be sad about? We will go for a walk together. It has been so long since I've seen the park."

"I go to the park all the time," Nora Jane said. "I never miss a Saturday. There's a grove of trees that is sacred to Apollo. My grandmother knew the man who planted them."

"She's Lydia Whittington's granddaughter," Chef Roland explained. "Remember that time Momma took us to hear her sing?"

"I heard your grandmother sing Madame Butterfly," Maurice said. "A long time ago when New Orleans was a center of the arts."

"We have a boomerang," Matthew said to Nora Jane. "We can go throw it in the park tomorrow. You want to throw our boomerang?"

"I don't know," Nora Jane said. Her sadness had lessened in the presence of Chef Roland and his family. Her sadness was turning back into rage. She remembered the real world. She was Lydia Whittington's granddaughter. She had a reputation to maintain. "I better go on home and see about Momma," she added.

"You stay with us," Chef Roland said. He turned the station wagon into the driveway and parked by the old garage. The twins got out and took off running into the house, planning on getting in a few minutes of worthless trashy television before someone turned it off. Betty went to look for her son Martin, who was on the baseball team but didn't get to play very much. She was always thinking about him when a game was going on, praying that he got to play, wondering if anyone had called him Four Eyes or hated him for striking out.

"I think I'll go on home," Nora Jane said, getting out. "Thanks for letting me go to the airport with you. It was nice to meet you, Father Maurice. I hope I'll see you again while you're here."

"Let me go talk to her," Chef Roland said. "Your mother likes me. I can talk to her."

"She'll be okay. She'll be asleep by the time I get home. I'm okay. I'll call you if I need any help. Thanks again for letting me go with you. I had a nice time." Nora Jane was moving away.

"Let me walk you home," Father Maurice said. "Let me go home with you."

"No, it's okay. I shouldn't have come over here. It's all right. It really is. I'll be okay." She had gained the sidewalk now. The man looked after her, not knowing what to do, not knowing where the lines were drawn in the problem of Nora Jane.

"I'm okay," she called back. "I really am." She waved again and hurried off down Webster Street. I am okay, she decided. It's all inside of me, heaven and hell and everything. I don't have to pay any attention to her. All I have to do is go to school and wait to get out of here. I'll get out sooner or later. That's for sure. At least I don't have a bunch of brothers and sisters to argue with. Their house is as bad as Momma's is.

She stopped on the corner and looked down the long green tunnel of Henry Clay. Past the houses where the rich satisfied people lived. "I'll get rich someday," she said out loud. "Whatever you want you get. Well, it's true." I'll be leaving here before too long. I'll have a job and a boyfriend and the things I need. Remember what I read in that poem. Oh, world, world, I cannot get thee close enough. Remember that and forget the rest.

THE FAMOUS POLL
AT JODY'S BAR

IT WAS NINETY-EIGHT DEGREES in the shade in New Orleans, a record-breaking day in August.

Nora Jane Whittington sat in a small apartment several blocks from Jody's Bar and went over her alternatives.

"No two ways about it," she said to herself, shaking out her black curls, "if Sandy wants my ass in San Jose, I'm taking it to San Jose. But I've got to get some cash."

Nora Jane was nineteen years old, a self-taught anarchist and a quick-change artist. She owned six Dynel wigs in different hair colors, a makeup kit she stole from Le Petit Theatre du Vieux Carre while working as a volunteer stagehand, and a small but versatile wardrobe. She could turn her graceful body into any character she saw in a movie or on TV. Her specialties were boyish young lesbians, boyish young nuns, and a variety of lady tourists.

Nora Jane could also do wonderful tricks with her voice, which had a range of almost two octaves. She was the despair of the sisters at the Academy of the Most Holy Name of Jesus when she quit the choir saying her chores at home didn't allow her to stay after school to practice.

The sisters made special novenas for the bright, lonely child whose father died at the beginning of the Vietnam War and whose pretty alcoholic mother wept and prayed when they called upon her begging her to either put away the bottle and make a decent home for Nora Jane or allow them to put her in a Catholic boarding school.

Nora Jane didn't want a decent home. What she wanted was a steady boyfriend, and the summer she graduated from high school she met Sandy. Nora Jane had a job selling records at The Mushroom Cloud, a record shop near the Tulane campus where rich kids came to spend their parents' money on phonograph records and jewelry made in the shape of coke spoons and marijuana leaves. "The Cloud" was a nice place, up a flight of narrow stairs from Freret Street. Nora Jane felt important, helping customers decide what records to buy.

The day Sandy came into her life she was wearing a yellow cotton dress and her hair was curling around her face from the humidity.

Sandy walked into the shop and stood for a long time reading the backs of jazz albums. He was fresh out of a Texas reform school with $500.00 in the bank and a new lease on life. He was a handsome boy with green eyes as opaque and unfathomable as a salt lake. When he smiled down at Nora Jane over a picture of Rahshaan Roland Kirk as The Five Thousand Pound Man, she dreamed of Robert Redford as The Sundance Kid.

"I'm going to dedicate a book of poems to this man's memory," Sandy said. "I'm going to call the book *Dark Mondays*. Did you know that Rahshaan Kirk died last year?"

"I don't know much about him. I haven't been working here long," Nora Jane said. "Are you really a writer?"

"I'm really a land surveyor, but I write poems and stories at night. In the school I went to in Texas a poet used to come and teach my English class once a month. He said the most important writing gets done in your head while you think you're doing something else. Sometimes I write in the fields while I'm working. I sing the poems I'm writing to myself like work songs. Then at night I write them down. You really ought to listen to this album. Rahshaan Kirk is almost as good as Coltrane. A boy I went to school with is his cousin."

"I guess I have a lot to learn about different kinds of music," Nora Jane answered, embarrassed.

"I'm new in town," Sandy said, after they had talked for a while, "and I don't know many people here yet. How about going with me to a political rally this afternoon. I read in the paper that The Alliance for Good Government is having a free picnic in Audubon Park. I like to find out what's going on in politics when I get to a new town."

"I don't know if I should," Nora Jane said, trying not to smile.

"It's all right," Sandy told her. "I'm really a nice guy. You'll be safe with me. It isn't far from here and we have to walk anyway because I don't have a car, so if you don't like it you can just walk away. If you'll go I'll wait for you after work."

"I guess I should go," Nora Jane said. "I need to know what's going on in politics myself."

When Nora Jane was through for the day they walked to Audubon Park and ate free fried chicken and listened to the Democratic candidate for the House of Representatives debate the Republican candidate over the ERA and the canal treaties.

It was still light when they walked back through the park in the direction of Sandy's apartment. Nora Jane was telling Sandy the story of her life. She had just gotten to the sad part where her father died when he stopped her and put his hands around her waist.

"Wait just a minute," he said, and he walked over to the roots of an enormous old live-oak tree and began to dig a hole with the heel of his boot. When he had dug down about six inches in the hard-packed brown soil he took out all the change he had in his pockets, wrapped it in a dollar bill and buried it in the hole. He packed the dirt back down with his hands and looked up at her.

"Remember this spot," he said, "you might need this some day."

Many hours later Nora Jane reached out and touched his arm where he stood leaning into the window frame watching the moon in the cloudy sky.

"Do you want to stay here for a while?" he asked, without looking at her.

"I want to stay here for a long time," she answered, taking a chance.

So she stayed for fourteen months.

Sandy taught her how to listen to jazz, how to bring a kite down without tearing it, how to watch the sun go down on the Mississippi River, how to make macrame plant holders out of kite string, and how to steal things.

Stealing small things from elegant uptown gift shops was as easy as walking down a tree-lined street. After all, Sandy assured her, their insurance was covering it. Pulling off robberies was another thing. Nora Jane drove the borrowed getaway car three times while Sandy cleaned out a drugstore and two beauty parlors in remote parts of Jefferson Parish. The last of these jobs supplied her with the wigs. Sandy picked them up for her on his way out.

"I'm heading for the west coast," he told her, when the beauty parlor job turned out to be successful beyond his wildest dreams, netting them $723.00. He had lucked into a payroll.

"I'll send for you as soon as I get settled," he said, and he lifted her over his head like a flower and carried her to the small iron bed and made love to her while the afternoon sun and then the moonlight poured in the low windows of the attic apartment.

Robbing a neighborhood bar in uptown New Orleans in broad daylight all by herself was another thing entirely. Nora Jane thought that up for herself. It was the plan she settled upon as the quickest way to get to California. She planned it for weeks, casing the bar at different times of the day and night in several disguises, and even dropping by one Saturday afternoon pretending to be collecting money to help the Crippled Children's Hospital. She collected almost ten dollars.

Nora Jane had never been out of the state of Louisiana, but once she settled on a plan of action she was certain all she needed was a little luck and she was as good as wading in the Pacific Ocean. One evening's work and her hands were back in Sandy's hair.

She crossed herself and prayed for divine intervention. After all, she told herself, robbing an old guy who sold whiskey and laid bets on athletic events was part of an anarchist's work. Nora Jane didn't like old guys much anyway. They were all wrinkled where the muscles ought to be and they were so sad.

She took the heavy stage pistol out of its hiding place under the sink and inspected it. She practiced looking tough for a few minutes and then replaced the gun in its wrapper and sat down at the card table to go over her plans.

Nora Jane had a methodical streak and liked to take care of details.

II

"THE FIRST NIGGER THAT COMES in here attempting a robbery is going to be in the wrong place," Jody laughed, smiling at Judge Crozier and handing him a fresh bourbon and Coke across the bar.

"Yes, sir, that nigger is gonna be in the wrong place." Jody fingered the blackjack that lay in its purple velvet sack on a small shelf below the antiquated cash register and warmed into his favorite subject, his interest in local crime fueled by a report in the *Times-Picayune* of a holdup in a neighborhood Tote-Sum store.

The black bandits had made the customers lie on the floor, cleaned out the cash register, and helped themselves to a cherry Icee on the way out. The newspaper carried a photograph of the Icee machine.

The judge popped open his third sack of Bar-B-Que potato chips and looked thoughtful. The other customers waited politely to see what he had to say for himself this morning concerning law and order.

"Now, Jody, you don't know how a man will act in an emergency until that emergency transpires," the judge began, wiping his hands on his worn seersucker pants. "That's a fact and worthy of all good men to be accepted. Your wife could be in here helping tend bar. Your tables could be full of innocent customers watching a ball game. You might be busy talking to someone like that sweet little girl who came in last Saturday collecting for the Crippled Children's Hospital. First thing you know, gun in your back, knife at your throat. It has nothing at all to do with being brave." The judge polished off his drink and turned to look out the door to where the poll was going on.

Jody's Bar didn't cater to just anyone that happened to drop by to get a drink or lay a bet. It was the oldest neighborhood bar in the Irish Channel section of New Orleans, and its regular customers included second- and third-generation drinkers from many walks of life. Descendants of Creole blue bloods mingled easily with house painters and deliverymen stopping by for a quick one on their route.

Jody ran a notoriously tight ship. No one but Jody himself had ever answered the telephone that sat beneath a framed copy of The Auburn Creed, and no woman, no matter what her tale of woe, had ever managed to get him to call a man to the phone.

"Not here," he would answer curtly, "haven't seen him." And Jody would hang up without offering to take a message. If a woman wanted a man at Jody's she had to come look for him in person.

There was an air of anticipation around Jody's this Saturday morning. All eight of the stools were filled. The excitement was due to the poll.

Outside of Jody's, seated at a small card table underneath a green-and-white-striped awning, Wesley Labouisse was proceeding with the poll in a businesslike manner. Every male passerby was interviewed in turn and his ballot folded into quarters and deposited in the Mason jar with a pink ribbon from an old Valentine's box wrapped loosely around it.

"Just mark it yes or no. Whatever advice you would give your closest friend if he came to you and told you he was thinking of getting married." Wesley was talking to a fourteen-year-old boy straddling a ten-speed bike.

"Take all the time you need to make up your mind. Think about your mother and father. Think about what it's like to have a woman tell you when to come home every night and when to get up in the morning and when to take a bath and when to talk and when to shut up. Think about what it's like to give your money to a woman from now till the day you die. Then just write down your honest feelings about whether a perfectly happy man ought to go out and get himself married."

Wesley was in a good mood. He had thought up the poll himself and had side bets laid all the way from The New Orleans Country Club to the Plaquemines Parish sheriff's office.

There was a big sign tacked up over the card table declaring THIS POLL IS BEING CONDUCTED WITHOUT REGARD TO SEX OR PREVIOUS CONDITION OF SERVITUDE. Wesley had made the sign himself and thought it was hilarious. He was well known in New Orleans society as the author of Boston Club Mardi Gras skits.

The leading man in the drama of the poll, Prescott Hamilton IV, was leaning into Jody's pinball machine with the dedication of a ballet dancer winding up The Firebird. He was twelve games ahead and his brand-new, navy blue wedding suit hung in its plastic see-through wrapper on the edge of the machine swaying in rhythm as Prescott nudged the laws of pinball machines gently in his favor. He was a lucky gambler and an ace pinball-machine player. He was a general favorite at Jody's, where the less aristocratic customers loved him for his gentle ways and his notoriously hollow leg.

Prescott wasn't pretending to be more interested in the outcome of the pinball-machine game than in the outcome of the poll that was deciding his matrimonial future. He was genuinely more interested in the pinball machine. Prescott had great powers of concentration and was a man who lived in the present.

Prescott didn't really care whether he married Emily Anne

Hughes or not. He and Emily Anne had been getting along fine for years without getting married, and he didn't see what difference his moving into Emily Anne's house at this late date was going to make in the history of the world.

Besides he wasn't certain how his Labradors would adjust to her backyard. Emily Anne's house was nice, but the yard was full of little fences and lacked a shade tree.

Nonetheless, Prescott was a man of his word, and if the poll came out in favor of marriage they would be married as soon as he could change into his suit and find an Episcopal minister, unless Emily Anne would be reasonable and settle for the judge.

Prescott was forty-eight years old. The wild blood of his pioneer ancestors had slowed down in Prescott. Even his smile took a long time to develop, feeling out the terrain, then opening up like a child's.

"Crime wave, crime wave, that's all I hear around this place anymore," the judge muttered, tapping his cigar on the edge of the bar and staring straight at the rack of potato chips. "Let's talk about something else for a change."

"Judge, you ought to get Jody to take you back to the ladies' room and show you the job Claiborne did of patching the window so kids on the street can't see into the ladies'," one of the regulars said. Two or three guys laughed, holding their stomachs.

"Claiborne owed Jody sixty bucks on his tab and the window was broken out in the ladies' room so Jody's old lady talked him into letting Claiborne fix the window to pay back part of the money he owes. After all, Claiborne is supposed to be a carpenter." Everyone started laughing again.

"Well, Claiborne showed up about six sheets in the wind last Wednesday while Jody was out jogging in the park and he went to work. You wouldn't believe what he did. He boarded up the window. He didn't feel like going out for a windowpane, so he just boarded up the window with scrap lumber."

"I'll have to see that as soon as it calms down around here," the judge said, and he turned to watch Prescott, who was staring passionately into the lighted TILT sign on the pinball machine.

"What's wrong, Prescott," he said, "you losing your touch?"

"Could be, Judge," Prescott answered, slipping another quarter into the slot.

The late afternoon sun shone in the windows of the bare apartment. Nora Jane had dumped most of her possessions into a container for The Volunteers of America. She had even burned Sandy's letters. If she was caught there was no sense in involving him.

If she was caught what could they do to her, a young girl, a first offender, the daughter of a hero? The sisters would come to her rescue. Nora Jane had carefully been attending early morning mass for several weeks.

She trembled with excitement and glanced at her watch. She shook her head and walked over to the mirror on the dresser. Nora Jane couldn't decide if she was frightened or not. She looked deep into her eyes in the mirror trying to read the secrets of her mind, but Nora Jane was too much in love to even know her own secrets. She was inside a mystery deeper than the mass.

She inspected the reddish-blond wig with its cascades of silky Dynel falling around her shoulders and blinked her black eyelashes. To the wig and eyelashes she added blue eye shadow, peach rouge, and beige lipstick. Nora Jane looked awful.

"You look like a piece of shit," she said to her reflection, adding another layer of lipstick. "Anyway, it's time to go."

On weekends six o'clock was the slow hour at Jody's, when most of the customers went home to change for the evening.

Nora Jane walked down the two flights of stairs and out onto the sidewalk carrying the brown leather bag. Inside was her costume change and a bus ticket to San Francisco zippered into a side compartment. The gun was stuffed into one of the Red Cross shoes she had bought to wear with the short brown nun's habit she had stolen from Dominican College. She hoped the short veil wasn't getting wrinkled. Nora Jane was prissy about her appearance.

As she walked along in the August evening she dreamed of Sandy sitting on her bed playing his harmonica while she pretended to sleep. In the dream he was playing an old Bob Dylan love song, the sort of thing she liked to listen to before he upgraded her taste in music.

Earlier that afternoon Nora Jane had rolled a pair of shorts, an old shirt, and some sandals into a neat bundle and hidden it in the low-hanging branches of the oak tree where Sandy had planted her money.

A scrawny-looking black kid was dozing in the roots of the tree. He promised to keep an eye on her things.

"If I don't come back by tomorrow afternoon you can have this stuff," she told him. "The sandals were handmade in Brazil."

"Thanks," the black kid said. "I'll watch it for you till then. You running away from home or what?"

"I'm going to rob a bank," she confided.

The black kid giggled and shot her the old peace sign.

Wesley walked into the bar where Prescott, Jody, and the judge were all alone watching the evening news on television.

"Aren't you getting tired of that goddamn poll," Prescott said to him. "Emily Anne won't even answer her phone. A joke's a joke, Wesley. I better put on my suit and get on over there."

"Not yet," Wesley said. "The sun isn't all the way down yet. Wait till we open the jar. You promised." Prescott was drunk, but Wesley was drunker. Not that either of them ever showed their whiskey.

"I promised I wouldn't get married unless you found one boy or man all day who thought it was an unqualified good idea to get married. I didn't ever say I was interested in waiting around for the outcome of a vote. Come on and open up that jar before Emily Anne gets any madder."

"What makes you think there is a single ballot in favor of you getting married?" Wesley asked.

"I don't know if there is or there isn't," Prescott answered. "So go on and let the judge open that goddamn jar."

"Look at him, Wesley," Jody said delightedly. "He ain't even signed the papers yet and he's already acting like a married man. Already worried about getting home in time for dinner. If Miss Emily Anne Hughes wakes up in the morning wearing a ring from Prescott, I say she takes the cake. I say she's gone and caught a whale on a ten-pound test line."

"Open the jar," Prescott demanded, while the others howled with laughter.

Nora Jane stepped into the bar, closed the door behind her, and turned the lock. She kept the pistol pointed at the four men who were clustered around the cash register.

"Please be quiet and put your hands over your heads before I kill one of you," she said politely, waving the gun with one hand and reaching behind herself with the other to draw the window shade that said CLOSED in red letters.

Prescott and the judge raised their hands first, then Wesley.

"Do as you are told," the judge said to Jody in his deep voice. "Jody, do what that woman tells you to do and do it this instant." Jody added his hands to the six already pointing at the ceiling fan.

"Get in there," Nora Jane directed, indicating the ladies' room at the end of the bar. "Please hurry before you make me angry. I ran away from DePaul's Hospital yesterday afternoon and I haven't had my medication and I become angry very easily."

The judge held the door open, and the four men crowded into the small bathroom.

"Face the window," Nora Jane ordered, indicating Claiborne's famous repair job. The astonished men obeyed silently as she closed the bathroom door and turned the skeleton key in its lock and dropped it on the floor under the bar.

"Please be very quiet so I won't get worried and need to shoot through the door," she said. "Be awfully quiet. I am an alcoholic and I need some of this whiskey. I need some whiskey in the worst way."

Nora Jane changed into the nun's habit, wiping the makeup off her face with a bar rag and stuffing the old clothes into the bag. Next she opened the cash register, removed all the bills without counting them, and dropped them into the bag. On second thought she added the pile of IOUs and walked back to the door of the ladies' room.

"Please be a little quieter," she said in a husky voice. "I'm getting very nervous."

"Don't worry, Miss. We are cooperating to the fullest extent," the judge's bench voice answered.

"That's nice," Nora Jane said. "That's very nice."

She pinned the little veil to her hair, picked up the bag, and walked out the door. She looked all around, but there was no one on the street but a couple of kids riding tricycles.

As she passed the card table she stopped, marked a ballot, folded it neatly, and dropped it into the Mason jar.

Then, like a woman in a dream, she walked on down the street, the rays of the setting sun making her a path all the way to the bus stop at the corner of Annunciation and Nashville Avenue.

Making her a path all the way to mountains and valleys and fields, to rivers and streams and oceans. To a boy who was like no other. To the source of all water.

JADE BUDDHAS,
RED BRIDGES,
FRUITS OF LOVE

She had written to him, since neither of them had a phone.

I'll be there Sunday morning at four. It's called the Night Owl flight in case you forget the number. The number's 349. If you can't come get me I'll get a taxi and come on over. I saw Johnny Vidocovitch last night. He's got a new bass player. He told Ron he could afford to get married now that he'd found his bass player. Doesn't that sound just like him. I want to go to that chocolate place in San Francisco the minute I get there. And lie down with you in the dark for a million years. Or in the daylight. I love you. Nora Jane

He wasn't there. He wasn't at the gate. Then he wasn't in the terminal. Then he wasn't at the baggage carousel. Nora Jane stood by the carousel taking her hat on and off, watching a boy in cowboy boots kiss his girlfriend in front of everyone at the airport. He would run his hands down her flowered skirt, then kiss her again.

Finally the bags came. Nora Jane got her flat shoes out of her backpack and went on out to find a taxi. It's because I was too cheap to get a phone, she told herself. I knew I should have had a phone.

She found a taxi and was driven off into the hazy early morning light of San Jose. The five hundred and forty dollars she got from the robbery was rolled up in her bag. The hundred and twenty she saved from her job was in her bra. She had been awake all night. And something was wrong. Something had gone wrong.

"You been out here before?" the driver said.

"It's the first time I've been farther west than Alexandria," she said. "I've hardly ever been anywhere."

"How old are you?" he said. He was in a good mood. He had just gotten a $100 tip from a drunk movie star. Besides, the little black-haired girl in the backseat had the kind of face you can't help being nice to.

"I'll be twenty this month," she said. "I'm a Moonchild. They used to call it Cancer but they changed. Do you believe in that stuff?"

"I don't know," the driver said. "Some days I believe in anything. Look over there. Sun's coming up behind the mountains."

"Oh, my," she said. "I forgot there would be mountains."

"On a clear day you can see Mount Diablo. You ought to go while you're out here. You can see eighty percent of California from it. You came out to visit someone?"

"My boyfriend. Well, he's my fiancé. Sometimes he has to work at night. He wasn't sure he could meet me. Is it far? To where I'm going?" They were in a neighborhood now, driving past rows of stucco cottages, built close together like houses in the Irish Channel. The yards looked brown and bare as if they needed rain.

"Couple of blocks. These are nice old neighborhoods. My sister used to live out here. It's called the Lewis tract." He turned a corner and came to a stop before a small pink house with an overgrown yard.

"Four fifty-one. Is that right?"

"That's right."

"You want me to wait till you see if anyone's here?"

"No, I'll just get out."

"You sure?"

"I'm sure." She watched as he backed and turned and went on off down the road, little clouds of dust rising behind the wheels. She stood looking up the path to the door. A red tree peeling like a sunburn shaded the yard. Here and there a few scraggly petunias bloomed in boxes. *Get your ass out here and see where the USA is headed,* Sandy had written her. *I've got lots of plans. No phone as yet. Bring some French bread. Everything out here is sourdough. Yours forever, Sandy.* He's here, she thought. I know he's here.

She walked on up the path. There was a spider's web across the screen door. They can make one overnight, she told herself. It's nothing to make one overnight.

She rang the doorbell and waited. Then she walked around to the back and looked in the window. It was a large room with a modern-looking stove and a tile floor. I'm going in, she decided. I'm worn out. I'm going in.

She picked up a rock and broke a pane of glass in the door, then carefully picked out all the broken pieces and put them in a pile under the steps. She reached her hand in the opening, undid the latch and went on in. It was Sandy's house all right. His old Jazzfest poster of Dr. John and the Mardi Gras Indians was hanging on a wall. A few clothes were in the closets. Not many. Still, Sandy traveled light. He'll be back, she thought. He's just gone somewhere.

She walked around the house looking for clues. She found only a map of San Francisco with some circles drawn on it, and a list, on an envelope, from something called the Paris Hotel. Willets, it said. Berkeley, Sebastopol, Ukiah, Petaluma, Occidental.

She walked back into the kitchen looking for something to eat. The refrigerator was propped open with a blue tile. Maybe he's in jail, she thought. Maybe I got here just in time.

She reached up a fingernail and flipped open a greeting card that was tacked up over the stove. It was a photograph of a snow-covered mountain with purple fields below and blue skies above. A hawk, or perhaps it was a buzzard, was flying over the mountain. FREEDOM IS THE GREATEST GIFT THAT ONE CAN GIVE ANOTHER, the card said. IT IS A GIFT BORN OF LOVE, TRUST, AND UNDERSTANDING. Nora Jane pulled out the pushpin and read the message inside.

Dear Sandy,

I am glad I am going to be away from you during our two weeks of abstinence. You were so supportive once you realized I was freaking out. I want to thank you for being there for me. We have climbed the mountain together now and also the valley. I hope the valley wasn't too low for you.

I know this has been hard on you. You have had to deal with a lot of new feelings and need time to adjust to them. We will both hopefully grow from this experience. I want us to have many more meaningful experiences together. I love you more than words can say. In deepest friendship.

Pam

I'm hungry, Nora Jane thought. I'm starving. She walked over to a bed in a corner. She guessed it was a bed. It was a mattress on top of a platform made of some kind of green stone. It looked more like a place to sacrifice someone than a place to sleep.

She put her pack up on the bed and began riffling through the pockets for the candy bar she had saved from a snack on the plane. When she found it she tore open the cardboard box and began to eat it, slowly at first, then faster. *I don't know,* she thought. *I just don't know.* She leaned up against the green stone platform eating the chocolate, watching the light coming in the window through the leaves of the red tree making patches on the mattress. That's all we are, she decided. Patches of light and darkness. Things that cast shadows.

She ate the rest of the candy, stopping every now and then to lick her fingers. When she was finished she folded the candy box and put it carefully away in her pack. Nora Jane never littered anything. So far in her life she had not thrown down a single gum wrapper.

During the next week there were four earthquakes in the Bay Area. A five point, then a four point, then a two, then a three. The first one woke her in the middle of the night. She was asleep in a room she had rented near the Berkeley campus. At first she thought a cat had walked across the bed. Then she thought the world had come to an end. Then the lights went on. Everyone in the house gathered in the upstairs hall. When the excitement wore down a Chinese mathematician and his wife fixed tea in their room. "Very lucky to be here for that one," Tam Suyin assured Nora Jane. "Sometimes have to wait long time to experience big one."

"I was in a hurricane once," Nora Jane said. "I had to get evacuated when Camille came."

"Oh," Tam said to her husband. "Did you hear that? Miss Whittington have to be evacuated during hurricane. Which one you find most interesting experience, Miss Whittington, earthquake or hurricane?"

"I don't know," Nora Jane said. She was admiring the room, which was as bare as a nun's cell. "I guess the hurricane. It lasted longer."

The next morning she felt better than she had in a week. She was almost glad to be alive. She bought croissants from a little shop on Tamalpais Street, then spent some time decorating her room to look like a nun's cell. She put everything she owned in the closet. She covered the bed with a white sheet. She took down the drapes. She put the rug away and cleaned the floor. She bought flowers and put them on the dresser.

That afternoon she found a theatrical supply store on Shattuck Avenue and bought a stage pistol. It was time to get to work.

"What are you doing?" the proprietor said.

"*Happy Birthday, Nora Jane.* Have you ever seen it?"

"The Vonnegut play? The one with the animal heads?"

"No, this is an original script. It's a new group on the campus."

"Bring a poster by when you get them ready. We like to advertise our customers."

"I'll do that," she said. "As soon as we get some printed."

"When's it scheduled for?"

"Oh, right away. As soon as we can whip it together."

Freddy Harwood walked down Telegraph Avenue thinking about everyone who adored him. He had just run into Buiji. She had let him buy her a café mocca at the Met. She had let him hold her hand. She had told him all about the horrible time she was having with Dudley. She told him about the au pair girl and the night he threatened her with a gun and the time he choked her and what he said about her friends. It was Freddy she loved, she said. Freddy she adored. Freddy she worshipped. Freddy's hairy stomach and strong arms and level head she longed for. She was counting the days until she was free.

I ought to run for office, he was thinking. And just to think, I could have thrown it all away. I could have been a wastrel like Augustine. But no, I chose another way. The prince's way. Noblesse oblige. Ah, duty, sweet mistress.

Freddy Harwood was the founder and owner of the biggest and least profitable bookstore in northern California. He had one each of every book worth reading in the English language. He had everything that was still in print and a lot that was out of print. He knew dozens of writers. Writers adored him. He gave them autograph parties and unlimited credit and kept their books in stock. He even read their books. He went that far. He actually read their books.

In return they were making him famous. Already he was the hero of three short stories and a science fiction film. Last month *California Magazine* had named him one of the Bay Area's ten most eligible bachelors. Not that he needed the publicity. He already had more women than he knew what to do with. He had Aline and Rita and Janey and Lila and Barbara Hunnicutt, when she was in between

tournaments. Not to mention Buiji. Well, he was thinking about settling down. *There are limits,* he said to himself. *Even to Grandmother's
money. There are perimeters and prices to pay.*

He wandered across Blake Street against the light, trying to
choose among his women. A man in a baseball cap took him by the
arm and led him back to the sidewalk.

"Nieman," he said. "What are you doing in town?"

"Looking for you. I've got to see three films between now and
twelve o'clock. Go with me. I'll let you help write the reviews."

"I can't. I'm up to my ass in the IRS. I'll be working all night."

"Tomorrow then. I'm at Gautier's. Call me for breakfast."

"If I get through. If I can."

"Holy shit," Nieman said. "Did you see that?" Nora Jane had just
passed them going six miles an hour down the sidewalk. She was
wearing black and white striped running shorts and a pair of canvas
wedgies with black ankle straps, her hair curling all over her head like
a dark cloud.

"This city will kill me," Freddy said. "I'm moving back to Gualala."

"Let's catch her," Nieman said. "Let's take her to the movies."

"I can't," Freddy said. "I have to work."

An hour later his computer broke. He rapped it across the desk several times, then beat it against the chair. Still no light. He laid it down
on a pile of papers and decided to take a break. An accountant, he was
thinking. They've turned me into an accountant.

Nora Jane was sitting by a window of the Atelier reading *The Bridge of
San Luis Rey.* She was deep into a description of Uncle Pio. "He pos-
sessed the six attributes of an adventurer—a memory for names and
faces; with the aptitude for altering his own; the gift of tongues; inex-
haustible invention; secrecy; the talent for falling into conversation with
strangers; and that freedom from conscience that springs from a

contempt for the dozing rich he preyed upon." That's just like me, Nora Jane was thinking. She felt in her bag for the gun. It was still there.

Freddy sat down at a table near hers. Your legs are proof of the existence of God. No, not that. What if she's an atheist? If I could decipher the Rosetta Stone of your anklestraps. My best friend just died. My grandmother owns Sears Roebuck.

"I haven't seen one of those old Time-Life editions of that book in years," he said. "I own a bookstore. May I look at that a minute?"

"Sure you can," she said. "It's a great book. I bought it in New Orleans. That's where I'm from."

"Ah, the crescent city. I know it well. Where did you live? In what part of town?"

"Near the park. Near Tulane."

"On Exposition?"

"No, on Story Street. Near Calhoun." She handed him the book. He took it from her and sat down at the table.

"Oh, this is very interesting, finding this," he said. "This series was so well designed. Look at this cover. You don't see them like this now."

"I've been looking for a bookstore to go to," she said. "I haven't been here long. I don't know my way around yet."

"Well, the best bookstore in the world is right down the street. Finish your coffee and I'll take you there. Clara, I call it. Clara, for light. You know, the patron saint of light."

"Oh, sure," she said. The stranger, she thought. This is the stranger.

They made their way out of the café through a sea of ice cream chairs and out onto the sidewalk. It was in between semesters at Berkeley, and Telegraph Avenue was quiet, almost deserted. When they got to the store Freddy turned the key in the lock and held the door open for her. "Sorry it's so dark," he said. "It's on an automatic switch."

"Is anyone here?" she asked.

"Only us."

"Good," she said. She took the pistol out of her purse and stepped back and pointed it at him. "Where is the office?" she said. "I am robbing you. I came to get money."

"Oh, come on," he said. "You've got to be kidding. Put that gun down."

"I mean it," she said. "This is not a joke. I have killed. I will kill again." He put his hands over his head as he had seen prisoners do in films and led the way to his office through a field of books, a bright meadow of books, one hundred and nineteen library tables piled high with books.

"Listen, Betty," he began, for Nora Jane had told him her name was Betty.

"I came to get money," she said. "Where is the money? Don't talk to me. Just tell me where you put the money."

"Some of it's in my pocket," he said. "The rest is locked up. We don't keep much here. It's mostly charge accounts."

"Where's the safe? Come on. Don't make me mad."

"It's behind that painting. Listen, I'll have to help you take that down. That's a Helen Watermeir. She's my aunt. She'll kill me if anything happens to that painting."

Nora Jane had moved behind his desk. "Try not to mess up those papers," he said. "I gave up a chance to canoe the Eel River to work on those papers."

"What's it a painting of?" she said.

"It's A.E."

"A.E.?"

"Abstract Expressionism."

"Oh, I know about that. Sister Celestine said it was from painters riding in airplanes all the time. She said that's what things look like to them from planes. You know, I was thinking about that flying up here.

We flew over all these salt ponds. They were these beautiful colors. I was thinking about those painters."

"I'll have to let you tell Aunt Helen that. She's really defensive about A.E. right now. That might cheer her up. Now, listen here, Betty, hasn't this gone far enough? Can't you put that gun down? They put people in Alcatraz for that." She was weakening. She was looking away. He pressed his luck. "Nobody with legs like yours should be in Alcatraz."

"This is what I do," she said. "I'm an anarchist. I don't know what else to do." The gun was pointing to the floor.

"Oh," he said. "There are lots of better things to do in San Francisco than rob a bookstore."

"Name one," she said.

"You could go with me," he said. He decided to pull out all the stops. He decided to go for his old standby. "We could go together 'while the evening is spread out against the sky, like a patient etherized upon a table. Oh, do not ask what is it. Let us go and make our visit.'"

"I know that poem," she said. "We had it in English." She wasn't pointing the gun and she was listening. Of course he had never known the "Love Song" to fail. He had seen hardhearted graduate students pull off their sweaters by the third line.

He kept on going. Hitting the high spots. Watching for signs of boredom. By the time he got to "tea and cakes and ices," she had begun to cry. When he got to the line about Prince Hamlet she laid the gun down on top of the computer and dissolved in tears. "My name isn't Betty," she said. "I hate the name of Betty. My name is Nora Jane Whittington and tomorrow is my birthday. Oh, goddamn it all to hell. Oh, goddamn everything in the whole world to hell."

He came around the desk and put his arms around her. She felt wonderful. She felt as good as she looked. "I'm going home and turn myself in," she was sobbing. "They've got my fingerprints. They've got my handwriting. I'm going to have to go live in Mexico."

"No, you aren't," he said. "Come along. Let's go eat dinner. I've been dreaming all day about the prawns at Narsai's."

"I don't want any prawns," she said. "I don't even know what prawns are. I want to go to that chocolate store. I want to go to that store Sandy told me about."

Many hours later they were sitting in the middle of a eucalyptus grove on the campus, watching the stars through the trees. The fog had lifted. It was a nice night with many stars.

"The woods decay, the woods decay and fall," Freddy was saying, but she interrupted him.

"Do you think birds live up there?" she said. "That far up."

"I don't know," he said. "I never thought about it."

"It doesn't look like they would want to nest that high up. I watch birds a lot. I mean, I'm not a birdwatcher or anything like that. But I used to go out on the seawall and watch them all the time. The seagulls, I mean. Feed them bread and watch them fly. Did you ever think how soft flying seems? How soft they look, like they don't have any edges."

"I took some glider lessons once. But I couldn't get into it. I don't care how safe they say it is."

"I don't mean people flying. I mean birds."

"Well, look, how about coming home with me tonight. I want you to spend the night. You can start off your birthday in my hot tub."

"You've got a hot tub in your house?"

"And a redwood deck and a vegetable garden, corn, okra, squash, beans, skylights, silk kimonos, futon, orange trees. If you come over you won't have to go anyplace else the whole time you're in California. And movies. I just got *Chariots of Fire*. I haven't even had time to see it yet."

"All right," she said. "I guess I'll go."

★　　　★　　　★

Much later, sitting in his hot tub, she told him all about it. "Then there was this card tacked up over the stove from this girl. You wouldn't believe that card. I wouldn't send anyone one of those cards for a million dollars. We used to have those cards at The Mushroom Cloud. Anyway, now I don't know what to do. I guess I'll go on home and turn myself in. They've got my fingerprints. I left them all over everything."

"We could have your fingers sanded. Did you ever see that movie? With Bette Davis as twin sisters? And Karl Malden. I *think* it was Karl Malden."

"I can't stay out here," she said. "I don't know how to take care of myself out here."

"I'll take care of you," he said. "Listen, N.J., you want me to tell you the rest of that quote I was telling you or not?"

"The one about the trees dying?"

"No, the one about the lice."

"All right," she said. "Go on. Tell the whole thing. I forgot the first part." She had already figured out there wasn't any stopping him once he decided to quote something.

"It's from Heraclitus. Now, listen, this is really good. 'All men are deceived by the appearances of things, even Homer himself, who was the wisest man in Greece; for he was deceived by boys catching lice; they said to him, 'What we have caught and what we have killed we have left behind, but what has escaped us we bring with us.'"

"Am I supposed to say something?" she said.

"Not unless you want to, come on, let's get to bed. Tomorrow we begin the F. Slazenger Harwood memorial tour of the Bay Area. The last girl who got it was runner-up for Miss America. It was wasted on her, however. She didn't even shiver when she put her finger in the passion fruit."

"What all do we have to do?" Nora Jane said.

"We have to see your chocolate store and the seismograph and the Campanile and the Pacific Ocean and the redwood trees. And a movie. At least one movie. There's this great documentary about Werner Herzog playing. He kills all these people trying to move a boat across a forest in Brazil. At the end he says, I don't know if it was worth it. Sometimes I don't know if movies are worth all this."

The tour moved from the Cyclotron to Chez Panisse, from Muir Woods to Toroya's, from the Chinese cemetery to Bolinas Reef.

It began with the seismograph. "That needle is connected to a drum deep in the earth," Freddy quoted from a high-school science lecture. "You could say that needle has its finger on the earth's heart. When the plates shift, when the mantle buckles, it tells us just how much and where."

"What good does that do," Nora Jane said, "if the building you're in is falling down?"

"Come on," he said. "We're late to the concert at the Campanile."

They drove all over town in Freddy's new DeLorean. "Why does this car have fingerprints all over it?" Nora Jane asked. "If I had a car this nice I'd keep it waxed."

"It's made of stainless steel. It's the only stainless steel DeLorean in town. You can't wax stainless steel."

"If I got a car I'd get a baby blue convertible," she said. "This girl at home, Dany Nasser, that went to Sacred Heart with me, had one. She kept promising to let me drive it but she never did."

"You can drive my car," he said. "You can drive it all day long. You can drive it anyplace you want to drive it to."

"Except over bridges," she said. "I don't drive over bridges."

"Why not?"

"I don't know. It always seems like there's nothing underneath them. Like there's nothing there."

★   ★   ★

He asked her to move in with him but she turned him down. "I couldn't do that," she said. "I wouldn't want to live with anyone just now."

"Then let's go steady. Or get matching tattoos. Or have a baby. Or buy a dog. Or call up everyone we know and tell them we can't see them anymore."

"There isn't anyone for me to call," she said. "You're the only one I know."

In August Sandy found her. Nora Jane was getting ready to go to work. She was putting in her coral earrings when Tam Suyin called her to the phone.

"I was in Colorado," he said. "I didn't get your letter until a week ago. I've been looking all over the place for you. Finally I got Ron and he told me where you were."

"Who's Pam," she said. "Tell me about Pam."

"So you're the one that broke my window."

"I'll pay for your window. Tell me about Pam."

"Pam was a mistake. She took advantage of me. Look, Nora Jane, I've got big plans for us. I've got something planned that only you and I could do. I mean, this is big money. Where are you? I want to see you right away."

"Well, you can't come now. I'm on my way to work. I've got a job, Sandy."

"A job?"

"In an art gallery. A friend got it for me."

"What time do you get off? I'll come wait for you."

"No, don't do that. Come over here. I'll meet you here at five. It's 1512 Arch Street. In Berkeley. Can you find the way?"

"I'll find the way. I'll be counting the minutes."

*   *   *

She called Freddy and broke a date to go to the movies. "I have to talk to him," she said. "I have to give him a chance to explain."

"Oh, sure," he said. "Do whatever you have to do."

"Don't sound like that."

"What do you want me to do? Pretend like I don't care? Your old boyfriend shows up at eight o'clock in the morning . . . the robber baron shows up, and I'm supposed to act like I think it's great."

"I'll call you tomorrow."

"Don't bother. I won't be here. I'm going out of town."

He worked all morning and half the afternoon without giving in to his desire to call her. By two-thirty his sinus headache was so bad he could hardly breathe. He stood on his head for twenty minutes reciting "The Four Quartets." Nothing helped. At three he stormed out of the store. I'm sitting on her steps till she gets home from work, he told himself. I can't make myself sick just to be a nice guy. Unless that bastard picks her up at work. What if he picks her up at work. He'll drag her into drugs. She'll end up in the state pen. He'll put his mouth on her mouth. He'll put his mouth on her legs. He'll touch her hands. He'll touch her hair.

Freddy trudged up Arch Street with his chin on his chest, ignoring the flowers and the smell of hawthorn and bay, ignoring the pines, ignoring the sun, the clear light, the cool clean air.

At the corner of Arch and Brainard he started having second thoughts. He stood on the corner with his hands stuck deep in the pockets of his pants. A white Lincoln with Colorado plates pulled up in front of Nora Jane's house. A tall boy in chinos got out and walked up on the porch. He inspected the row of mailboxes. He had an envelope in his hand. He put it into one of the boxes and hurried back down the steps. A woman was waiting in the car. They talked a moment, then drove off down the street.

That's him, Freddy thought. That's the little son-of-a-bitch. The

Suyins' Pomeranian met him in the yard. He knocked it out of his way with the side of his foot and opened Nora Jane's mailbox. The envelope was there, in between an advertisement and a letter from a politician. He stuck it into his pocket and walked up the hill toward the campus. He stopped in a playground and read the note.

Angel, I have to go to Petaluma on business. I'll call tonight. After eight. Maybe you can come up and spend the weekend. I'm really sorry about tonight. I'll make it up to you. Yours forever.

Sandy

When he finished reading it he wadded it up and stuck it into a trash container shaped like a pelican. "All right," he said to the pelican. "I'll show him anarchy. I'll show him business. I'll show him war."

He walked back down to Shattuck Avenue and hailed a taxi. "Where's the nearest Ford place?" he asked the driver. "Where's the nearest Ford dealer?"

"There's Moak's over in Oakland. Unless you want to go downtown. You want me to take you to Moak's?"

"That's fine," Freddy said. "Moak's is fine with me."

"I wouldn't have a Ford," the driver said. "You couldn't give me a Ford. I wouldn't have a thing but a Toyota."

Moak Ford had just what he was looking for. A pint-sized baby blue convertible sitting in the display window with the sunlight gleaming off its chrome and glass. The interior was an even lighter blue with leather seats and a soft blue carpet. "I'll need a tape deck," he said to the salesman. "How long does it take to install a tape deck?"

At six-thirty he called her from a pay phone near her house. "I don't want to bother you," he said. "I just want to apologize for this morning. I just wanted to make sure you're okay."

"I'm not okay," she said. "I'm terrible. I'm just terrible."

"Could I come over? I've got a present for you."

"A present?"

"It's blue. I bought you something blue."

She was waiting on the porch when he drove up. She walked down the steps trying not to look at it. It was so blue. So very blue. He got out and handed her the keys.

"People don't give other people cars," she said. "They don't just give someone a car."

"I do whatever I need to do," he said. "It's my charm. My fabled charisma."

"Why are you doing this, Freddy?"

"So you'll like me better than old Louisiana Joe. Where is he, by the way? I thought you had a big date with him."

"I broke the date. I didn't feel like seeing him right now. Did you really buy me that car?"

"Yes, I really did. Get in. See how good it smells. I got a tape deck but they can't put it in until Thursday. You want the top down or not?"

She opened the car door and settled her body into the driver's seat. She turned on the key. "I better not put it down just yet. I'll put it down in a minute. I'll stop somewhere and put it down later."

She drove off down Arch Street wondering if she was going crazy. "You don't have to stop to put it down," he said. He reached across her and pushed a button and the blue accordion top folded down like a wing, then back up, then back down again.

"Stop doing that," she said. "You'll make me have a wreck. Where should I go, Freddy? I don't know where to go."

"We could go by the Komatsu showroom and watch ourselves driving by in their glass walls. When I first got the DeLorean I used to do that all the time. Don't look like that, N.J. It's okay to have a car. Cars are all right. They satisfy our need for strong emotions."

"Just tell me where to go."

"I want to take you to the park and show you the Brundage collection but I'm afraid they're closed this time of day. They have this jade Buddha. It's like nothing you've ever seen in your life. I know, let's give it a try. Go down University. We'll drive across a couple of bridges. You need to learn the bridges."

"I can't drive across a bridge. I told you that."

"Of course you can. We'll do the Oakland first, then the Golden Gate. You can't live here if you can't go across the bridges. You won't be able to go anywhere."

"I can't do it, Freddy. I can't even drive across the Huey P. Long, and it's only over the Mississippi."

"Listen to me a minute," he said. "I want to tell you about these bridges. People like us didn't built these bridges, N.J. People like Teddy Roosevelt and Albert Einstein and Aristotle built those bridges. People like my father. The Golden Gate is so overbuilt you could stack cars two deep on it and it wouldn't fall."

"Go on," she said. "I'm listening." She was making straight for the Oakland Bridge, *with the top down*. In the distance the red girders of the Golden Gate gleamed in the sun. She gripped the wheel and turned onto University Avenue leading to the bay.

"All right," he continued, "about these bridge builders. They get up every morning and put on a clean shirt and fill their pockets with pencils. They go out and add and subtract and read blueprints and put pilings all the way down to the bedrock. Then they build a bridge so strong their great-grandchildren can ride across it without getting hurt. My father helped raise money for the Golden Gate. That's how strong it is."

Nora Jane had driven right by the sign pointing to the Oakland Bridge. The little car hummed beneath her fingers. She straightened her shoulders. She kept on going. "All right," she said. "I'll try it. I'll give it a try."

"I wish to hell the Brundage was open. You've got to see this Buddha. It's unbelievable. It's only ten inches high. You can see every wrinkle. You can see every rib. The jade's the color of celadon. Oh, lighter than that. It's translucent. It just floats there."

"Don't talk so much until I get through the gate," she said. She almost sideswiped a black Mazda station wagon. There was a little boy in the backseat wearing a crown. He put his face to the window and waved.

"Did you see that?" Nora Jane said. "Did you see what he's wearing?" She drove through the toll gate and out onto the bridge. She was into it now. She was doing it.

"Loosen up," Freddy said. "Loosen up on the wheel. This Buddha I was telling you about, N.J. It's more the color of sea foam. You've never seen jade like this. It's indescribable. It's got a light of its own. Well, we'll never make it today. I know what, we'll stop in Chinatown and have dinner. I want you to have some Dim Sum. And tomorrow, tomorrow we're going to Mendocino. The hills there are like yellow velvet this time of year. You'll want to put them on and wear them."

I haven't been to confession in two years, Nora Jane was thinking. What am I doing in this car?

The Mazda passed them again. The boy with the crown was at the back window now. Looking out the open window of the tailgate, eating a package of Nacho Cheese Flavored Doritos and drinking a Coke. He held up a Dorito to Nora Jane. He waved it out the window in the air. The Mazda moved on. A metallic green Buick took its place. In the front seat was a young Chinese businessman wearing a suit. In the backseat, a Chinese gentleman wearing a pigtail.

A plane flew over, trailing a banner. HAPPY 40th, ED AND DEB, the banner said. Things were happening too fast. "I just saw an airplane fly by trailing bread crumbs," she said.

"What did you say?" he said. *"What did you just say?"*

"I said . . . oh, never mind. I was thinking too many things at once. I'm going over there, Freddy, in the lane by the water." She put the turn signal on and moved over into the right-hand lane. "Now don't talk to me anymore," she said, squeezing the steering wheel, leaning into it, trying to concentrate on the girders and forget the water. "Don't say any more until I get this car across this bridge."

THE DOUBLE
HAPPINESS BUN

NORA JANE WHITTINGTON was going to have a
baby. There was no getting around that. First Freddy Harwood talked
her into taking out her Lippes Loop. "I don't like the idea of a piece of
copper stuck up your vagina," he said. "I think you ought to get it out."

"It's not in my vagina. It's in my womb. And it's real small. I saw
it before they put it in."

"How small?" he said. "Let me see." Nora Jane held up a thumb and
forefinger and made a circle. "Like this," she said. "About like this."

"Hmmmmmmmmm . . ." he said, and let it go at that. But the idea
was planted. She kept thinking about the little piece of copper. How
it resembled a mosquito coil. Like shrapnel, she thought. Like having
some kind of weapon in me. Nora Jane had a very good imagination
for things like that. Finally imagination won out over science and she
called the obstetrician and made an appointment. There was really
not much to it. She lay down on the table and squeezed her eyes shut
and the doctor reached up inside her with a small cold instrument and
the Lippes Loop came sliding out.

"Now what will you do?" the doctor said. "Would you like me to
start you on the pill?"

"Not yet," she said. "Let me think it over for a while."

"Don't wait too long," he said. "You're a healthy girl. It can happen very quickly."

"All right," she said. "I won't." She gathered up her things and drove on over to Freddy's house to cook things in his gorgeous redwood kitchen.

"Now what will we do?" she said. "You think I ought to take the pill? Or what?" It was much later that evening. Nora Jane was sitting on the edge of the hot tub looking up at the banks of clouds passing before the moon. It was one of those paradisial San Francisco nights, flowers and pine trees, eucalyptus and white wine and Danish bread and brie.

Nora Jane's legs were in the hot tub. Her back was to the breeze coming from the bay. She was wearing a red playsuit with a red and yellow scarf tied around her forehead like a flag. Freddy Harwood thought she was the most desirable thing he had ever seen in his whole life.

"We'll think of something," he said. He took off his Camp Pericles senior counselor camp shorts and lowered himself into the water. He was thirty-five years old and every summer he still packed his footlocker full of tee-shirts and flashlight batteries and went off to the Adirondacks to be a counselor in his old camp. That's how crazy he was. The rest of the year he ran a bookstore in Berkeley.

"What do you think we'll think of?" she said, joining him in the water, sinking down until the ends of the scarf floated in the artificial waves. What they thought of lasted half the night and moved from the hot tub to the den floor to the bedroom. Freddy Harwood thought it was the most meaningful evening he had spent since the night he lost his cherry to his mother's best friend. Nora Jane didn't think it was all that great. It lacked danger, that aphrodisiac, that sugar to end all sugars.

"We have to get married," he told her in the morning. "You'll have to marry me." He walked around a ladder and picked up a kimono and pulled it on and tied the belt into a bowline. The ladder was the only furniture in the room except the bed they had been sleeping

in. Freddy was in the process of turning his bedroom into a planetarium. He was putting the universe on the ceiling, little dots of heat-
absorbing cotton that glowed in the night like stars. Each dot had to
be measured with long paper measuring strips from the four corners
of the room. It was taking a lot longer to put the universe on the ceiling than Freddy had thought it would. He turned his eyes to a spot he
had reserved for Aldebaran. It was the summer sky he was re-creating,
as seen from Minneapolis where the kits were made. "Yes," he said, as
if he were talking to himself. "We are going to have to get married."

"I don't want to get married," she said. "I'm not in love with you."

"You are in love with me. You just don't know it yet."

"I am not in love with you. I've never told you that I was. Besides,
I wouldn't want to change my name. Nora Harwood, how would that
sound?"

"How could you make love to someone like last night if you didn't
love them? I don't believe it."

"I don't know. I guess I'm weird or abnormal or something. But I
know whether I'm in love with someone or not. Anyway, I like you
better than anyone I've met in San Francisco. I've told you that." She
was getting dressed now, pulling a white cotton sweater over a green
cotton skirt, starting to look even more marvelous than she did with
no clothes on at all. Freddy sighed, gathered his forces, walked across
the room and took her in his arms. "Do you want to have a priest? Or
would you settle for a judge. I have this friend that's a federal judge
who would love to marry us."

"I'm not marrying you, Freddy. Not for all the tea in China. Not
even for your money and I want you to stop being in love with me. I
want you to be my friend and have fun like we used to. Now listen, do
you want me to give you back that car you gave me? I'll give you back
the car."

"Please don't give me back the car. All my life I wanted to give
someone a blue convertible. Don't ruin it by talking like that."

"I'm sorry. That was mean of me. I knew better than to say that. I'll keep that car forever. You know that. I might get buried in that car." She gave him a kiss on his freckled chest, tied a green scarf around her hair, floated out of the house, got into the blue convertible and away she went, weaving in and out of the lanes of traffic, thinking about how hard it was to find out what you wanted in the world, much less what to do to get it.

It was either that night that fertilized one of Nora Jane Whittington's wonderful, never to be replaced or duplicated as long as the species lasts, small, wet, murky, secret-bearing eggs. Or it was two nights later when she heard a love song coming out an open doorway and broke down and called Sandy Halter and he came and got her and they went off to a motel and made each other cry.

Sandy was the boy Nora Jane had lived with in New Orleans. She had come to California to be with him but there was a mix-up and he didn't meet her plane. Then she found out he'd been seeing a girl named Pam. After that she couldn't love him anymore. Nora Jane was very practical about love. She only loved people that loved her back. She never was sure what made her call up Sandy that night in Berkeley. First she dreamed about him. Then she passed a doorway and heard Bob Dylan singing. "Lay, lady, lay. Lay across my big brass bed." The next thing she knew she was in a motel room making love and crying. Nora Jane was only practical about love most of the time. Part of the time she was just as dumb about it as everybody else in the world.

"How can we make up?" she said, sitting up in the rented bed. "After what you did to me."

"We can't help making up. We love each other. I've got some big things going on, Nora Jane. I want you working with me. It's real money this time. Big money." He sat up beside her and put his hands on his knees. He looked wonderful. She had to admit that. He was as tan as an Indian and his hair was as blond as sunlight and his mind as faraway and unavailable as a star.

"Last night I dreamed about you," she said. "That's why I called you up. It was raining like crazy in my dream and we were back in New Orleans, on Magazine Street, looking out the window, and the trees were blowing all over the place, and I said, Sandy, there's going to be a hurricane. Let's turn on the radio. And you said, no, the best thing to do is go to the park and ride it out in a live oak tree. Then we went out onto the street. It was a dream, remember, and Webster Street and Henry Clay were under water and they were trying to get patients out of the Home for the Incurables. They were bringing them out on stretchers. It was awful. It was raining so hard. Then I got separated from you. I was standing in the door of the Webster Street Bar calling to you and no one was coming and the water was rising. It was a terrible dream. Then you were down the street with that girl. I guess it was her. She was blond and sort of fat and she was holding on to you. Pam, I guess it was Pam."

"I haven't seen Pam since all that happened. Pam doesn't mean a thing to me. Pam's nothing."

"Then why was I dreaming about her?"

"Don't ruin everything, Nora Jane. Let's just love each other."

"You want to make love to me some more? Well, do you?"

"No, right now I want a cigarette. Then I want to take you to this restaurant I like. I want to tell you about this outfit I'm working for. I'll tell you what. Tomorrow's Saturday and I have to take Mirium's car back so I'll take you with me and show you what's going on."

"I've been wondering what you were up to."

"Just wait till you meet Mirium. She's my boss. I've told her all about you. Now come on, let's get dressed and get some dinner. I haven't eaten all day." Sandy had gotten out of bed and was putting on his clothes. White linen pants and a blue shirt with long full sleeves. He liked to dress up even more than Nora Jane did.

Sandy's boss, Mirium Sallisaw, was forty-three years old. She lived in a house on a bluff overlooking the sea between Pacifica and Montara. It was a very expensive house she bought with money she made arranging trips to Mexico for people that wanted to cure cancer with Laetrile. The Laetrile market was dying out but Mirium wasn't worried. She was getting into Interferon as fast as she could make the right connections. Interferon and Energy. Those were Mirium's key words for 1983.

"Energy," she was fond of saying. "Energy. That's all. There's nothing else." She imagined herself as a little glowworm in a sea of dark branches, spreading light to the whole forest. She was using Sandy to keep her batteries charged. She liked to get in bed with him at night and charge up, then tell him her theories about energy and how he could have all the other women he wanted, because she, Mirium Sallisaw, was above human jealousy and didn't care. Sandy was only twenty-two years old. He believed everything she told him. He even believed she was dying to meet Nora Jane. He thought of Mirium as this brilliant businesswoman who would jump at a chance to have someone as smart as Nora Jane help drive patients back and forth across the border.

Nora Jane and Sandy got to Mirium's house late in the afternoon. They parked in the parking lot and walked across a lawn with Greek statues set here and there as if the decorator hadn't been able to decide where they should go. Statues of muses faced the parking lot. Statues of heroes looked out upon the sea. Twin statues of cupid guarded the doorway.

Nora Jane and Sandy opened the door and stepped into the foyer. It was dark inside the house. All the drapes were closed. The only light came from recessed fixtures near the ceiling. A young man in a silk shirt and elegant pointed shoes came walking toward them. "Hello, Sandy," he said. "Mother's in the back. Go tell her you're here."

"This is Maurice," Sandy said. "He's Mirium's son. He's a genius, aren't you, Maurice? Listen, did you give Mirium my message? Does she know Nora Jane's coming?"

"We've got dinner reservations at Blanchard's. They have fresh salmon. Mimi called. Do you like salmon?" he said to Nora Jane. "I worship it. It's all I eat."

"I've never given it much thought," she said. "I don't think much about what I eat."

"Maurice takes chemistry courses at the college," Sandy said. "Mirium's making him into a chemist."

"That's nice," she said. "That must be interesting."

"Well, profitable. I'll make some dough if I stick to it. Sandy, why don't you go on back and tell her you're here. She's in the exercise room with Mimi. Tell her I'm getting hungry." Sandy disappeared down a long hall.

Maurice took Nora Jane into a sunken living room with sofas arranged around a marble coffee table. There were oriental boxes on the table and something that looked like a fire extinguisher.

"Sit down," he said. "I'll play you some music. I've got a new tape some friends of mine made. It's going to be big. Warner's has it and Twentieth Century–Fox is interested. Million Bucks, that's the name of the group. The leader's name is Million Bills. No kidding, he had it changed. Listen to this." Maurice pushed some buttons on the side of the marble table and the music came on, awful erratic music, a harp and a lot of electronic keyboards and guitars and synthesizers. The harp would play a few notes, then the electrical instruments would shout it down. "Pretty chemical, huh? Feel that energy? They're going to be big." He was staring off into the recessed light, one hand on the emerald embedded in his ear.

Nora Jane couldn't think of anything to say. She settled back into the sofa cushions. It was cool and dark in the room. The cushions she was leaning into were the softest things she had ever felt in her life. They felt alive, like some sort of hair. She reached her hands behind her. "What are these cushions?" she said. "What are they made of?"

"They're Mirium's old fur coats. She wanted drapes but there wasn't enough."

"They're made of fur coats?"

"Yeah. Before that they were animals. Crazy, huh? Chemical? Look, if you want a joint they're different kinds in those boxes. That red one's Colombian and the blue one is some stuff we're getting from Arkansas. Heavy. Really heavy. There's gas in the canister if you'd rather have that. I quit doing it. Too sweet for me. I don't like a sweet taste."

"Could I have a glass of water?" she asked. "It was a long drive." She was sitting up, trying not to touch the cushions. "Sure," he said. "I'll get you some. Just a minute." He had taken a tube of something out of his pocket and was applying it to his lips. "This is a new gloss. It's dynamite. Mint and lemon mixed together. Wild!" Then, so quickly Nora Jane didn't have time to resist, Maurice sat down beside her and put his mouth on hers. He was very strong for a boy who looked so thin and he was pressing her down into the fur pillows. Her mouth was full of the taste of mint and lemon and something tingly, like an anesthetic. For a moment she thought he was trying to kill her. "Get off of me," she said. She pushed against him with all her might. He sat up and looked away. "I just wanted you to get the full effect."

"How old are you?"

"Sixteen. Isn't it a drag?"

"I don't know. I'd never have guessed you were a day over four. Three or four."

"I guess it's my new stylist," he said, as if he didn't know what she meant. "I've got this woman in Marin. Marilee at Plato's. It takes forever to get there. But it's worth it. I mean, that woman understands hair. . . ."

Sandy reappeared with a woman wearing gray slacks and a dark sweater. She looked as if she smiled about once a year. She held out her hand, keeping the other one on Sandy's arm. "Well," she said. "We've been hearing about you. Sandy's told us all about your exploits together in New Orleans. He says you can do some impressive tricks with your voice. How about letting us hear some."

"I don't do tricks," Nora Jane said. "I don't even sing anymore."

"Well, I guess that's that. Did Sandy fill you in on the operation we've got going down here? It isn't illegal, you know. But I don't like our business mouthed around. Too many jealous people, if you know what I mean."

"He told me some things . . ." Nora Jane looked at Sandy. He wouldn't meet her eyes. He picked up one of the canisters and took out a joint and lit it and passed it to Maurice.

"We have dinner reservations in less than an hour," Mirium said. "Let's have some wine, then get going. I can't stand to be late and lose our table. Maurice, try that buzzer. See if you can get someone in here."

"These are sick people you send places," Nora Jane said. "That you need a driver for?"

"Oh, honey, they're worse than sick. These people are at the end. I mean, the end. We're the last chance they've got."

"They don't care what it costs," Sandy said. "They pay in cash."

"So what does it do for them?" Nora Jane said. "Does it make them well?"

"It makes them happy," Maurice said.

"It makes them better than they were," Mirium said. "If they have faith. It won't work without faith. Faith makes the energy start flowing. You see, honey, the real value of Laetrile is it gets the energy flowing. Right, Sandy?" She moved over beside him and took the joint from between his fingers. "Like good sex. It keeps the pipes open, if you know what I mean." She put her hand on Sandy's sleeves, caressing his sleeve.

"Do you have a powder room?" Nora Jane said. "A bathroom I mean."

"There's one in the foyer," Mirium said. "Or you can go back to the bedroom."

"The one in the foyer's fine." Nora Jane had started moving. She was up the steps from the sunken area. She was out of the room and into the hall. She was to the foyer. The keys are in the ignition, she was thinking. I saw him leave them there. And if they aren't I'll walk. But I am getting out of here. Then she was out the door and past the cupids and running along the paving stones to the parking lot. The Lincoln was right where Sandy had parked it. She got in and turned the key and the engine came on and she backed out and started driving. Down the steep rocky drive so fast she almost went over the side. She slowed down and turned onto the ocean road. Slow down, she told herself. You could run over someone. They can't do anything to me. They can't send the police after me. Not with all they have going on in there. All I have to do is drive this car. I don't have to hurry and I don't have to worry about a single thing. And I don't have to think about Sandy. Imagine him doing it with that woman. Well, I should talk. I mean, I've been doing it with Freddy. But it isn't the same thing. Well it isn't.

She looked out toward the ocean, the Pacific Ocean lying dark green and wonderful in the evening sun. I'll just think about the whales, she decided. I'll concentrate on whales. Tam says they hear us thinking. She says they hear everything we do. Well, Chinese people are always saying things like that. I guess part of what they say is true. I mean they're real old. They've been around so long.

It was dark when Nora Jane got to Freddy's house. The front door was wide open. He was in the hot tub with the stereo blaring out country music. "Oh, I'm a good-hearted woman, in love with a good-timing man." Waylon Jennings was filling the house with dumb country ideas.

"I'm drunk as a deer," Freddy called out when he saw her. "The one I love won't admit she loves me. Therefore I am becoming an alcoholic. One and one makes two. Cause and effect. Ask Nieman. He'll tell you. He's helping me. He's right over there, passed out on the sofa. In his green suit. Wake him up. Ask him if I'm an alcoholic or not. He'll tell you." Freddy picked up a bottle of brandy from beside an art deco soap dish and waved it in the air. "Brandy. King of elixirs. The royal drink of the royal heads of France, and of me. Frederick Slazenger Harwood, lover of the cruel Louisiana voodoo queen. Voodooooed. I've been voodooooed. Vamped and rendered alcoholic."

"Get out of there before you drown yourself. You shouldn't be in there drunk. I think you've started living in that hot tub."

"Not getting out until I shrivel. Ask Nieman. Go ahead, wake him up. Ask him. Going to shrivel up to a tree limb. Have myself shipped to the Smithsonian. Man goes back to tree. I can see the headlines."

"I stole a car. It's in the driveway."

"Stay me with flagons," he called out. "Comfort me with apples, for I am sick with love. Nieman, get up. Nora Jane stole a car. We have to turn her in. Why did you steal a car? I just gave you a car." He pulled himself up on the edge of the hot tub. "Why on earth would you steal a car?"

So, first there was the night she spent with Freddy, then there was the night she spent with Sandy, then there was the night she stole the car. Then three weeks went by. Then five weeks went by and Nora Jane Whittington had not started menstruating and she was losing weight and kept falling asleep in the afternoon and the smell of cigarettes or bacon frying was worse than the smell of a chicken plucking plant. The egg had been hard at work.

A miracle, the sisters at the Academy of the Most Sacred Heart of

Jesus would have said. Chemistry, Maurice would say. Energy, Mirium Sallisaw would declare. This particular miraculous energetic piece of chemistry had split into two identical parts and they were attached now to the lining of Nora Jane's womb, side by side, the size of snow peas, sending out for what they needed, water and pizza and sleep, rooms without smoke or bacon grease.

"Well, at least its name will start with an H," Nora Jane said. She was talking to Tam Suyin, a Chinese mathematician's wife who was her best friend and confidante in the house on Arch Street where she lived. It was a wonderful old Victorian house made of boards two feet wide. Lobelia and iris and Madonna lilies lined the sidewalk leading to the porch. Along the side poppies as red as blood bloomed among daisies and snapdragons. Fourteen people lived in the twelve bed-rooms, sharing the kitchen and the living quarters.

Nora Jane had met Tam the night she moved in, in the middle of the night, after an earthquake. Tam and her husband Li had taught Nora Jane many things she would never have heard of in Louisiana. In return Nora Jane was helping them with their English grammar. Now, wherever they went in the world, the Suyins' English would be colored by Nora Jane's soft southern idioms.

"And it probably will have brown eyes," she continued. "I mean, Sandy has blue eyes, or, I guess you could call them gray. But Freddy and I have brown eyes. That's two out of three. Oh, Tam, what am I going to do? Would you just tell me that?" Nora Jane had just come back from the doctor. She walked across the room and lay down on the bed, her face between her hands.

"Start at the beginning. Tell story all over. Leave out romance. We see if we figure something out. Tell story again."

"Okay. I know I started menstruating about ten days before I took the IUD out. I had to wait until I stopped bleeding. I used to bleed like a stuck pig when I had that thing. That's why I took it out. So then I made love to Freddy that night. Then Sandy called me, or, no, I called him because I heard this Bob Dylan song. Anyway, I was glad to see him until I met these people he's been living with. This woman that gives drugs to her own kid. But first I made love to him and we cried a lot. I mean, it was really good making love to him. So I think it must be Sandy's. Don't you? What do you think?"

Tam came across the room and sat down on the bed and began to rub Nora Jane's back, moving her fingers down the vertebrae. "We can make abortion with massage. Very easy. Not hurt body. Not cost anything. No one make you have this baby. You make up your mind. I do it for you."

"I couldn't do that. I was raised a Catholic. It isn't like being from China. Well, I don't mind having it anyway. I thought about it all the way home from the doctor's. I mean, I don't have any brothers or sisters. My father's dead and my mother's a drunk. So I don't care much anyway. I'll have someone kin to me. If it will be a girl. It'll be all right if it's a girl and I can name her Lydia after my grandmother. She was my favorite person before she died. She had this swing on her porch." Nora Jane put her face deeper into the sheets, trying to feel sorry for herself. Tam's hands moved to her shoulders, rubbing and stroking, caressing and loving. Nora Jane turned her head to the side. A breeze was blowing in the window. The curtains were billowing like sails. Far out at sea she imagined a whale cub turning over inside its mother. "It will be all right if it's a girl and I can name it Lydia for my grandmother."

"Yes," Tam said. "Very different from China."

"Who do you think it belongs to?" Nora Jane said again.

"It belong to you. You quit thinking about it for a while. Think one big grasshopper standing on leaf looking at you with big eyes. Eyes made of jade. You sleep now. When Li come home I make us very special dinner to celebrate baby coming into world. Li work on problem. Figure it out on calculator."

"If it had blond hair I'd know it was Sandy's. But black hair could be mine or Freddy's. Well, mine's blacker than his. And curlier . . ."

"Go to sleep. Not going to be as simple as color of hair. Nothing simple in this world, Nora Jane."

"Well, what am I going to do about all this?" she said sleepily. Tam's fingers were pressing into the nerves at the base of her neck. "What on earth am I going to do?"

"Not doing anything for now. For now going to sleep. When Li come home tonight he figure it out. Not so hard. We get it figured out." Tam's fingers moved up into Nora Jane's hair, massaging the old brain on the back of the head. Nora Jane and Lydia and Tammili Whittington settled down and went to sleep.

"Fifty-five percent chance baby will be girl," Li said, looking up from his calculations. "Forty-six percent chance baby is fathered by Mr. Harwood. Fifty-four percent chance baby is fathered by Mr. Halter. Which one is smartest gentleman, Nora Jane? Which one you wish it to be?"

"I don't know. They're smart in different ways."

"Maybe it going to be two babies. Like Double Happiness Bun. One for each father." Li laughed softly at his joke. Tam lowered her head, ashamed of him. He had been saying many strange things since they came to California.

"You sure it going to be good idea to have this baby?" he said next.

"I guess so," Nora Jane said. "I think it is." She searched their faces trying to see what they wanted to hear but their faces told her nothing. Tam was looking down at her hands. Li was playing with his pocket calculator.

"How you going to take care of this baby and go to your job?" he said.

"That's nothing," Nora Jane said. "I've already thought about that. It isn't that complicated. People do it all the time. They have these little schools for them. Day-care centers. I used to work in one the Sisters of Mercy had on Magazine Street. I worked there in the summers. We had babies and little kids one and two years old. In the afternoons they would lie down on their cots and we would sit by them and pat their backs while they went to sleep. It was the best job I ever had. The shades would be drawn and the fan on and we'd be sitting by the cots patting them and you could hear their little breaths all over the room. I used to pat this one little boy with red hair. His back would go up and down. I know all about little kids and babies. I can have one if I want to."

"Yes, you can," Tam said. "You strong girl. Do anything you want to do."

"You going to tell Mr. Harwood and Mr. Halter about this baby?" Li said.

"I don't know," she answered. "I haven't made up my mind about that."

Then for two weeks Nora Jane kept her secret. She was good at keeping secrets. It came from being an only child. When Freddy called she told him she couldn't see him for a while. She hadn't talked to Sandy since she called and told him where to pick up Mirium's car.

At night she slept alone with her secret. In the mornings she dressed and went down to the gallery where she worked and listened to people talk about the paintings. She felt very strange, sleepy and secretive and full of insight. I think my vision is getting better, she told herself, gazing off into the pastel hills. I am getting into destiny, she said to herself at night, feeling the cool sheets against her legs. I am part of time, oceans and hurricanes and earthquakes and the history of man. I am the aurora borealis and the stars. I am as crazy as I can be. I ought to call my mother.

⋆   ⋆   ⋆

Finally Freddy Harwood had had as much as he could stand. There was no way he was letting a girl he loved refuse to see him. He waited fourteen days, counting them off, trying to get to twenty-one, which he thought was a reasonable number of days to let a misunderstanding cool down. Only, what was the misunderstanding? What had he done but fall in love? He waited and brooded.

On the fourteenth day he started off for work, then changed his mind and went over to his cousin Leah's gallery where he had gotten Nora Jane a job. The gallery was very posh. It didn't even open until 11:00 in the morning. He got there about 10:30 and went next door to Le Chocolat and bought a chocolate statue of Aphrodite and stood by the plate-glass windows holding the box and watching for Nora Jane's car. Finally he caught a glimpse of it in the far lane on Shattuck Boulevard heading for the parking lot of the Safeway store. He ran out the door and down to the corner and stood by a parking meter on the boulevard.

She got out of the car and came walking over, not walking very fast. She was wearing a long white rayon shirt over black leotards, looking big-eyed and thin. "You look terrible," he said, forgetting his pose, hurrying to meet her. "What have you been doing? Take this, it's a chocolate statue I bought for you. What's going on, N.J.? I want you to talk to me. Goddammit, we are going to talk."

"I'm going to have a baby," she said. She stepped up on the sidewalk. Traffic was going by on the street. Clouds were going by in the sky. "Oh, my God," Freddy said.

"And I don't know who the father is. It might be your baby. I don't know if it is or not." Her eyes were right on his. They were filling up with tears, a movie of tears, a brand-new fresh print of a movie of tears. They poured down her cheeks and onto her hands and the white cardboard box holding the chocolate Aphrodite. Some even fell on her shoes.

"So what," Freddy said. "That's not so bad. I mean, at least you don't have cancer. When I saw you get out of the car I thought, leukemia, she's got leukemia."

"I don't know who the father is," she repeated. "There's a forty-six percent chance it's you."

"Let's get off this goddamn street," he said. "Let's go out to the park."

"You aren't mad? You aren't going to kill me?"

"I haven't had time to get mad. I've hardly had time to go into shock. Come on, N.J., let's go out to the park and see the Buddha."

"He has blue eyes, or gray eyes, I guess you'd call them. And you have brown eyes and I have brown eyes. So it isn't going to do any good if it has brown eyes. Li said it's more the time of month anyway because sperm can live several days. So I've been trying and trying to remember . . ."

"Let's don't talk about it anymore," Freddy said. "Let's talk less and think more." They were in the De Young Museum in Golden Gate Park. Freddy had called his cousin Leah and told her Nora Jane couldn't come in to work and they had gone out to the park to see a jade Buddha he worshipped. "This all used to be free," he said, as he did every time he brought her there. "The whole park. Even the planetarium. Even the cookies in the tea garden. My father used to bring me here." They were standing in an arch between marble rooms.

"Let's go look at the Buddha again before we leave," Nora Jane said. "I'm getting as bad about that Buddha as you are." They walked back into the room and up to the glass box that housed the Buddha. They walked slowly around the case looking at the Buddha from all angles. The hands outstretched on the knees, the huge ears, the spine, the ribs, the drape of the stole across the shoulder. Sakyumuni as an Ascetic. It was a piece of jade so luminous, so rounded and perfect and alive that just looking at it was sort of like being a Buddha.

"Wheeewwwwwwwww," Nora Jane said. "How on earth did he make it?"

"Well, to begin with, it took twenty years. I mean, you don't just turn something like that out overnight. He made it for his teacher, but the teacher died before it was finished."

Nora Jane held her hands out to the light coming from the case, as if to catch some Buddha knowledge. "I could go see your friend Eli, the geneticist," she said. "He could find out for me, couldn't he? I mean he splices genes, it wouldn't be anything to find out what blood type a baby had. How about that? I'll call him up and ask him if there's any way I can find out before it comes."

"Oh, my God," Freddy said. "Don't go getting any ideas about Eli. Don't go dragging my friends into this. Let's just keep this under our hats. Let's don't go spreading this around."

"I'm not keeping anything I do under my hat," she said. She stepped back from him and folded her hands at her waist. Same old, same old stuff, she thought. "You just go on home, Freddy," she said. "I'll take BART. I don't want to talk to you anymore today. I was doing just fine until you showed up with that chocolate statue. I've never been ashamed of anything I've done in my life and I'm not about to start being ashamed now." She was backing up, heading for the door. "So go on. Go on and leave me alone. I mean it. I really mean it."

"How about me?" he called after her retreating back. "What am I supposed to do? How am I supposed to feel? What if I don't want to be alone? What if I need someone to talk to?" She held her hands up in the air with the palms turned toward the ceiling. Then she walked on off without turning around.

Several days later Nora Jane was at the gallery. It was late in July. Almost a year since she had robbed the bar in New Orleans and flown off to California to be with Sandy. So much had happened in that time. Sometimes she felt like a different person. Other times she felt like the same old Nora Jane. That morning while she was dressing for work she had looked at her body for a long time in the mirror, turning this way and that to see what was happening. Her body was beginning to have a new configuration, strange volumes like a Titian she admired in one of Leah's art books.

It was cool in the gallery, too cool for Nora Jane's sleeveless summer dress. Just right for the three-piece suit on the man standing beside her. They were standing before one of Nora Jane's favorite paintings. The man was making notes on a pad and saying things to the gallery owner that made Nora Jane want to sock him in the face.

"What is the source of light, dear heart? I can't review this show, Leah. This stuff's so old-fashioned. It's so obvious, for God's sake. Absolutely no restraint. I can't believe you got me over here for this. I think you're going all soppy on me."

"Oh, come on," Leah said. "Give it a chance, Ambrose. Put the pad away and just look."

"I can't look, angel. I have a trained eye." Nora Jane sighed. Then she moved over to the side of the canvas and held the edge of the frame in her hand. It was a painting of a kimono being lifted from the sea by a dozen seagulls. A white kimono with purple flowers being lifted from a green sea. The gulls were carrying it in their beaks, each gull in a different pose. Below the painting was a card with lines from a book.

On some undressed bodies the burns made patterns . . . and on the skin of some women . . . the shapes of flowers they had had on their kimonos. . . .

Hiroshima, *by John Hersey*

"Hummmmmmmm . . ." Nora Jane said. "The source of light? This is a painting, not a lightbulb. There's plenty of light. Every one of those doves is a painting all by itself. I bet it took a million hours just to paint those doves. This is a wonderful painting. This is one of the most meaningful paintings I ever saw. Anybody that doesn't know this painting is wonderful isn't fit to judge a beauty contest at a beach, much less a rock of art, I mean, a work of art."

"Leah," the man said. "Who is this child?"

"I used to work here," she said. "But now I'm quitting. I'm going home. I'm going to have a baby and I don't want it floating around inside me listening to people say nasty things about other people's paintings. You can't tell what they hear. They don't know what all they can hear."

"A baby," Leah said. She moved back as though she was afraid some of it might spill on her gray silk blouse. "My cousin Freddy's baby?"

"I don't know," Nora Jane said. "It's just a baby. I don't know whose it is."

I'm doing things too fast, she thought. She was driving aimlessly down University Avenue, headed for a bridge. I'm cutting off my nose to spite my face. I'm burning my bridges behind me. I'll call my mother and tell her where I am. Yeah, and then she'll just get drunker than ever and call me up all the time like she used to at The Mushroom Cloud. Never mind that. I'll get a job at a day-care center. That's what I'll do. This place is full of rich people. I bet they have great ones out here. I'll go find the best one they have and get a job in it. Then I'll be all set when she comes. Well, at least I can still think straight. Thank God for that. Maybe I'll drive out to Bodega Bay and spend the day by the ocean. I'll get a notebook and write down everything I have to do and make all my plans. Then tomorrow I'll go and apply for jobs at day-care centers. I wonder what they pay. Not much I bet. Who cares? I'll live on whatever they pay me. That's one thing Sandy taught me. You don't have to do what they want you to if you don't have to have their stuff. It was worth living with him just to learn that. I've got everything I need. It's a wonderful day. I loved saying that stuff to that man, that Ambrose whatever his name is. I'll bet he's thinking about

it right this minute. YOU AREN'T FIT TO JUDGE A BEAUTY CON-
TEST AT THE BEACH MUCH LESS A WORK OF ART. That was
good, that was really good. I bet he won't forget me saying that. I bet
no one's said anything to him in years except what he wants to hear.

Nora Jane turned on the radio, made a left at a stoplight and drove
out onto the Richmond–San Rafael bridge. She had the top down on
the convertible. The radio was turned up good and loud. Some
lawyers down in Texas were saying the best place to store nuclear
waste would be the salt flats in Mexico. Nora Jane was driving along,
listening to the lawyers, thinking about the ocean, thinking how nice
it would be to sit and watch the waves come in. Thinking about what
she'd stop and get to eat. I have to remember to eat, she was thinking.
I have to get lots of protein and stuff to make her bones thick.

She was just past the first long curve of the bridge when it happened.
The long roller coaster of a bridge swayed like the body of a snake,
making a hissing sound that turned into thunder. The sound rolled
across the bay. Then the sound stopped. Then a long time went by.
The car seemed to be made of water. The bridge of water. Nora
Jane's arms of water. Still, she seemed to know what to do. She turned
off the ignition. She reached behind her and pulled down the shoulder harness and put it on.

The bridge moved again. Longer, slower, like a long cold dream.
The little blue convertible swerved to the side, rubbing up against a station wagon. The bumper grated and slid, grated and slid. Then everything was still. Everything stopped happening. The islands in the bay
were still in their places. Angel Island and Morris Island and the Brothers
and the Sisters and the sad face of Alcatraz. An oil tank had burst on
Morris Island and a shiny black river was pouring down a hill. Nora Jane
watched it pour, then turned and looked into the station wagon.

A woman was at the wheel. Four or five small children were jump-
ing up and down on the seats, screaming and crying. "Do not move

from a place of safety," the radio was saying. "The aftershocks could begin at any moment. Stay where you are. If you have an emergency call 751-1000. Please do not call to get information. We are keeping you informed. Repeat. Do not move from a place of safety. The worst shock has passed. If you are with injured parties call 751-1000." I think I'm in a place of safety, Nora Jane thought.

The children were screaming in the station wagon. They were screaming their heads off. I have to go and see if they're hurt, she thought. But what if a shock comes while I'm going from here to there? I'll fall off the bridge. I'll fall into the sea. "The Golden Gate is standing. The approaches are gone to the Bay Bridge and the Richmond–San Rafael. There is no danger of either bridge collapsing. Repeat, there is no danger of either bridge collapsing. Please do not move from a place of safety. If you are with injured parties call 751-1000. Do not call to get information. Repeat . . ."

That's too many children for one woman. What if they're hurt? Their arms might be broken. I smashed in her side. I have to go over there and help her. I have to do it. Oh, shit. Hail Mary, full of grace, blessed art thou among women and blessed is the fruit of thy womb, Jesus. Womb, oh, my womb, what about my womb . . . ? Nora Jane was out of the car and making her way around the hood to the station wagon. Holy Mary, Mother of God, pray for us sinners now and at the hour of our death. . . . She reached the door handle of the backseat and opened the door and slid in. The children stopped their screaming. Five small faces and one large one turned her way. "I came to help," she said. "Are any of them hurt? Are they injured?"

"Thank God you're here," the woman said. "My radio doesn't work. What's happening? What's going on?"

"It's a big one. Almost a seven. The approaches to this bridge are gone. Are the children all right? Are any of them hurt?"

"I don't think so. We're a car pool. For swimming lessons. I think they're all right. Are you all right?" she said, turning to the children. "I think they're just screaming." None of them was screaming now but one small boy was whining. "Ohhhhhhhh . . ." he was saying very low and sad.

"Well, now I'm here," Nora Jane said. "They'll come get us in boats. They'll come as soon as they can."

"I'm a doctor's wife. My husband's Doctor Johnson, the plastic surgeon. I should know what to do but he never told me. I don't know. I just don't know."

"Well, don't worry about it," Nora Jane said. She set the little whining boy on her lap and put her arm around a little girl in a yellow bathing suit. "Listen, we're all right. They'll come and get us. The bridge isn't going to fall. You did all right. You knew to stop the car."

"I'm scared," the little girl in the yellow suit said. "I want to go home. I want to go where my momma is."

"It's all right," Nora Jane said. She pulled the child down beside her and kissed her on the face. "You smell so nice," she said. "Your hair smells like a yellow crayon. Have you been coloring today?"

"I was coloring," the whining boy said. "I was coloring a Big Bird book. I want to go home too. I want to go home right now. I'm afraid to be here. I don't like it here."

"He's afraid of everything," the little girl said. "He's my brother. He's afraid of the dark and he's afraid of frogs." "Ohhhhhhhhhhhhh-hhh," he cried out, louder than ever. "See," the girl said. "If you just say frog he starts crying."

"Celeste, please don't make him cry," the plastic surgeon's wife said. "I'm Madge Johnson," she went on. "That's Donald and Celeste, they belong to the Connerts that live next door and that's Lindsey in the back and this is Starr and Alexander up here with me. They're mine. Lindsey, are you all right? See if she's all right, would you?"

Nora Jane looked into the back of the station wagon. Lindsey was curled up with a striped beach towel over her head. She was sucking her thumb. She was so still that for a moment Nora Jane wasn't sure she was breathing. "Are you all right?" she said, laying her hand on the child's shoulder. "Lindsey, are you okay?"

The child lifted her head about an inch off the floor and shook it from side to side. "You can get up here with us," Nora Jane said. "You don't have to stay back there all alone."

"She wants to be there," Celeste said. "She's a baby. She sucks her thumb."

"I want to go home now," Donald said, starting to whine again. "I want to go see my momma. I want you to drive the car and take me home."

"We can't drive it right now," Madge said. "We have to wait for the men to come get us. We have to be good and stay still and in a little while they'll come and get us and take us home in boats. Won't that be nice? They'll be here as soon as they can. They'll be here before we know it."

"I want to go home now," Donald said. "I want to go home and I'm hungry. I want something to eat."

"Shut up, Donald," Celeste said.

"How old are they?" Nora Jane said.

"They're five, except Lindsey and Alexander, they're four. I wish we could hear your radio. I wish we could hear what's going on."

"I could reach out the front window and turn it back on, I guess. I hate to walk over there again. Until I'm sure the aftershocks are over. Look, roll down that window and see if you can reach in and turn the radio on. You don't have to turn on the ignition. Thank God the top's down. I almost didn't put it down."

Madge wiggled through the window and turned on the radio in the convertible. "In other news, actor David Niven died today at his home in Switzerland. The internationally famous actor succumbed to a long battle with Gehrig's disease. He was seventy-three. . . . Now for an update on earthquake damage. The department of geology at the University of California at Berkeley says—oh, just a minute, here's a late report on the bridges. Anyone caught on the Bay Bridge or the Richmond–San Rafael bridge please stay in your cars until help arrives. The Coast Guard is on its way. Repeat, Coast Guard rescue boats are on their way. The danger is past. Please stay in your cars until help arrives. Do not move from a place of safety. The lighthouse on East Brother has fallen into the sea. . . ."

"I want to go home now," Donald was starting up again. Lindsey rose up in the back and joined him. "I want my momma," she was crying. "I want to go to my house."

"Come sit up here with us," Nora Jane said. "Come sit with Celeste and Donald and me. You better turn that radio off now," she said to Madge. "It's just scaring them. It's not going to tell us anything we don't already know."

"I don't want to come up there," Lindsey cried, stuffing the towel into her mouth with her thumb, talking through a little hole that was all she had left for breath. She was crying, big tears were running down the front of her suit. Madge climbed out the window again and turned off the radio.

"You're a big baby," Celeste said to Lindsey. "You're just crying to get attention."

"Shut up, Celeste," Madge said. "Please don't say things to them."

"I want to go to my house," Donald said. "I want you to drive the car right now."

"ALL RIGHT," Nora Jane said. "NOW ALL OF YOU SHUT UP A MINUTE. I want you all to shut up and quit crying and listen to me. This is an emergency. When you have an emergency everybody has to stick together and act right. We can't go anywhere right now. We have to wait to be rescued. So, if you'll be quiet and act like big people I will sing to you. I happen to be a wonderful singer. Okay, you want me to sing? Well, do you?"

"I want you to," Donald said, and cuddled closer.

"Me too," Celeste said, and sat up very properly, getting ready to listen.

"I want you to," Lindsey said, then closed her mouth down over her thumb. Starr and Alexander cuddled up against Madge. Then, for the first time since she had been in California, Nora Jane sang in public. She had been the despair of the sisters at the Academy of the Most Sacred Heart of Jesus because she would never use her voice for the glory of God or stay after school and practice with the choir. All Nora Jane had ever used her voice for was to memorize phonograph albums in case there was a war and all the stereos were blown up.

Now, in honor of the emergency, she took out her miraculous voice and her wonderful memory and began to sing long-playing albums to the children. She sang Walt Disney and *Jesus Christ Superstar* and Janis Joplin and the Rolling Stones and threw in some Broadway musicals for Madge's benefit. She finished up with a wonderful song about a little boy named Christopher Robin going to watch the changing of the guards with his nanny. "They're changing guards at Buckingham Palace. Christopher Robin went down with Alice."

The children were entranced. When she stopped, they clapped their hands and yelled for more.

"I've never heard anyone sing like that in my whole life," Madge said. "You should be on the stage."

"I know," Nora Jane said. "Everyone always says that."

"Sing some more," Donald said. "Sing about backwards land again."

"Sing more," Alexander said. It was the first time he had said a word since Nora Jane got in the car. "Sing more."

"In a minute," she said. "Let me catch my breath. I'm starving, aren't you? I'll tell you one thing, the minute we get off this bridge I'm going somewhere and get something to eat. I'm going to eat like a pig."

"So am I," Celeste said. "I'm going to eat like a pig, oink, oink."

"I'm going to eat like a pig," Donald said. "Oink, oink."

"Oink, oink," said Alexander in a small voice.

"Oink, oink," said Starr.

"Oink, oink," said Lindsey through her thumb.

"There's a seagull," Nora Jane said. "Look out there. They're lighting on the bridge. That must mean it's all right now. They only sit on safe places."

"How do they know?" Celeste said. "How do they know which place is safe?"

"The whales tell them," Nora Jane said. "They ask the whales."

"How do the whales know?" Celeste insisted. "Who tells the whales? Whales can't talk to seagulls." Celeste was really a very questionable little girl to have around if you were pregnant. But Nora Jane was saved explaining whales because a man in a yellow slicker appeared on the edge of the bridge, climbing a ladder. He threw a leg over the railing and started toward the car. Another man was right behind him. "Here they come," Alexander said. "They're coming. Oink, oink, oink."

"Here they come," Celeste screamed at the top of her lungs. She climbed up on Nora Jane's stomach and stuck her head out the window, yelling to the Coast Guard. "Here we are. Oink, oink. Here we are."

What is that? Tammili Whittington wondered. She was the responsible one of the pair. Shark butting Momma's stomach? Typhoon at sea? Tree on fire? Running from tiger? Someone standing on us? Hummmmmmmmmmm, she decided and turned a fin into a hand, four fingers and a thumb.

Here they come, Nora Jane was thinking, moving Celeste's feet to the side. Here come the rescuers. Hooray for everything. Hooray for my fellow men.

"Oh, my God," Madge said, starting to cry. "Here they are. They've come to save us."

"Oink, oink," Celeste was screaming out the window. "Oink, oink, we're over here. Come and save us. And hurry up because we're hungry."

DRUNK WITH LOVE

FREDDY HARWOOD SAT IN HIS OFFICE at his bookstore in Berkeley, California, with his feet up on the desk and chewed the edge of his coffee cup. Francis came to the door three times to see if he would talk but he wouldn't even look at her. "You've got to send back those calligraphy books," she said. "We haven't sold a single one. I told you not to get that many."

"I don't want to send them back," he said. "I want them right where they are. Don't talk to me now, Francis. I'm thinking."

"Are you okay?"

"No. Now go on. Close the door."

"What's wrong?"

"Nora Jane's pregnant."

"Oh, my God."

"Leave me alone, Francis. Please shut the door."

"You need someone to talk to. You need—"

"Go run the bookstore, Francis. Please don't stand there."

She left the door open. Freddy got up and closed it. He laid his feet on a stack of invoices and stuck the edge of his thumb into his mouth. Manic-depressive, he decided. I was perfectly all right five minutes ago, a normal average neurotic walking down the street on my way to do my share of the world's work, on my way to add my light to the store of light, on my way to run the single most financially depressed bookstore in Northern California and maybe the world. Perfectly, absolutely all right. Normal. And the minute I came in this room I started thinking about her and all she ever did in this room in my life was try to rob me. My God, I love her.

He raised his hands to his face. He made a catcher's mitt out of his hands and laid his face into that container. This is it, he decided, what all the science and art and philosophy and poetry and literature and movies were supposed to deliver me from and they have failed. A baby inside of her and it might not even be mine. A curved universe, low and inside, coming at me below the knees.

The first shock passed up the desk and through his hands and into his jaw. Books fell from their shelves, a chair slid into a window, there were crashes downstairs. She's in the car, he thought. She's in that goddamn convertible. He got up and pulled the door open and moved out into the hall. The stairway was still there. He ran down the stairs and found Francis in the History section holding on to a man in a raincoat. Several customers were huddled around the cash register. Willis and Eileen were on the floor with their arms over their heads. "Get out in the street," Freddy yelled. "For Christ's sake, get out of here. There's too much to fall. Let's go. Let's get outside." He pushed a group of customers through the turnstile. The second shock came. A section of art books fell across Children's Fantasy.

"Out the door," he was screaming. "For Christ's sake get out the door. Francis, get over here. Get out that door before it shatters." He dragged the customers along with him. They were barely out the door when the third shock came. The front window collapsed around the sign *Clara Books, Clara For Light*. His baby. The whole front window caved in upon a display of photography books. It moved in great triangular plates right down on top of Irving Penn and Ansel Adams and Disfarmer and David Hockney and Eugene Smith. A five-thousand-dollar print of "Country Doctor" fell across the books. "Is anyone else in there?" Freddy yelled. "Willis, where is Allison? Was she in the storeroom?"

"She's here," Willis said. "Right here by me." Telegraph Avenue was full of people. They were streaming out of the stores. A woman in a sari was running toward them. She grabbed Freddy's arm and pulled him toward a door. "In there," she was screaming. "My babies in there. You save them. In there." She pulled him toward the door of a restaurant. "In there," she kept saying, pointing to the door, pulling on his arm. "My babies in there. In the kitchen. In there." He pushed her behind him and walked into the restaurant. He moved between the tables, past the barstools and the bar, and turned into a narrow hall. He went down a hallway and into a kitchen and pushed a fallen counter out of his way and there they were, huddled beneath a sink, two little boys. He covered them with wet tablecloths and picked them up, one under each arm, and walked back out the way he had come. He handed them to a policeman and sank down onto the pavement on top of a tablecloth and began to cry. He rolled up in a ball on the wet white tablecloth and cried his heart out. Then he went to sleep. And into a terrible dream. In the dream Nora Jane's retreating back moved farther and farther away from him through the length of Golden Gate Park. Come back, he yelled after her, come back, I'm sorry I said it. I'm sorry. You goddamn unforgiving, Roman Catholic bitch, come back. Don't you dare break my heart, you heartless uneducated child. Come back to me.

He woke up in a hospital room with his best friend, Nieman Gluuk, standing beside his bed. Nieman was a film critic for the *San Francisco Chronicle*. On the other side of the bed was his mother. His hands were bandaged and there were newspapers piled up on a tray. "You're a hero," Nieman said. "Coast to coast. Every paper in the U.S.A."

"My hands hurt," he said. "My hands are killing me."

"It's only skin," his mother said. "Stuart's been here all night. He said they're going to heal. You're going to be all right."

"Where is Nora Jane? Nieman, WHERE IS NORA JANE?"

"She's on her way. She was on a bridge. She's in Sausalito with some plastic surgeon's wife."

"What day is it?"

"It's Friday. The city's a mess. It's the worst quake in fifty years. Do you want some water?"

"She's pregnant. Nora Jane's going to have a baby. Where is she, Nieman? I want to see her."

"She's coming. It's hard to get around right now, Freddy. She's on her way."

"Get me something for my hands, will you? Goddammit, where is Stuart? Tell him to get me some butter. You have to put butter on it, for Christ's sake. Mother, get Stuart in here. That bastard. Where is he? If he was all burned up I wouldn't be wandering around somewhere. Tell him to get me some butter for my goddamn hands." Stuart was a heart surgeon. He was Freddy's older brother. "I want some butter, for God's sake. Go tell him to get in here." A nurse appeared and slipped a needle out of a cone and put it into Freddy's arm and he drifted back down into his dreams. These dreams were better. It was the beach at Malibu on a windy day, the undertow signs were up and the sun was shining and everyone was sitting around under umbrellas drinking beer. Nieman was filming it. It was a movie about Malibu. They were going to make a million dollars by just being themselves on a beach telling stories and letting Nieman film it.

"She's pregnant?" Mrs. Harwood said, looking at Nieman. "His little girlfriend's pregnant?"

"It's been quite a day," Nieman said. "Well, your son's a hero," he added.

"Do you think his hands will be all right?"

"Medical science can do anything now."

★   ★   ★

Nora Jane Whittington was on the Richmond–San Rafael bridge when the earthquake moved across the beautiful city of San Francisco, California. She got out of her car and made her way around the front and climbed into a station wagon full of babies being driven by one Madge Johnson of Sausalito, California. After Nora Jane and Madge were rescued by the Coast Guard they went to Madge's house in Sausalito and Madge's husband, who was a plastic surgeon, took everyone's pulse and the maid fed them supper and Nora Jane told the Johnsons the story of her life, up to and including the fact that she was pregnant and wasn't sure if the father was Freddy Harwood or her old boyfriend, Sandy. "You can have an amnio," Doctor Johnson suggested. "That way you'll at least know if it's a girl or a boy." He laughed at his joke.

"My God, Arnold, that's incredible you would joke at a thing like this," Madge said. "I am really upset with you."

"That is how men face the facts of conception." Doctor Johnson straightened his shoulders and went into his lecture mode. "Men always get dizzy and full of fear and hilarity at the idea of children being conceived. It's a phenomenon that has been documented in many cultures. They have photographed men everywhere, including some very remote tribes in New Guinea, being presented with the fact that a conception has taken place and they uniformly begin to joke about the matter, many going into this sort of uncontrolled smiling laughing state. In much the same way people are often filled with laughter at funerals. It seems to be a clue to the darkness or fear of death hiding in us all. . . ."

"Oh, please," Madge said. "Not now. About this amnio. I think you should consider it, Nora. It would at least tell the blood type."

"What exactly do they do?" Nora Jane said. "They stick a needle down where the baby is? I don't like that idea. How do they know where it is? I don't see how that could be a good idea, to make a hole in there, a germ might get in."

"Oh, they've got it all on a sonar screen while they're doing it," Doctor Johnson said. "There's no chance a good technician would injure the baby. For your own peace of mind you ought to go on and clear this up. It's the modern world, Nora Jane. Take advantage of it. Well, it's up to you."

"Of course it's up to her," Madge said. "Let's turn on the television again. I want to see what happened in the city."

The television came on. Scenes of downtown San Francisco, followed by shots of firemen escorting people from buildings. There were broken monuments, stretchers, smashed automobiles. Then Freddy Harwood's face appeared, a shot Nieman had taken years ago at a Berkeley peace rally. "Bookstore owner walks into burning building," the announcer was saying. "In an act of unparalleled daring and courage a Telegraph Avenue bookstore owner walked into a Vietnamese restaurant and carried out two small children through what firemen described as an inferno. He was taken to Mount Sinai Hospital where he is being treated for burns of the hands and legs. The governor has sent greetings and in a press release the President of the United States said . . ."

"It's Freddy," Nora Jane said. "Oh, my God, Madge, that's him. How can I call him?"

Now Nora Jane stood at the foot of the hospital bed. Madge and Doctor Johnson were with her. Nieman had moved back. Mrs. Harwood was still stationed by her son's head. "He said you were going to have a baby," she said. "I think that's wonderful. I want you to know I will do anything I can to help." She lifted her hands. She held them out to the girl.

"How is he?" Nora Jane said. "Are his hands going to be okay?"

"They'll heal," Nieman said. "He's a hero, Nora Jane. He's gone the distance. That's the important thing. After you do that you can fix the rest."

"I don't know what to say," Nora Jane said. "I never knew a hero." She moved closer to the bed. She lay her head down on Freddy's crazy hairy chest. She very softly lay her head down upon his heart. He was breathing. No one spoke. Mrs. Harwood looked down at the floor. Madge rolled her hips into Doctor Johnson's leg. Nieman closed his mind.

"Nora Jane was a hero too," Madge said. "She helped me so much on the bridge. I never would have made it without her. I had a whole carpool with me."

"I didn't do anything," Nora Jane said. "I just came over there because I was afraid to be alone." She stood up, put her hand on Freddy's head, looked at his mother. She was thinking about something he did when he made love to her. He pretended he was retarded. "Oh, Missy Nora Jane, you so good to come and see us at the home," he would say. "Miss Dater, she say we should be so good to you. You want me to do what I do for Miss Dater? Miss Dater, she say I'm so good at it. She say I get all the cookies and candy I can eat. She say—"

"Shut up," Nora Jane would say whenever he started that. "I won't make love to you if you pretend to be retarded." Now that he was a hero she wished she had let him do it. She giggled.

"I'm sorry," she said. "I was just thinking about something he does that's funny. He does a lot of real crazy things."

"Don't tell me," Mrs. Harwood said. "I'm his mother."

"He's waking up," Nieman said. "Don't talk about him. He can hear." Freddy opened his eyes, then closed them again, then waved his hands in the air, then moaned. He opened one eye, then the other. He was looking right at her. Nora Jane's heart melted. "Oh, Freddy," she said. "I'm so glad you're here."

"You're going to marry me," he said. He sat up on his elbow. "You are going to marry me, goddammit. You can't play with somebody's affections like that. I'm a serious man and SERIOUS PEOPLE GET MARRIED. Goddammit, my hands are killing me. Mother, would you get Stuart to come in here. That GODDAMN STUART, THEY OUGHT TO TAKE HIS LICENSE AWAY . . . NORA JANE."

She put her hands on his chest. It seemed the best place to touch him. "I'll get a test," she said. "Doctor Johnson's going to fix it up."

"I don't want a test," he said. "I want you to marry me." He sank back down on the pillows. He was starting to cry again. Tears were starting to run down his face. His mother looked away. Nieman was writing it. I admire your passion, he was writing. I always admire passion. Freddy kept on crying. Madge and Doctor Johnson clutched each other. Nora Jane moved her hands up onto his shoulder. "Please don't cry anymore," she said. "You have a good time. You have a happy life. You watch movies all the time and read books and go up to Willits and camp out and build your solar house. Freddy, please stop crying. We're alive, aren't we? I mean, we're lucky to be alive. A lot of people got killed." He stopped at that.

"Wipe off my face, will you, Mother? And tell Stuart to get in here and put something on my hands. Oh, shit. Could I have another shot? I really want another shot."

"I love you," Nora Jane said. "I really love you, Freddy. I'm not just saying that. You are the best friend I've ever had."

"Good," he said. "I'm glad you do." Then the nurse came in the room with Freddy's brother right behind her and they moved everyone out into the hall and put him back to sleep.

Twelve injections of Demerol, seven days on Valium and Tylenol Number Three, four days on Bayer aspirin, failed attempts at transcendental meditation, self-hypnosis, and positive thinking, three days of walking all over the Mount Sinai Hospital behind the bookmobile, and Freddy was dismissed, with his hands still bandaged, to resume his normal life. Nora Jane picked him up at the emergency entrance. Three nurses helped him into the car, piling the backseat with flowers and plants.

"Stop off somewhere and get rid of these goddamn flowers,"

Freddy said, as soon as they pulled out onto the freeway. "I had to take them."

"I never saw anybody get that many flowers in my life, even when the archbishop died."

"Let's go to Peet's. I want a cup of real coffee so goddamn much."

"I made an appointment to get an amnio. They said I could come in tomorrow. I, well, never mind that."

"What? Never mind what? Cut down Redwood."

"I know. I was going to. Listen, I think you'll be sorry I did it. Well, anyway, what difference does it make?"

"It makes a difference to me."

"It might not even tell me anything. I don't even know what blood type Sandy is. Well, never mind it. I don't know how we got into this." She parked the car across from Peet's and turned around in the seat and put her hands on his bandages. "I like you the most of anyone I've ever made love to or run around with. That's true and you know it. You're the best friend I've ever had. But I am not in love with you and that is also true." Her black curls were violet in the sun. Her shoulders were bare beneath the straps of her sundress. If he could not have her there was no reason for anything. If he could not have her there was no reason in the world, all was madness and random evil and stupid jokes being played by the galaxy and all its real and imagined gods. Gods, yes, if he could not have her there must be gods after all, only something in the image of man could be so dumb, mistaken, ignorant and cruel. The sun beat down on Nora Jane's blue convertible, it beat down on her head and shoulders and Freddy Harwood's bandaged hands. "You don't have to love me, Nora Jane. As long as that baby belongs to me."

"I don't think it does."

"Well, get out and let's go see if I can figure out a way to drink a cup of coffee without making a goddamn fool of myself." He knocked the door open with his elbow and stepped out onto Telegraph Avenue. Seven people were around him by the time Nora Jane could come around the other way. Three people who already knew and loved him and four more who wanted to. He's a hero, Nora Jane was thinking. Why would anybody like that want to like me anyway?

The next morning Nora Jane went down to the Berkeley Women's Clinic and had the amniocentesis. Afterwards she was going to meet Nieman and Freddy for lunch. She got up early and dressed up in a jade green silk dress, which was beginning to be too tight around the hips, and she screwed her face together and walked into the clinic determined to go through with it.

The first thing she had to do was take off the dress. Next she had to lie down on a bed surrounded by machinery, and in a moment she was watching the inside of her uterus on a television screen. "Oh, oh," the technician said. The doctor laughed.

"What happened?" Nora Jane said. "What's wrong?"

"There're two of them," the doctor said. "I thought so by the heartbeats. You've got twins." He squeezed her hand. The technician beamed, as delighted as if he had had something to do with it.

"What do you mean?" Nora Jane sat up on her elbow.

"Two babies in there. Identical by the looks of it. I think it's one sac. Can't be sure."

"Oh, my God."

"Be still now. Lie back. We're going to begin the amnio. It won't take long. It's all right. Don't worry. Hold Jamie's hand. Oh, that's a good girl." Then Nora Jane squeezed her eyes and her fists and the needle penetrated her skin and moved down into the sac Lydia and Tammili were swimming in and took one ounce of amniotic fluid and withdrew. The doctor secured the test tube, rubbed a spot on Nora Jane's stomach with alcohol and patted her on the leg. "You're a good girl," he said. "Now we'll get you out of here so you can celebrate."

"I can't believe it," she said. "I just don't believe it's true."

"We'll give you a picture to take home with you. How about

that?" An hour later Nora Jane left the clinic carrying in her purse an envelope containing a photograph of Tammili and Lydia floating around her womb. This is too much knowledge, she decided. This is more than I need to know.

"What's this all about?" Nieman said. He was at an upstairs table at Chez Panisse holding Freddy's hand while the test went on. "Stop chewing your bandages, Freddy. Talk to me."

"She fucked this crazy bastard she used to go with in New Orleans. One afternoon when she was mad at me, so she doesn't know if the baby's mine. I should have killed him the minute I saw him. He's a goddamn criminal, Nieman. I ought to have him put in jail. Well, never mind, he isn't here anyway. So she's having this amniocentesis and she won't get the results for about a month anyway. I'm going crazy. You know that. Everything happens to me. You know it does. I'm probably going to lose my left hand."

"No you aren't. Stuart said it was healing. Besides, you're a hero. It was worth it."

"That's easy for you to say."

"So when will she find out?"

"I don't know. Who knows anything anymore. Well, I'm marrying her anyway if I can talk her into it. I can't live without her. You wouldn't believe how goddamn much my hands hurt at night. That goddamn Stuart won't give me a thing."

"Have you heard from the kids, the ones you saved?"

"Of course I have. They write me every other day. They've written me about ten letters. I'm going to get them into Camp Minnesota next year. I was thinking about that this morning. I'll take them up there as soon as they're old enough." Freddy still went to his old camp every summer. He was a senior counselor. Nieman looked away. Freddy's friends never mentioned his camp to him. They liked to talk about that behind his back. "Well," Nieman said. "Here she comes. You want me to leave?"

"Of course not, Nieman. This is Berkeley. Not Ohio. What's happening?" He stood up and held out a chair for Nora Jane and gave her a small quick kiss on the side of the face. Freddy was in extremely high gear this morning. Even for him he was running very tight and hot. He handed Nora Jane her napkin, laid it in her lap. "What did they say?"

"It's two babies. It's going to be twins. I have a picture of them if you'd like to see it." She fished it out of her purse and Freddy held it up to the light and looked at it.

"A month?" Freddy said. "Well, let's eat lunch. A month, huh? Thirty days."

"I don't think they're yours," she said. She was looking straight at him. "The right time of month when I was with Sandy. You never listen when I tell you that." Nieman coughed and drank his wine and signaled to the waiter for some more.

"The role of will is underrated in human affairs," Freddy said. "To tell the truth, Miss Whittington, you have driven me crazy. Have I told you that today?"

"I didn't mean to," she answered. "You're the one that thought up sleeping with me." Nieman rose a few inches from his chair and caught the waiter's eye. Nothing human is foreign to me, he said to himself, as he did about a hundred times a day.

II

SANDY, THE BEAUTIFUL AND MYSTERIOUS Sandy George Wade of Louisiana and Texas and nowhere. Abandoned when he was six years old, after which he roamed the world playing out that old scenario, doing things to please people and make them love him, then doing things to make them desert him. It was all he knew. One of the people he talked into caring for him was a drunken poet who taught English at his reform school in Texas. The poet taught him to love poetry and to wield it with his voice and eyes. Nora Jane was a sucker for poetry. When they lived together in New Orleans Sandy had been able to get her to forgive him anything by quoting Dylan Thomas or A. E. Housman or a poem by Auden called "Petition," which ends with a plea to "Look shining at, new styles of architecture, a change of heart." Nora Jane always took that to mean she was supposed to think anything Sandy did was all right with advanced thinkers like poets.

Now, on the same day that Nora Jane was having her amniocentesis, Sandy was sitting alone in his room in Mirium Sallisaw's tacky West Coast mansion thinking of ways to get Nora Jane to forgive him and take him back as her mate and child and live-in boyfriend. Sandy worked for Mirium Sallisaw in her cancer business. She sold trips to Mexico for miracle cures. She had made several million dollars collecting the life savings of terminally ill cancer patients and she paid Sandy well to be her driver.

In his spare time Sandy had been talking to Mirium's psychoanalyst and he was beginning to see that some of the things he had done might actually be affecting the lives of other people, especially and specifically Nora Jane, who was the best thing that had ever happened to him. He paced around his room and lay down on his bed and thought up a thousand tricks to get her back. Finally he decided to sit down and write out his frustration in a poem and have Mirium's Federal Express service deliver it. By the time he had finished it he was so excited he abandoned the Federal Express idea and drove into town and delivered it himself. She was not there, so he left it in the mailbox.

Nora Jane found the poem when she got home from lunch at Chez Panisse. She had spent the afternoon arguing with Freddy about whether they should get married and finally, when she left him at his house, she had agreed to consider a trial marriage for the duration of her pregnancy.

Now she walked up onto the porch of the beige and green house where she had a room and saw the piece of paper sticking out of her mailbox. She knew what it was. No one in her life had left her things sticking out of mailboxes except Sandy. Sandy was one of the few young men left in the Western world who understood the power of written communications. There it was, sticking out and beckoning to her as she walked by the red salvia and the madrone hedge and the poppies. She pulled it out and sat down on the stairs to read.

Jane, Jane, where can you be?
Flown so very far from me.

The golden rain trees are blooming now
Above the house where we once lived.
Could we go there once again?
Could we recapture the love we had?

She folded it up and put it back into its envelope and went into the house and called him up.

"Come on over," she said. "I have a lot to tell you."

"What is that?" he answered.

"You won't believe it, I'm going to have two babies about six months from now."

"You mean that, don't you?"

"I think they're yours, but I'm not sure. Are you coming?"

"As fast as I can get there."

"Do you think it's funny?"

"No."

"Neither do I."

He arrived at eight o'clock that night, pulling up to the curb in Mirium Sallisaw's white Cadillac Coupe de Ville. It was the car he used to drive her clients down to Mexico to the Laetrile clinic and to Las Vegas to get their bootleg Interferon. It was weird and depressing work and Sandy had been saving his money so he could quit. He was up to about four thousand dollars in savings on the night Nora Jane told him she was pregnant. He sped along the freeway thinking what a small sum it was, wondering where in the world he would get some more.

Nora Jane was waiting for him on the steps. He took her into his arms and the old magic was as good as new. The poem he had written to her was true. Back in New Orleans the golden rain trees were covering their old roof with golden dust. "That stuff is made of stars," Sandy had told her once. "And we are too."

"I love you," he told her now. "God, I've been missing you."

"I miss you too," she answered.

"I'm sorry I've been such an asshole. I don't know what makes me act that way."

"It's okay. It was half my fault. Come on in. I've got a lot to tell you."

It was some hours later and the moon was shining in on her small white bed with her new lace-trimmed sheets and the lace-trimmed pillowcases and the yellow lilies in a vase she had run out and bought when she knew he was coming. She was wrapped up in his arms. She had told him all she knew. Now she was finishing her speech. "I'm going to have them no matter whose they are. It's all I know for sure. I don't care what anyone says. Or who gets mad at me."

"Don't sound like that. I want them. I want them to be mine so much I'd reach inside and touch them." He ran his hands across her stomach. "Listen, baby, we're going to get out of here and get a place together and start living like white people. I've had all I can take of loneliness. You can call the shots. You tell me what you want and I'll deliver. I'm quitting Mirium. I've got four grand saved up in the bank and that will tide us over. I'm going to an employment agency tomorrow and see what they can offer. I'll take anything they offer me." He got up from the bed and pulled a package of cigarettes out of his pants and lit one and stood in the window smoking. The moonlight was on his body.

He was so graceful it broke Nora Jane's heart to look at him. He was the most beautiful and graceful person she had ever watched or seen. Everything he did made sense in the beauty of movement department. Watching him now, so beautiful and perfect, she thought about a terrible story he told her about being left somewhere when he was small and standing by the door for days waiting for his mother to come back but she didn't come. "Oh, Sandy." Nora Jane got up and stood behind him, holding him in her arms. "I will never leave you again no matter what happens or what you do. I will stick by you if you want me to." Then she was crying tears all over his beautiful graceful back.

Across the campus of the University of California at Berkeley Freddy Harwood was in his hot tub getting drunk. His bandaged hand was propped up on a shoe rack and a bottle of VVSOP Napoleon brandy was by the soap dish and he was talking on the remote-control phone. "She hasn't even called and she isn't there. It means she's with him. I know it. She's bound to be. I've had it, Nieman. Life's not doing this to me. I'm getting out. I mean it. I'm getting into dope or moving to New York or paddling up to Canada in a birchbark canoe. None of it is funny anymore. The whole thing sucks and you know it. The whole show. You goddamn well know it. I would take any age over this age. Fuck it all to goddamn bloody fucking hell. That's all I've got to say. I'm through."

Nieman said he would come over.

"Well, hurry up. I'm in deep, old buddy. I lost my sense of reality a while ago. I mean, I didn't do anything to deserve this. This is fucking unfair. I don't know. I just don't know."

Nieman said he was on his way. He called up Freddy's old girlfriend, Buiji Dalton, and told her to meet him there. Then he called a friend of theirs named Teddy who was a psychotherapist and told him to get in his car. They converged on Freddy's house. It was a wooden house with great glass wings that swept the horizon for miles across San Francisco and the bridges and the bay.

It had cost three hundred and fifty thousand dollars. It had paintings by every major painter who had worked in the United States in the last twenty years. It had books in six languages and light and air and was full of food and wine and bottled water from Missouri that tasted like honey. In the middle of the patio, looking out on the bay, was the hot tub where Freddy was contemplating suicide or having a prefrontal lobotomy or taking heroin every day. "The pain," he was saying into his tape recorder. "This is real pain. This is not some figment of my imagination. This is not just trying to get something that's hard to get. I don't want her because she's hard to get. I want her because I like to look at her and if those aren't my babies in there it's all over, she will never marry me. I risked my life to save two small children. I walked into a burning building. It isn't fair. IT IS NOT FAIR. I'M MAD AS HELL AND I'M NOT GOING TO TAKE IT ANYMORE." He turned off the recording machine and called Nieman back. "You haven't left yet?"

"I was going out the door."

"Have you got a tape of *Network*, that movie with Peter Finch as the television announcer who gets all the people yelling out the windows?"

"I think so."

"Bring it over, will you?"

Freddy laid down the phone and turned the recorder back on. "Bitter," he said into the microphone. "Bitter, bitter, bitter, jaded, tired of life and cynical. No good for anything anymore. Nothing works. The system fucks."

Clouds of vapor were rolling in from the Pacific Ocean. In a petri dish near the Berkeley campus Tammili and Lydia Whittington's DNA began to give up its secrets to the Chinese student who was working overtime to make money to bring his sister to the United States from Singapore. "Very interesting," he thought. He added one drop of a chemical and watched the life below him form and re-form. *AB posi-*

tive, universal donors, he wrote on a pad. He translated it into Chinese with a few brief strokes of his pen. This case interested him very much. He wrote down the name, Nora Jane Whittington. Yes, when he got home he would cast the *I Ching* and see what else was in store for these baby girls with the lucky blood. Lin Tan, for that was his name, moved the dish to one side and picked up the next one.

Sandy got back into bed with Nora Jane and cuddled her up into his arms. He kissed her hair and then her eyes. He arranged their bodies so they fit against each other very comfortably and perfectly. He heaved a sigh. It was so fragile. It never stayed. It always deserted him. It always went away. It was here now. It would go away. It would leave him alone. "Calm down," she said. "Don't get scared. We don't have to be unhappy if we don't want to."

"When will you know?"

"They said a month. They're busy. So what kind of blood do you have anyway? I'm B positive."

"It's some weird shit. I've forgotten. I'll call and find out."

"Go to sleep. We'll make it."

"Do you love me?"

"Yes, I do."

"Well, I love you too."

Freddy got out of the hot tub. He was the color of a sunset at Malibu when there were plenty of clouds. Buiji Dalton took a big white towel and began to dry him off. She'd been trying to marry him for his money for five years and she wasn't giving up now. Not with all she had to offer. Not after she had divorced Dudley and only kept the house. "I couldn't believe it when I read it in the paper. I cut it out and showed it to everyone. I made a hundred copies and mailed them to people. I'm so proud of you."

"Hey, stop that, will you?"

"What?"

"Drying me. I'm okay. Come on. Let's go in the bedroom and watch this movie. It's the greatest movie made in the United States in four years and Nieman had to go and trash it. He trashed it. Wait till you see it. I want you to tell him what you think when it's over."

"Do you want anything to eat?"

"No, just get me that brandy, will you?" Freddy draped the towel over his shoulder and pulled the other part across his stomach to cover his reproductive organs and went into his bedroom and got into bed with his best friend and his old girlfriend on either side of him and pushed a button and the movie started. Freddy had changed his mind about suicide. After all, Nora Jane was practically illiterate. She had never even read Dostoyevsky. The copyright warning appeared on the screen. His psychiatrist friend, Teddy, came tearing into the room waving a bag from the deli. He took up the other side of Buiji Dalton and the movie began.

"This will go away," Sandy was saying. "It will disappear."

"It might not," Nora Jane answered. "Don't get scared. We don't have to be miserable if we don't want to be."

Down inside Nora Jane's womb Tammili signaled to her sister. "Nice night tonight."

"I wish it could always be the same. She's always changing. Up and down. Up and down."

"Get used to it. We'll be there soon."

"Let's don't think about it."

"You're right. Let's be quiet."

"Okay."

THE STARLIGHT
EXPRESS

NORA JANE was seven months' pregnant when Sandy disappeared again. *Dear Baby,* the note said. *I can't take it. Here's all the money that is left. Don't get mad if you can help it. I love you, Sandy.*

She folded up the note and put it in a drawer. Then she made up the bed. Then she went outside and walked along the water's edge. At least we are living on the water, she was thinking. I always get lucky about things like that. Well, I know one thing. I'm going to have these babies no matter what I have to do and I'm going to keep them alive. They won't die on me or get drunk or take cocaine. Freddy was right. A decent home is the best thing.

Nora Jane was on a beach fifty miles south of San Francisco, beside a little stucco house Sandy's old employer had been renting them for next to nothing. Nora Jane had never liked living in that house. Still, it was on the ocean.

The ocean spread out before her now, gray and dark, breaking against the boulders where it turned into a little cove. There were places where people had been making fires. Nora Jane began to pick up all the litter she could find and put it in a pile beside a fire site. She walked around for half an hour picking up cans and barrettes and half-burned pieces of cardboard and piled them up beside a boulder. Then she went back to the house and got some charcoal lighter and a match and lit the mess and watched it burn. It was the middle of October.

December the fifteenth was only two months away. I could go to Freddy, she was thinking. He will always love me and forgive me anything. But what will it do to him? Do I have a right to get around him so he'll only love me more? This was a question Nora Jane was always asking herself about Freddy Harwood. Now she asked it once again.

A cold wind was blowing off the ocean. She picked up a piece of driftwood and added it to the fire. She sank down upon the sand. She was carrying ten pounds of babies but she moved as gracefully as ever. She wiggled around until her back was against the boulder, sitting up very straight, not giving in to the cold or the wind. I'm one of those people that could go to the Himalayas, she decided. Because I never give in to cold. If you hunch over it will get you.

Freddy Harwood stood on the porch of his half-finished house, deep in the woods outside of Willits, California, and thought about Nora Jane. He was thinking about her voice, trying to remember how it sounded when she said his name. If I could remember that sound, he decided. If I could remember what she said that first night it would be enough. If that's all I get it will have to do.

He looked deep into the woods, past the madrone tree, where once he had seen a bobcat come walking out and stop at the place where the trees ended and the grass began. A huge yellow cat with a muff around its neck and brilliant eyes. A poet had been visiting and they had made up a song about the afternoon called "The Great Bobcat Visit and Other Mysteries of Willits." If she was here I could teach it to her, Freddy thought. So, there I go again. Everything either reminds me of her or it doesn't remind me of her, so everything reminds me of her. What good does it do to have six million dollars and two houses and a bookstore if I'm in love with Nora Jane? Freddy left his bobcat lookout and walked around the side of the house toward the road. A man was hurrying up the path.

It was his neighbor, Sam Lyons, who lived a few miles away up an impassable road. Freddy waved and went to meet him. He's coming to tell me she's dead, he decided. She died in childbirth in the hands of a midwife in Chinatown and I'm supposed to go on living after that. "What's happening?" he called out. "What's going on?"

"You got a call," Sam said. "Your girlfriend's coming on the train. I'm getting tired of this, Harwood. You get yourself a phone. That's twice this week. *Two calls in one week!*"

In a small neat room near the Berkeley campus a young Chinese geneticist named Lin Tan Sing packed a change of clothes and his toilet articles, left a note for himself about some things to do when he returned, and walked out into the beautiful fall day. He had been saving his money for a vacation and today was the day it began. As soon as he finished work that afternoon he would ride the subway to the train station and get on board the Starlight Express and travel all the way up the California coast to Puget Sound. He would see the world. My eyes have gone too far inside, Lin Tan told himself. Now I will go outside and see what's happening at other end. People will look at me and I will look at them. We will learn about each other. Perhaps the train will fall off cliff into the ocean. There will be stories in the newspapers. Young Chinese scientist saves many lives in daring rescues. President of United States invites young Chinese scientist to live in White House and tutor children of politicians. Young Chinese scientist adopted by wealthy man whose life he saves in train wreck. I am only a humble scientist trying to unravel genetic code, young Chinese scientist tells reporters. Did not mean to be hero. Do not know what came over me. I pushed on fallen car and great strength came to me when it was least expected.

Lin Tan entered the Berkeley campus and strolled along a sidewalk leading to the student union. Students were all around. A man in black was playing a piano beneath a tree. The sky was clear with only a few clouds to the west. The Starlight Express, Lin Tan was thinking. All Plexiglas across the top. Stars rolling by while I am inside with something nice to drink. Who knows? Perhaps I will find a girl on the train who wishes to talk with me. I will tell her all things scientific and also of poetry. I will tell her the poetry of my country and also of England. Lin Tan folded his hands before him as he walked, already he was on the train, speeding up the California coast telling some dazzling blonde the story of his life and all about his work. Lin Tan worked at night in the lab of the Berkeley Women's Clinic. He did chemical analyses on the fluid removed during amniocentesis. So far he had made only one mistake in his work. One time a test had to be repeated because he knocked a petri dish off the table with his sleeve. Except for that his results had proved correct in every single instance. No one else in the lab had such a record. Because of this Lin Tan always kept his head politely bowed in the halls and was extra-nice to the other technicians and generous with advice and help. He had a fellowship in the graduate program in biology and he had this easy part-time job and his sister, Jade Tan Sing, was coming in six months to join him. Only one thing was lacking in Lin Tan's life and that was a girlfriend. He had what he considered a flaw in his character and wished to be in love with a Western girl with blond hair. It was only fate, the *I Ching* assured him. A fateful flaw that would cause disaster and ruin but not of his own doing and therefore nothing to worry about.

On this train, he was thinking, I will sit up straight and hold my head high. If she asks where I come from I will say Shanghai or Hong Kong as it is difficult for them to picture village life in China without thinking of rice paddies. I am a businessman, I will say, and have only taken time off to learn science. No, I will say only the truth so she may gaze into my eyes and be at peace. I will buy you jewels and perfume, I will tell her. Robes with silken dragons eating the moon, many pearls. Shoes with flowers embroidered on them for every minute of the day. Look out the Plexiglas ceiling at the stars. They are whirling by and so are we even when we are off the train.

*   *   *

Nora Jane bought her ticket and went outside to get some air while she waited for the train. She was wearing a long gray sweatshirt with a black leather belt riding on top of the twins. On her legs were bright yellow tights and yellow ballet shoes. A yellow and white scarf was tied around her black curls. She looked just about as wonderful as someone carrying ten pounds of babies could ever look in the world. She was deserted and unwed and on her way to find a man whose heart she had broken only four months before and she should have been in a terrible mood but she couldn't work up much enthusiasm for despair. Whatever chemicals Tammili and Lydia were pumping into her bloodstream were working nicely to keep Nora Jane in a good mood. She stood outside the train station watching a line of cirrus clouds chugging along the horizon, thinking about the outfits she would buy for her babies as soon as they were born. Nora Jane loved clothes. She couldn't wait until she had three people to dress instead of only one. All her life she had wanted to be able to wear all her favorite colors at one time. Now she would have her chance. She could just see herself walking into a drugstore holding her little girls by the hand. Tammili would be wearing blue. Lydia would be wearing red or pink. Nora Jane would have on peach or mauve or her old standby, yellow. Unless that was too many primaries on one day. I'll start singing, she decided. That way I can work at night while they're asleep. I have to have some money of my own. I don't want anyone supporting us. When I go shopping and buy stuff I don't want anybody saying why did you get this stuff and you didn't need that shirt and so forth. As soon as they're born I'll be able to work and make some money. Nieman said I could sing anyplace in San Francisco. Nieman should know. After all, he writes for the newspaper. If they don't like it then I'll just get a job in a day-care center like I meant to last fall. I'll do whatever I have to do.

A whistle blew. Nora Jane walked back down the concrete stairs. "Starlight Express," a black voice was calling out. "Get on board for the long haul to Washington State. Don't go if you're scared of stars. Stars all the way to Marin, San Rafael, Petaluma, and Sebastopol. Stars all the way to Portland, Oregon, and Seattle, Washington. Stars to Alaska and points north. Stars to the North Pole. Get on board this train. . . ."

Nora Jane threw her backpack over her shoulder and ran for the train. Lin Tan caught a glimpse of her yellow stockings and reminded himself not to completely rule out black hair in his search for happiness.

Freddy Harwood was straightening up his house. He moved the wooden table holding his jigsaw puzzle of the suspended whale from the Museum of Natural History. He watered his paper-white narcissus. He got a broom out of a closet and began to sweep the floor. He found a column Nieman did about *My Dinner with André* and leaned on the broom reading it. It was two o'clock in the afternoon and there was no reason to leave for the station before five. They aren't my babies, he reminded himself. She's having someone else's babies and they aren't mine and I don't want them anyway. Why do I want her at all? Because I like to talk to her, that's why. I like to talk to her more than anyone in the world. That's that. It's my business. Mine and only mine. I like to look at her and I like to talk to her. Jesus Christ! Could I have a maid? I mean would it violate every tenet if I had a maid once a week?

He threw the broom into a closet and pulled on his boots and walked out into the yard to look for the bobcat.

The house Freddy was stamping out of was a structure he had been building on and off for years. It was in Mendocino County near the town of Willits and could only be reached by a long winding uphill road that became impassable when it rained. Actually, it was impassable when it didn't rain but Freddy and his lone neighbor put their four-wheel jeeps in gear and pretended the rock-covered path was a road. Sometimes it even looked like a road, from the right angle and if several trips had been made in a single spell of dry weather.

The house sat on high ground and had several amazing views. To the west lay the coastal ranges of northern California. To the east the state game refuge of the Mendocino National Forest. In any direction were spruce trees and Douglas fir and Northern pine. Freddy had bought the place with the first money he ever earned. That was years ago, during the time when he stopped speaking to his family and smoked dope all day and worked as a chimney sweep. He had lived in a van and saved twelve thousand dollars. Then he had driven up the California coast until he found Douglas fir on land with no roads leading to it. He bought as much as twelve thousand dollars would buy. Two acres, almost three. Then he set up a tent and started building. He built a cistern to catch water and laid pipes to carry it to where the kitchen would later be. He leveled the land and poured a concrete foundation and marked off rooms and hauled stones for a fireplace. He planted fruit trees and a vineyard and put in root plants and an herb garden for medical emergencies. He had been working on the house off and on for twenty-three years. The house was as much a part of Freddy Harwood as his skin. When he was away from Willits for long stretches of time, he thought about the house every day, the red sun of early morning and the redder sun of sundown. The eyes of the bobcat in the woods, the endless lines of mountains in the distance. The taste of the air and the taste of the water. His body sleeping in peace in his own invention.

Now she's ruined my house for me, he was thinking, leaning against the madrone tree while he waited for the bobcat. She's slept in all the rooms and sat on the chairs and touched the furniture. She's used all the forks and spoons and moved the table. I'm putting it back where it goes today. Well, let her come up here and beg for mercy. I don't care. I'll give it to her. Let her cry her dumb little Roman Catholic heart out. I guess she looks like hell. I bet she's as big as a house. Well, shit, not that again.

He turned toward the house. A redbird was throwing itself against the windows. Bird in the house means bad luck. Well, don't let it get in. I'll have to put some screens on those windows. Ruin the light.

The house was very tall with many windows. It was a house a child might draw, tall and thin. Inside were six rooms, or areas, filled with books and mattresses and lamps and tables. Everything was white or black or brown or gray. Freddy had made all the furniture himself except for two chairs by Mies van der Rohe. A closet held all of Buiji Dalton's pottery in case she should come to visit. A shelf held Nieman's books. On a peg behind the bathroom door was Nora Jane's yellow silk kimono.

When she comes, Freddy was saying to himself as he trudged back up the hill to do something about the bird, I won't say a word about anything. I'll just act like everything is normal. Sam came over and said you'd be on the train and it was getting into Fort Bragg at eight and would I meet you. Well, great. I mean, what brought you here? I thought you and the robber baron had settled down for the duration. I mean, I thought I'd never see you again. I mean, it's okay with me. It's not your fault I am an extremely passionate and uncontrollably sensitive personality. I can tell you one thing. It's not easy being this sensitive. Oh, shit, he concluded. I'll just go on and get drunk. I'm a match for her when I'm drunk. Drunk, I'm a match for anyone, even Nora Jane. He opened the closet and reached in behind one of Buiji Dalton's hand-painted Egyptian funeral urns and took out a bottle of Red Aubruch his brother had sent from somewhere. He found a corkscrew and opened it. He passed the cork before his nose, then lifted the bottle and began to drink. "There ain't no little bottle," he was thinking. "Like that old bottle of mine."

At about the same time that Freddy Harwood was resorting to this time-honored method of acquiring courage, Lin Tan Sing was using a similar approach aboard the Starlight Express. He was drinking gin and trying not to stare at the yellow stockings which were all he could see of Nora Jane. She was in a high-backed swivel chair turned around to look out the glassed-in back of the train. She was thinking about whales, how they had their babies in the water, and also about Sandra Draine, who had a baby in a tub of salt water in Sausalito while her husband videotaped the birth. They had shown the tape at the gallery when Sandra had her fall show. It won't be like that for me, Nora Jane was thinking. I'm not letting anyone take any pictures or even come in the room except the doctor and maybe Freddy, but no cameras. I know he'll want to bring a camera, if he's there. He's the silliest man I have ever known.

But I love him anyway. And I hate to do this to him but I have to do what I have to do. I can't be alone now. I have to go somewhere. The train rounded a curve. The wheels screeched. Nora Jane's chair swiveled around. Her feet flew out and she hit Lin Tan in the knee with a ballet shoe.

"Oh, my God," she said. "Did I hurt you?"

"It is nothing."

"We hit a curve. I'm really sorry. I thought the chair was fastened down."

"You are going to have a baby?" His face was very close to her face. It was the largest oriental face Nora Jane had ever seen. The darkest eyes. She had not known there were eyes that dark in all the world, even in China. She lowered her own.

"Yes," she said. "I am."

"I am geneticist. This interests me very much."

"It does me too."

"Would you like to talk with me?"

"Sure. I'd like to have someone to talk to. I was just thinking about the whales. I guess they don't even know it's cold, do they?"

"I have gone out in kayak to be near them. It is very mysterious. It was the best experience I have had in California. A friend of mine in lab at Berkeley Women's Clinic took me with him. He heads a team of volunteers to collect money for whales. Next summer I will go again."

"Oh, my God. That's where I go. I mean, that's my doctor. I'm going to have twin baby girls. I had an amnio at your clinic. That's how I know what they are."

"Oh, this is very strange. You are Miss Whittington of 1512 Arch Street, is it not so? Oh, this is very strange meeting. I am head technician at this lab. Head technician for night lab. Yes. I am the one who did the test for you. I was very excited to have these twin girls show up. It was an important day for me. I had just been given great honor at the university. Oh, this is chance meeting like in books." He stood up and took her hand. "I am Lin Tan Sing, of the province of Suchow, near Beijing, in Central China. I am honored to make your acquaintance." He stood above her, waiting.

"I am Nora Jane Whittington, of New Orleans, Louisiana, and San Jose, California. And Berkeley. I am glad to meet you also. What all did the tests show? What did they look like under the microscope? Do you remember anything else about it?"

"Oh, it is not in lab that I learn things of substance. Only chip away at physical world in lab. Very humble. Because it was a memorable day in my own life I took great liberty and cast *I Ching* for your daughters. I saw great honors for them and gifts of music brought to the world."

"Oh, my God," Nora Jane said. She leaned toward him. "I can't believe I met you on this train." Snowy mountains, Lin Tan was thinking. Peony and butterfly. Redbird in the shade of willows.

Later a waiter came through the club car and Lin Tan advised Nora Jane to have an egg salad sandwich and a carton of milk. "I am surprised they allow you to travel so far along in your pregnancy. Are you going far?"

"Oh, no one said I could go. I mean, I didn't ask anyone. They said I could travel until two months before they came." She put her hand to her mouth. "I guess I should have asked someone. But I was real upset about something and I needed to come up here. I need to see this friend of mine."

"Be sure and get plenty of rest tonight. Very heavy burden for small body."

"My body's not so small. I have big bones. See my wrists." She held out her wrists and he pretended to be amazed at their size. "All the same, be sure and rest tomorrow. Don't take chances. Many very small babies at clinic now. I am worrying very much about so many months in machine for tiny babies. Still, it is United States and they will not allow anything to die. It is the modern age."

"I want my babies no matter what size they are." She folded her hands across her lap. "I guess I shouldn't have come up here. Well, it's too late now. Anyway, where did you learn to speak English so well? Did you have it in school?"

"I studied your writers. I studied Ernest Hemingway and William Faulkner and John Dos Passos. Also, many American poets. Then, since I am here, I am learning all the time with my ears."

"I like poetry a lot. I'm crazy about it to tell the truth."

"I am going to translate poetry of women in my country for women of America. I have noticed there is much sadness and menustation in poetry of women here. But is not sadness in life here. In my country poetry is to overcome sadness, help people to understand how things are and see beauty and order and not give in to despair."

"Oh, like what? Tell me some."

"Here is poem by famous poet of the T'ang Dynasty. The golden age of Chinese poetry.

> *A branch is torn from the tree*
> *The tree does not grieve*
> *And goes on growing*

"Oh, that's wonderful."

"This poet is called the White Poppy. She has been dead for hundreds of years but her poems will always live. This is how it is with the making of beautiful things, don't you find it so?"

"Whenever I think of being on this train I'll remember you telling me that poem." She was embarrassed and lowered her eyes to be talking of such important things with a stranger.

"A poem is very light." Lin Tan laughed, to save the moment. "Not like babies. Easy to transport or carry." Nora Jane laughed with him. The train sped through the night. The whales gave birth in the water. The stars stayed on course. The waiter appeared with the tray and they began to eat their sandwiches.

Freddy was waiting on the platform when the train arrived at the Noyo–Point Cabrillo Station. He was wearing his old green stadium coat and carrying a blanket. Nora Jane stepped down from the train and kissed him on the cheek. Lin Tan pressed his face against the window and smiled and waved. Nora Jane waved back. "That's my new friend," she said. "He gave me his address in Berkeley. He's a scientist. Get this. He did the amnio on Lydia and Tammili. Can you believe it? Can anybody believe the stuff that happens?"

Freddy wrapped the blanket around her shoulders. "I thought you might like to see a movie before we go back. *The Night of the Shooting Stars* is playing at the Courthouse in Willits."

"He ran off and left me," she said. "I knew he would. I don't think I even care."

"You met the guy on the train that did the amnio? I don't believe it."

"He knew my name. I almost fainted when he said it."

"Look, we don't have to go to a movie unless you feel like it. I just noticed it was playing. It's got a pregnant woman in it."

"I've seen it three times. We went last year, don't you remember? But I'll go again if you want to."

"We could eat instead. Have you eaten anything?"

"I had a sandwich on the train. I guess we better go on to the house. I'm supposed to take it easy. I don't have any luggage. I just brought this backpack. I was too mad to pack."

"We'll get something to eat." He took her arm and pulled her close to him. Her skin beneath her sleeve was the same as the last time he had touched her. They began to move in the direction of the car. "I love the way you smell," she said. "You always smell just like you are. Listen, Freddy, I don't know exactly what I'm doing right now. I'm just doing the best I can and playing it by ear. But I'm okay. I really am okay. Do you believe everything that's happened?"

"You want to buy anything? Is there anything you need? You want to see a doctor or anything like that?"

"No, let's just go up to the house. I've been thinking about the house a lot. About the windows. Did you get the rest of them put in?"

"Yeah, and now the goddamn birds are going crazy crashing into them. Five dead birds this week. They fight their reflections. How's that for a metaphor." He helped her into the car. "Wear your seat belt, okay? So, what's going on inside there?"

"They just move around all the time. If I need to I can sell the car. I don't want anybody supporting us, even you. I'm really doing great. I don't know all the details yet but I'm figuring things out." He started the motor and began to drive. She reached over and touched his knee. They drove through the town of Fort Bragg and turned onto the road to Willits. Nora Jane moved her hand and fell asleep curled up on the seat. She didn't wake again until they were past Willits and had started up the long hill leading to the gravel road that led to the broken path to Freddy's house. "He said they were going to give great gifts to the world, gifts of music," she said when she woke. "I think it means they won't be afraid to sing in public. I want to call Li Suyin and talk to her about it. I forgot you didn't have a phone. I need to call and tell her where I am. If she calls San Jose she'll start worrying about me."

"You can call tomorrow. Look, how about putting your hand back on my leg. That way I'll believe you're here." He looked at her. "I want to believe you're here."

"You're crazy to even talk to me."

"No, I'm not. I'm the sane one, remember, the control in the modern world experiment." She was laughing now so he could afford to look at her as hard as he liked. She looked okay. Tired and not much color in her face, but okay. Perfect as always from Freddy Harwood's point of view.

II

"I WANT TO TAKE THEM on the grand tour as soon as they're old enough," Freddy was saying. They were lying on a futon on top of a mattress in the smallest of the upstairs rooms. "My grandmother took me when I was twelve. She took my cousin, Sally, and hired a gigolo to dance with her in Vienna. I had this navy blue raincoat with a zip-in lining. God, I wish I still had that coat." Nora Jane snuggled down beside him, smelling his chest. It smelled like a wild animal. There were many things about Freddy Harwood that excited her almost as much as love. She patted him on the arm. "So, anyway," he continued. "I have this uncle in New Orleans and he's married two women with three children. He's raised six children that didn't belong to him and he's getting along all right. He says at least his subconscious isn't involved. There's a lot to be said for that. . . . What I'm saying is, I haven't lived in Berkeley all my life to give in to some kind of old worn-out masculine pride. Not with all the books I've read."

"All I've ever done is make you sad. I always end up doing something mean to you."

"Maybe I like it. Anyway, you're here and that's how it is. But we ought to go back to town in a few days. You can stay with me there, can't you?" He pulled her closer, as close as he dared. She was so soft.

The babies only made her softer. "I ought to call Stuart and tell him you're here."

"He's a heart doctor. He doesn't know anything about babies."

"Wait a minute. One of them did something. Oh, shit, did you feel that?"

"I know. They're in there. Sometimes I forget it but not very often. Tell me some more about when you went to Europe. Tell me everything you can remember, just the way it happened. Like what you had to eat and what everyone was wearing."

"Okay. Sally had a navy blue skirt and a jacket and she had some white blouses and in Paris we got some scarves. She had this scarf with the Visigoth crowns on it and she had it tied in a loop so a whole crown showed. She fixed it all the time she wore it. She couldn't leave it alone. Then they went somewhere and got some dresses made out of velvet but they only wore them at night."

"What did you wear?" She had a vision of him alone in a hotel room putting on his clothes when he was twelve. "I bet you were a wonderful-looking boy. I bet you were the smartest boy in Europe."

"We met Jung. We talked to him. So, what else did you talk about to this Chinese research biologist?"

"A genetic research biologist. He's still studying it. He has to finish school before he can do his real work. He wants to do things to DNA and find out how much we remember. He thinks we remember everything that ever happened to anyone from the beginning of time because there wouldn't be any reason to forget it, and if you can make computer chips so small, then the brain is much larger than that. We talked all the way from Sausalito. His father was a painter. When his sister gets here they might move to Sweden. He believes in the global village."

"He says they're musicians, huh?"

"Well, it wasn't that simple. It was very complicated. He had the biggest face of any oriental I've met. I just love him. I'm going to talk to him a lot more when we both get back to San Francisco." Her voice was getting softer, blurring the words.

"Go to sleep," Freddy said. "Don't talk anymore." He felt a baby move, then move again. They were moving quite a bit.

"I'm cold," she said. "Also, he said the birth process was the worst thing we ever go through in our life. He told me about this boy in England that's a genius, his parents are both doctors and they let him stay in the womb for eighteen months for an experiment and he can remember being born and tells about it. He said it was like someone tore a hole in the universe and jerked you out. Get closer, will you. God, I'm tired."

"We ought to go downstairs and sleep in front of the fire. I'm going to make a bed down there and come get you."

Freddy went downstairs and pulled a mattress up before the fireplace and built up the fire and brought two futons in and laid them on top of the mattress and added a stack of wool blankets and some pillows. When he had everything arranged, he went back upstairs and carried her down and tucked her in. Then he rubbed her back and told her stories about Vienna and wondered what time it was. I am an hour from town, he told himself, and Sam is twenty minutes away and probably drunk besides. It's at least three o'clock in the morning and the water's half frozen in the cistern and I let her come up here because I was too goddamn selfish to think of a way to stop it. So, tomorrow we go to town.

"Freddy?"

"Yes."

"I had a dream a moment ago . . . a dream of a meadow. All full of light and this dark tree. I had to go around it."

"Go to sleep, honey. Please go to sleep."

When she fell asleep he got up and sat on the hearth. We are here as on a darkling plain, he thought. We forget who we are. Branching plants, at the mercy of water. But tough. Tough and violent, some of us anyway. Oh, shit, if anything happened to her I couldn't live. Well, I've got to get some air. This day is one too many.

He pulled on a long black cashmere coat that had belonged to his father and went outside and took a sack of dog food out of the car and walked down into the hollow to feed the bobcat. He spread part of the food on the ground and left the open sack beside it. "I know you're in there," he said out loud. "Well, here's some food. Come and get it. Nora Jane's here. I guess you know that by now. Don't kill anything until she leaves." He listened. The only sound was the wind in the trees. It was very cold. The stars were very clear. There was a rustle, about forty yards away. Then nothing. "Good night then," Freddy said. "I guess this dog food was grown in Iowa. The global village. Well, why not." He started back up the hill, thinking the bobcat might jump on him at any moment. It took his mind off Nora Jane for almost thirty seconds.

At that moment the Starlight Express came to a stop in Seattle, Washington, and Lin Tan climbed down from the train and started off in search of adventure. Before the week was over he would fall in love with the daughter of a poet. His life would be shadowed for five years by the events of the next few hours but he didn't know that yet. He was in a wonderful mood. All his philosophical and mystical beliefs were coming together like ducks on a pond. To make him believe in his work, fate had put him on a train with a girl whose amnio he had done only a few months before. Twin baby girls with AB positive blood, the luckiest of all blood. Not many scientists have also great feeling for mystical properties of life, he decided, and see genetic structure when they gaze at stars. I am very lucky my father taught me to love beauty. Moss on Pond, Light on Water, Smoke Rising Beneath the Wheels of Locomotive. Yes, Lin Tan concluded, I am a fortunate man in a universe that really knows what it is doing.

* * *

Freddy let himself back into the house. He built up the fire, covered Nora Jane and lay down beside her to try to sleep. This is not paranoia, he told himself. I am hyper-aware, which is a different thing. If it weren't for people like me the race would have disappeared years ago. Who tends the lines at night? Who watches for the big cats with their night vision? Who stays outside the circle and guards the tribe?

He snuggled closer, smelling her hair. "What is divinity if it can come only in silent shadows and in dreams?" Barukh atah Adonai eloheinu, melekh ha-olam. Praised be thou, Lord our God, King of the Universe, who has brought forth bread from the earth. Nora Jane, me. Jesus Christ!

It was five-thirty when she woke him. "I'm wet," she said. "I think my water broke. I guess that's it. You'd better go and get someone."

"Oh, no, you didn't do this to me." He was bolt upright, pulling on his boots. "You're joking. There isn't even a phone."

"Go use one somewhere. Freddy, this is serious. I'm in a lot of pain, I think. I can't tell. Please go on. Go right now."

"Nora Jane. This isn't happening to me." He was pulling on his boots.

"Go on. It'll be okay. This Chinese guy said they were going to be great so they can't die. But hurry up. How far is it to Sam's?"

"Twenty minutes. Oh, shit. Okay, I'm going. Don't do anything until I get back. If you have to go to the bathroom, do it right there." He leaned fiercely down over her. His hands were on her shoulders. "I'll be right back here. Don't move until I come." He ran from the house, jumped into his car, and began driving down the rocky drive. It was impossible to do more than five miles an hour over the rocks. The whole thing was impossible. The sun was lighting up the sky behind the mountains. The sky was silver. Brilliant clouds covered the western sky. Freddy came to the gate he shared with the other people on the mountain and drove right through it, leaving it torn off the post. He drove as fast as he dared down the rocky incline and turned onto gravel and saw the smoke coming from the chimney of Sam Lyons's house.

Nora Jane was in great pain. "I'm your mother," she was pleading. "Don't hurt me. I wouldn't hurt you. Please don't do it. Don't come now. Just wait awhile, go back to sleep. Oh, God. Oh, Jesus Christ. It's too cold. I'm freezing. I have to stop this. Pray for us sinners." The bed filled with water. She looked down. It wasn't water. It was blood. So much blood. What's going on? she thought. Why is this happening to me? I don't want it. Holy Mary, Mother of God, pray for us sinners now and at the hour of our death, Amen. Hail Mary, Mother of God, blessed art thou among women and blessed is the fruit of your womb, Jesus. Oh, Christ, oh, shit, oh, goddamnit all to hell. I don't know what's so cold. I don't know what I'm going to do. Someone should be here. I want to see somebody.

The blood continued to pour out upon the bed.

Sam came to the door. "A woman's up there having babies," Freddy said. "Get on the phone and call an ambulance and the nearest helicopter service. Try Ukiah but call the hospital in Willits first. Do it now. Sam, a woman's in my house having babies. Please." Sam turned and ran back through the house to the phone. Freddy followed him. "I'm going back. Get everyone you can get. Then come and help me. Make sure they understand the way. Or wait here for them if they don't seem to understand. Be very specific about the way. Then come. No, wait here for them. Get Selby and tell him to come to my house. I'm leaving." He ran back out the door and got back into his car and turned it around and started driving. His hands burned into the wheel. He had never known anything in his life like this. Worse than the earthquake that ruined the store. He was alone with this. "No," he said out loud as he drove. "I couldn't love them enough to let them call me on the phone. No, I had to have this goddamn fucking house a million miles from nowhere. She'll die. I know it. I have known it from the first moment I set eyes on her. Every time I ever touched her I knew she would die and leave me. Now it's coming true." The car hit a boulder. The wheel was wrenched from his hand but he straightened it with another wrench and went on driving. The sky was lighter now. The clouds were blowing away. He parked the car a hundred yards from the house and got out and started running.

Lydia came out into the space between Nora Jane's legs. Nora Jane reached for the child and held her, struggling to remember what you did with the cord. Then Freddy was there and took the baby from her and bit the cord in two and tied it and wrapped the baby in his coat and handed it to her. Tammili's head moved down into the space where Lydia's had been. Nora Jane screamed a long scream that filled all the spaces of the house and then Nora Jane didn't care anymore. Tammili's body moved out into Freddy's hands and he wrapped her in a pillowcase and laid her beside her sister, picking up one and then the other, then turning to Nora Jane. Blood was everywhere and more was coming. There was nothing to do, and there was too much to do. There wasn't any way to hold them and help her too. "It's all right," she said. "Wipe them off. I don't want blood all over them. You can't do anything for me."

"I want you to drink something." He ran into the kitchen and pulled open the refrigerator door. He found a bottle of Coke and a bottle of red wine and held them in his hands trying to decide. He took the wine and went back to where she lay. "Drink this. I want you to drink this. You're bleeding, honey. You have to drink something. They'll be here in a minute. It won't be a minute from now."

She shook her head. "I'm going to die, Freddy. It's all right. It looks real good. You wouldn't believe how it looks. Get them some good-looking clothes . . . get them a red raincoat with a hood. And yellow.

Get them a lot of yellow." He pulled her body into his. She felt as if she weighed a thousand pounds. Then nothing. Nothing, nothing, nothing. "Wake up," he screamed. "Wake up. Don't die on me. Don't you dare die on me." Still, there was nothing. He turned to the babies. He must take care of them. No, he must revive Nora Jane. He laid his head down beside hers. She was breathing. He picked up the bottle of wine and drank from it. He turned to the baby girls. He picked them up, one at a time, then one in each arm. Then he began to count. One, two, three, four, five, six, seven, eight. He laid Lydia down beside Nora Jane, and, holding Tammili, he began to throw logs on the fire. He went into the kitchen and lit the stove and put water on to boil. He dipped a kitchen towel in cold water, then threw that away and took a bottle of cooking oil and soaked a rag in it and carried Tammili back to the fire and began to wipe the blood and mucous from the child's hair. Then he put Tammili down and picked up Lydia and cleaned her for a while. They were both crying, very small yelps like no sound he had ever heard. Nora Jane lay on the floor covered with a red wool blanket soaked in blood and Freddy kept on counting. Seven hundred and seventeen. Seven hundred and eighteen. Seven hundred and nineteen. He found more towels and made a nest for the babies in the chair and knelt beside them, patting and stirring them with his hands until he heard the cars drive up and the helicopter blades descending to the cleared place beside the cistern. Barukh atah Adonai eloheinu, melekh ha-olam, he was saying. Praised be thou, Lord our God, King of the Universe, who has brought forth bread from the earth. Praised be thou, inventor of helicopters, miner of steel, king of applied science. Oh, shit, thank God, they're here.

When Nora Jane came to, the helicopter pilot was on top of her, Freddy was doing something with her arms, and people were moving around the room. A man in a leather jacket was holding the twins. "They're going to freeze," she said. "I want to see them. I think I died. I died, didn't I?" The pilot moved away. Freddy propped her body up with his own and Sam tucked a blanket around her legs. "The ambulance is coming," he said. "It's okay. Everyone's okay."

"I died and it was light, like walking through a field of light. A fog made out of light. Do you think it's really like that or only shock?"

"Oh, honey," Freddy crooned into her hair. "It was the end of light. Listen, they're so cute. Wait till you see them. They're like little kittens or mice, like baby mice. They have black hair. Listen, they imprinted on my black cashmere coat. God knows what will happen now."

"I want to see them if nobody minds too much," she said. The man in the leather jacket brought them to her. She tried to reach out for them but her arms were too tired to move. "You just be still," the pilot said. "I'm Doctor Windom from the Sausalito Air Emergency Service. We were in the neighborhood. I'm sorry it took so long. We had to make three passes to find the clearing. Well, a ground crew is coming up the hill. We'll take you out in a ground vehicle. Just hold on. Everything's okay."

"I'm holding on. Freddy?"

"Yes."

"Are we safe?"

"For now." He knelt beside her and buried his face in her shoulder. He began to tremble. "Don't do that," she whispered. "Not in front of people. It's okay."

Lydia began to cry. It was the first really loud cry either of the babies had uttered. Tammili was terrified by the sound and began to cry even louder than her sister. Help, help, help, she cried. This is me. Give me something. Do something, say something, make something happen. This is me, Tammili Louise Whittington, laying my first guilt trip on my people.

PERHAPS
A MIRACLE

IT WAS THE WORST ARGUMENT they had had in months. Nora Jane almost never argued with Freddy Harwood. In the first place she thought he was smarter than she was and in the second place he always went rational on her and in the third place there were better ways to get what she wanted. The best way was to say she wanted something and then not mention it for a week or two. All that time he would be arguing with himself about his objection and in the end he would decide he didn't have the right to impose his ideas on any other human being, not even his wife. Freddy had not gone to Berkeley in the sixties for nothing. *The Greening of America* and *The Sorcerer of Bolinas Reef* were still among his favorite books. Once a reporter had asked Freddy to name his ten favorite books and he had left out both those books because this was the nineties and Freddy was famous in the world of publishing and independent bookstores and he didn't want to seem too crazy in public. If someone had asked him the ten things he regretted most, leaving *The Greening of America* and *The Sorcerer of Bolinas Reef* off his list would have been right up there with the butterfly tattoo on his ankle.

"It doesn't matter what you take," he said out loud. "It's none of my business."

"You don't care what I take?"

"All I said is that sociology is a pseudoscience and you're too good for that kind of mush. I didn't mean you shouldn't take it. I should never have asked what you are going to take. I'm embarrassed that I asked. All I care about is that you be home by three so the girls won't come home to an empty house."

"You don't want me to go to college. I can tell."

"I want you to go to college fiercely. I wish I could quit work and go with you. My biology is about twenty years behind the field."

"Freddy." She climbed down off the ladder. She had been putting up drapes while Freddy read. She was wearing a white cashmere sweater and a pair of jeans. She was wearing ballet shoes.

"You wear that stuff to drive me crazy," Freddy said. "If they sold that perfume Cleopatra used on Caesar, you'd wear it every day. How can I let you go to college? Every man at Berkeley will fall in love with you. Education will come to a grinding halt. No one will learn a thing. No one will be able to teach. It's my civic duty to keep you at home. I owe it to the culture." He pulled her across the room and began to dance with her. He sang an old Cole Porter song in a falsetto voice and danced her around the sofas. One thing about Nora Jane. She could move into a scenario. "Where are the girls?" she asked.

"In the den doing homework. I told them I'd take them down to Berkeley to get an ice-cream cone when they were finished."

"Meet me in the pool house. Hurry." She smiled the wild, hard-won smile that worked on Freddy Harwood better than all the perfumes of the East.

"Yes, yes, yes," he answered, and let her go and she walked away from him and out of the room and down the stairs and across the patio to the guest house beside the swimming pool. She went into the bedroom and took off her clothes and waited. In a moment he was there. He turned off the lights to the pool with a switch on the wall. He locked the door and lay down beside her and began to make love to her.

It was Freddy's theory that the way you made love to a woman was to worship every inch of her body with your heart and mind and soul. This was easy with Nora Jane. He had worshiped every inch of Nora Jane since the night he met her. He loved beauty, had been raised to know and worship beauty, believed beauty was truth, balance, order. He worshiped Nora Jane and he loved her. Ten years before, on a snow-covered night in the Northern California hills, he had delivered the twin baby girls who were his daughters. With no knowledge of how to do it and nothing to guide him but love, he had kept them all alive until help came. Nora Jane had another lover at the time and no one knew whose sperm had created Lydia and Tammili. The other man had disappeared before they were born and had not been heard from since. It was a shadow, but all men have shadows, Freddy knew. Where it was darkest and there was no path. This was Freddy's credo. Each knight entered the forest where it was darkest and there was no path. If there was a path, it was someone else's path.

Freddy ran his hand up and down the side of Nora Jane's body. He trembled as he touched her small round hip. I cultivate this, he decided. Well, some men gamble.

II

A FOUR-YEAR-OLD BOY named Zandia, who was visiting his grandmother in the house next door, had been trying all week to get to the Harwoods' heated swimming pool. He didn't necessarily want to get in the water. He wanted to get the blue and white safety ring he could see from his grandmother's fence. All these days and his grandmother had not noticed his fascination with the pool. Perhaps she had noticed it but she hadn't given it enough weight. She trusted the lock on the gate, and besides, Zandia was such a wild little boy. He could have four or five plans of action going at the same time. His latest fascination was with vampires, and Clyda Wax, for that was his grandmother's name, had been occupied with overcoming his belief in them. "Where did you ever see a vampire?" she kept asking. "There is no such thing as a vampire, Zandia. There are vampire bats. I'll admit that. But they live in caves and they are very stupid and blind and I could kill a hundred of them with a broom."

"They would fly up and eat your blood. They can fly."

"I'd knock them down with the broom. They are blind. It would be easy as pie. I'd have a bushel basket full of them."

"They'd fly up and stick to the trees. What would you do then?"

"I'd get a giraffe to eat them."

"But giraffes live in Africa."

"So what? I can afford to import one."

"What about Count Dracula? You couldn't kill him."

"There isn't any Count Dracula. There's just that vulgar, disgusting, imbecilic Hollywood trash that you are exposed to in L.A. I shudder to think what they let you watch down there. Did the baby-sitter show it to you? Did the baby-sitter tell you about vampires? Vampires are not true. Now go and play with your Jeep for a while. I want to rest." Clyda closed her eyes and lay back on the lawn chair. She didn't mean to go to sleep but she was exhausted from taking care of him. She had volunteered for one week. It had turned into three. He had been up that morning at five rummaging around in her kitchen drawers. "When your mother comes to get you I'm going to a spa," she said sleepily. "I'm going to Maine Chance and stay a month."

As soon as he saw she was asleep he walked over to the fence and undid the latch. He pushed the latch open and disappeared through the gate. There it was, shimmering in the moonlight, the swimming pool with all its chairs and the red rubber raft and the safety ring. He walked under the window of the bedroom where Nora Jane and Freddy lay in each other's arms. He walked around the chairs and up to the edge of the water. He bent over and saw his reflection in the water. Then he began to fall.

* * *

"Something's wrong." Nora Jane sat up. She pushed Freddy away from her. She jumped up from the bed. She tore open the door and began to run. She got to the pool just as Zandia was going under. She ran around the edge. She jumped in beside him and found him and they began to struggle. She pulled and dragged him through the water. When she got to the shallow end she pulled him up into the air. Then the lights were on and Freddy was in the water with her and they lifted him from the water and turned him upside down and Freddy was on the mobile phone calling 911.

"How did you know?" they asked her. After it was over and Zandia was in his grandmother's arms eating cookies and the living room was full of uniformed men and Tammili and Lydia had seen their naked parents performing a miracle and were the most cowed ten-year-old girls in the Bay Area.

"I don't know. I don't know what I knew. I just knew to go to the pool."

"You've never even met this kid?" one of the men in uniform asked.

"I've seen him in the yard. He's been in the yard next door."

Later that night, after Zandia and his grandmother had been walked to their house and Tammili had been put to bed reading *The Voyage of the Dawn Treader* and Lydia had been put to bed reading a catalog from *American Girl* and they were alone in their room, Freddy had opened all the windows and the skylight above the bed and they had lain in each other's arms, awed and pajamaed, talking of time and space and life at the level of microbiology and wave and particle theory and why Abraham Pais was their favorite person in New York City and how it was time to take the girls to the Sierra Nevada to see the mountains covered with snow. "We need to do something to mark it. Plant some trees at Willits. Lay bricks for a path."

"You could rearrange the books in the den. It's such a mess in there Betty won't even go in to clean. It's unhealthy to have that many books in a room. It's musty. It's like a throwback to some other age. It doesn't go with the rest of the house."

"Go on to sleep if you can."

"I can. You're the one who doesn't sleep."

"We should both sleep tonight. Something's on our side. I never felt that as strongly as I do right now." He patted her for a while. Then he began to dream his old dream of building the house at Willits. The solar house he and Nieman had built by hand to prove it could be done and to prove who they were. Our rite of passage into manhood house, Freddy knew. The house to free us from our mothers. In the recurrent dream it was a clear, cold day. They had finished the foundation and were beginning to set the posts at the sides. The mountain lions came and sat upon the rise and watched them. "You think I'm nuts to go to all this trouble to make a nest," he told the lions. "Well, you're wrong. This is what my species does."

In that magical house Tammili and Lydia were born and sometimes Freddy thought the house had been built to serve that purpose. To make them so much his that nothing could sever the bond. So what if one or both of them were Sandy George Wade's biological spawn? So what if maybe Tammili was his and Lydia was not? So what in a finite world if there was love? Freddy always ended up deciding.

Next door, it was Zandia's grandmother who couldn't sleep. She was talking to Zandia's mother on the phone. "You just come up here tomorrow afternoon as soon as they finish shooting and spend the night. He's lonely for you. Four-year-old boys shouldn't be away from their mother for this many days."

"I can't. We have to look at rushes every night. It's the first time Sandy and I have had a chance to be in a film together. I'm a professional, Mother. I have to finish my work, then I'll come get him.

There's no reason you can't hire a baby-sitter for him, you know. He stays with baby-sitters here."

"He almost died, Claudine. I don't think you understand what happened here. You never listen to me, do you know that? You only half listen to anything I say. The child almost died. Also, he is obsessed with vampires. Who let him see a movie about vampires? That's what I'd like to know. I'm taking him to my psychiatrist tomorrow for an evaluation."

"All right then. I'll send someone to get him. I thought you wanted him, Mother. You always do this. You say you want him, then you change your mind in about four days."

"He almost drowned."

"Could we talk in the morning? I'll call you at seven."

Claudine hung up the phone, then went into the bedroom to find Sandy. He was in bed smoking and reading the script. He put the cigarette out when he saw her and shook his head. "Where have you been?" he asked. "What took you so long?"

"Zandia fell in a swimming pool and Mother's neighbor had to fish him out. They're acting like it was some sort of big, big deal. God, she drives me crazy. This is the last time he's going up there. From now on if she wants to see him she can come down here."

"We'll be finished in a week or ten days. It can't drag on much longer than that. You think we ought to send for him?"

"She can bring him. I'll tell her in the morning. I'll line up a sitter and he can go back to the Montessori school in the mornings. I knew better than to do this."

"How'd he fall in a pool?"

"Mother's neighbors left the gate open or something. The police came. He's fine. Nothing happened to him. It's just Mother's insanity."

Then Sandy George Wade, who was the father of Lydia Harwood, as anyone who looked at them would immediately know, began to flip channels on the television set, hoping to find a commercial starring either Claudine or himself, as that always cheered him up and made him think he wouldn't end up in a poor folks home. He reached for Claudine, to believe she was there, and sighed deep inside his scarred, motherless, fatherless heart. His main desire was to get a good night's sleep so he would be beautiful for the cameras in the morning.

Claudine pulled away from him. She got up and went into the other room to call her mother back. When she returned she had a different plan. "We have to go to San Francisco and pick him up. She won't bring him. Well, to hell with it. She wants me to meet the woman who pulled him out of the pool. I probably ought to sue them for having an attractive nuisance. Anyway, we have to go. Will you take me?"

"Of course I will. As soon as we have a break. Come on, get in bed. I like San Francisco. It's a nice drive. We'll take the BMW. It's driving good since I got the new tires. Get in bed. Let's get some sleep." Then Claudine gave up for the day and climbed into the bed and let Sandy cuddle up to her. Their neuroses fit like gloves. They were really very happy together. They hated the same things. They liked to make love to each other and they liked to sleep in the same bed. It was the best thing either of them had ever known. They even liked Zandia. Neither one of them liked to take care of him but they didn't hate or resent him. Sometimes they even thought he was funny.

LUNCH AT THE
BEST RESTAURANT
IN THE WORLD

So WHY WAS I CHOSEN for this? That's what I keep
asking myself. It's like a tear in the fabric of reality. Maybe I heard him
walking by the window. I have a perfect ear for music. Well, I do. Maybe
I saw him by the fence and knew he'd be wanting to get to the pool. All
mothers are wary of pools. I've been watching to make sure no one
drowns in our pool for years. Maybe there's a logical explanation. I'm
sure there is. It only seems like a miracle." Nora Jane was talking. She
and Freddy and Freddy's best friend, Nieman Gluuk, were at Chez
Panisse having lunch. Nora Jane was wearing yellow. Freddy had on his
plaid shirt and chinos. Nieman wore his suit. It was the first time the
Harwoods had been out in public since the night Nora Jane pulled the
child from the swimming pool. Nieman had been with them almost
constantly since the event. Actually he had been with them almost constantly since they were married ten years before. Nieman and Freddy
saw each other or talked on the phone nearly every day. They had done
this since they were five years old. No one thought anything about it or
ever said it was strange that two grown men were inseparable.

"Three knights were allowed to see the Grail," Freddy said. "Bors
and Percival and Galahad. They were pure of heart. You're pure of
heart, Nora Jane. And besides, you're an intuitive. The first time

Nieman met you he told me that. He says you're the most intuitive person he's ever known."

"Maybe this means I shouldn't go to college. It means something, Freddy. Something big."

"You think I don't know that? I was there too, wasn't I? I watched it happen. What it means is that there's a lot more going on than we are able to acknowledge. Thought is energy. It creates fields. You picked up on one. You're a good receiver. That's what intuitive means. Maybe I'll go to school with you. Just dive right into a freshman science course and see if I sink or swim."

Nieman sighed and shook his head from side to side. "I can't believe you had this experience just when you were getting ready to try your wings at Berkeley. It's a coincidence, not a warning. It doesn't mean the girls are in danger or that we are in danger. No, listen to me. I know you think that but you shouldn't. The point is that you saved his life, not that his life was in danger. You will always save lives in many ways. It's all the more reason to go back to school and gain more knowledge and more power. Knowledge is power, even if it does sound trite to say it."

"I wish they hadn't put it in the papers." Nora Jane turned to Nieman and touched his hand. She was one of the three people in the world who dared to touch the esteemed and feared Nieman Gluuk, the bitter and hilarious movie critic of the *San Francisco Chronicle.* "The whole thing only lasted about six minutes. I can barely remember any of it except the moment I knew to do it. Freddy remembers pulling him out better than I do."

"We must never forget it," Nieman said.

"A man who had it happen to him last year called last night. He went through a glass door to get to a pool and saved his nephew. He thinks it has something to do with water. Water as a conductor."

"It proves a lot of theories," Freddy added. "I was there too, Nieman. I witnessed it. I was in bed with her."

"Excuse me." They were interrupted by a waiter, who took their orders for goat cheese pie and salads and wine. "It was the single most profound thing that ever happened to me in my life," Freddy went on. "I will be thinking about it every day for the rest of my life. A tear in the cover, a glimpse of a wild, or perhaps exquisitely orderly, reality that is lost to us most of the time. Think of it, Nieman. The brain can't stand to consciously process all it senses and knows. We'd go crazy. The brain is a filter and its first job is to keep the body healthy. Occasionally, perhaps by accident, it sees a larger reality as its domain. Altruism. Well, it's so humbling to be part of it." He looked down, afraid they would think he wanted them to remember what he had done in the earthquake of 1986. But they knew better. He had forbidden his friends ever to speak of that. "Well, let's don't talk it all away. It's Nora Jane's miracle. I want to take her up to Willits for a while to think it over but she can't go. She starts school in three days, you know."

The waiter put bread down in front of them, the best French bread this side of New Orleans. Nieman held out a loaf to Nora Jane and they broke the bread. They ate in silence for a while.

"Fantastic about Berkeley," Nieman said at last. "Brilliant. I wish I could go. I feel like a dinosaur with my old knowledge. My encyclopedia is twenty years old. Every year I say I'll get another one but I never do."

The waiter brought more bread. Nieman buttered a piece and examined it, calculating the fat grams and wondering if it mattered. "Our darling Nora Jane," he went on. "Loose on the campus in the directionless nineties. I should write a modern opera for you. The problem is the ending. Shakespeare knew what to do. He poured in outrageous action, tied up all the loose ends, piled up some bodies, and danced off the stage on the wings of language. Ah, those epilogues. 'As you from crimes would pardoned be. Let your indulgence set me free.' Oh, he could lift the language! The modern stage can't bear the weight of so much beauty, so much fun. It's too large an insult to the modern fantasy, boredom, and self-pity. I went to three movies last week that were so bad I didn't last for the first hour. I just walked out. They began hopefully enough, were well acted by fine actors, then you could see the money mold begin to grow, the meetings where the money people in group think begin to decide how to corrupt the script. Well, let's not ruin lunch with such thoughts. After lunch shall we go over to the campus and walk around and get you accustomed to your new domain, Miss Nora? I heard the brilliant translator Mark Musa is here for the semester to teach *The Divine Comedy*. You might want to take that. We could go by and see if he's in his office and introduce ourselves."

"There you go," Freddy said. "Trying to take over what she takes. I pray to God every day to make me stop caring what classes she takes."

"The only answer is for you to go to school with me," Nora Jane said. "You too, Nieman. Why not? Life is short, as you both tell me a thousand times a month."

"Life is short," Nieman agreed. "We could do it, Freddy. We could think of it as a donation to the university. Pay tuition as special students, sign up for classes, and go as often as we are able. I could take Monday and Tuesday off. I'm going to list the names of seven movies and then leave a blank white space. Think of us back on the campus, Freddy. Freddy was valedictorian of our class, Nora. But you know that."

"His mother's told me a million times. I think it was the high point of her life."

"That's what she wants you to think. The high point of her life was when she flew that jet to Seattle in the air show. No, I guess it was when she played Martha in *Who's Afraid of Virginia Woolf?* You know who she's going out with now, don't you, Nieman?"

"I heard. It's a terrible shadow, Freddy, but you have survived so far. Well, shall we do it then? Register for classes?"

"Yes. I'm taking biology, physics, and a history course. I want to see what they're teaching. It can't be as bad as I've heard it is."

"I'll take Musa's Dante in Translation and a playwriting course. I'll go incognito and write the play for Nora Jane and we'll put it on next year as an AIDS benefit."

"I'll sing 'Vissi d'arte' from the side of the stage while twelve little girls in long white dresses run around the stage doing leaps. Would that be a conclusion? Then a poet can run out on the stage and read part of 'Little Gidding.' Imagine us all going to college together."

"Meeting for coffee at Aranga's. When I was a student I was touched by old people going back to school. We will touch their silly little hearts. At least, Freddy and I will. You'll drive them crazy. I don't know, Freddy, maybe she's overeducated already."

"I want a degree. I'm embarrassed not to have a college degree. I'm the first person in my family in three generations not to have one." She sat up very straight and tall and Nieman and Freddy understood this was not to be taken lightly.

"Then let's go," Freddy said. "If you will allow us, we will accompany you on this pilgrimage." She turned her head to look at him and he fell madly in love with the sweep and whiteness of her neck and Nieman watched this approvingly. After all, someone has to be in love and get married and continue the human race.

An hour later they were on the Berkeley campus, walking along the sidewalks where Freddy and Nieman had walked when they were young. Nora Jane had been on the campus many times but never as a student. It was very strange, very liberating, and she felt her spirit open to the world she was about to enter. "I'll be Virgil and you be Dante and Nora Jane can be Beatrice," Nieman was saying. "The possibility of vast fields of awareness, that's what this campus always says to me. I used to think I could get vibrations from the physics building when the first reactor was installed and all those brilliant minds were here. I used to feel the force of them would dissolve the harm my mother did to me each morning. She would pour fear and anxiety over me and I would step onto the campus and feel it eaten up by knowledge. She was enraged that I was studying theater. She was very hard on me."

"You had to live at home with her?" Nora Jane took his arm to protect him from the past.

"She wanted me to go to medical school and be a psychiatrist, as she was seeing one. I would say to her, Mother, theater is psychotherapy writ large. The actors on the stage do what people do in ordinary life, keep secrets, say half of what they're thinking, manipulate, lie. Because it's writ large on the stage or screen the audience is on to them. They leave the theater and go out into the world more aware of other people's behaviors, if not of their own. Still, she was not convinced. She still thinks what I do is frivolous."

"She can't, after all these years?"

"Can she not? I'm an only child, don't forget that."

"I am too and so is Freddy. We're the only-child league. Like the redheaded league in Sherlock Holmes."

They linked arms, coming down the wide sidewalk to the student union. "This is like *The Wizard of Oz*," Nieman said. "In *The Divine Comedy* they walked single file."

"Well, these are not the legions of the damned either," Freddy added, "although they certainly look the part." They were passing students, some with rings in their ears and noses and lips and some wearing chic outfits and some looking like they were only there because they didn't have anything better to do.

"Let's go to the registrar's office and get that over with," Freddy suggested.

"I will fill out any number of forms but I am not sending off for transcripts," Nieman decreed. "If they start any funny stuff about transcripts I'll drop my disguise and call the president of the university."

"We aren't pulling rank, Nieman," Freddy said. "We go as pilgrims or not at all."

"You go your way and I'll go mine, as always. Yes, it's beginning to feel like old times."

"Don't talk about the sixties or I'll hit you," Nora Jane said. "I was in a convent school kneeling in the gravel before the statue of the Virgin and you were here getting to read literature and hear lectures by physicists. It isn't fair. You're too far ahead. I'll never catch up."

"No competition please. We're in this together."

By five that afternoon it was done. Freddy was signed up to audit World History and Physics I and Biology I. Nieman was taking Dante and had met Mark Musa and promised to brush up on his Italian and Nora Jane had her books and notebooks for English, History, Algebra, and Introduction to Science. They had sacks of books from Freddy's bookstore and the campus bookstore.

When they were through collecting all the books they went to a coffeehouse across the street from the campus and picked out a table where they could meet. "I don't know if this table will be large enough," Nieman said. "Students will be flocking to us, don't you think?"

"Don't scare me like that," Freddy said.

"Don't turn my education into an anecdote," Nora Jane decreed. "Or I'll get my own table and have my own following." She piled her books up in front of her and looked at them. She was proud of them. She was on fire at this beginning.

THE INCURSIONS OF
THE GODDAMN
WRETCHED PAST

IT WAS THE SUNDAY MORNING after the won-
derful Friday when Nora Jane, Freddy, and their best friend, Nieman,
spent the afternoon on the Berkeley campus signing up for classes and
being filled with happiness and hope.

It was Sunday morning and Freddy and Nora Jane were on the
patio reading the Sunday newspapers and watching Zandia, who was
brandishing a plastic sword in the air. He was standing on a ladder by
the fence that separated the houses and pretending to poke them with
the sword to punish them for ignoring him.

Because Nora Jane had saved Zandia's life he thought he had a
claim on her. He thought she was a mean, bad girl to sit there reading
the newspapers when he didn't have a thing to do. "I'm killing you,"
he called out in his annoying, high-pitched voice. "You are Nora Jane
Captain Hook. I'm swording you."

"You think I should go get him?" Nora Jane asked Freddy. "Clyda
said his mother was coming this afternoon. Can you stand him for a
while?"

"Sure. Why not? Did that man call about the new pool cover?"

"He's coming Monday afternoon. Betty will let him in if I'm not
here." Nora Jane got up from her chair and walked down across the

lawn to Zandia, who was continuing to threaten her. His grandmother met her at the fence.

"Let me take him for a while," Nora Jane said. "We like to watch him play."

"If you're sure you want him. I swear to God I'm worn out with him. I'm going to Maine Chance for two weeks the minute that he's gone. I was going to the Golden Door but they're full."

"Let us have him for a while. It will keep Freddy from reading the editorial page. It drives him crazy to read the editorials. Actually he shouldn't even be allowed to read the papers." Nora Jane helped Zandia over the fence and he stood beside her, poking his sword in the direction of his grandmother.

"Claudine ought to be here by three or four. They sent me some stills from the set. You want to see them? She really is a pretty girl. I guess I'm too proud of her." Clyda pulled some photographs out of the pocket of her jacket. She handed them over the fence, still talking. "That's Kevin Kline in the background. That's a Mardi Gras parade. These were made while they were still filming in New Orleans. That's Claudine and the other one's her boyfriend, Sandy Wade. They're pretty handsome, aren't they?"

Nora Jane took the photographs. It was Sandy George Wade, her old lover. Ten years older and stronger looking and wider and twelve times as handsome, if it were possible for anyone that handsome to look any better. It was Sandy, on his way to San Francisco to ruin her life.

"That's her boyfriend?"

"Yes. He's very good-looking, isn't he? They'll be here this afternoon to get Zandia. Claudine wants to meet you and thank you in person. She'll never forgive me if she doesn't have a chance to thank you for what you did."

"I don't know if we'll still be here. We're going to Berkeley starting tomorrow. There's so much we have to do. Well, thanks for

showing these to me." Nora Jane handed them back over the fence.
"I'll bring him back in half an hour. We have to leave pretty soon." She
took Zandia's hand and hurried back across the lawn to Freddy.
Tammili and Lydia were with him. Tammili had on a blue and white
dress and Lydia had on shorts and a white T-shirt advertising an Amos
Oz book.

Lydia is his, Nora Jane said to herself. If he sees her he will know.
Anyone will know. We know. Freddy will go crazy when he finds out
Sandy's coming. Well, I can't wait. I have to tell him now. We have to
leave. What hell is this? That we have to pay for the past forever. The
terrible past. The mean past. It's here every moment of our lives,
weighing us down, ruining everything we do.

"Take Zandia," she said to Tammili. "Go find him some cookies.
I have to talk to your father."

She pulled Freddy up from his chair and led him into the living room.
It was a perfect room. High glass walls that looked out onto the bay.
White marble floors with soft blue handmade cotton rugs. A long
gold sofa. A Japanese tea box for a coffee table. A bowl of white roses
beside the fireplace. Nora Jane pushed a button and the music of
Johann Sebastian Bach began to play. Freddy had not spoken. He
thought she was going to tell him someone had died. He was going
over a list in his head. It had to be something Zandia's grandmother
told her. It wouldn't be Nieman, or someone would have called.

"Sit down," she said. "Don't go crazy when you hear this. We can
deal with this. We are not hopeless in the face of what I'm going to
tell you."

"Say it."

"Sandy Wade is the boyfriend of Zandia's mother. They're coming
here today. This is real, Freddy. I just saw a photograph of him. We
can't let him see Lydia. He's a human being. It would break his heart
and then I don't know what he'd do. He's in a film with Zandia's

mother. Clyda has photographs of the girls with Zandia at the pool. He'll see them. We can get the girls out of here but what about the pictures? Even if we could do something about that, Clyda will talk about them. He thinks they're his. Both of them. I lived with him the whole time I was pregnant. Don't forget that."

"We'll steal the photographs. That's easy. Say you want to borrow them." He had stood up. He was walking around the room.

"She gave us a set."

"I'm going to get them now. We'll sell the house. We'll move. I'll sell the house tomorrow."

"That's overreacting."

"No, it's not. Call Mother. Tell her we're coming over there for a few days. Then we'll go get the photographs. You keep her busy and I'll steal them."

Twenty minutes later Nora Jane and Freddy were in the kitchen of Clyda's house. "We want to see those photographs you took," Freddy said. "We need to borrow the negatives. We can't find the ones you gave us. The girls must have put them somewhere."

"Oh, they are good, aren't they? I can't believe how well they turned out." Clyda left the room to get the photographs. Zandia stuck his sword into the space between the refrigerator and the wall. The cat climbed up on a counter and sat beside a plate of fruit. The doorbell was ringing. Then the phone was ringing also. Nora Jane started to answer it, then couldn't touch it. Zandia picked up the phone. It was Lydia, looking for her mother. "Put my mother on the phone, Zandia. Zandia, can you hear me? Is my mother there?"

There were excited voices in the hall. Zandia dropped the phone and ran down the hall and then they were there. His mother and his grandmother and Sandy George Wade, moving into the kitchen all talking. Freddy had never met Sandy Wade but he had lived with Lydia for ten years and it was as though she had stepped into the room. The hair, the eyes, the body English, the expression on Sandy's face, quizzical, waiting.

"I have wondered where you were," Nora Jane began. "I'm glad to see you well. This is my husband, Freddy. Sandy is an old friend from New Orleans," she explained to Clyda. "We went to school together."

"We went to the same church," Sandy added. "We knew each other a long time ago."

"We have to be going," Nora Jane said. "We have people waiting on us."

"May I borrow the photographs to show them?" Freddy took them from Clyda's hand and led Nora Jane toward the back door.

"This is who saved Zandia's life," Clyda was saying. "This is Nora Jane."

"I don't know what to say," Claudine put in. "I brought you a present. Sandy, go get my suitcase, will you?" She was very tall, very thin, nervous and excited. She had picked up Zandia but she was not paying much attention to him. She was trying to figure out what was wrong. "Mother," she added, "get that goddamn cat off the counter, will you? I told you Zandia's allergic to them. Has that cat been inside the whole time?"

"We really have to leave. We'll see you later." Freddy put the photographs into his pocket and he and Nora Jane disappeared through the door.

"I'll call you later," Nora Jane called over her shoulder. "We'll get together later."

They made it through the gate and started up the hill to their house. "Get the girls," she said. "Let's get out of here."

They walked back across the yard, holding hands, tight against each other's bodies. Freddy's shoulders barely came an inch higher than Nora Jane's. "Yet I feel the breadth of them," she said, and he did not ask the meaning. They had grown to talk this way when they were alone together. In sentence fragments, long hints, musings. Perhaps she had learned it from him, or perhaps she had only learned to do it aloud, since she had always whispered parts of secrets to herself and to her cats. Lonely little only child that she had been, always up in trees with a cat, spinning worlds she could inhabit without fear. Now, into this world she had created with this man, a real world of goodness and light, peace and hope, came this moment and they must bear it and survive it.

"He cannot mean to harm us," Freddy answered. "Still, she is his and he will know it. What do we do now? First we think."

"He thinks they both are his. We should never have kept this secret. Nothing should be a secret. Secrets are dynamite, weapons-grade uranium."

"Who would we have told? Tammili and Lydia? We can't do that."

"Call your mother and tell her we're coming over there. We'll move if we have to. He knows where we live."

"Leave the house?"

"There are millions of houses. Think of the stuff we could throw away."

"All right. Go get the girls. Let's go. A house on the beach. That's what you've always wanted, isn't it?"

"This is what money is for, Freddy. This is the difference in being rich and being poor." They had arrived at the cobbled path that led to the back door. It was sheltered by azalea bushes and they stopped beneath one and moved into each other's arms. Frozen still, on guard, but moving. This was the thing Nieman envied them, this marriage, this shield they had created, the ability to plan and move as one.

Nora Jane disappeared into the house and began to throw clothes for the girls into a suitcase. Freddy got the station wagon out of the garage and drove it to the side door. He went into the living room and turned on the CD player. Then he called his mother. The strains of the Sixth Symphony were in the background while he talked to her.

"It's dire, Mother. Someone who is a threat to us is staying next door. We're coming there, for perhaps a week."

"What will you tell the girls?"

"What do you suggest?"

"Say I need them. Say I was frightened."

"You've never been frightened in your life. They'd never believe that."

"Then tell them they can't know."

"I'll say the air-conditioner's broken. Hell, I'll say the power's going off."

"Come on then. I'm waiting."

"We're going to buy another house. Will you go with Nora Jane this afternoon and help her look?"

"Whatever you need."

Ann Harwood hung up the phone and sat staring out the leaded glass doors into the morning light. Then she picked up the phone and called her lover and told him she couldn't drive to the desert as they had planned. "The children need me," she said. "This is why there's no point in getting married."

"Can I help?"

"I don't think so. I'll call you later." She hung up the phone and walked down the hall and began to open doors to unused rooms.

Sandy George Wade stood by himself in Clyda's pink and white guest bedroom feeling the way he had felt most of his life. Frightened, deserted, in the way, waiting for the next blow to fall. I guess I'd like to see those kids she had, he decided. See how they turned out, but what the hell, nobody offered to show them to me, did they?

Zandia came into the room and brandished his plastic sword. Sandy struck a pose and pretended to fence with him. They moved around the room thrusting and pointing at one another. Zandia began to laugh, he ran in little circles, faster and faster, then he jumped up on the bed and held the sword in both hands and began to jump on the mattress. Sandy picked him up and carried him upside down to his mother. "You've been had, Zorro," he said to him. "You've met your match when you fence with Captain Sandy Hook, the master swordsman of the deep." Zandia whacked him on the leg with the sword, then dissolved in upside-down giggles.

Sandy set him upright and took his hand. "Back to Montessori for you, old buddy," he said. "Tomorrow morning bright and early. And this time don't bring home any colds while I'm filming."

Freddy and Lydia had promised to go to movies with Nieman, so only Tammili went with Nora Jane and Ann Harwood to hunt for houses. "I came to California to live by the ocean," Nora Jane said. "I want to live where breakers beat upon the shore. I want to look out the window and see my girls playing in the sand."

"What's she been smoking?" Tammili dissolved in laughter. They were in Ann's Bentley, going to meet a real estate broker. "It's because Zandia fell in the pool, I bet," she added. "She probably wouldn't let us in the ocean if we lived by it."

At five-fifteen that afternoon they found it. A three-story frame house on a promontory where the Pacific Ocean beat against the shore. Nora Jane stood on a slope and watched the waves break against a tall, triangular rock. She walked to the water's edge and watched her footprints come and go. She thought, I did mean to live by the water, where the land meets the sea. "I was on the ocean's edge when I decided you were about to be born," she said to Tammili. "I think you should be excited by the sound of the waves."

"I know. Then you got on the train and went to Willits and that's why we were born there. How many times do I have to hear that story?"

"But do you like the house?" Ann asked. "We'll restore it and paint it and change the landscaping. But the basic plan, the house, how do you feel about it, Tammili?"

"Who wouldn't want that mansion? But I don't want to move. How are we going to get to school? How will Daddy get to work?"

"It isn't that far. We'll keep the other house too. In case we need it. We won't throw it away."

"I don't see how we'll get to school. We'll have to get up at six o'clock in the morning."

"Details," her grandmother said. "Three months and we can have it done. Paint, new bathrooms, new kitchen. I know just the people. I've been wanting to get them some work. This young contractor who's helpful with Planned Parenthood."

"Do you want to see the other two houses?" the real estate agent asked.

"No, we're mad about this house. We'll go back to my house and talk about an offer. Oh, Freddy has to see it. I forgot about that."

"Can we show him tonight?" Nora Jane asked. "Are the lights on?"

"Yes."

"Why are we getting this house?" Tammili asked. "You can tell me the truth. You can trust me."

"Would you wait a few days and let us tell you then?" her grandmother asked. "Could you trust us?"

"Okay. I guess so. But I know why. I know anyway." She walked off from them and stood looking at the house, smirking to herself. They think I'm so dumb. It's because the people next door are anti-Semitic. Dad's afraid they'll be snotty to us or something. He's so protective it's pitiful. Now Grandmother will have to spend a million dollars or something to move us all out here so we won't have any neighbors. It's ridiculous. If they're snotty to me I'll dump the cat litter in their yard. She walked closer to the house. Actually, it was four houses joined together to make one. A colonial house like one in some faraway country in another time. She was drawn to it. She wanted to go back inside and pick out some rooms for herself and Lydia.

"We aren't ever going to tell them or admit it to them," Nora Jane said. "We made up our mind. Can you live with that, Ann? With never letting them know there is any difference in them to you? You have to leave them the same amount of money in your will and things like that. If we keep this from them and they find it out, the older they are when they find out the madder they are going to be. But it's a chance we have to take. I don't want them to meet Sandy. I don't want him trying that charm on them."

"I always knew this, Nora Jane. I didn't know how exactly. I studied science as a girl, you know. I knew Lydia wasn't kin to me, but it's never mattered one way or the other. I adore her. I would rather be her grandmother than any little girl in the world. She's ten times as lovable as Tammili. Tammili reminds me too much of my mother to be able to pull the strings of my heart. Look at her, she's probably going up there to stake out territory. That's what Big Ann would have done. She was a weaver when she got old, did you know that? She had a loom and made twenty or so rugs and we don't know what she did with them. She never gave us one of them. I think she sold them."

"Are you sure you want to buy this house? It costs so much."

"A sound investment. They don't make any more beaches. It would be a good investment if the lot were empty. I might fix it up for myself if you decide you don't want it or Freddy doesn't like it."

"Oh, he'll like it. He'll go crazy. I know his taste. He'll start wanting to fill it with period pieces."

"Let's go find him. We can send Tammili into the movies if they're still at the Octoplex. Were they really going to three movies?"

"Parts of three. That's how Nieman does it, you know. If he comes to one he likes well enough to stay that one gets a review."

II

OF COURSE NIEMAN started seeing the Harwoods' problems as a play. It had everything. Confused passions (the great overbearing winds of the first circle of the Inferno), uncertain parentage, innocence slaughtered, random ill. He was walking around his house listening to Kiri Te Kanawa sing Puccini and thinking of Nora Jane's amazing singing voice, which she almost never let anyone hear. He was musing on the story of her childhood: a father slaughtered in a senseless war, a mother drinking herself into dementia, the portrait of her grandfather in the robes of a supreme court justice, the grandmother in the blue house with the piano and the phonograph records.

"Unfair, unfair, always unfair." Nieman strode around the living room and waved his arms in the air to the music. *Vissi d'arte,* the consolations of art. There was nothing else. Struggle and death, and in the meantime, beauty. Tammili and Lydia and Nora Jane and his best friend, Freddy, who was born to bear the suffering of anyone who came his way. He bore mine, Nieman remembered, when my own father died within a month of his, both taking their cigarette-scarred lungs to the Beth Israel Cemetery. We were fourteen years old but it was Freddy who became the father. It was Freddy who saw to it that our holidays were never sad, Freddy who sent off for the folders and found the wilderness camp where we could learn the things our fathers would have taught us. Freddy who went to Momma and made her let me go. "I won't let him die, Miss Bela," he told her. "I'll see to it personally that Nieman isn't involved in anything that's dangerous. His safety will be more important to me than my own."

Four weeks later they were stuck all night in a canyon in the Sierra Nevada with half the rangers in the area looking for them.

The phone was ringing. It was Freddy, catching Nieman up on the events of the afternoon. "They bought a mansion on the beach. Up by Mendelin Pass. You wouldn't believe what they bought. It looks like

Gatsby's house. Mother's in ecstasy, as you can imagine. She's been trying to get me in a house she understands for twenty years. Well, on a higher note, I'm taking two days off for this education jaunt. You want to meet us somewhere or shall we come and pick you up?"

"We all have to be in different buildings at different times. Let's meet at Aranga's at noon and have lunch. I've got to work all night to get caught up. Is that all? They bought a house? You haven't been home?"

"I'm going over later and see if he's left."

"Can I do anything to help?"

"Not yet."

"He has no legal rights. Your name is on the birth certificate, isn't it?"

"We don't want him to know where they are, Nieman. Hide your treasures. You're the one who taught me that. If he sees them he might want them."

"Perhaps you should confront him. Pay him off. Who is he anyway? You need more information. Call Jody and get him to put a tail on him and do a profile. I thought you read murder mysteries."

"That's the best idea you've had. Tammili has decided we are moving to escape anti-Semitism. It's a sore spot with her that she can't experience prejudice."

"The angel. Well, I'll meet you at noon tomorrow. Call Jody Wattes. Get more information. Don't let your imagination run this. Athena's the goddess you need. Balance, knowledge, cool head."

"See you tomorrow then."

Sandy walked around the perimeter of Nora Jane and Freddy's house. It was eight o'clock at night and there were lights on in the living room and central hall but the garage was locked and no one seemed to be there. "They've run off because of me," he said out loud. "Well, I deserve that. I never sent her a penny. I guess they have a good life, her and her Jewish husband and my kids. I wonder what they look like. She always said they might not be mine. What if they were his kids and I'd been supporting them all these years? Well, things will change for me after this picture is released. I'll come see them then." He shook his head. I'll just go up and look around. See what kind of stuff they keep around. You can tell a lot about someone by the things they keep around. Life never lets up on me, does it? If I get happy for fifteen minutes, something comes along to throw me to the mat. Well, I better get back or Claudine will get worried. She's the best thing to come down the pike for me in years. I even like the little kid. Yeah, Zandia's a kick. He's got a criminal mind. And Clyda's okay for an old lady even if she is a nervous wreck. Yeah, Claudine's good for me.

Sandy walked up on the front porch and listened for guard dogs, then tried the door. It opened. In their hurry, Nora Jane and Freddy had left it unlocked. He walked into the foyer and called out, "Anybody here? I brought a message from Clyda next door." He walked into the living room and came face to face with a huge portrait of Tammili when she was nine years old. Her short black hair, her intense, worried black eyes stared out at him. They were in sharp contrast to the frilly white lace dress Nora Jane had made her wear. It was a powerful, no-nonsense face. A forbidding IQ, an analytical mind, a wide, flared nose, the painter had captured them all. It was a portrait of a Medici.

Not very pretty, Sandy decided. She sure doesn't look like me. The face followed him when he tried to turn away. That is not my kid, he decided. It hardly even looks like a kid.

The painting, the empty house, the strangeness of a life he could not imagine, began to work on Sandy's mind. If they were mine they might not like me, he decided. They wouldn't know anything about me. Maybe when the movie comes out I'll send N.J. a print and she can show it to them if she wants to. If they're mine. That kid's not mine. I'm out of here.

He went back out the way that he had come, wiping his prints off the door handle, locking, then unlocking the door. He walked across the yard and climbed over the fence and let himself down into Clyda's backyard. "Where have you been?" Claudine asked. "Zandia's been looking for you. I want to take him down and rent him a video. You want to go with us?"

"I used to know that woman who lives next door," Sandy said. "I knew her in New Orleans. So what are they, rich Jews or something?"

"They run a bookstore," Clyda answered. "I'll go with you to the video store. I need to get out of the house myself."

Claudine sighed. "Well, Momma, I just wanted to get Zandia off to myself for a while. I don't like to have everyone in one car."

The next morning Claudine and Zandia and Sandy got into Claudine's BMW and started driving back to L.A. "I know she got her feelings hurt," Claudine was saying. "But I couldn't take any more. I don't know how I grew up with her working on me morning, noon, and night. It's a wonder I survived. My analyst says it proves what a powerful personality I have that I got away from her. What was all that shit she was telling you about Scientology?"

"She's just lonely, baby. She's an old lady and she's lonely. It was nice of her to keep the kid for so long. Don't go bad-mouthing your mother. You should have seen the one I had. When I had one, which wasn't long. I like your old lady. I think she looks good for her age and she leaves you alone."

"Well, it's over. We did it. Let's go home and get back to our own life. That's what I told her. I said, Mother, I have a life of my own, believe it or not, and I need to get back to it." Claudine bent over the wheel, pulled out onto the eight-lane that runs along the coast. "At least it isn't raining."

III

AT FIVE MINUTES TO TEN on Monday morning Nora Jane was settling into a seat in the back of the history class. A tall man in a gray shirt came into the room and put his books on the professor's desk. He was overweight and soft in the face but he had intelligent eyes and huge black-rimmed glasses and he rolled up his sleeves as he waited for the class to assemble. There were thirty or forty students when all the seats were filled. Nora Jane got out a notebook and a pencil. She began to write. "Walls and foyer, decorator white. Porch ceilings, French blue. Tammili and Lydia's rooms, sunshine yellow, ask them. Go by Goyer's Paints this afternoon."

"Where to begin to talk about the history of the world? How to begin to sort out the threads that led to the Golden Age of Greece and the first historian, Thucydides? Agriculture, the domestication of animals, the wheel, pots to store food, ways to carry water, the idea that man has a soul. Where does history begin? Is history a concept of the brain? Does time move in one direction? What is a Zeitgeist? What is an inventor? Is he only a sort of point man, the natural next step created by the force or need of many brains, or is he a lone individual stumbling onto a good idea? What is an idea? Who drilled the first well? Was it a pipe in the ground or a boy or girl sucking moisture from the earth with a straw or reed? Tell me the difference in a hat, a roof, and an umbrella.

"Water, food, shelter, keeping the young alive. Are these the things man needs? When there is an earthquake in San Francisco, what are the first things the survivors do? You do not run into the living room to save the video recorder or the Nikonos. You run to save the babies. . . ." The professor's voice was deep and soothing. Nora Jane got chills listening to him talk. She was thrilled to be here in this class with her books beside her on the floor. If only Sandy doesn't go over to their school today and kidnap them. They wouldn't go with him. The school wouldn't let them go. I have the mobile phone. I could go out in the hall and call the school. I will in a minute. I have to. I can't stand it.

"Our hold on the earth is tenuous at best," the voice was saying. "It doesn't seem so if you are an English-speaking citizen of the United States of America and don't live in a ghetto. We wake up with our automobiles and jet helicopters and computers and video cameras and houses full of every imaginable sort of thing and we know we have gotten rid of the lions and tigers and bears and wolves and bacteria. Unfortunately we have replaced them with the AIDS virus and antibiotic-resistant tuberculoses, by threats to the very air we breathe and polluted lakes and rivers. Also, the same comets that perhaps destroyed the dinosaurs are aiming at us in the sky. . . ."

"Excuse me," Nora Jane muttered to the girl on her right, and leaving her books, went out into the hall and called the twins' school and talked to the receptionist. "Their grandmother is picking them up at three-thirty," she told the girl. "Mrs. Ann Harwood. She has a pale gray Bentley or else a black Porsche. Don't let them leave with anyone else for any reason. Unless you call me first. Here's the mobile phone number. . . . Okay, I know. Well, thank you."

She went back into the classroom and took her seat and listened to the rest of the lecture. Then she put the books into her backpack and put it on her shoulder and struck out across the campus to find Nieman and Freddy.

Nieman and Freddy were at their designated table at Aranga's waiting for her. "I may sell Clara too," Freddy was saying. "Now that he knows where we are. Of course, Nora Jane always told him they might not be his. The whole time she was pregnant she told him that. Isn't that just like her, the darling. Of course the thing is he's AB positive and so am I and so are both of them. It's such a bizarre coincidence."

"Is he bright enough to remember all that and call it into play? I thought he drank."

"Well, obviously he doesn't anymore for what it's worth. He's bright, Nieman. Lydia tests at 130. Just because she's not as smart as Tammili. Of course, psychopathic personalities are never dumb. That's been proven." Freddy played with his coffee cup. "I hope she's all right. Where is she? She got out at eleven."

"It's ten after eleven. Maybe you should prepare to buy him off. I hate to keep bringing this up, but you could just offer him money."

"Solicit blackmail? So we can spend the rest of our days wondering when he'll show up wanting more? It's frightening, Nieman. We can't know what he's thinking. What he's up to."

IV

"I DON'T KNOW WHY that woman who saved him never came back to get the present," Claudine was saying. They had stopped at San Jose to get lunch and were still on the road. Claudine was driving and Sandy was watching Zandia and manning the CD player. "Two ounces of Joy I bought her. I wish I'd just taken it home with me. I thought she was rude, didn't you? I keep thinking they think I'll sue for letting him fall in. I keep reading fear of lawsuits, don't you? Did you see the way they beat it out of there?"

"I told you, I used to know her. Maybe there's something she doesn't want her husband to know that she thinks I'll tell him."

"She had a bad reputation, huh?"

"I didn't really know her. She just went to our church. Well, that's over, baby. You're right about one thing. If your mother wants to see the kid she can come and visit us."

"If she ever saw our condo maybe she'd buy me a bigger one. She's got tons of money but her shrink tells her not to give it to me. I hate his guts, the son-of-a-bitch."

"Think about something good. You're making wrinkles, baby,

worrying about things like that. We've got plenty going on. I hope that deal down in Mexico works out. We could have a lot of fun living down there for a while. I love it down there. The more I think about it, the more I think it's a breakthrough script for you."

"Sandy, Sandy, Sandy," Zandia yelled from the car seat. "Sandy, Sandy, Sandy."

"He's crazy about you," Claudine said. "I think he likes you better than he does me."

Later that afternoon, while Claudine was at the store, Sandy found a piece of stationery and wrote a letter to Nora Jane.

Dear N.J.,

It was really good to see you looking so happy. Your husband looks like a nice guy. You shouldn't have run off like that. I saw you leave. I thought, there she goes. She always did think she was invisible when she had her head in the sand.

Don't worry about me, baby. I'm glad you got a life. I got one too. We're doing a film in Mexico as soon as we finish this one.

Thanks for saving Zandia. I really like this kid even if I do wish sometimes the little helicopter blade on his hat would fly him off to cloud land for a couple of weeks. Around here we call him IN YOUR FACE.

Take care of yourself. Love always,

Sandy

He carried the letter around for a couple of days, then he tore it up.

Freddy Harwood called his old friend Jody Wattes, who had given up a profitable law practice to be a private investigator, and asked him to put a tail on Sandy. Then he and Nora Jane and Tammili and Lydia moved back into their house while they waited for the new one to be renovated.

"I still don't know why we went over to Grandmother's to begin with," Tammili was saying. "Or why all of a sudden we have to have a house on the beach. It's because the neighborhood is anti-Semitic, isn't it? You just don't want us to know. I don't think people should move because of things like that. So is that what's going on?"

"No, it is not." Nora Jane was doing all the lying on this matter. Not that she was good at it, but she was better than Freddy was. "I have always wanted a house on the beach. I never really liked this house. This house is pure nineteen seventy. I want to look out a window and see you playing on a beach. If we are going to live near an ocean, we might as well live on it."

"We want room to grow and change," Freddy added. "We might want some foreign exchange students. More dogs. Anything can happen. Besides, think how happy it is making Grandmother Ann."

"I'll have to get up at six in the morning to get to school."

"Maybe you'll want to change schools in the next few years. We'll go and look at some. You might want to go to a different school that's closer."

"You aren't telling me." Tammili stood with her hands on her hips.

"We're evolving," Freddy said. "Rilke said, You must change your life. Are you afraid to live in a different house, Tammili?"

"No. I just want to know what's going on. You all are up to something and I want to know what it is. Grandmother's getting married to that guy, isn't she? Is that it?"

"I doubt it," Freddy answered. "It wouldn't be like her to get married."

Nora Jane went to her daughter and put her arm around her shoulders. "Your college student mother is going to write a report on the new cave they found in France. Come help me pull up the data on the computer. Will you do that?"

"They told us about it." Tammili got excited. "They showed us a picture of the paintings. There was a herd of animals so good no one could paint it any better. I almost fainted. They showed it to us today in art class. You had that too? They talked about it in college?"

"Uncle Nieman knows about it." Lydia had come into the room from the shadow of the door where she had been listening. "Uncle Nieman's been inside the one at Lascaux. He's one of the few people in America who ever got to see it."

"It was a religion." Tammili took her mother's hand, began to lead her in the direction of the room with the computer. "They weren't very big or they wouldn't have fit through the crawl spaces. I bet they weren't any bigger than Lydia and me. I can't believe you guys are going to college. It's amazing. Come on. I know exactly where to find it. It was all in the newspapers a while ago. Uncle Nieman made me copies of the stories. I've got them in my room somewhere."

Lydia and Tammili and Nora Jane disappeared in the direction of the computer and Freddy walked out onto the patio and looked up at the stars and started making deals. Just keep them safe, he offered. That's all. Name your price. I'm ready. Don't I always keep my word? Have I ever let you down?

Going to live on the beach, his father answered. Well, that's all right until the big storms come.

What's it like up there? Freddy asked.

I don't know, his father answered. I'm too busy watching you to care.

YOU MUST CHANGE
YOUR LIFE

IN JANUARY of nineteen hundred and ninety-five the esteemed movie critic of the *San Francisco Chronicle* took an unapproved leave of absence from his job and went back to Berkeley full time to study biochemistry. He gave his editor ten days' notice, turned in five hastily written, unusually kind reviews of American movies, and walked out.

Why did the feared and admired Nieman Gluuk walk out on a career he had spent twenty years creating? Was it a midlife crisis? Was he ill? Had he fallen in love? The Bay Area arts community forgot about the Simpson trial in its surprise and incredulity.

Let them ponder and search their hearts. The only person who knows the truth is Nieman Gluuk and he can't tell because he can't remember.

The first thing Nieman did after he turned in his notice was call his mother. "I throw up my hands," she said. "This is it, Nieman. The last straw. Of course you will not quit your job."

"I'm going back to school, Mother. I'm twenty years behind in knowledge. I have led the life you planned for me as long as I can lead it. I told you. That's it. I'll call you again on Sunday."

"Don't think I'm going to support you when you're broke," she answered. "I watched your father ruin his life following his whims. I swore I'd protect you from that."

"Don't protect me," he begged. "Get down on your knees and pray you won't protect me. I'm forty-four years old. It's time for me to stop pacing in my cage. I keep thinking of the poem by Rilke."

> His vision, from the constantly passing bars,
> has grown so weary that it cannot hold
> anything else. It seems to him there are
> a thousand bars; and behind the bars, no world. . . .

"You are not Rilke," his mother said. "Don't dramatize yourself, Nieman. You have a lovely life. The last thing you need is to go back to Berkeley and get some crazy ideas put in your head. This is Freddy Harwood's doing. This has Freddy written all over it."

"Freddy's in it. I'll admit that. He and Nora Jane and I have gone back to school together. I wish I hadn't even called you. I'm hanging up."

"Freddy has a trust fund and you don't. You never remember that, Nieman. Don't expect me to pick up the pieces when this is over. . . ." Nieman had hung up the phone. It was a radical move but one to which he often resorted in his lifelong attempt to escape the woman who had borne him.

Nieman's return to academia had started as a gesture of friendship. Nieman and Freddy had attended Berkeley in the sixties but Nora Jane was fifteen years younger and had never attended college, not even for a day.

"Think how it eats at her," Freddy told him. "We own a bookstore and she never even had freshman English. If anyone asks her where she went to school, she still gets embarrassed. I tell her it's only reading books but she won't believe it. She wants a degree and I want it for her."

"Let's go with her," Nieman said, continuing a conversation they had had at lunch the day before. "I mean it. Ever since she mentioned it I keep wanting to tell her what to take. Last night I decided I should go and take those things myself. We're dinosaurs, Freddy. Our education is outdated. We should go and see what they're teaching."

"Brilliant," Freddy said. "It's a slow time at the store. I could take a few weeks off."

"Here's how I figure it." Nieman stood up, got the bottle of brandy, and refilled their glasses. "We sign up for a few classes, pay the tuition, go a few weeks, and then quit. The university gets the tuition and Nora Jane gets some company until she settles in."

"We have spent vacations doing sillier things," Freddy said, thinking of the year they climbed Annapurna, or the time they took up scuba diving to communicate with dolphins.

"I need a change," Nieman confessed, sinking down into the water until it almost reached his chin. "I'm lonely, Freddy. Except for the two of you I haven't any friends. Everyone I know wants something from me or is angry with me for not adoring their goddamn, whorish movies. It's a web I made and I've caught myself."

"We'll get applications tomorrow. Nora Jane's already registered. Classes start next Monday."

Nieman went to the admissions office the next day and signed up to audit Dante in Translation and Playwriting One. Then, suddenly, after a night filled with dreams, he changed the classes to biochemistry and Introduction to the Electron Microscope.

This was not an unbidden move. For several years Nieman had become increasingly interested in science. He had started by reading books by physicists, especially Freeman Dyson. Physics led to chemistry, which led to biology, which led to him, Nieman Gluuk, a walking history of life on earth. Right there, in every cell in his body, was the whole amazing panorama that led to language and conscious thought.

The first lecture on biochemistry and the slides from the microscopes excited Nieman to such an extent he was trembling when he left the building and walked across the campus to the coffee shop where he had agreed to meet Freddy and Nora Jane. A squirrel climbed around a tree while he was watching. A girl walked by, her hair trailing behind her like a wild tangled net. A blue jay landed on a branch and spread his tail feathers. Nieman's breath came short. He could barely put one foot in front of the other. Fields of wonder, he said to himself. Dazzling, dazzling, dazzling.

"This is it," he told Freddy and Nora Jane, when they were seated at a table with coffee and croissants and cream and sugar and butter and jam and honey before them on the handmade plates. "I'm quitting the job. I'm going back to school full time. I have to have this body of information. Proteins and nucleic acids, the chain of being. This is not some sudden madness, Freddy. I've been moving in this direction. I'll apply for grants. I'll be a starving student. Whatever I have to do."

"We don't think you're crazy," Nora Jane said. "We think you're wonderful. I feel like I did this. Like I helped."

"Helped! You are the Angel of the Annunciation is what you are, you darling, you."

"Are you sure this isn't just another search for first causes?" Freddy warned. "Remember those years you wasted on philosophy?"

"Of course it is. So what? This isn't dead philosophical systems or Freudian simplicities. This is real knowledge. Things we can measure and see. Information that allows us to manipulate the physical world."

"If you say so."

"May I use the house at Willits for the weekend? I need to be alone to think. I want to take the textbooks up there and read them from start to finish. I haven't been this excited in years. My God, I am in love."

"Of course you can borrow the house. Just be sure to drain the pipes when you leave."

"It might snow up there this weekend," Nora Jane put in. "The weather station warned of snow."

Two days later Nieman was alone in the solar-powered house he and Freddy had built on a dirt road five miles from Willits, California. The house was begun in 1974 and completed in 1983. Many of the boards had been nailed together by Nieman himself with his delicate hands.

The house stood in the center of one hundred and seven acres of land and overlooked a pleasant valley where panthers still hunted. In any direction there was not a power line or telephone pole or chimney. The house had a large open downstairs with a stone bathroom. A ladder led from the kitchen area to a loft with sleeping rooms. There were skylights in the roof and a wall of glass facing east. There was a huge stone fireplace with a wide hearth. Outside there was a patio and a deep well for drinking water. "This well goes down to the center of the earth," Freddy was fond of saying. "We cannot imagine the springs from which it feeds. This could be water captured eons ago before the crust cooled. This water could be the purest thing you'll ever taste."

"It tastes good," his twin daughters, Tammili and Lydia, would always answer. "It's the best water in the world, I bet."

Nieman stood in the living room looking out across the valleys, which had become covered with snow while he slept. He had arrived late the night before and built up the fire and slept on the hearth in his sleeping bag. "It was the right thing to do to come up here," he said out loud. "This holy place where my friends and I once made our stand against progress and the destruction of the natural world. This holy house where Tammili and Lydia were born, where the panther once came to within ten yards of me and did not strike. I am a strange man and do not know what's wrong with me. But I know how to fix myself when I am broken. You must change your life, Rilke said, and now I am changing mine. Who knows, when I come to my senses, somebody will have taken my job and I'll be on the streets writing travel articles. So be it. In the meantime I am destined to study science and I am going to study science. I cannot allow this body of information to pass me by and I can't concentrate on it while attempting to evaluate Hollywood movies."

Nieman moved closer to the window so he could feel the cold permeating the glass. Small soft flakes were still falling, so light and small it seemed impossible they could have turned the hills so white and covered the trees and the piles of firewood and the well. I can trek out if I have to, he decided. I won't worry about this snow. This snow is here to soothe me. To make the world a wonderland for me to study. Life as a cosmic imperative, de Duve says. I will read that book first, then do three pages of math. I have to learn math. My brain is only forty-four years old, for Christ's sake. Mother taught math. The gene's in there somewhere. It's just rusty. Before there was oxygen there was no rust. Iron existed in the prebiotic oceans in a ferrous state. My brain is like that. There are genes in there that have never been exposed to air. Now I will use them.

Nieman was trembling with the cold and the excitement of the ideas in his head. Proteins and nucleic acids, the idea that all life on earth came from a single cell that was created by a cosmic imperative. Given the earth and the materials of which it is created, life was inevitable. Ever-increasing complexity was also inevitable. It was inevitable that we would create nuclear energy, inevitable that we would overpopulate the earth. It was not as insane as it had always seemed. And perhaps it was not as inevitable once the mind could recognize and grasp the process.

Nieman heaved a great happy sigh. He left watching the snow and turned and climbed the ladder to the sleeping loft. There, on that bed, in that corner beneath the skylight, on a freezing night ten years before, Freddy and Nora Jane's twins had been born, his surrogate children, his goddaughters, his angels, his dancing princesses. Nieman lay down upon the bed and thought about the twins and the progress of their lives. Not everything ends in tragedy, he decided. My life has not been tragic, neither has Freddy's or Nora Jane's. Perhaps the world will last another hundred years. Perhaps this safety can be stretched to include the lives of Tammili and Lydia. So what if they are not mine, not related to me. All life comes from one cell. They are mine because they have my heart. It is theirs. I belong to them, have pondered over them and loved them for ten years. How can this new knowledge I want to acquire help them? How can this new birth of curiosity and wonder add to the store of goodness in the world?

Well, Nieman, don't be a fool. It isn't up to you to solve the problems of the world. But it might be. There were ninety-two people in that lecture room but I was the only one who had this violent a reaction to what the professor was saying. I was the only one who took what he was saying as a blow to the solar plexus. This might be my mission. It might be up to me to learn this stuff and pass it on. It is not inevitable that we overpopulate and destroy the world. Knowledge is still power. Knowledge will save us.

Nieman was crying. He lay on the bed watching the snow falling on the skylight and tears rolled down his face and filled his ears and got his fringe of hair soaking wet. He cried and he allowed himself to cry.

I had thought it was art, he decided. Certainly art is part of it. Cro-Magnon man mixing earth with saliva and spitting it on the walls of caves was a biochemist. He was taking the elements he found around him and using them to explore and recreate and enlarge his grasp of reality. After the walls were painted he could come back and stare at them and wonder at what he had created. Perhaps he cried out, terrified by the working of his mind and hands. I might stare in such a manner at this house we built. I could go outside and watch the snow falling on those primitive solar panels we installed so long ago. It is all one, our well and solar panels and the cave paintings at Lascaux and microscopes at Berkeley and de Duve in Belgium writing this book to blow my mind wide open and Lydia and Tammili carrying their backpacks to school each morning. The maker of this bed and the ax that felled the trees that made the boards we hammered and Jonas Salk and murderers and thieves and Akira Kurosawa and I are one. This great final truth, which all visionaries have intuited, which must be learned over and over again, world without end, amen.

Nieman fell asleep. The snow fell faster. The flakes were larger now, coming from a cloud of moisture that had once been the Mediterranean Sea, that had filled the wells of Florence, in the time of Leonardo da Vinci, and his royal patron, Francis, King of France.

The young man was wearing long robes of dark red and brown. His hair was wild and curly and his feet were in leather sandals. His face was tanned and his eyes were as blue as the sky. He had been knocking on the door for many minutes when Nieman came to consciousness and climbed down the ladder to let him in. "Come in," Nieman said. "I was asleep. Are you lost? I'm Nieman Gluuk. Come in and warm yourself."

"It took a while to get here," the young man said. "That's a kind fire you have going."

"Sit down. Do you live around here? Could I get you something to drink? Coffee or tea or brandy? Could I get you a glass of water? We have a well. Perhaps you're hungry." The young man moved into the living room and looked around with great interest. He walked over to the window and laid his palms against the glass. Then he touched it with his cheek. He smiled at that and turned back to Nieman.

"Food would be nice. Bread or cheese. I'll sit by the fire and warm myself."

Nieman went into the kitchen and began to get out food and a water glass. The young man picked up the book by the biochemist de

Duve, and began to read it, turning the pages very quickly. His eyes would move across the page, then he would turn the page. By the time Nieman returned to the fireplace with a tray, the young man had turned half the pages. "This is a fine book," he said to Nieman, smiling and taking a piece of bread from the tray. "It would be worth the trip to read this."

"You aren't from around here, are you?" Nieman asked.

"You know who I am. You called me here. Don't be frightened. I come when I am truly called. Of course, I can't stay long. I would like to finish this book now. It won't take long. Do you have something to do while I'm reading?" The young man smiled a dazzling smile at Nieman. It was the face of the Angel of the Annunciation in Leonardo's painting. It was the face of David. "You knew me, didn't you?" the young man added. "Weren't there things you wanted to tell me?"

Nieman walked back toward the kitchen, breathing very softly. The young man's face, his hair, his feet, his hands. It was all as familiar as the face Nieman saw every day in the mirror when he shaved. Nieman let his hands drop to his sides. He stood motionless by the ladder while the young man finished reading the book.

"What should I call you?" Nieman said at last.

"Francis called me da Vinci."

"How do you speak English?"

"That's the least of the problems."

"What is the most?"

"Jarring the protoplasm. Of course, I only travel when it's worth it. I will have a whole day. Is there something you want to show me?"

"I want to take you to the labs at Berkeley. I want to show you the microscopes and telescopes, but I guess that's nothing to what you've seen by now. I could tell you about them. Did you really just read that book?"

"Yes. It's very fine, but why did he waste so many pages pretending to entertain superstitious ideas? Are ideas still subject to the Church in this time?"

"It's more subtle, but they're there. The author probably didn't want to seem superior. That's big now."

"I used to do that. Especially with Francis. He was so needy. We will go to your labs if you like. Or we could walk in this snow. I only came to keep you company." He smiled again, a smile so radiant that it transported Nieman outside his fear that he was losing his mind.

"Why to me?"

"Because you might be lonely in the beginning. Afterward, you will have me if you need me." The young man folded the book very carefully and laid it on a cushion. "Tell me how cheese is made now," he said, beginning to eat the food slowly and carefully as he talked. "How is it manufactured? What are the cows named? Who wraps it? How is it transported?"

"The Pacific Ocean is near here," Nieman answered. He had taken a seat a few feet from the young man. "We might be able to get out in the Jeep. That's the vehicle out there. Gasoline powered. I don't know what you know and what you don't know. Do you want to read some more books?"

"Could we go to this ocean?"

"I guess we could. I have hiking gear. If we can't get through we can always make it back. I have a mobile phone. I'd like to watch you read another book. I have a book of algebra and a book that is an overview of where we are in the sciences now. There's a book of plays and plenty of poetry. I'd be glad to sit here and read with you. But finish eating. Let me get you some fruit to go with that."

"Give me the books. I will read them."

Nieman got up and collected books from around the room and brought them and put them beside the young man. Then he brought in firewood and built up the fire. He took a book of poetry and sat near the young man and read as the young man read. Here is the poem he turned to and the one he kept reading over and over again as he sat by the young man's side with the fire roaring and the wind picking up outside and the snow falling faster and faster.

> *. . . Still, if love torments you so much and you so much need*
> *To sail the Stygian lake twice and twice to inspect*
> *The murk of Tartarus, if you will go beyond the limit,*
> *Understand what you must do beforehand.*
> *Hidden in the thick of a tree is a bough made of gold*
> *And its leaves and pliable twigs are made of it too.*
> *It is sacred to underworld Juno, who is its patron,*
> *And it is roofed in by a grove, where deep shadows mass*
> *Along far wooded valleys. No one is ever permitted*
> *To go down to earth's hidden places unless he has first*
> *Plucked this golden-fledged growth out of its tree*
> *And handed it over to fair Proserpina, to whom it belongs*
> *By decree, her own special gift. And when it is plucked,*
> *A second one always grows in its place, golden again,*
> *And the foliage growing on it has the same metal sheen.*
> *Therefore look up and search deep and when you have found it*
> *Take hold of it boldly and duly. If fate has called you,*
> *The bough will come away easily, of its own accord.*
> *Otherwise, no matter how much strength you muster, you never will*
> *Manage to quell it or cut it down with the toughest of blades.*

"Now," the young man said, when he finished the biochemistry textbook. "Tell me about these infinitesimal creatures, amoebas, proteins, acid chains, slime molds, white cells, nuclei, enzymes, DNA, RNA, atoms, quarks, strings, and so on. What an army they have found. I could not have imagined it was that complicated. They have seen these creatures? Many men have seen them?"

"We have telescopes and microscopes with lenses ground a million times to such fineness and keenness, with light harnessed from electrons. They can magnify a million times. A thousand million. I don't know the numbers. I can take you to where they are. I can take you to see them if you want to go."

"Of course. Yes, you will take me there. But it must be soon. There is a limited amount of time I will be with you."

"How much time?"

"It will suffice. Will your vehicle travel in this snow?"

"Yes. Perhaps you would like to borrow some modern clothes. Not that there's anything wrong with your clothes. They are very nice. I was especially admiring the cape. The weave is lovely. They're always worrying about security. I want to take you to the laboratories at Berkeley. I can call the head of the department. He will let us in."

"You may have the cloak since you admire it. It can remain here." He removed the long brown garment and handed it to Nieman.

"I'll give you a parka." Nieman ran for the coatrack and took down a long beige parka Freddy had ordered from L.L. Bean. He held it out to the young man. "I guess I seem nervous. I'm not. It's just that I've wanted to talk to you since I was ten years old."

"Yes. You've been calling me for some time."

"I thought you would be old. Like of the time when you died. Did you die?"

"I thought so. It was most uncomfortable and Francis wept like a child, which was not altogether unpleasant." He laughed softly. "It is better to come with my young eyes. In case there is something to see."

"Where are you when you aren't here?"

"Quite far away."

"Will it matter that you came here? I mean in the scheme of things, as it were?"

"It will matter to me. To read the books and see these instruments you are describing. I have always wished to have my curiosity satisfied. That was always what I most dreamed of doing. Francis never understood that. He could never believe I wouldn't be satisfied to eat and drink and be lauded and talk with him. It kept me from loving him as he deserved."

"I meant, will it change the course of anything?"

"Not unless you do it."

"I wouldn't do it. Could I do it by accident?"

"No. I will see to that. Do you want to go out now, in the vehicle in the snow?" There it was again, the smile that soaked up all the light and gave it back.

"Let's get dressed for it." Nieman led his guest upstairs and gave him a warm shirt and socks and shoes and pants and long underwear. While he was changing Nieman banked the fire and put the food away and set the crumbs out for the birds and locked the windows and threw his things into a bag. He forgot to drain the pipes.

"Well, now," he said out loud. "I guess I can drive that Jeep in this snow. Let's assume I can drive. Let's say it's possible and I will do it." He turned on the mobile phone and called the department at Berkeley and left a message saying he was bringing a senator to see the labs. Then he called the president of the university at his home and called in his markers. "Very hush-hush," he told the president. "This could be very big, Joe. This could be millions for research but you have to trust me. Don't ask questions. Just tell the grounds people to give me the keys when I come ask for them. I can't tell you who it is. You have to trust me."

"Of course, Nieman," the president answered. "After everything you and Freddy have done for us. Anything you want."

"The keys to everything. The electron microscopes, the physics labs, the works. We could use one of your technical people for a guide but no one else."

"There'll be people working in the labs."

"I know that. We won't bother anyone. I'll call you Monday and tell you more."

"Fine. I'll look forward to hearing about it." After he hung up the phone the university president said to his wife, "That was Nieman Gluuk. Did you know he's quitting writing his column? Took a leave of absence to go back to school."

"Well, don't you go getting any ideas like that," his good-looking wife giggled. "All he ever wrote about were foreign films. He'd gotten brutal in his reviews. Maybe they let him go. Maybe he just pretended that he quit."

There was a layer of ice beneath the snow. Nieman tested it by walking on it, then put Leonardo into the passenger seat and buckled him in and got behind the wheel and started driving. He drove very carefully in the lowest gear across the rock-strewn yard toward the wooden gate that fenced in nothing since the fence had been abandoned as a bad idea. "Thank God it's downhill," he said. "It's downhill most of the way to the main road. So, when was the last time you were here?" He talked without turning his head. The sun was out now. Birds were beginning to circle above the huge fir trees in the distance. "Have you been to the United States? To the West Coast?"

"Once long ago. I saw the ocean with a man of another race. I walked beside it and felt its power. It is different from the ocean I knew."

"We can go there first. It won't take long once we get to the main road. I'm sorry if I keep asking you questions. I can't help being curious."

"You can ask them if you like. I was visited by Aristotle in my turn. We went to a river and explored its banks. He was very interested in my studies of moving water. He said the flow of water would impede the mixture of liquids and we talked of how liquid forms its boundaries within a flow. He had very beautiful hands. I painted them later from memory several times. Of course everyone thought they were Raphael's hands. Perhaps I thought so too finally. After he left I had no real memory of it for a while. More like the memory of a dream, bounded, uncertain, without weight. I think it will be like that for you, so ask whatever you wish to ask."

"I don't think I want to ask anything now. I think we should go to the ocean first since we are so near. I forget about water. I forget to look at it with clear eyes, and yet I was watching the snow when I fell asleep. Also, I was crying. Why are you smiling?"

"Go on."

"I was thinking that when I was small I knew how to appreciate the ocean. Later, I forgot. When I was small I would stand in one place for a very long time watching the waves lap. Every day I came back to the same spot. I made footprints for the waves to wash away. I made castles farther and farther up the beach to see how far the tide could reach. I dug into the sand, as deep as it would allow me to dig. I was an infatuate of ocean, wave, beach. Are you warm enough? Is that coat comfortable?"

"I am warm. Tell me about this vehicle. What do you call it?"

"Automobile. Like auto and mobile. It's a Jeep, a four-wheel drive. We call it our car. Everyone has one. We work for them. We fight wars over the fuel to power them. We spend a lot of time in them. They have radios. We listen to broadcasts from around the world while we drive. Or we listen to taped books. I have a book of the Italian language we could listen to. You might want to see how it's evolved. It might be the same. It might be quite similar to what you spoke. Would you like to hear it?" Nieman shifted into a higher gear. The road was still steep but lay in the lee of the mountain and was not iced beneath the snow. "We'll be on the main road, soon," he added. "We're in luck it seems. I wouldn't have driven this alone. One more question. How do you read the books so fast?"

"I'm not sure." Leonardo laughed. "It's been going on since I quit the other life. It's getting better. At first it was not this fast. I'm very fond of being able to do it. It's the nicest thing of all."

"Where do you stay? When you aren't visiting? I mean, going someplace like this."

"With other minds."

"Disembodied?"

"If we want to be. Is that the main road?" It was before them, the road to Willits. Plows had pushed the snow in dirty piles on either side of the road. In the center two vehicles were moving in one lane down the mountain. A blue sedan and a white minivan were bouncing down the road in the ripening sunlight.

"I believe this," Nieman said. "I'm in my red Jeep driving Leonardo da Vinci down from the house to see the ocean. My name is Nieman Gluuk and I have striven all my life to be a good man and use my talents and conquer resentment and be glad for whatever fate dumped me in Northern California the only child of a bitter woman and a father I almost never saw, and I never went into a movie theater expecting to hate the movie and was saddened when I did. Maybe this is payback and maybe this is chance and maybe I deserve this and the only thing I wish is that my friend, Freddy, could be here so it won't destroy our friendship when I am driven to tell him about it."

"You won't remember it." Leonardo reached over and touched his sleeve. He smiled the dazzling smile again and Nieman took it in without driving off the road and took the last curve down onto the highway. "You will have it," Leonardo added. "It is yours, but you won't have the burden of remembering it."

"I want the burden." Nieman laughed. "Burden me. Try me. I can take it. I'll write a movie script and publicize intelligence. *Nel mezzo del cammin di nostra vita mi ritrovai per una selva oscura, che la diritta via era smarrita. Ahi quanto a dir qual era e cosa dura esta selva selvaggia e aspra e forte.* That's the beginning of *The Divine Comedy.* That's what I went back to Berkeley to take. Instead, I'm in this forest of biochemistry. I'm dreaming the things I'm reading. They put literature into a new light. The artist intuits what the mind knows and the mind knows everything, doesn't it? Past, present, and forevermore."

"Some wake to it gradually. Some never know."

"I've worked for it," Nieman said. "I have worked all my life to understand, to see myself as the product of five hundred million years of evolution. You seem to have known it always."

"I was taken from my mother's house when I was four years old. On the walk to my father's house, the fields and the wonder of the earth came to console me. But I worked also. I always worked." He laid his hand on Nieman's arm. Nieman steered the Jeep across a pile of snow and turned onto the road leading down to Willits. Around them the snow-covered hills with their massive fir trees were paintings of unspeakable complexity. Neither of them spoke for many miles.

It was past noon when they drove through the small town of Willits and turned onto Highway 20 leading to the Pacific Ocean. "I'm going to stop for gasoline for the automobile," Nieman said. "We collect it in foreign countries. The countries of the Turks and Muslims, although some of it is under the ground of this country. We store it underneath these filling stations in large steel tanks. Steel is an alloy made of iron and carbon. It's very strong. Then we drive up to the pumping stations and pump the fuel into our tanks. Even young children do this, Leonardo. I don't know what you know and what you don't know, but I feel I should explain some things."

"I like to hear you speak of these phenomena. Continue. I will listen and watch."

Nieman spotted a Conoco station and stopped the Jeep and got out. He took down one of the gasoline hoses and inserted it in the fuel tank of the Jeep. Leonardo stood beside the tank watching and not speaking. "Don't smile that smile at anyone else," Nieman said. "We'll be arrested for doing hallucinogens."

"They never explode?" Leonardo moved in for a closer look, took a sniff of the fumes, then put both hands in the pockets of the jacket. There was a package of Kleenex in one pocket. He brought it out and examined it.

"It's called Kleenex. We blow our noses on it," Nieman explained. "It's a disposable handkerchief."

"Could one draw on it?" Leonardo held a sheet up to the light. "It's fragile and thin."

"Wait a minute." Nieman pulled a notepad and a black felt-tip pen out of the glove compartment and handed them to Leonardo. Leonardo examined the pen, took the top from it, and began to draw, leaning the pad against the top of the Jeep. Nieman put the hose back on the pump, then went inside and paid for the gasoline. When he returned, Leonardo had covered a page with the smallest, most precise lines Nieman had ever seen. Leonardo handed the drawing to him. It was of the mountains and the trees. In the foreground Nieman was standing beside the Jeep with the gasoline hose in his hand.

Nieman took the drawing and held it. "You are a microscope," he said. "Perhaps you will not be impressed with the ones we've made."

"Shall we continue on our way?" Leonardo asked. "Now that your tank is full of gasoline."

They drove in silence for a while. The sun was out in full violence now, melting the snow and warming the air. "The air is an ocean of currents," Nieman said at last. "I suppose you know about that."

"Always good to be reminded of anything we know."

"You want to hear the Italian tape? I'd like to hear what you think of it."

"That would be fine."

Nieman reached into a pack of tapes and extracted the Beginning Italian tape and stuck it into the tape player. "This Jeep doesn't have very good speakers," he said. "We have systems that are much better than this one." The Italian teacher began to teach Italian phrases.

Leonardo began to laugh. Quietly at first, then louder and louder until he was shaking with laughter.

"What's so funny?" Nieman asked. He was laughing too. "What do you think is funny? Why am I laughing too?"

"Such good jokes," Leonardo answered, continuing to laugh. "What questions. What news. What jokes."

It was thirty-six miles from Willits to the Pacific Ocean. The road led down between mountains and virgin forests. They drove along at fifty miles an hour, listening to the Italian tape and then to Kiri Te Kanawa singing arias from Italian opera. Nieman was lecturing Leonardo on the history of opera and its great modern stars. Long afterward, when he had forgotten everything about the day that could be proven, Nieman remembered the drive from Willits to the ocean and someone beside him laughing. "Are you sure you weren't with me?" he asked Freddy a hundred times later in their lives. "Maybe we were stoned. But Kiri Te Kanawa didn't start recording until after we had straightened up so we couldn't have been stoned. I think you were with me. You just don't remember it."

"I never drove in a Jeep with you from Willits to the ocean while listening to Italian tapes. I would remember that, Nieman. Why do you always ask me that? It's a loose wire in your head, a precursor of dreaded things to come." Then Freddy would smile and shake his head and later talk about it to his psychiatrist or Nora Jane. "Nieman's fixated on thinking I drove with him in a Jeep listening to an Italian tape," he would say. "About once a year he starts on that. It's like the budding of the trees. Once a year, in winter, he decides the two of us took that trip and nothing will convince him otherwise. He gets mad at me because I can't remember it. Can you believe it?"

Outside the small town of Novo, Nieman found a trail he had used before. It led to a beach the townspeople used during good weather.

He parked the Jeep in a gravel clearing and they got out and climbed down a path to the water. The ocean was very dramatic, with huge boulders jutting into the entrance of a small harbor. The snow was melting on the path. Even now, in the heart of winter, moss was forming on the rocks. "'The force that through the green fuse drives the flower,'" Nieman said.

"Dylan is happy now," Leonardo answered. "A charming man. I go to him quite often and he recites poetry. It makes the poetry he wrote when he was here seem primitive. I should not tell you that, of course. We try never to say such things."

"Look at the ocean," Nieman answered. "What mystery could be greater. Shouldn't this be enough for any man to attempt to understand? This force, this power, this place where land and air meet the sea? '. . . this goodly frame, the earth . . . this most excellent canopy, the air . . . this brave o'erhanging firmament, this majestical roof fretted with golden fire . . .'"

"Will loved the sea and wrote of it but had little time for it. Plato was the same. He talked and wrote of it but didn't take the time to ponder it as we are doing. Of course, in other ages time seemed more valuable. Life was short and seemed more fleeting."

They were walking along a strip of sand only ten to twenty feet wide. It was low tide. Later in the day it would have been impossible to walk here and they would have had to use the higher path.

"We could just stay here," Nieman said. "We don't have to go to the labs. I just thought you might want to see the microscopes."

"We have all day."

"They're leaving the labs open in the biochemistry building. We can go to Berkeley or we can stay here. I saw you looking at the atlas. Did you memorize it? I mean, is that how you do it?"

"I remember it. It is very fine how they have mapped the floor of the oceans. Is it exact, do you think?"

"Pretty much so at the time of mapping. The sand shifts,

everything shifts and changes. They map the floor with soundings, with radar. When you leave here, where do you have to be? Is there some gathering place? Do you just walk off? Where do you go?"

"I just won't be here."

"Will the clothes be here? I only wondered. That's Freddy's coat. I could get him another one but he's pretty fond of that one. He took it to Tibet."

Nieman moved nearer to Leonardo, his eyes shifting wildly. The day had a sort of rhythm. Sometimes it was just beating along. Then suddenly he imagined it whole and that made his heart beat frantically. "I don't care, of course. You can take it if you need to. You can have anything I have."

"I will leave the clothes. It would be a waste to take them."

"When will you go? How long will it be? You have to understand. I never had a father. No man ever stayed long enough. I was always getting left on my own. It's been a problem for me all my life."

Leonardo turned to face him. "This is not a father who leaves, Nieman. This is the realm of knowledge, which you always longed for and long for now. It is always available, it never goes away, it cannot desert you, it cannot fail you. It is yours. It belongs to whoever longs for it. If you desert it, it is always waiting, like those waves. It comes back and back like the sea. I am only a moment of what is available to you. When I am gone the clothes will be here and you can wear them when you are reading things that are difficult to understand. You will read everything now. You will learn many languages. You will know much more than you know now. Tell me about the microscopes."

"I haven't used one yet. But I can tell you how it works. It concentrates a beam of electrons in a tube to scan or penetrate the thing you want magnified. It makes a photograph using light and dark and shadow. The photograph is very accurate and magnified a million times. Then a portion of that photograph can be magnified several million more times. It's so easy for me to believe the photographs so I think it must be something I know. My friend, Freddy, thinks we know everything back to the first cell, that all discovery is simply plugging into memory banks. Memory at the level of biochemistry. Which is why I can't believe it took me so long to begin to study this. I had to start in the arts. My mother is a frustrated actress. I've been working her program for forty-four years. Now it's my turn. But this is plain to you. You're the one who saw the relationship between art and science. It never occurred to you not to do both."

"I am honored to be here for your birth of understanding. Where I am, the minds are past their early enthusiasms. I miss seeing the glint in eyes. I miss the paintbrush in my hand and the smell of paints. If you wish to show me this microscope we can go there now. The sea is very old. We don't have to stay beside it all day."

It was a two-and-a-half-hour drive to Berkeley. They drove along the western ridge of the Cascade Range, within a sea breeze of the Mendocino Fracture Zone. Beside the Russian River. They drove to Mendocino, then Littleriver, then Albion. At Albion they cut off onto Highway 128 and drove along the Navarro River to Cloverdale. They went by Santa Rosa, then Petaluma, then Novato, and down and across the Richmond–San Rafael Bridge and on to Berkeley.

It was six o'clock when they arrived at the campus. It was dark and the last students were mounting their bicycles as they left the biochemistry building. Nieman nosed the Jeep into a faculty parking space and they got out and entered the building through iron doors and went down a hall to an elevator.

"Have you been on one of these?" Nieman asked, holding the elevator door with his hand. "It's a box on a pulley, actually. It's quite safe. When they were new sometimes they would get stuck. Some pretty funny jokes and stories came out of that. Also, there were tragedies, lack of oxygen and so forth. This one is thirty years old at least, but it's safe."

"Arabic," Leonardo said, touching the numbered buttons with his finger. "I thought it would continue to be useful."

"The numbers? Oh, yes. Everyone uses the same system. Based on the fingers and toes. Five fingers on each hand. Two arms, two legs. Binary system and digital system. We run our computers on the binary system. It's fascinating. What man has done. There's one playwright dealing with it, a man named Stoppard." Leonardo stepped back and stood near Nieman. Nieman pressed 2 and the box rose in space on its pulley and the door opened.

Waiting for them on the second-floor hall was the head of university security. He was wearing a blue uniform with silver buttons. "Hello," he said. "If you're Mr. Gluuk they have a lady waiting for you. President Culver said to tell you she'd show you the machines."

"Oh, that wasn't necessary. We only wanted to look at them." He took Leonardo's arm. So he looks like a genius who has spent a thousand years on a Buddhist prayer bench. So the smile is so dazzling it hypnotizes people. No one would imagine this. No one would believe it.

"Don't I know you from when I was a student?" Nieman asked. "I'm Nieman Gluuk. I used to edit the school paper. In the seventies. Didn't you guard the building when we had the riots in seventy-five?"

"I thought I knew you. I'm Abel Kennedy. I was a rookie that year and you kept me supplied with cookies and coffee in the newspaper office. I'm head of security now." Captain Kennedy held out his hand and Nieman shook it. He was trying to decide how to introduce Leonardo when a door opened down the hall and a woman came walking toward them. She was of medium height with short blond hair. She was wearing a pair of blue jeans and a long-sleeved white shirt. Over the shirt was a long white vest. There were pencils and pens in the pockets of the vest. A pair of horn-rimmed glasses was on her head. Another pair was in her hand.

"I was wondering if one could wear bifocals to look into the scope," Nieman said. "I was afraid I'd have to get contact lenses to study science."

"It's a screen." She laughed. "I'm Stella Light. My parents were with the Merry Pranksters. Some joke. I meant to have it changed but I never did." She held out her hand to Nieman. Long slender fingers. Nails bitten off to the quick. No rings. She smiled again.

"I'm Nieman Gluuk. This is our distinguished guest, Leo Gluuk, a cousin from Madrid. I mean, Florence. Also from Minneapolis."

"Make up your mind. Nice to meet you. I've read your stuff. I'm from Western Oregon. Well, what exactly can we do for you?"

"Just let us see the microscopes. Leo is very interested in the technology. It's extremely nice of you to stay late like this. I know your days are long enough already."

"I was here anyway. We've had an outbreak of salmonella in the valley. We're trying to help out with that. It gets on the chicken skin in the packing plants or if they are defrosted incorrectly. Well, I'll let you see slides of that. They're fresh."

They walked down a hall to a room with the door ajar. Inside, on a long curved table, was the console. In the center, covered with a metal that looked more like gold than brass, was the scanning electron microscope. The pride of the Berkeley labs.

They moved into the open doorway. Leonardo had been completely quiet. Now he gave Stella the smile and she stepped back and let him precede her into the room. She and Leonardo sat down at the console. She got out a box of slides and lifted one from the box with a set of calipers. She slid it into a notch and locked it down. Then she pushed a button and an image appeared on the screen. "To 0.2 nanometers," she said. "We can photograph it and go higher."

Nieman leaned over their shoulders and looked into the screen. It was a range of hills covered with cocoons. "A World War 1 battlefield," he said. "Corpses strewn everywhere. Is that the salmonella?"

"Yes. Let's enlarge it." She pushed another button. The hill turned into crystal mountains. Now it was the Himalayas. Range after range of crystals. Nieman looked down at his own arm. In a nanometer of skin was all that wonder.

Leonardo began asking questions about the machine, about the metal of which it was made, about the vacuum through which the electrons traveled, how the image was created. Stella answered the questions as well as she could. She bent over him. She put pieces of paper in front of him. She put slides into the microscope. She asked no questions. She had been completely mesmerized by the smile. She would remember nothing of the encounter. Except a momentary excitement when she was alone in the room at night. She thought it was sexual. She thought it was about Nieman. There I go, she would scold herself, getting interested in yet another man I cannot understand. The daddy track, chugging on down the line to lonesome valley.

They stayed in the laboratory for half an hour. Then they wandered out into the hall and found a second microscope and Stella took the thing apart and let Leonardo examine the parts. Then she let him reassemble it. She stood beside Nieman. She sized him up. He was better looking than his photograph in the paper. His skin was so white and clear. He was kind.

"You really quit your job?" she asked.

"A leave of absence. I was burned out."

"Who is he?" she asked. "I don't think I've ever met anyone I liked as much."

"We all love him. The family adores him. But it's hard to keep track of him. He travels all the time."

Leonardo put everything back into its place. He laid Stella's pencil on top of the stack of papers and got up from the chair. "We are finished now," he said. "We should be leaving. We thank you for your kindness."

Stella walked them to the elevator. They got on and she stood smiling after them. When they had left she went back into the labo-

ratory and worked until after twelve. Two children had died in the salmonella outbreak. Twenty were hospitalized. The infected food had
reached a grade school lunchroom.

When they left the building there was a full moon in the sky. There
was so much light it cast shadows. Leonardo walked with Nieman to
the Jeep. "I am leaving," he said. "You will be fine." He kissed Nieman
on the cheek, then on the forehead. Then he was gone. Nieman tried
to follow him but he did not know how. When he got back to the Jeep,
the clothes Leonardo had been wearing were neatly stacked on the
passenger seat. On top of the clothes was a pencil. A black and white
striped pencil sharpened to a fine point. Nieman picked it up and held
it. He put it in his pocket. I might write with this, he decided. Or I
might draw.

He got into his Jeep and drove over to Nora Jane and Freddy
Harwood's house and parked in the driveway and walked up on the
porch and rang the doorbell. The twins let him in. They pulled him
into the room. "Momma's making étouffée and listening to the
Nevilles," Tammili told him. "She's having a New Orleans day. Come
on in. Stay and eat dinner with us. Daddy said you'd been in Willits.
How is it there? Was it snowing?"

They dragged him into the house. From the back Freddy called
out to him. Nora Jane emerged from the kitchen wearing an apron. It
was already beginning to fade. Whatever had happened or almost
happened or seemed to happen was fading like a photograph in acid.

"Come on in here," Freddy was calling out. "Come tell us what
you were doing. We have things to tell you. Tammili made all-stars in
basketball. Lydia got a role in the school play. Nora Jane got an A on
her first English test. I think I'm going bald. We haven't seen you in
days. Hurry up, Nieman. I want to talk to you."

"He's your best friend," Lydia giggled, half whispering. "It's so
great. You just love each other."

THE BROWN CAPE

TAMMILI AND LYDIA were supposed to be cleaning up the loft. Their father was working on the well. Their mother was cooking breakfast and it was their job to make the beds and straighten up the loft and clean the windows with vinegar and water.

"Why can't we clean them with Windex like we do at home?" Lydia complained. "Just because we come to Willits for spring vacation they go environmental and we have to use vinegar for the windows. The windows are okay. I'm not cleaning them."

"You shouldn't have come then. You could have stayed with Grandmother. You didn't have to come if you're just going to complain."

"Why can't we have a ski lodge or something? Why do we have to have a solar house? We can't bring anybody. It's too little to even bring the dogs."

"It's a solar-powered house, not a solar house, and I don't want to take dogs everywhere I go. There're wolves and panthers in these woods. Those dogs wouldn't last a week up here. Dooley is so friendly he'd let a wolf carry him off in his teeth."

"You clean the windows and I'll get all this stuff out from under the bed. Everyone's always sticking stuff under here. I hate piles of junk like this." Lydia was pulling boxes and clothes out from underneath the bed where she and Tammili had been sleeping. It was the bed on which they had been born, in the middle of the night, ten and a half years before.

"What are you thinking about?" Tammili asked, but she knew. She and Lydia always thought about things at the same time. It was the curse and blessing of being twins. You were never lonely, not even in your thoughts. On the other hand there was no place to hide.

"Who put this here?" Lydia dragged a long brown cloak out from underneath the bed. It had a cowl and a twisted cord for the waist and it was very thick, as thick as a blanket. It smelled heavenly, like some wonderful mixture of wildflowers and mist. She pulled it out and spread it on the bed. Then she wrapped it around her shoulders.

"I've never seen this before." Tammili drew near the cape and touched it. "It smells like violet. I bet it belongs to Nieman. No one but Nieman would leave a cape here. Let me wear it too, will you?" She moved into one half of the cape. They wrapped it around themselves like a cocoon and fell down on the bed and started laughing.

"Once upon a time," Lydia began, "there were two little girls and they were so poor they didn't have any firewood for the fireplace. All the trees had been cut down by ruthless land developers and there weren't any twigs left to gather to make a fire. They only had one thing left and that was their bed. We better cut up the bed and burn it, one of them said, or else we won't live until the morning. We will freeze to death in this weather. Okay, the other one said. Pull that bed over here and let's burn it up. Then they saw something under the bed. It was a long warm cape that their father had left for them when he went away to war. There was a note on it. 'This is for my darling daughters in case they run out of firewood. Love, your dad.' "

"Tammili." It was their mother calling. "You girls come on down. I want you to help me with the eggs." Tammili and Lydia put their faces very close together. They giggled again, smothering the sound.

"We're coming," Lydia called. "We'll be down in a minute." They folded the cape and laid it on the bed by Tammili's backpack. Then they climbed down the ladder to help their mother with the meal.

*　　*　　*

That was Wednesday morning. On Wednesday night their father decided they should go on an expedition. "To where?" their mother asked. "You know I have to study while I'm here. I can't go off for days down a river or in the mountains. One-day trips. That's all I'm good for this week."

"I thought we might overnight up in the pass by Red River," Freddy Harwood said. "Nieman and I used to camp there every spring. It might be cold but we'll take the bedrolls and I'll have the mobile phone. You can't go for one night?"

"I should stay here. Do you need me?"

"We don't need you," Tammili said. "We can take care of things. I want to go, Dad. We've been hearing about Red River for years but no one ever takes us. We're almost eleven. We can do anything."

"Get another adult," Nora Jane insisted. "Don't go off with both of them and no one to help."

"We are help," Lydia said. "Is it a steep climb, Daddy? Is it steep?"

"No. It's long but it's not that steep. Nieman and I used to do the trail to the top in three hours. Two and a half coming down. There's a bower up there under thousand-year-old pine trees. You don't need a sleeping bag. We'll take them but we could sleep on the ground. I haven't been up there to camp in years. Not since I met your mother. So, we'll go. It's decided."

"Tomorrow," they both screamed.

"Maybe tomorrow. Maybe Friday. Let me think about it." They jumped on top of him and started giving him one of their famous hug attacks. They grabbed pillows and hugged him with them until he screamed for mercy. "Tomorrow, tomorrow, tomorrow," they kept saying. "Don't make us wait."

"Then we have to get everything ready tonight because we have to leave at sunup. It takes an hour to drive to the trail. Then three hours to climb. I want to have camp set up by afternoon."

"What do we need?"

"Tent, food, clothes, extra socks. Vaseline for blisters, ankle packs for sprains, snakebite kit, Mag Lites, sleeping bags."

"We're going to carry all that?"

"Whatever we want we have to carry. We'll have extra water in the car. We'll take small canteens and the purifying kit. Go start pumping at the well, Tammili. Fill two water bags."

"Can't I fill them at the sink?"

"No, the idea is to know how to survive without a sink. That's what Willits is for, sweeties."

"We know." They gave each other a look. "So no matter what happens your DNA is safe." They started giggling and their mother put down the dish she was drying and started giggling too.

Freddy Harwood was an equipment freak. He had spent the summers of his youth in wilderness camps in Montana and western Canada. When he graduated to camping on his own, he took up equipment as a cause. If he was going camping he had every state-of-the-art device that could be ordered on winter nights from catalogs. He had Mag Lites on headbands and Bull Frog sunblock. He had wrist compasses and Ray-Ban sunglasses and Power Bars and dehydrated food. He had two lightweight tents, a Stretch Dome and a Lookout. The Lookout was the lightest. It weighed five pounds, fifteen ounces with the poles. He had Patagonia synchilla blankets and official referee whistles and a Pur water purifier and drinking water tablets in case the purifier broke. He had two-bladed knives for the girls and a six-bladed knife for himself. He had stainless-steel pans and waterproofing spray and tent repair kits and first aid kits of every kind.

"Bring everything we think we need and put it on the table," Freddy said. "Then we'll decide what to take and what to leave. Bring everything. Your boots and the clothes you're going to wear. It's eight o'clock. We have to be packed and in bed by ten if we're going in the morning."

The girls went upstairs and picked out clothes to wear. "I'm taking this cape," Tammili said. "I've got a feeling about this cape. I think it's supposed to go to Red River with us."

"Nieman saw baby panthers up there once," Lydia added. "The mother didn't kill him for looking at them, she was so weak with hunger because there had been a drought and a forest fire. Nieman left them all his food. He got to within twenty feet of their burrow and put the food where she could get it. Dad was there. He knows it's true. Nieman's so cool. I wish he was going with us."

"He has to study. He's going for a Nobel prize in biochemistry. That's what Dad told Grandmother. He said Nieman wouldn't rest until he won a Nobel."

The girls brought their clothes and backpacks down from the loft and spread the things out on the table. "What's this?" Freddy asked, picking up the cloak.

"Something we found underneath the bed. We think it's Nieman's. I was going to take it instead of a sleeping bag. Look how warm it is."

"I wouldn't carry it if I were you. You have to think of every ounce." Tammili went over and took the cape from him and folded it and laid it on the hearth. Later, when they had finished packing all three of the backpacks and set them by the kitchen door, she picked up the cape and pushed it into her pack. I'm taking it, she decided. I like it. It looks like the luckiest thing you could wear.

In a small, neat condominium in Berkeley, the girls' godfather, Nieman Gluuk, was finishing the last of twenty algebra problems he had set himself for the day. His phone was off the hook. His flower gardens were going wild. His cupboards were bare. His sink was full of dishes. His bed was unmade.

He put the last notation onto the last problem and stood up and began to rub his neck with his hand. He was lonely. His house felt like a tomb. "I'm going to Willits to see the kids," he said out loud. "I'm going crazy all alone in this house. Starting to talk to myself. They are my family and I need them and it's spring vacation and they won't be ten forever."

He went into his bedroom and began to throw clothes into a suitcase. It was three o'clock in the morning. He had been working on the algebra problems for fourteen hours. When Nieman Gluuk set out to conquer a body of knowledge, he did it right. When he had studied philosophy he had learned German and French and Greek. Now he was studying biochemistry and he was learning math. "If my eyes hold out I will learn this stuff," he muttered. "If my eyes give out, I'll learn it with my ears." He pushed the half-filled suitcase onto the floor and turned off the lights and pulled off his shirt and pants and fell into his bed in his underpants. It would be ten in the morning before he woke. Since he had quit his job at the newspaper he had been sleeping nine and ten hours a night. The day he canceled his subscription he slept twelve hours that night.

"The destination," Freddy was saying to his daughters, "is the high caves above Red River. They aren't on this map but you can see the cliff face in these old photographs. Nieman and I took these when we were about twenty years old. We developed them in my old darkroom in Grandmother Ann's house. See all the smudges? We were experimenting with developers." He held the photograph up. "Anyway, we follow the riverbed for a few miles, then up and around the mountain to this pass. Four rivers rise on this mountain. All running west except this one. Red River runs east and north. It's an anomaly, probably left behind from some cataclysm when the earth cooled or else created by an earthquake eons ago. It's unique in every way. If there was enough snow last winter the falls will be spectacular this time of year. Some years they are spectacular and sometimes just a trickle. We won't know until we get there. Even in dry years the sound is great. Where we are camping we will be surrounded by water and the sound of water. It's the best sleeping spot in the world. I'll put it up against any place you can name. I wish your mother was going with us. She doesn't know what she's missing." He took the plate of pancakes Nora Jane handed him and began to eat, lifting each mouthful delicately and dramatically, meeting her violet-blue eyes and saying secrets to her about the night that had passed and the one she was going to be missing.

Tammili and Lydia played with their food. Neither of them could eat when they were excited and they were excited now.

"Is this enough?" Lydia asked her mother. "I really don't want any more."

"Whatever you like. It's a long way to go and the easy way to carry food is in your stomach."

"It weighs the same inside or out," Tammili said. "We're only taking dehydrated packs. In your stomach it's mixed with water so it really weighs less if you carry it in the pack."

Lydia giggled and got up and put her plate by the sink. Tammili followed her. "Let's go," they both said. "Come on, let's get going."

"I wish you had a weather report," Nora Jane put in. "If it turns colder you just come on back."

"Look at that sky. It's as clear as summer. There's nothing moving in today. I've been coming up here for twenty years. I can read this weather like the back of my hand. It's perfect for camping out."

"I know. The world is magic and there's nothing to fear but fear itself." Nora Jane went to her husband and held him in her arms. "Go on and sleep by a waterfall. I wish I could go but I have to finish this paper. That's it. I want to turn it in next week."

"Let's go," Tammili called out. "What's keeping you, Dad? Let's get going." Freddy kissed his wife and went out and got into the driver's seat of the Jeep Cherokee and the girls strapped themselves into the seats behind him and plugged their Walkmans into their ears.

Nora Jane went back into the house and stacked the rest of the dishes by the sink and sat down at the table and got her papers out. She was writing a paper on Dylan Thomas. " 'The force that through the green fuse drives the flower / Drives my green age;' " she read, " 'that blasts the roots of trees / Is my destroyer. . . .' "

Freddy took a right at the main road to Willits, then turned onto an old gold-mining trail that had been worn down by a hundred years of rain. "Hold on," he told the girls. "This is only for four miles, then we'll be on a better road. It will save us hours if we use this shortcut." The girls took the plugs out of their ears and held on to the seats in front of them. The mobile phone fell from its holder and rattled around on the floor. Tammili captured it and turned it on to see if it was working. "It's broken," she said. "You broke the phone, Dad. It wasn't put back in right."

"Good," he said. "One less hook to civilization. When we get rid of the Jeep we'll be really free. The wilderness doesn't want you to bring a bunch of junk along. It wants you to trust it to provide for you."

"Trusting the earth is trusting yourself. Trusting yourself is trusting the earth. This is our home. We were made for it and it for us." The girls chanted Freddy's credo in unison, then fell into a giggling fit. The Jeep bounced along over the ruts. The girls giggled until they were coughing.

"You have reached the apex of the silly phase," Freddy said, in between the bumps. "You have perfected being ten years old. I don't want this growing up to go a day further. If you get a day older, I'll be mad at you." He gripped the steering wheel, went around a boulder, and came down a steep incline onto a blacktop road that curved around and up the mountain. "Okay," he said. "Now we're railroading. Now we're whistling Dixie."

"He hated that mobile phone," Tammili said to her sister. "He's been dying for it to break."

"It's Momma's phone so she can call us from her school," Lydia answered. "He's going to have to get her another one as soon as he gets back."

Nieman woke with a start. He had been dreaming about the equations from the day before. They lined up in front of the newspaper office. Gray uniformed and armed to the teeth, they barred his way to his typewriter. When he tried to reason with them, they held up their guns. They fixed their bayonets.

"I hate dreams," he said. He put his feet down on the floor and looked around at the mess his house was in. He lay back down on the bed. He dialed a number and spoke to the office manager at Merry Maids. Yes, they would send someone to clean the place while he was gone. Yes, they would tell Mr. Levin hello. Yes, they would be sure to come.

I'm out of here, Nieman decided. I'll eat breakfast on the way. They know I'm coming. They know I wouldn't stay away all week. I'll go by the deli and get bagels and smoked salmon. I'll take the math book and do five more problems before Monday. Only five. That's it. I don't have to be crazy if I don't want to be. An obsessive can pick and choose among obsessions.

He put the suitcase back onto the unmade bed. He added a pair of hiking shorts and a sun-resistant Patagonia shirt he always wore in Willits. He closed the suitcase and went into the bathroom and got into the shower and closed his eyes and tried to think about the composition of water. Hydrogen, he was thinking. So much is invisible to us. We think we're so hot with our five senses but we know nothing, really. Ninety-nine percent of what is going on escapes us. Ninety-nine percent to the tenth power or the thousandth power. The rest we

know. We are so wonderful in our egos, dressed out in all our igno-
rance and bliss. Our self-importance, our blessed hope.

Freddy went up a last long curve, cut off on a dirt road for half a mile,
then stopped the Jeep at the foot of an abandoned gold mine. "Watch
your step," he said to the girls. "There are loose stones everywhere.
You have to keep an eye on the path. It's rough going all the way to
where the trees begin."

"It's so nice here," Lydia said. "I feel like no one's been here in
years. I bet we're the only people on this mountain. Do you think we
are, Dad? Do you think anyone else is climbing it today?"

"I doubt it. Nieman and I never saw a soul when we were here. Of
course, we have managed to keep our mouths shut about it, unlike
some people who have to photograph and publish every good spot
they find."

"Feel the air," Tammili added. "It tastes like spring. I'm glad we're
here, Dad. This is a thousand times better than some old ski resort."

"Was a ski resort a possibility?" Freddy was trying not to grin.

"No. But some people went to them. Half the school went to Sun
Valley. I don't care. I'd lots rather be in the wilderness with you."

"I'm glad you approve. Look up there. Not a cloud in the sky.
What a lucky day."

"There's a cloud formation in the west," Tammili said. "I've been
watching it for half an hour." They turned in the direction of the sea.
Sure enough. On the very tip of the horizon a gray cloud was
approaching. Nothing to worry about. Not a black system. Just a very
small patch of gray on the horizon.

"Gather up the packs," Freddy said. "Let's start climbing. The
sooner we make camp the sooner we don't have to worry about the
weather. Those trees up there have withstood a thousand years of
weather. We'd be safe there in a hurricane."

"What about a map check?" Tammili asked. She was pulling the straps of her pack onto her strong, skinny shoulders. Lydia was beside her, looking equally determined. This will never come again, Freddy thought. This time when they are children and women in the same skin. This innocence and power. My angels.

"Daddy. Come to." Lydia touched his sleeve, and he turned and kissed her on the head.

"Of course. Get a drink of water out of the thermos we're leaving. Then we'll climb up to that lookout and take our bearings." He handed paper cups to them and they poured water from a thermos and drank it, then folded the cups and left them in the Jeep. They hiked up half a mile to a lookout from where they could see the terrain between them and the place they were going. "Take a reading," Freddy said. "We'll write the readings down, but I want you to memorize them. Paper can get lost or wet. As long as the compass is on your wrist and you memorize the readings, you can find your way back to any base point."

"The best thing is to look where you're going," Tammili said. "Anyone can look at the sun and figure out where the ocean is."

"We won't always be hiking in Northern California," Freddy countered. "We'll do the Grand Canyon soon and then Nepal."

"Momma's friend Brittany got pregnant in Nepal," Lydia said. "She got pregnant with a monk. We saw pictures of the baby."

"Well, that isn't going to happen to either of you. I'm not going to let either of you get pregnant until you have an M.D. or a Ph.D., for starters. I may not let you get pregnant until you're forty. I was thinking thirty-five, now I'm thinking forty."

"We know. You're going to buy a freezer so we can freeze our eggs and save them until we can hire someone to have the babies." They started giggling again. When Lydia and Tammili decided something was funny, they thought it was funnier and funnier the more they laughed.

"Maps and compasses," Freddy said. "Find out where we are. Then find out where we're going, then chart a course."

"Where are we going?"

"Up there. To that cliff face. Around the corner is the waterfall that is the source of Red River." He watched as their faces bent toward their indescribably beautiful small wrists. The perfect bones and skin of ten-year-olds, burdened with the huge wrist compasses and watches. I could spend the day worshiping their arms, Freddy thought, or I could teach them something. "This is the Western Cordillera," he added. "Those are Douglas fir, as you know, and most of the others are pines, several varieties. Are the packs too heavy?"

"They're okay. We can stash things on the trail if we have to."

"In twenty minutes, we'll rest for five. All right?"

"I think I hear the waterfall," he said. "Can you hear it?"

"Not if you're talking," Tammili said. "You have to be quiet to get nature to give up its secrets."

"Stop it, Tammili. Stop teasing him."

"Yeah, Tammili. Stop teasing me." They walked in silence then, up almost a thousand feet before they stopped to rest. The path was loose and slippery and the landscape to the east was barren and rough. To the west it was more dramatic. The cloud formation they had noticed earlier was growing into a larger mass.

"A gathering storm," Freddy said. "We'll be glad I put the waterproofing on the tent last night."

"I am glad," Lydia said. "I don't like to get wet when I'm camping."

"Let's go on then," Tammili said. "That might get here sooner than we think it's going to."

They shouldered the packs and began to climb again. Freddy was drawing the terrain in his mind. He had planned on camping at a site that was surrounded by watercourses. It was so steep that even if there was a deluge it would run off. Still, there was a dry riverbed that had to be crossed to get to the site. We could make for the caves, he was thinking. There wouldn't be bears this high but there are always snakes. Well, hell, I should have gotten a weather report but I didn't. That was stupid but we'll be safe.

"He's worrying," Tammili said to her sister.

"I knew he would. He thinks we'll get wet."

"I don't know about all this." Freddy stopped on the path above them and shook his head. "That cloud's worrying me. Maybe we should go back and camp by the Jeep. We could climb all around down there. We can go to Red River another time."

"We're halfway there," Tammili said. "We can't turn back now. We've got the tent. We'll get it up and if it rains, it rains."

"Yeah," Lydia agreed. "We'll ride it out."

In the solar-powered house Nora Jane was watching the sky. She would study for a while, then go outside and watch the weather. Finally, she started the old truck they kept for emergencies and tried to get a station on the radio. A scratchy AM station in Fort Bragg came on but it was only playing country music. She was about to drive the truck to town when she saw dust on the road and Nieman came driving up in his Volvo. "Thank God you came," she said, pulling open the door as soon as he parked. "Freddy took the girls to Red River and now it's going to storm. I could kill him for doing that. Why does he do such stupid things, Nieman? He didn't get a weather report and he just goes driving off to take the girls to see a waterfall."

"We'll go and find them," Nieman said. "Then we'll kill him. How about that?"

The adventurers climbed until they came to a dry riverbed that had to be crossed to gain the top. It was thirty feet wide and abruptly steep at the place where it could be crossed. The bed was a jumble of boulders rounded off by centuries of water. Some were as tall as a man. Others were the size of a man's head or foot or hand. Among the dark rounded boulders were sharper ones of a lighter color. "The sharp-looking pieces are granite," Freddy was saying. "It's rare in the coastal ranges. God knows where it was formed or what journeys it took to get here. Hang on to the large boulders and take your time. We are lucky it's dry. Nieman and I have crossed it when it's running, but I wouldn't let you." He led the girls halfway across the bed, then let them go in front of him, Tammili, then Lydia. They were surefooted and careful and he watched them negotiate the boulders with more than his usual pride. When they were across he started after them. A broken piece of granite caught his eye. He leaned over to pick it up. He stepped on a piece of moss and his foot slipped and kept on slipping. He stepped out wildly with his other foot to stop it. He kept on falling. He twisted his right ankle between two boulders and landed on his left elbow and shattered the humerus at the epicondyle.

"Don't come back here," he called. "Stay where you are. I'll crawl to you."

"Don't listen to him," Tammili said. She dropped her pack on the ground and climbed back over the boulders to where he lay gasping with pain. "Cut the pack strap," he said. "Use the big blade on your knife. Cut it off my shoulder if you can."

"What time did they leave?" Nieman asked. He had called the weather station and gotten a report and put in a preliminary request for information on distress flares in the area.

"They left about six-thirty this morning. Maybe they're on their way back. Freddy can see this front as well as we can. He wouldn't go up the mountain with a storm coming. All they have is that damned little tent. It barely sleeps three."

"They could go to the caves. I'm going to try to call him on the mobile phone. If they're driving, he'll answer." Nieman tried raising Freddy on the mobile phone, then called the telephone company and had them try. "Nothing. They can't get a thing. We are probably crazy to worry. What could go wrong? The girls are better campers than I am. They're not children."

"Tammili only weighs eighty pounds. I want to call the park rangers."

"Then call them. We'll tell them to be on the alert for flares from that area. I know he has flares with him. He loves flares. He always has them. Then we'll get in the Volvo and go look for them. I guess it will go down that road. Maybe we better take the truck."

"We have to make a stretcher and carry him to the trees," Tammili was saying. Freddy was slowly moving his body but he wasn't making much progress. He couldn't stand on his left ankle and he couldn't use his right arm and he could barely breathe for the pain. There were pain pills in the kit but he wouldn't take them. "At least I can think," he kept saying. "I can stand it and I can think. We have to get a shelter set up before the rain hits. I want you to go on over there and wait for me. I can make it. I'll get there." Then he went blank and the girls were standing over him.

"Let's go over to that stand of trees and tie down the supplies and get the tent cover and drag him on it," Tammili said. "If you start crying I'll smack you. What do you think we went to all those camps for? This is the emergency they trained us for. Come on. Help me drag his pack to the trees. Then we'll come back and get him. Nothing's going to happen to him. We can leave him for a minute."

They pulled Freddy's pack to the stand of pine trees where they had left their own. They tied the straps around a sapling and then found the tent cover and went back for him. The sky was very dark now but they did not notice it because they were ten years old and could live in the present.

They laid the tent cover down beside their father and tried to wake him. "You have to wake up and help us," Tammili was saying. "You have to roll over on the cover so we can drag it up the trail. Come on, Dad.

It's going to rain. You'll get washed down the river. Come on. Move over here if you can." Freddy came to consciousness. He rolled over onto the tent cover with his left shoulder and tried to find a comfortable position. "Clear the rocks off the path," Lydia said. "Come on, Tammili. Let's clear the path." They began to throw the rocks to the side. Working steadily they managed to clear a way from the riverbed to the trees. Freddy lay on the cover with the pain coming and going like waves on the sea. He rocked in the pain. He let the pain take him. There was no way to escape it. Nora Jane will call for help, he was thinking. I know her. This is where her worrying will come in handy. The truck runs. She will drive it into town and call for help. The rain was beginning. He felt it on his face. Then the pain won and he didn't feel anything.

Lydia and Tammili came back down the path to the unconscious body of their father. They folded the tent cover around his body and began to pull him along the path they had cleared. Every two or three feet they would stop and try to wake him. Then they would scour the next few feet for branches and rocks. Then they would move him a few feet more. The rain was still falling softly, barely more than a mist. "It's good to get the ground wet," Tammili was saying. "It makes the tent slide."

"You aren't supposed to move wounded people. We could be making him worse."

"We aren't making him worse. His ankle's right there. We aren't moving it and his arm isn't moving. We're just going to that tree. We have to get away from the riverbed, Lydia. That thing could turn into a torrent. Keep pulling. Don't start crying. Nothing's going to happen. We're going to pull him to that tree and stay there until this storm is over."

"I don't believe this happened. How did it happen to us? We shouldn't have come up here."

"We only have a little more to go. Keep pulling. Don't talk so much." Tammili dug in her heels and pulled the weight of her father six more inches up and to the right of the path. Wind came around the side of the mountain and blew rain into their faces. She went to her father and pulled the tent cover more tightly around his body. She looked up at her sister. Their eyes met. Lydia was holding back her tears. "We only have one move," Tammili said. "We take the king to a place of safety. I'm a bishop and you're a rook. We're taking Dad to that tree, Lydia. We can do it if we will."

"I'm okay," Freddy said. "I can crawl up there. I'm okay, Lydia. Help me up, Tammili. This is just a rain. Just a rain that will end."

He half stood with Tammili supporting his side. He managed to hobble a few more feet in the direction of the tree. Lydia dragged the tent cover around in front of him and they laid him back down on it and pulled him the rest of the way.

Nora Jane and Nieman climbed into the Volvo and started across the property toward the old gold-mining road that Freddy and the girls had taken earlier that morning. "It's too low," Nieman said, after five minutes of driving. "It will never make it down that riverbed. Let's go back and get the truck."

"The truck barely runs."

"Well, we'll make it run."

"Let's call the ranger station again. I don't think we can overdo that. My God, Nieman, what's that noise?"

"I think it's a tire. It feels like something's wrong with a tire." He stopped the car and got out and stood looking at the left front tire. It was almost completely flat and getting flatter.

"You have a spare, don't you?" Nora Jane asked. She had gotten out and was standing beside him.

"No. I left it months ago to be repaired and never went back to pick it up. We'll have to walk back and get the truck."

"Call the ranger station first, then we'll get the truck." Nieman didn't argue. He got the ranger station on the phone. "No, we don't know they're lost. We just know they didn't know this weather was coming. You can put it in the computer, can't you? So if anyone sees a warning flare in that area they'll report it? He always has flares. . . . Because I know. Because I've been camping with him a hundred times. . . . Okay. Just so you're on the alert. We're going there now. It's the old gold-mining camp below Red River Falls. The waterfall that is the source of Red River. Surely you have it on a map. . . . All right. Thanks again. Thank you."

"Insanity. Bureaucrazy. Okay, my darling Nora Jane, let's get out and walk."

Halfway to the house it began to rain. By the time they reached the house they were soaking wet. They changed into dry clothes and got into the truck and started driving. This time they didn't talk. They didn't curse. They didn't plan. They just moved as fast as they could go in the direction of the people that they loved.

Tammili and Lydia had managed to drag Freddy almost to the tree. There was a reasonably flat patch of ground there and they surveyed it. "Let's put the tent up over him," Lydia suggested.

"We'd have to move him twice to do that. We haven't got time and besides we shouldn't move him any more than we have to."

"So what are we going to do?"

"We'll cover him up with the tent and put all the packs and some rocks around to hold it down."

"Water's going to run in."

"Not if we fix it right. Get it out." Tammili was pulling things out of the packs. "We'll get him covered up, then I'll set off flares."

"You better set them off before it rains any more."

"Then hurry." They dragged the tent over to their father and draped it over his body. Lydia took the cape and wrapped it around his legs and feet. They pulled the tent cover up to make a rain sluice and set rocks against it to hold it in place.

"Finish up," Tammili said. "I'm going over there by the riverbed and set off flares." She had found a pack of them in the bottom of Freddy's pack. She pulled it out and read the directions. "Keep out of the hands of children. This is not a toy. Approved by the Federal Communications Commission and the Federal Bureau of Standards. Remove plastic cap carefully. Point in the direction of clear sky. Da. Pull down lever with a firm grasp. If three pulls does not release flare, discard and try another flare. Okay, here goes." She walked over to the cleared place. She pulled the lever down and a huge point of light rose to the sky and spread out and held.

"Do some more," Lydia called to her. Tammili set off four more flares. Then waited. Then set off two more. Rain was beginning to fall in earnest now. She went back to the pack and put the leftover flares where she had found them. Then she buckled up the pack and put the smaller packs on top of it. Then she dragged the synchilla blanket underneath the tent and she and Lydia lay down on each side of their father. The rain was falling harder. They arranged the synchilla blanket over Freddy's body and then covered that with the cape. They found each other's hands. The fingers of Lydia's right hand fit into the fingers of Tammili's left hand as they had always done.

A volunteer fire lookout worker was in a fire tower ten miles from where they lay covered with the cape and tent. He was a twenty-year-old student who had always been good at everything he did. He prided himself on being good at things. Every other Thursday when he spent his three hours in the tower he was on the lookout every second. He didn't go down and fill his coffee cup. He didn't read books. He kept his eyes on the sky and the land. That was what he had volunteered to do and that is what he did. Earlier, before he began his stint, he had pulled up all the local data on a computer and read it carefully. He had especially noted the memo about Red River because his mother was a geologist and had taken him there as a child. He saw the first flare out of the corner of his eye just as it was dying. He saw the second and the third and fourth flares, but lost the last two in the approaching storm. "I will be damned," he decreed. "I finally saw something. It finally paid off to stay alert." He called the ranger station and reported what he had seen.

Nora Jane and Nieman were driving the four miles of rocky trail between blacktop and blacktop. They were driving in a blinding rain. Nieman was at the wheel. Nora Jane was pushing back into the seat imagining her life without her husband and her daughters. I don't know why we built that crazy house to begin with, Nieman was thinking. I hate it there. Grass doesn't grow. You can't take a hot shower half the time. It's a dangerous place. We should have been down in the inner city building houses for people to live in. Not some goddamn, lonely, scary, dangerous trap on a barren hillside. He shouldn't have taken them up there, much less to Red River. As though they are expendable. As though we could ever breathe again if anything happened to them. But what could happen? Nothing will happen. They'll get wet, then we'll get them dry. He steered the old red truck down onto the blacktop and pushed the pedal to the floor. "I'm gunning it," he said to Nora Jane. "Hold on."

"Don't worry, Daddy," Tammili was crooning. "Momma will send someone to get us. Remember when Lydia broke her arm and it got all right. Her hand was hanging off her wrist like nothing and it grew back fine."

"It sure did," Lydia said. "It grew right back."

"Get behind the rocks," Freddy said. "Don't stay here. I'm okay. I'm doing fine." A sheet of lightning blazed a mile away. It seemed to be beside them. "It's okay," Freddy said. "Cuddle up. Rain always stops. It always stops. It always does."

"Sometimes it rains for two days," Lydia put in. She snuggled down into a ball beside her father. She patted her father's chest. She patted his ribs. She patted his heart. Another burst of lightning flashed even closer. Then the rain began to fall twice as hard as it had before. The earth seemed to sink beneath the force of the rain, but they were warm beneath the cape and the tent and they were together.

"These are Franciscan rocks," Tammili said. "The whole Coast Range is made up of the softest, weirdest rocks they know. Geologists don't know what they are. They used to be the ocean floor. Where we are, right now, as high as it seems, used to be stuff on the floor of the ocean."

"That's right," Lydia added. "Before that it was the molten center of the earth."

"The continents ride on the seas like patches of weeds in a marsh," Tammili went on. "Fortunately for us it all moves so slowly that we'll be dead before it changes enough to matter. Unless the big earth-quake puts it all back in the sea."

"Who told you that?" Freddy tried to rise up on his good arm. The pain in the other one had subsided for a moment. He was beginning to be able to move his foot. "When the storm subsides we'll put up the rest of the flares. They'll be looking for us. Someone's looking for us now."

"We could drive the car," Lydia whispered. A third network of lightning had covered the mountain with clear blue light. Far away the thunder rumbled, but the lightning seemed to be only feet away. "One of us could stay with you and the other one could get in the Jeep and go for help."

"They'll find us," Freddy said. "Your mother will be right on top of this. If we don't come back, she'll send for help." The rain was harder now, beating on the flattened tent. Still, they seemed to be warm and dry. "This cape wicks faster than synchilla," Freddy added. "Just like Nieman to find this and leave it lying around." The pain returned full force then and Freddy felt himself going down. Don't think, he told himself. Turn it off. Don't let it in.

"Hold my hand," Lydia said and reached for her sister. "Tell more about the coast and the ocean. Tell the stuff Nieman tells us."

"It was a deep trench, the whole coast, the whole state of California. And the ocean and the hot middle of the earth keep churning and pushing and hot stuff comes up from the middle, like melted fire, only more like hot, hot honey, and it's very beautiful and red and gold and finally it turns into rocks and mud and gets pushed up to make mountains. Then the trench got filled with stuff and it rose up like islands and made California. Then the Great Plains got in the middle of the Coast Range and the Sierra Nevada and the Cascades. They are real thick mountains and all crystallized together with granite. But not the Coast Range. The Coast Range is made of strange rocks and there is jade left here by serpentine. And maganese and mercury and bluechist and gold and everything you could want."

"Serpentinite," Freddy said. "Manganese."

Nieman was saying, "You stay in the truck and wait for the rangers. Work on the phone in Freddy's Jeep. You might get it working. I'm going up."

They were standing at the base of the path. It was still pouring rain. Nieman was wearing a foul-weather parka and was laden with signal devices, everything they had found in the house and cars.

"Go on then. Start climbing. I'll do what I can."

"Do whatever you decide to do." He looked at her then, this beautiful, whimsical creature whom his best friend adored, and he understood the adoration as never before. Her whole world was in danger and she was breathing normally and was not whining. Nieman gave her a kiss on the cheek and turned and began to climb. The rain was coming down so fast it was difficult to see, but he knew the path and he was careful. Maybe we should have gone for help instead of coming here. Maybe we should have done a dozen things. The rangers know. Surely to God they are on their way.

The ranger helicopter had turned back from the lightning and now a truck carrying a medic was headed in their direction but the road had been washed out in two places and they had had to ford it. "Plot the coordinates of the flares again," the driver said. "Are you sure twenty-four is the nearest road?"

"There's an old creek bed we might navigate, but not in this weather. An old mining road leads to within a mile. I'd rather take that. Here, you look at the map."

"Jesus, what a storm. A frog strangler, that's what we call them where I come from."

"Two little girls and their father. I'd like to kill some people. What the hell does a man want to go off for with kids this far from nowhere? It kills me. I used to teach wilderness safety at the hospital. What a waste of breath."

"Land of the free. Home of the foolhardy. Okay, I think I can make it across that water. Let's give it a try." He drove the vehicle across a creek and made it to the other side. As soon as they were across, the medic put on his seat belt and pulled it down tight across his waist and chest.

"Four hundred and three," Nieman was counting. "Four hundred and four. Four hundred and five."

Nora Jane sat in the passenger seat of the Jeep and worked on the phone. Once or twice she was able to hear static and she kept on trying. She took the batteries out and wiped them on her shirt and put them back in. She moved every movable part. She prayed to her old Roman Catholic God. She prayed to Mary. She made promises.

*　　　*　　　*

The storm was moving very slowly across the chaos of disordered rocks that is the Coast Range of Northern California. The birds pulled their wings over their heads. The panthers dreamed in their lairs. The scraggly vegetation drank the water as fast as it fell. When the sun came back out it would use the water to grow ten times as fast as vegetation in wetter climates. Tammili and Lydia held hands. Freddy slept. An infinitesimal part of the energy we call time became what we call history.

"Six thousand and one," Nieman counted. He wanted to stop and wipe his glasses but he could not bring himself to waste a second. Some terrible intuition led him on. Some danger or unease that had bothered him ever since the night before. He had come to where he was needed. It was not the first time that had happened to him. That's why I hated those movies, he told himself. When no one believed what they knew. When no one learned anything. The beginning of *Karate Kid* was okay. The beginning of it was grand.

He had come to a creek bed that was now a torrent of rushing water. I know this, he remembered. But how the hell will I cross it now? He stood up straight. He pushed the hood back from his parka and reached for his glasses to wipe them. A huge bolt of lightning shook the sky. It illuminated everything in sight. By its light Nieman saw the pile of tent and figures on the ground on the other side of the water. "Freddy," he screamed at the top of his lungs. "It's me. It's Nieman. Freddy, is that you?"

The rest was drowned by thunder. Then Nieman saw a small figure rise up from the pile. She came out from under the tent and began waving her hands in the air.

"I'll get there," he yelled. "Stay where you are." The rain was slacking somewhat. Nieman found a flat place a few yards down the creek and began to make his way across the rocks. Lydia met him on the other side. "Dad's broken his arm and foot," she told him. "We need to get him to a doctor."

*   *   *

The medic spotted the Jeep and the truck. "There they are," he yelled at the driver. "There're the fools. Let's go get them."

An hour later Freddy was on a stretcher being brought down the mountain by four men. The clearing was filled with vehicles. The brown cape was thrown into the back of an EMS van. It would end up at the city laundry. Then on the bed of a seven-year-old Mexican girl who had been taken from her mother. But that is another story.

Ten days later a party gathered at Chez Panisse to eat an early dinner and discuss the events of the past week. There were nine people gathered at Freddy Harwood's favorite table by the window in the back room. The young man who had seen the flares, the medic, the driver, Nieman, Freddy, Nora Jane, Tammili, Lydia, and a woman biochemist who was after Nieman to marry him. Her name was Stella Light and this was the first time Nieman had taken her out among his friends. It was the first time he had taken her to Chez Panisse and the first time he had introduced her to Nora Jane and Freddy and the twins. Stella Light was dressed in her best clothes, a five-year-old gray pantsuit and a white cotton blouse. She had almost added a yellow scarf but had taken it off minutes after she put it on.

"We had this magic cape we found under the bed," Lydia was telling her. "The minute we say something's magic, it is magic, that's what Uncle Nieman says. It's probably his cape but he can't remember it. He leaves his stuff everywhere. Did you know that? He's absentminded because he is a genius. Do you go to school with him? Is that how you met him?"

"Well, I teach in the department. Tell me about the cape."

"It kept us warm. Dad thinks it was synchilla. Anyway, it was raining so hard it felt like rocks were falling on us."

"It was lightning like crazy," Tammili added. "There was lightning so near it made halos around the trees."

"Tammili!" Freddy shook his head.

"You don't know. You were incoherent from pain."

"Incoherent?" Stella laughed.

"She always talks like that," Lydia said. "It's Uncle Nieman. He's been working on our vocabularies since we were born."

"I'm having goat cheese pie and salad," Nieman said. "I think he wants to take our orders. Menus up, ladies. Magic cape, my eye. Magic forest rangers and volunteer distress signal watchers." He stood up and raised his glass to the medic and the driver and the young man. "To your honor, gentlemen. We salute thee."

"To all of us," Freddy added, raising his glass with his good hand. "My saviors, my family, my friends."

Nieman caught Stella's eye as they drank. A long sweet look that was not lost on Tammili and Lydia. We could be the bridesmaids, Lydia decided. We never get to be in weddings. None of Mom and Dad's friends ever get married. Pretty soon we'll be too old to be bridesmaids. It will be too late.

"Stop it," Tammili whispered to her sister, pretending to be bending over to pick up a napkin so she wouldn't be scolded for telling secrets at the table. "Stop wanting that woman to marry Uncle Nieman. Uncle Nieman doesn't need a girlfriend. He's got everything he needs. He's got Mom and Dad and you and me." When she sat up she batted her eyes at her godfather. Then, for good measure, she got up and walked around the table and gave him a hug and stood by his side. Oh, my God, Stella was thinking. Well, that's an obstacle that can be overcome. Children are such little beasts nowadays. It makes you want to get your tubes tied.

"Go back to your chair," Nora Jane said to her daughter. "Let Uncle Nieman eat his goat cheese pie."

THE AFFAIR

NIEMAN GLUUK was finally going to be taken to bed. Not that he hadn't had love affairs before. He had had them but they hadn't meant to him what they mean to most of us. They hadn't thrown him to the mat. They hadn't given him a taste of what men kill and die for, dream about. One Stella Light of Salem, Oregon, was going to be the one to do it. Thirty-seven years old, five feet six inches tall, dark haired and dark eyed, a physicist, a biochemist, and a distance runner. A control freak. An expert on viral diseases of poultry. The only child of a high school science teacher and a librarian. A small-breasted woman who had dyed her hair platinum blond the week before she met Nieman and begun wearing a devastatingly expensive perfume called Joy. Her clock was ticking and her hours staring at photographs taken by electron microscopes had not given her any reason to put off doing anything she wanted to do.

It is dawn. Stella gets up and makes the bed. She puts on a white T-shirt and a pair of cutoff blue jeans and some high-tech Nike running shoes. She rubs sunblock lotion on her arms and face. She pours a cup of coffee that was made automatically at five o'clock by her combination clock radio and coffeemaker.

She walks out onto her porch. She surveys the mist that has come in the night before. She imagines the coast of California swaying on its shaky underpinnings. She goes down the stairs and begins to run.

In five minutes the endorphins kick in. In five minutes the blood is in her legs instead of her cerebral cortex, and for the only time during the day she is free of thinking, thinking, thinking.

She runs uphill for a mile, then cuts over to the Berkeley campus. She runs the length of the campus three times, back and forth, and back again. She stops once to pick up a curled leaf that has fallen from a tree. It has been infested with a bole. She scratches the bole open and squints at it, then puts it in the pocket of her shorts. She has been inspecting leaves since she was three years old.

Nothing surprises Stella. And everything interests her. Of late, she has found herself musing on reproduction more than she thinks is healthy. Leaf, bole, tree, nuts, seeds, eggs. Not to mention the terrible viral splittings on the screens of the microscopes. As Stella runs through the campus she forces her mind to stay in the realm of vertebrates. I should use one of my eggs, her mind keeps repeating. No one else carries Grandfather Bass's genes. No one else carries Mother's or Aunt Georgia's. I am the last. I should go deeper into life. Life is dangerous and awful. Still, it is all we have. I am tired of being perfect. Perhaps I am tired of being alone. Perhaps this is true. Perhaps it is a trick the hormones play.

Nieman had been laid before. He had slept with prostitutes and he had slept with a girl from Ohio for five months in 1973. He had slept with a French girl one summer when he and Freddy went to study French at the Sorbonne. What he had not done was fall in love. All he had seen around him were the ruins of love. His parents' marriage had been a disaster. He barely knew his father. The hundreds of movies he had reviewed and all the books he had read taught him that love was a wasteland, a tornado, an earthquake, a fire. Men and women in love were like children, given over to childlike jealousies and self-loathing and despair.

*   *   *

When he ran into Stella late one afternoon as they were both leaving the biochemistry building and knocked her papers out of her hand, he had no idea that his life was being changed. He had a premonition, a terrible sense of déjà vu, and so did she, but Nieman thought it was the weather and Stella thought it was because she was about to begin her period.

"They weren't numbered," she said, as she knelt to pick up the papers. "Well, that's not your fault, is it?"

"Oh, God, oh, please let me pick them up. Don't do that. I'm so sorry. Let me help you?"

"Have we met?" She was kneeling only feet away from him. She was wearing a blue denim skirt, a soft blue shirt, little blue sneakers like you see on sale at the grocery store. She smelled of some heavenly perfume, some odor of divinity. Underneath the shirt was a soft white camisole with lace along the edges. In the center of the camisole was a small pink flower. "I'm having a déjà vu," she added. "It's such an odd sensation. I'm probably hungry. I get crazy when I don't eat. Blood sugar. Oh, well."

"That's dangerous. Let me feed you. Please. Come with me." He had gathered up the rest of the papers. He stood up. He took her hand and pulled her up beside him. "Please. Come have dinner with me. I'll help you straighten up the papers. I'm hungry too."

"Well, if you'll go someplace near. How about the Grill across from the library?"

"Great. I like it there. I go there all the time. I'm Nieman Gluuk. I'm a student."

"I know who you are. You're the talk of the department. Did you really quit the paper to study science?"

"I wish that story hadn't gotten out. I'm a neophyte. A bare beginner. It's pitiful how far I have to go."

"Oh, I doubt that."

★   ★   ★

Twenty minutes later they were sitting in a booth at the Grill eating French fries and waiting for their omelets. They were telling each other the stories of their lives.

"So when they quit the Merry Pranksters, they moved back to Salem and had me. They were worried they had fucked up their DNA with all the acid they had done so they had me tested all the time. It turned out I test well. Then they decided I'm a genius. I'm not. I just learned to take the tests. So, out of their relief that I wasn't an idiot, they turned into the worst bourgeois you can imagine. They collect furniture. You wouldn't believe the furniture my mom can cram into a room. Danish modern, English antiques . . . Anyway, I like them. They leave me alone, considering I'm an only child. They work for environmental groups and they have a lot of friends. They're pretty people. Both of them are a lot prettier than I am. I look like my maternal grandfather, who invented dental floss, by the way. He was a dentist in New Orleans."

"You're very pretty. You're as pretty as you can be. You don't think you're pretty?"

"I'm okay. You ought to see them. They look like early-retirement poster people. So, what set of events made you?"

"An undependable father and an unhappy mother. No wonder I started going to the movies. She's a frustrated actress. I grew up thinking the theater was real life."

"Well, I'm a fan. I always read your column. I loved the things you wrote. I can't believe you just quit doing it."

"Twenty years. It got so unpleasant at the end. I couldn't please anyone. Even people I praised didn't think the praise went far enough. Now I want to know the rest. The things you know. I can't wait to use an electron microscope."

"They haven't let you use it?"

"They were supposed to last week, then the class was canceled."

"Oh, I know what happened. The Benning-Rohrer was down and

we had to double up on the SEM. I'll show them to you. We can go there after dinner if you like."

The waiter appeared and put plates of steaming omelets in front of them. This is not what I thought would happen, Nieman was thinking. Always what you least expect. I already feel the air getting thin. Freddy told me someday this would happen to me but I thought he was projecting.

Look at that forebrain, Stella was thinking. The cerebral cortex. The verbal skills. I could breed with that, if I am being driven to breed. She sat very still. She picked at her food. She lifted a hand and touched her mouth with her finger.

"Are you left-handed?" Nieman asked.

"Yes."

"I am too."

When they had finished eating they walked back across the campus to the biochemistry building and went up to Stella's office and left the papers, which they had forgotten to put in order, on her desk. Then they went into the laboratory and sat down in the chairs before the scanning electron microscope. "How much do you know?" Stella asked.

"'The scanning electron microscope . . . a beam of electrons is scanned over the surface of a solid object and used to build up an image of the details of the surface structure. There are also several special types of electron microscope. Among the most valuable is the electron-probe microanalyzer, which allows a chemical analysis of the composition of materials to be made by using the incident electron beam to excite the emission of characteristic X radiation by the various elements composing the specimen. These X rays are detected and analyzed by spectrometers built into the instrument. Such probe microanalyzers are able to produce an electron-scanning image so that structure and composition may be easily correlated.'"

"My heavens. How did you do that?"

"My brand-new Encyclopædia Britannica, Macropædia, volume twenty-four, page sixty-six. Do you want more?" Nieman was leaned back in the chair. He was smiling. He was almost laughing. He was wearing thin khaki pants. His legs were strong and spread out on the chair.

"Go on."

" 'Fundamental research by many physicists in the first quarter of the twentieth century suggested that cathode rays (i.e., electrons) might be used in some way to increase microscopic resolution. Louis de Broglie, a French physicist, in 1924 opened the way with the suggestion that electron beams might be regarded as a form of wave motion. De Broglie derived the formula for their wavelength, which showed, for example, that, for electrons accelerated by sixty-thousand volts, the effective wavelength . . .' What? Why are you laughing?"

"Photographic memory?"

"Of course. It's selective, and I have to be interested in something to imprint it. I've seen movies I can't remember at all. That was a test. If I couldn't remember them, I didn't review them."

Stella was looking at his pants. He sat up straighter in the chair. He pulled his legs together. He coughed. " 'The electron image must be made visible to the eye by allowing the electrons to fall on a fluorescent screen. Such a screen is satisfactory for quick observations and for focusing and aligning the instrument. A low-power binocular optical microscope fitted outside the column allows the flower on the screen, I mean the image on the screen, to be inspected at a magnification of about ten magnitudes. . . .' "

"You want to see the AIDS virus?" Stella asked. She pulled a box of slides from a drawer and inserted one into a locked compartment at the base of the instrument. "This is the virus on a human T-cell. I really hate this slide." She pushed a button and the lights came on the screen. Then an image appeared. Long tubular cells covered with watery stars of death.

"I've been to one hundred and seven funerals since this thing started," Nieman said. "Have you been tested?"

"Dozens of times. This job has its drawbacks. I essentially hate viruses. I'm not one of those biologists who love nature. Nature is not on our side. It's always trying to take us back. I'm for the higher mammals straight out. How about you? Have you been tested?"

"My dentist tested me. He never called me back so I assumed I was all right. How accurate do you think the tests are?" Nieman leaned forward to study the screen. It was terrible to behold. "Cut it off," he said and went back to looking at the flower in the center of the camisole under Stella's blouse.

Stella pressed a button. The screen went blank. The room was quiet. The overwhelming sense of déjà vu returned.

"I keep thinking I've been here before," Nieman said. "In this room with you. It's the damnedest thing."

"I feel it too," she answered. "I'm thirty-seven. I keep thinking about breeding. It's probably hormonal. We are primates, don't forget that." She turned around on the swivel chair and looked at him.

"Should we resign ourselves to that?"

"We could welcome it."

"You think so?" Nieman stood up. "There it is again," he said. "It's the damnedest thing. Déjà vu, it means *already seen*. Of course we must have met somewhere. Then, of course, the gene pool is wide. These things might be chemical. See, I'm beginning to think like one of you." He smiled down at her and she reached up and touched, first his sleeve, then his hand. She didn't take his hand or grab it. She brushed her fingers across the back of his hand, then left them only inches away from him. "I don't have much experience with women, sexually, that is." Nieman kept on smiling at her and at himself, at the strangeness of the moment, the silliness and divinity of it. "But I haven't given up on myself. I'd like to have an affair with someone, something that mattered, that might matter to them also. Am I out of line here? You can hit me or dismiss me."

"I haven't had a lover in three years. If I had a love affair I'd be the inexperienced one. I always start thinking what I'm doing is funny. Not the sexual part, per se, you know, but the thing entire, as it were. Well, what are we talking about here?"

"I think we are saying we like each other more than ordinary. I am saying that. I am saying, would you imagine some day, in your time, on your terms, having me as a candidate for a lover?"

"We could get an AIDS test in the morning and have the results back in a day. Then, if we still wanted to, we could explore this further. I have some time after my nine o'clock class." She went on and put her hands on his hands. "I'll admit this is partly about your verbal skills."

"For me it's the flower on your undershirt and your Ph.D." Nieman laughed. "Or the electrical systems in this building are affecting our brains. Tell me where to meet you. I'll be there."

"Would we really do this?"

"I think we are doing it. In my old life I always maintained that thought was action. So the question is: Would we actually carry it out?"

"It's what the young people do, but not the first time they knock the papers out of someone's hands."

"How long do they wait?"

"I think three days. I heard three days from someone who was confessing something to me. I'm a student adviser part-time."

"Then grown people only have to wait one day because we have a shorter time to live."

"That's a theory? Shall we leave now?"

"I suppose we should. Let me help you turn things off."

"All right. The switches are on the wall." They turned off the lights in the laboratory and walked to the elevator holding hands. They went down on the elevator and Nieman walked her to her car. "What time in the morning?" he asked.

"You're serious?"

"More than I've ever been in my life."

"Do you know where the student health center is now?"

"Yes."

"Meet me there at quarter past ten." It was very still in the tree-bordered parking lot. The earth smelled like birth and death and love. There were stars in the sky and a new moon above the physics building. Luckily they were both intuitive, feeling types. A sensate might have swooned.

At ten-fifteen the next morning they met at the student health center and asked to be tested for the AIDS virus. They filled out forms and sat in the waiting room reading magazines and were called in and blood was drawn and the nurse told them to call that afternoon for the results. "Sometimes it takes a couple of days if they're backed up but it's been slow this week. I'll tell them it's for you, Doctor Light. I think you'll get these back by five." She smiled a professional smile and Nieman held open the door for Stella and they walked back out into the waiting room and out the door onto the blooming spring campus. "Are you free tomorrow?" he asked.

"Pretty much. I have some papers to grade."

"I was thinking we could drive up Highway One to Mendocino and spend the weekend together. I mean, no matter how the tests come out. I want to talk to you. I want to be with you some more. I don't know how to say all this."

"I would love to go to Mendocino with you."

"Will you have dinner with me tonight?"

"Yes. Yes, I will."

"I don't know where you live."

"Then you'll find out, won't you? Call me at six. If we're positive, we'll get drunk. If we're negative, we'll, I don't know."

"We'll be negative. Perhaps all we are supposed to do about that is be grateful. I'll call then. I'll call at six."

A young technician named Alice Yount put the slides underneath the microscope and watched the fine, free T-cells swim in their sea. She called the health center and made the report and then sent the papers over. It was a good morning. Only one test had come back positive and that was a man who had known it already. Some happiness, Alice was thinking as she took off her apron and washed her hands. Some good news.

At seven o'clock that night Nieman appeared at Stella's door. He was wearing a blue shirt he bought in Paris. He was wearing his best silk socks and seersucker pants and he had taken off his watch and ring. I am putting myself in the path of pain and suffering and life, he told himself. I am a Mayan sacrifice. I have seen this movie but I have never played in it. I can't believe it is this exciting and terrible and irresistible. I want to burn every word I've ever written. What did I know?

Then she was there and they walked into her kitchen and poured glasses of water and sipped them and were shy. They walked around her house looking at the books, the bare stone floors, the clean windows, the stark white walls, the wide white bed.

It was not silly when it happened and neither of them was afraid. "Nice scar," he told her later, examining her knee.

"Bike wreck when I was ten," she answered. "What do you have to show me?"

"Navel?" he asked. "Appendix scar? Cut on eyebrow?"

At two in the morning Nieman went home to pack for the weekend. "I forgot my sleeping pills," he explained. "There are limits to what the psyche can take. I might keep you up all night."

"Go on," she answered. "We're pushing the envelope. I'd like to be alone for a few hours. What do you take?"

"Ambien. Benadryl. Xanax if I travel. If I'm at home I usually just stay awake."

"Distressing, all the people who can't sleep. Do you think it's the modern world?"

"No. I think it's always been that way. Neurotic from the start. That's how I view our history. Short lived and neurotic. Now we're long lived and neurotic. I call that progress, any way you look at it."

"Me too."

At ten the next morning Nieman picked her up in Freddy Harwood's Jeep Cherokee and they drove out over the Golden Gate Bridge and took the Stinson Beach exit and began the 1,500-foot climb into the coastal hills. At Muir Woods they got out of the car and held hands and looked at the ocean for a long time. Already their bodies were joined at the hip. Already there was nothing that could keep them apart.

"Where's Nieman?" Nora Jane was asking. "What did he want the Cherokee for?"

"I think he's in love," Freddy answered. "It's the damnedest thing you've ever seen. He's trying to keep it a secret."

"Who is she?"

"I don't know. He wouldn't even look at me."

"He's getting laid. My God, imagine that."

"He had on a brand-new polo shirt."

"You're kidding."

"I am not. May lightning strike me if I am. It still had the creases in it. He hadn't even washed it."

"My folks drove this highway on the bus," Stella was saying. "I wish they didn't disavow that so much. They were just kids. Everything is in a state of anarchy, Nieman. Every single thing we see about us. Our universe is a nanosecond, the blink of an eyelash, and yet, we are here and this experience seems vast. Last night, after you left, I fell asleep giggling. I kept seeing us marching into the student health center to be tested. That will be all over the campus by the time we get back. Technically I can't date you, you know. Since you are a student."

"We aren't dating." Nieman slowed down. He drove the car to a wide place that overlooked the sea. He turned off the motor and turned to her and took her hands. "I am in love with you. That's been clear since Friday afternoon at six o'clock. I have waited all my life for you. I want to marry you, or live with you, or do whatever you want to do. I have three hundred and forty-seven thousand dollars in assets and no responsibilities I can't get rid of in an hour. I will go anywhere you want to go. I will live any life you want to live."

"My goodness."

"I wrote that down several times this morning. There's a draft of it in my jacket pocket. You can have it."

"Let's get something to eat first. I can't get engaged on an empty stomach."

"This is real, Stella. This is deadly serious on my part."

"I know that. I'm serious too. Don't you think I know a miracle when one slaps me in the face?" Then Nieman was extremely glad he had borrowed Freddy's Cherokee, because it had an old-fashioned front seat and Stella slid over next to him and stayed there all the way to Stinson Beach.

Which is how Tammili and Lydia Harwood finally got to be brides-maids in a wedding. "I thought it would never happen," Lydia told her friends. "The last person I thought would give us this window of opportunity was Uncle Nieman. I am wearing pink."

"And I am wearing blue," Tammili would add. "It's going to be at our beach house. There will be two cakes and lots of petits fours and Jon Ragel from *Vogue* is going to take the photographs."

"Uncle Nieman will never get a Nobel now," Lydia would sigh. "Dad says Nieman has forgotten all about wanting a Nobel prize for biochemistry."

A WEDDING
BY THE SEA

THE WEDDING HAD BEEN PLANNED for June. Then for August. Now it was the tenth of September and at last Nieman Gluuk and Stella Light had set a date they wouldn't break.

"We are mailing the invitations today," Stella told Nora Jane. They were having tea on the patio of the Harwoods' house on the beach. It was Friday morning. Stella was missing a faculty meeting about grants for the graduate students, but the dean had let her go. No one was expecting much of Stella or Nieman this year. The world will always welcome lovers. This is especially true on the Berkeley campus, where many people have thought themselves almost out of the emotional field. "We have set a deadline. Every invitation in the mail before we sleep. Are you sure you want to have it here? This close to the baby coming?"

The women were sitting on wicker chairs with a small table between them. The table held cheese and crackers and wild red strawberries and small almond wafers Stella had brought for a gift. "I told the department head I had to have a week and he said, Take two weeks." Stella shook her head. "I think we'll just go to the Baja and lie in the sun and read. I have never imagined myself being married. It seems like such an odd, old rite of passage. Are you sure you want to have it here?"

"Freddy Harwood would die if he couldn't have this wedding

here. He is fantastically excited about it. So are the girls. Did you bring a list?"

Stella fished it out of her jacket pocket and handed it over. "It's seventy names. This one is my cousin in Oklahoma City. The one who lost a child in the bombing. They have two foster children they're trying to adopt. So I think they will bring them. Two little girls they found in a Catholic home down on the border. One's eleven and the other's seven. My mother's been very involved in it. She specializes in children with learning disorders. They had to round up all sorts of counseling. They were kids no one else wanted to adopt. Anyway, they are coming to the wedding."

"Maybe they should be bridesmaids. Tammili and Lydia would love some help." Nora Jane stretched her legs out in front of her. She was eight months' pregnant. Sometimes she forgot about it for hours, then the baby would start moving and remind her.

"I should have thought of that. Of course they can be in the wedding. But how will we get them dresses? Don't the dresses all have to match?"

"That's easy. Bridesmaids' dresses are big business. I'll have a shop here send them things or they can send measurements and we'll have dresses waiting for them. Where are they going to stay?"

"I made reservations at the Intercontinental."

"Let your cousin's family stay with us. The guest house is just sitting there. Four little bridesmaids. This is starting to sound like a wedding."

"I'll call Jennifer tonight. Momma said they were nice little girls. She said it's working out a lot better than anyone thought it would. It's been a godsend to me. It kept Momma off my back while Nieman and I decided what to do."

That was Friday morning. By Monday afternoon a bridal shop in San Francisco and one in Oklahoma City were deep in consultation on the subject of four pink bridesmaids' dresses that must be ready by

October the sixteenth. The four little girls had been introduced on a conference call and Nora Jane Harwood and Jennifer Williams had gone past discussing dresses and hats and shoes and flowers and were into the real stuff. "You just went down there and got them?" Nora Jane asked. It was the fourth time they had talked.

"We had to live. When I saw them, my heart almost burst. They aren't a thing alike. Annie looks like she belongs in Minnesota. We still haven't figured out how she ended up in Potrero. But Gabriela is a little Mexican Madonna. Her ambition is to be a singer and get rich. She is very interested in getting rich."

"Can you adopt them?"

"We don't know yet. It's pretty certain we can have Annie but there aren't any papers on Gabriela. We're just living from day to day. I think if anyone tried to take them Allen would run away to Canada with them. Actually, the people here seem to think it will be all right. We're trying not to worry about it."

"This wedding is going to be amazing. It keeps growing. Freddy and Nieman found a string quartet and it's been in the papers twice. 'The famous iconoclastic bachelor Nieman Gluuk,' that's what they're calling Nieman."

"What are they calling Stella?"

"'Brilliant, reclusive scientist' was in the *Chronicle*. Freddy's teasing them to death about it."

"We will be there," Jennifer said. "I don't think either of them have ever been to a big wedding."

It was several weeks before eleven-year-old Annie started worrying about going to California to the wedding. Once she started, the worry fed upon itself. She began lying on her bed in the afternoon pretending to be asleep. Also, she started eating everything in sight.

"Don't you want to jump on the trampoline?" seven-year-old Gabriela asked her. "Don't you want to do anything?" She had known something was wrong with Annie for several days but this was the first time she had felt like doing anything about it. It was nice living in Oklahoma City, but Gabriela was getting worn out with all the things she had to do to keep it together. Keeping Jennifer happy, letting Allen teach her to play the piano, trying to learn the arithmetic at school, talking Annie into taking her pills. The doctor had given Annie some pills that were supposed to keep her from getting mad at people, but she was afraid they would poison her and Gabriela had to help talk her into swallowing them. Sometimes Annie was afraid she would choke to death swallowing them and sometimes she just thought they might be poison. Gabriela would get on one side of Annie and Jennifer would get on the other side and Gabriela would say, "Would I let you get poisoned? Jennifer got them at a drugstore, Annie. She knows the guy who sold them to her. You swallow food all the time and it doesn't choke you, does it? It would take a lot of pills to make a French fry." Then Gabriela would take a piece of cereal or bread and demonstrate swallowing it and in the end they would usually get Annie to take the pill.

"You better let us keep them in our room," Gabriela advised Jennifer and Allen. "That way she'll know nobody's trying to slip her something."

"I'll take her to the drugstore to get the prescription filled," Allen suggested.

"Yeah, well, I knew a guy who worked in a place where they made pills." Annie was backed into a corner of the living room sofa. They were all around her. "He said they threw in rat shit when they got in a bad mood. He said you wouldn't believe what all was in pills you buy at the store."

Allen and Jennifer looked at each other. Both of them sort of half believed it. It was not the first revelation these girls from the lost half-world of the Mexican border had brought them.

Allen sat down on the floor. "Well, look at it like this," he began. "We have a system of trust in our culture. We all eat and drink things all day long that other people have handled and we have to believe that our inspectors, the people who go into factories where pills are made, are doing a good job of seeing that the things they sell us are clean and made out of the right things, not out of rat feces. Most of the people who make things for us do a good job of it, just like we would if we worked there. I'll find out where the pills come from, Annie. I'll find out where the factory is and I'll call them and see if they're doing a good job before you take any more of them."

"That's right," Gabriela added. "I guess you got to think of it as getting lucky. If your luck's good, you don't get poisoned or raped or anything. If your luck runs out, you're fucked." She looked at Jennifer. She was trying not to say *fuck* around Jennifer. Jennifer smiled and went to her and touched her shoulder.

"It's okay," she said. "Say anything you want to say. So, Annie, what should we do? Should we trust the doctor and this druggist and take these pills or not? I don't want you to be scared every day when you have to take them."

"She'll take them." Gabriela went to her friend. "You're going to take them, aren't you? Look at me, Annie. Say something about it."

"I'm taking her to the drugstore to see where they come from," Allen said. "We'll find out where they're made. Maybe we can call the company and check on them."

"Okay. Give it here." They handed Annie a pill and watched as she swallowed it.

"Okay," Gabriela said. "Now let's talk some more about what we're going to get for our birthdays."

The next afternoon Allen took Annie to the drugstore and they talked to the druggist about where the pills were made and looked them up in the *PDR* and the druggist let Annie watch him put them in the bottle.

"You can keep them in your room," Allen said. "In a safe place. Every morning when you take one you can write it down in a notebook." They found the stationery department and picked out a pink notebook with a pencil attached. When they got home Annie put the pills and the notebook on a shelf in her closet.

"Tell us that again," she asked Allen that night. "That part about everybody trusts everybody else not to poison them."

"You think it's wise to let her keep them in her room?" Jennifer asked later.

"She needs to learn to write down dates. It will serve several purposes. I don't want her taking that stuff for long, Jennifer. The warnings in the PDR are pretty scary. It's just a form of Dexedrine. Why did Doctor Cole think she needed it?"

"Just to calm her down until we can get her settled in school. He says she's plenty bright. He just wants to make sure she doesn't get further behind and get the idea that she's dumb. Thank God for the sisters. She's going to stay in the fifth grade no matter what we have to do."

"She liked the notebook. I don't think she's had much of her own. Did you see the way she arranged her things in the room? She touches my heart, Jennifer. I can't believe how much I am attached to her already."

"Gabriela wants a savings account. She asked me to take her to my bank. Where did she find out about banks?"

"I'd be afraid to ask." They shook their heads in disbelief at what they had brought into their lives. Neither of them said Adelaide and neither of them had to. She was there, alive in their hearts and in every moment. World without end, amen.

On top of everything else she had to do, when Annie started acting funny about going to the wedding, Gabriela decided it was up to her to fix it. "I'll talk to her," she told Jennifer. "I can always get her to say what's wrong with her."

"How do you do it?" Jennifer asked.

"I just keep after her until she tells me. She's never afraid of anything except stuff that isn't true. She gets ideas in her head. She may be worrying about the airplane. She didn't like flying here too much but we didn't want to tell you."

That afternoon after school Gabriela cornered Annie in their room while she was changing clothes and started in on her. "Are you afraid of going on the airplane?" she asked. "You think it's going to crash or something?"

"I think they won't bring us back. I think they'll leave us there. They'll take us back to the home."

"No they won't. Jennifer says we're the reason she and Allen are alive."

"It's costing too much money. They have to pay the doctor and they have to buy me those pills. They cost twenty-four dollars. When I went to the drugstore with Allen to meet that guy that bottles them up I saw the bill. Twenty-four dollars for that little bottle that wasn't even full. They have to buy us all that food. They're going to get tired of that. They'll send us back."

Gabriela moved over and began to stroke Annie's hair. "They don't want to get rid of us. Would they buy us all these clothes if they weren't going to keep us? Not to mention that saddle Allen got you. Listen, you were so cute in that play last week. I bet Allen and Jennifer think you're the cutest girl they could ever get in the world. Come on, don't hide your face." Annie was starting to smile, thinking about the applause at her school play. Gabriela pressed her advantage. "If you'll stop worrying about going on the plane, I'll tell you what we'll do."

"What?"

"We won't be taking any chances. Wait a minute." Gabriela walked over to a painted chest at the foot of her bed and opened it and took out the brown cape. She arranged the cowl. "All right. Here's what we'll do. We will take this cape with us. This cape has been very lucky for us. The day we got it Sister Maria Rebecca told me about Allen and Jennifer coming to meet me. And it made you remember your lines last week when I made you sleep with it, didn't it? Admit it. Say something, Annie."

"Where do you think it came from?"

"I think some old monk had it in Nevada or somewhere, or else it's real old. Lucky stuff doesn't have to come from somewhere. You know when something's lucky for you."

"Okay. It's lucky for us."

"Then we'll take it to California to keep our luck going. Those girls we talked to on the phone are waiting for us. They're rich as they can be. They're going to make their dad take us to an amusement park. This is going to be a vacation, Annie. I never went on a vacation in my life. I want to go on one."

"All right," Annie said. "I'll go to this wedding. If I get to carry the cape."

"You can carry it. But if you lose it, I'll kick your butt. Do you get that?"

"I'd like to see you try." Annie stood up and grabbed her smaller friend around the waist and wrestled her to the bed. They fought for a minute, then they started laughing. The cape had gotten tangled around their legs. Besides, it was hard to fight without making any noise and it scared Jennifer to death if they punched each other. They had almost given up having fights, which was a shame because they were beautifully matched, despite the difference in their sizes. Annie was a wrestler, who liked to get holds on people and then sit on them or twist their arms. Gabriela was a stomach puncher and a shin kicker and a biter. She was also a good spitter and had won several battles at the home by spitting on people at crucial points in a fight.

The bridal shop in San Francisco mailed the dresses to the bridal shop in Oklahoma City. They were dresses by Helen Morley, who had also designed the dress Stella was going to wear. Stella's dress was elegant and simple, thick white silk with embroidery down the back and capped sleeves and a high neck.

The dresses for the girls were made of pale pink lace over satin slips. There were tiers of lace ten inches wide going down to the ankles and high-waisted bodices and full soft sleeves. When the owner of the shop in Oklahoma City pulled the first dress from the box a sigh went around the room. "Well," she said. "California always has to outdo everybody."

"They have all those Asian ideas," a saleslady comforted her. "Plus Hollywood."

"Yeah," said a third. "What do you expect?" Then the ladies recovered from their moment of jealousy and one ran off to comb the neighborhood for shoes. Another ran out to a rival store for gloves. A third began to work on the veils, which had been crushed in the mail.

At five that afternoon Jennifer and Annie and Gabriela arrived at the store and were ushered into a huge dressing room with golden chairs and a golden sofa. The girls took off their school clothes and were dressed in the pink lace costumes.

"I wasn't expecting this," Annie said. "How much does this dress cost?"

"This is for the Queen of Sheba," Gabriela agreed. "How are we going to wear this on a sandy beach?"

"Shit," Annie added, turning to see the back in the three-way mirror. "We look like a bunch of hibiscus flowers by the well."

"Fucking merde." Gabriela went to stand by her taller friend in the mirror. Even then the dresses looked perfect.

"Fucking-A," Annie agreed.

"Well, let's try on the gloves and shoes," the owner said. "We sent Roberta all over town to find shoes. We think white patent sandals since it's by the water."

The saleslady named Roberta began to open the shoeboxes that were stacked in the corner. "Every size they could possibly wear," she said proudly. "I looked all over town. We aren't going to be outdone by anyone in California. They will arrive with everything they need." Except mouthwash, she was thinking, and then chastised herself for being mean. Everyone in Oklahoma City knew the Williamses' story.

Annie sat down on the sofa and allowed Roberta to try the shoes on one by one. "You might consider shaving her legs," Roberta said. "I started shaving mine in the sixth grade."

Annie bent over and looked at the elegant little sandals on her feet. She examined the small, light-colored hairs showing along her bones. She pursed her lips.

"Her legs are perfect," Jennifer was saying. "She doesn't need to shave her legs."

"She's right," Annie muttered. "That looks like shit. I know how to shave it off. I seen a girl in the home doing it. You get me a razor and a bar of soap and I'll take care of that."

"Do you like the shoes? Is that pair comfortable? Get up and walk around in them."

Annie got up from the couch and began to parade around in front of the mirrors. What would it be like, being in a wedding? The priest would be fixing the wine. The altar boys would be swinging incense. Everyone would be looking at her. She stood very still, lost in thought. Gabriela moved across the room and took her arm. "Don't start getting moody," she said in a whisper. "Ask them if we're just going to wear these dresses, or if we're going to get to keep them."

"I need the shoes with the heels on them," she said in a louder voice to Jennifer. "If I wear those little ones I'll look like a midget."

It was seven that night when Jennifer and the girls got home from the store. They had gloves and hats and shoes in an assortment of sacks and boxes. The dresses had been left to be altered and hemmed. "So now do you think they would get rid of you?" Gabriela asked Annie, when they were alone in their room getting ready for bed. "After they got you a dress that cost about two hundred dollars and all that other stuff that matches it?"

"I've got to get me a razor," Annie answered. "I've got to shave these fucking hairs off my legs."

It stormed in the night. A huge thunderstorm that roared in about twelve o'clock and woke up the town. Jennifer and Allen lay in bed listening to the hail hit the roof. Then they went into the kitchen and got out food. They got out potato chips and sliced chicken and mayonnaise and lettuce and tomatoes and chocolate chip cookies and Gatorade. Since the girls had been there they had completely altered their diet and gone back to eating things that tasted good. "Something's bothering Annie," Jennifer said. "She's worrying about something and I don't know how to ask her what it is. I don't know if I should wait for Doctor Cole to find out or ask her. I don't know how far to pry into her mind. What would it be like, to be here with us, to think you were on probation, whether you were or not? What else can we do?"

"She's been knocked around from pillar to post all her life. How could she keep from worrying? If she's breathing, we're ahead. But I don't like her taking Ritalin, Jenny. That's a class four drug. Ever since we went through that business with going to the drugstore I've been reading up on it. I don't think they ought to be giving her drugs for anything, even to make her do better in school."

"Did you ask your brother?"

"He agrees it isn't the best idea but Cole is the only child psychiatrist he could find us on short notice. He said it would be all right to let her take it for a month or so until he can find another doctor."

"It seems to help."

"Drugs are for sick people. She's not sick. I thought we weren't going to care if they didn't act like normal children. I thought they were going to tear things up. I was hoping they'd break some of that bric-a-brac of Mother's in the living room. I hate that bric-a-brac. I was looking forward to seeing it in piles on the floor." Allen brandished his chicken sandwich. He added more mayonnaise and took a bite.

"I didn't know you hated the bric-a-brac. I hate it too. If you hate it, let's go take it down. We have those boxes the encyclopedia came in. We'll take it down and put it in them."

"Okay. Let's do it." Allen ate one last bite of his sandwich, grabbed a couple of potato chips, and led the way into the living room. There, behind the sofa, was a wall of shelves holding the remnants of his childhood, little cups and saucers and figurines and glass statues and vases and bookends. "I used to be late for baseball practice because I had to dust that stuff on Saturdays," he said. "Now I shall have my revenge." He began to take the things from the shelves. Jennifer brought in a bag of newspapers they were saving to recycle and began to wrap the pieces and put them in the encyclopedia boxes. They were almost finished removing every piece when Annie appeared in the door.

"That rain woke me up," she said. "You guys have the noisiest weather I ever heard in my life."

"No mountains," Allen said. He went to her and put his arms around her shoulders. He pulled her with him over to where Jennifer was packing a kneeling Cupid into the last box. "Jennifer thinks you're worrying about something," he began. "So we're worrying about you worrying. If you worry, we worry. We know something's worrying you because we love you and we are thinking about you. You want to tell us what's wrong, so we can worry about the right thing?"

"Why are you taking all this stuff down?" she asked.

"Because I'm sick of looking at it. We're going to put it in the garage. You don't want to talk about if something is worrying you?"

"I'm worried about going on that plane," she answered. "I don't see what holds it up."

"I'll show you what holds it up." Allen hugged her tighter, then let her go. "You have come to the right place with that question, Miss Annie. Did you know that I just so happen to know how to fly airplanes? Did you know that I also know how to fly a helicopter and flew them for three years in the United States Air Force?" He took the little girl to a table and opened a volume of the new encyclopedia which was still stacked in a corner waiting for him to get around to assembling the bookshelf that had come with it. He spread the encyclopedia down on a table and began to teach her the principles of aeronautics.

Two weeks went by. In Berkeley, everyone was busy getting ready for the wedding. The guest list kept expanding as friends Nieman and Stella hadn't heard from in months kept calling and asking where to send gifts. The gossip columns were full of the news. Also, the story of the girls from the home in Potrero had leaked out, adding to the public's interest.

In Salem, Oregon, Stella's mother was working out at a gym every afternoon hoping to lose weight so she wouldn't embarrass Stella by being fat. Stella's father was reading back issues of the *National Geographic* and pretending to ignore the whole thing. Nieman's mother was so mad she couldn't sleep. She had intended Nieman to marry a wealthy Jewish girl, preferably from New York City, and instead he had chosen this thirty-seven-year-old woman who didn't even wear eye makeup. "You can barely see her eyes," Bela Gluuk told her friends. "I doubt if she'll have her hair done for the ceremony. . . . No, of course not. No rabbi, not even a minister or a priest. Some woman judge, just to make me miserable, no doubt. What else has Nieman ever done?"

In Oklahoma City the day finally arrived to board the plane and fly to San Francisco. Annie clutched Allen's hand and climbed aboard the plane. She had the cape slung across her shoulder. "Why are you bringing that?" Jennifer asked. "They have blankets on the plane."

"It's something lucky we have," Gabriela explained. "I let her carry it for luck."

"Fine with me," Allen said. They found their seats on the DC-9. Allen and Jennifer were together with a seat in between them and Gabriela and Annie were across the aisle. "There is nothing to fear on this plane but the food," Allen whispered. "Don't lose that sack with the sandwiches and cookies."

"Allen," Jennifer said. "Keep your voice down. Don't let the stewardess hear you."

"At least I know it's my lucky day." Gabriela reached underneath the cape and took Annie's hand. "At least I lived long enough to have a vacation."

Annie squeezed the hand Gabriela had put in hers. She pushed the sack with the lunch around until she was holding it with both her feet. Allen and Jennifer tried not to laugh out loud. "She lived to go on a vacation," Jennifer whispered to him. "I have to start writing down the things she says."

Stella and Tammili met the Williams family at the airport. Lydia had not been able to come as she had a class on Friday afternoons. "So, how was your flight?" Tammili asked. She picked up Gabriela's backpack and carried it. Gabriela picked up Annie's pack and carried that. Annie carried the cape.

"I threw up," Annie said. "Allen told me why the plane stays up, but I stopped believing it when we were halfway here."

"I made her look out the window at the mountains. That's when it happened," Gabriela added. "I thought you had a twin sister. Where's the other girl?"

"She's at an acting class. We have to take a lot of classes so we'll have different interests. I don't do it anymore, but Lydia does everything they think up for her. So, how are things going in Oklahoma? You all getting along all right?"

"Except for storms," Gabriela answered. "Just when I thought I was going to live someplace that doesn't have earthquakes, I get adopted by some people who live in Tornado Alley. That's what they call it there. It's okay, though. People wear a lot of colored clothes. Like all these old ladies have these pink outfits they wear to the mall. Do you all have malls around here?"

"We have Chinatown. Did you ever go to it when you lived out here?"

"Are you kidding? The nuns never took us anywhere. So, where's this wedding going to be anyway?"

"At our house. That's the best part. We don't have to ride in a car in our dresses and get them wrinkled. All we have to do is put them on and walk out to the patio." They had come to the baggage carousel and were standing beside the grown people, waiting for the luggage to come. Tammili moved nearer to Annie. She reached up and touched the cape. "That's weird," she said. "My sister and I had a cape like that. We lost it on a camping trip when Dad broke his arm. Where do you get those capes? Did you buy it in Oklahoma?"

"It's magic," Gabriela said. "It's got powers in it."

"So did the one we had. Listen, it stayed dry in this terrible rain. This synchilla blanket we had that's supposed to wick faster than anything you can buy, got wet, but that cape was still as dry as a bone."

"She thinks some monks in Nevada probably make them." Annie moved the cape until it was around both of her shoulders. "Gabriela thinks they make them and sell them to people to give them luck. We seen some monks in Potrero. A bunch of them came and stayed with us on their way to Belize. We had them there for a week but that was before Gabriela came. She never got to see them."

"I saw them. Where'd you think I saw monks if it wasn't for that bunch that came and stayed at the home? I got there the day they were leaving. I saw them all sleeping on the ground. This cape is just like the stuff they were wearing."

"We're Jewish," Tammili said. "We don't have any monks."

The bags arrived and a man in a uniform appeared and helped them carry the bags outside to a limousine.

"The limo's just for fun," Tammili said. "My dad thought you'd like a limo, so we got you one. There're things to drink inside. Get in. See how you like it. Lydia and I adore limousines but we never get to get them because Dad usually says they're for movie people and Eurotrash."

The grown people got into the back and the girls got into the seats facing backward. Tammili was sitting next to Annie. She reached out and touched the cape again. She felt the softness of the weave caress her hand. "This is going to be the best wedding anyone ever had," she said. "I've been waiting all my life to be a bridesmaid. I don't care if it's bourgeois or not. I think it's the best."

"Well, I've never been in a wedding. I never even gave it much thought. I just hope I don't do something stupid."

"My parents' friends almost never get married. They just cohabit and have serial monogamy. So we are lucky this happened. You see, the groom is our godfather. He means a lot to us."

Annie and Tammili were deep in conversation, their heads turned to each other. Gabriela started getting jealous. "Did you take your pill this morning?" she put in, leaning toward them. "Where are they, Annie? Where did you put them?"

"I don't know," Annie answered. "I don't know where they are."

"Dad found this article in the *New York Times* about these people who have been getting orphaned babies from China," Tammili was saying. "We saved it to show you. Lydia and I are begging Mom and Dad to adopt some to go with the baby we're having. They said if we both made the honor roll for a year they'd think about it. Anyway, we saved the article for you. I mean, what you're doing is not that unusual. Well, this is San Francisco. That's the Golden Gate Bridge up there. We have to cross it to get to our house."

"She forgot her pills," Gabriela said to Jennifer. "Annie forgot her Ritalin."

"Good," Allen said. "She doesn't need any pills. I think that doctor's crazy to give pills to that child."

"She's taking Ritalin?" Stella asked. "I didn't think they still prescribed that to children. What are they giving her Ritalin for?"

"To get her adjusted to school," Jennifer answered. "Why? What do you know that we don't know?"

"It's just a very old-fashioned drug. Primitive, compared to the things we have now. How long has she been taking it?"

"A month. Almost a month. What's wrong with it, Stella?"

"I took a couple of them," Gabriela put in. "It didn't do anything to me but make me talk all the time. And, yeah, that day at school I did all that arithmetic so fast. I was wondering if that had anything to do with that."

"You took one?" All three of the adults leaned her way.

"I sure wasn't feeding them to Annie without knowing what she was taking. I seen, saw. I saw that happen with a girl in this place I stayed once. She took some pills this guy gave her and she ended up almost dying."

"You took a Ritalin?" Allen took both her hands in his. Stella began to breathe into a Zen koan.

"I cut one in two. I know about drugs. I used to help out at the home when kids got sick. Sister Elena Margarite said she might make a nurse of me."

"Where are they now?" Stella asked. "I'd like to see these pills."

"She left them at home. She wouldn't ever take them if I didn't remind her."

"It's all right," Jennifer said. "Forget about the Ritalin. When we get home we'll find another doctor."

"Was this my mother's doing?" Stella asked. "Is this some of Momma's old hippie connections she put you on to? Damn that woman. She and Dad are at a Ramada Inn waiting to hear from us. I've been praying for weeks they wouldn't come."

"Stella, how can you talk like that about your parents?"

"I'm an unnatural child. Nieman is too. That's why we're marrying each other. I finally met a man who isn't interested in meeting my family."

Annie had slid back into the seat, listening. These were the strangest adults she had ever encountered. All these days and weeks and they kept on acting just like they had the day she met them. As if life was funny, an adventure, something amazing to be watched and commented on. As if some light was in them that did not go out. She raised her eyes and they were smiling on her. Stella was looking at Gabriela.

"You got any crabs on this beach where your house is?" Gabriela asked Tammili. "I went to the beach a couple of times. These old birds were pecking for food in the sand and there were crabs underneath a log. I'd like to catch one in a bucket and get a good look at that if I could."

"We're almost there," Tammili told her. "We are almost to our house."

As soon as they arrived at the Harwoods' house, Stella excused herself and got into her car and drove to her office in the biochemistry building and started making phone calls and pulling things up on her computer. In an hour she had talked to child psychiatrists in New Orleans and New York City and Pittsburgh. She had researched recent antidepressants and had missed her appointment for a haircut. She stopped on her way home at a walk-in beauty parlor and let them even up the back and sides of her very short, severe haircut. She shook out the navy blue dress she was wearing to her rehearsal dinner and got into the shower still running the statistics on antidepressants through her head. Not good, she decided. Feeding Ritalin to a perfectly healthy child. She probably needs a shrink and Jennifer and Allen need to find out where she's been and what happened to her but I could figure that out if I had her alone for a week. Anxieties are like fingerprints but they are easily traced. What a fantastic cousin I have to think up something this crazy and wonderful and brave. I really like that girl. And the other one, the small one, is as pretty as a picture. What a lovely, ancient face. She looks like she's thirty years old inside. She took one of the pills! God, the human race. You can't see that underneath a microscope, Stella. There is nothing in RNA and DNA to account for our behavior, except the attachments we form are in the pattern, aren't they? Each of us has our receivers, what the old Jungians called the anima and animus, and someone comes along that fits the pattern and we meld. I am getting married in the morning to Nieman Gluuk. I am going to be his wife and make a home with him and be with him when we are old. Scary and wonderful, I guess.

She turned up the water in the shower and decided to stay there until the hot water ran out. The phone started ringing as soon as she got comfortable. She got out and answered it. "Stella," Nieman moaned on the telephone. "Where are you? I can't be alone waiting to get married. I'm coming over right this minute."

"Then I won't get dressed," she giggled. "Come on. Let's see what terror does to the parasympathetic nervous system."

"I'm in the car. I'll be there in ten minutes."

The living room of the Harwoods' house at the beach was an inspiration of the movers. They had moved all the musical instruments into one room while they waited for someone to arrive and give them orders. The Harwoods had left it that way. The room contained two baby grand pianos and a harpsichord and a harp. That was it. Except for a long thin table holding a Bose music system the size of a book.

"Fucking-A," Gabriela said when she saw it, forgetting her vow not to curse at the wedding.

"My grandmother bought it for us," Tammili said. "Don't worry about it being big. Most of it is wasted space. It was a wreck when we got it. We had to have the roof replaced and all the plumbing and the windows. The windows were so loose they rattled when it rained. So, there's the ocean. I guess that makes up for everything. And the guest house is nice. You'll like it there."

"What do you do with all these pianos?" Gabriela asked.

"We play them. Go ahead, try one. Come on. You can't hurt it. Momma's got a piano tuner who used to work for the symphony. He comes out every other month. Go on, play it. See how it sounds."

Gabriela walked over to the harpsichord and ran her fingers soundlessly across the keyboard. Nora Jane watched them from the doorway. "Would you like me to show you how?" she asked. "I have all these pianos because I was an orphan too. I have these pianos so I won't have to put up with feeling bad in case I ever do. I just come in here and start making noise. Come on, sit down by me." She sat down at one of the baby grand pianos. Gabriela sat beside her. Annie came and sat on the other side. She was still holding the cape over her shoulder like a shawl. Tammili stood behind her and laid her left hand very lightly on the cape. Nora Jane began to play show tunes, songs from Broadway musicals.

Tammili moved away from the piano. She began to dance. Gabriela got up and danced beside her. When Lydia came in the front door she found them dancing and joined them.

The wedding of Nieman Gluuk to Miss Stella Ardella Light began with children dancing.

The day of the wedding dawned bright and clear. By nine in the morning all four of the bridesmaids were dressed and wandering around the house getting in the way of the caterers. "Dahlias," Freddy Harwood declared. "The house is full of dahlias." Freddy was dressed in his morning suit and was videotaping everything in sight. He video-taped the bridesmaids in the music room and on the patio and in the kitchen. He videotaped the judge arriving with her twenty-six-year-old boyfriend. He videotaped Nieman and Stella getting out of Nieman's car and walking up the pathway to the back door. "He's scared to death," Freddy said into the microphone. "He's terrified. He can barely walk. He's making it. He's opening the door for her. It's nine-fifteen. Forty-five minutes until ground zero."

Nieman's mother arrived in a limousine. Stella's parents came in their Mazda van. The guests were crowding in. The driveway became packed with cars. The cars spread out across the lawn. The string quartet was playing Bach. Between nine-thirty and nine-forty-nine, a hundred and fifty people made their way up the front steps and filled the house. Someone handed bouquets to the bridesmaids. They formed a semicircle around the altar. The judge stepped into the mid-dle. Nieman appeared. The quartet broke into a piece by Schubert. Stella joined her groom and the judge read a ceremony in which the bride and groom promised to do their best to take care of each other for as long as they lived and loved each other. Nieman kissed his bride. The audience heaved a sigh of relief and champagne began to be passed on silver trays.

"That's it?" Annie said.

"I guess so," Lydia answered. "You want to get some petits fours and go play in my room?"

"We had a cape like this," she was saying later. She and Annie were lying on her bed with a plate of petits fours and wineglasses full of grape juice on her dresser. "We found a cape like this in this house we have that's in the hills. We took it on this hike with us and then we lost it."

"Your sister said the same thing. She said your dad broke his arm."

"We thought it was a lucky cape. Then we lost it."

"This one's lucky. As soon as Gabriela got it we got adopted. Just like that."

"I wish we could get another one. Do you know where to get them?"

"No. But I can't let you have this. It's Gabriela's. She just let me borrow it to fly on the airplane. So, is your dad going to take us to this amusement park?"

"He said he would if he could. If it opens before you have to leave tomorrow. I wish you could stay a few more days. There're a lot of things we could show you. We could take you on BART." Lydia lay facedown upon the cape, smelling the wonderful smell of wildflowers. "I think they make these out of some kind of flowers they grow somewhere. Like linen is made of flax. Where do you think they make them?"

"I think, Italy." Annie had no idea how she had decided to say Italy, but as soon as she said it she felt it was true. "I think they have this town in Italy and all they do is grow the flowers to make these capes."

"They think the cape is magic," Jennifer was saying. "They think they have a magic cape."

"What?" Nieman asked. "What are you talking about?"

"Like Michael Jordan wearing number twenty-three," Allen put in. "They believe in it, but they don't know we know they think it's magic. They just keep dropping hints."

They were on the side porch of the Harwoods' house. The wedding was winding down. The guests had nearly all gone home. The string quartet was in the kitchen talking to Freddy and Nora Jane. Jennifer and Allen Williams and the bride and groom were on the porch. It was the first time the Williamses had had a chance to be alone with the pair. Nieman had been commenting on how well the adopted girls had managed to fit into a scene they could not possibly have imagined. "Perhaps they saw it on a film," he had been saying. "I've written several times about how film teaches manners. Not just the obvious bad things, like violence, but also niceties, like how to hold your wedding bouquet. Do you think they were exposed to many films?"

"I don't know about that," Allen said. "But they have a cape they think is magic."

"They found the cape in a box of Salvation Army things a few days before we came to the home and met them. So they think it brought them luck. Technically, it's Gabriela's cape, but she lets Annie share it. She let Annie carry it on the plane. They pretended they wanted it for a blanket."

"I'm having a déjà vu," Stella said. She took Nieman's arm. She pressed herself into his side. "What is this all about?"

"I have it too," he said. "Just then. When Jennifer started talking about the cape. You have to understand," he said to Jennifer and Allen. "The first time we met we had this huge mutual déjà vu. Is this part of love, do you think? A harkening back to the mother–child relationship?"

"It's probably blood sugar," Stella said. "A magic cape. Well, that's a wonderful thing to believe you have. I found a really fine psychiatrist in Oklahoma City who will see her, Jennifer. I had to beg, but he'll see her once a week. Don't take her back to that man who gave her Ritalin. Promise you won't go back to him."

"Whatever you say, brilliant cousin," Jennifer answered. "It's unbelievable how much you learn to love a child, any child." She looked at Allen. "It's hard enough to suffer when you're old. Eleven years old should be a happy time and we want to make it one for her. If you found someone, we'll go and see him. I believe in psychiatry. I always have."

"I've thought of going into it," Stella said. "Sometimes I think I've taken molecular biology as far as it will go. Maybe I'll abandon the field to Nieman and get myself a new career." She closed her eyes, then opened them. "A dog runs across the street in front of your car. In a nanosecond the entire chemistry of the body changes. There are Buddhist monks who can regulate their heartbeat, control pain, choose when to die. There is so much to learn, so much to know." She turned to Nieman and kissed him on the lips. Jennifer clapped her hands, then kissed Allen long and passionately. It was the best kiss they had kissed in many months. A storm was brewing on the ocean. The negative ions were thick in the clean, sweet air.

"We'll come see you in August," Tammili was saying. "And you'll come here at Christmas when it's snowing where you live. We'll do that every year as long as we live and always be friends."

"We swear by the cape to be friends," Lydia added. The four little girls were sitting on the floor in their dresses. The cape was spread out between them. They were each holding part of it.

"Every time we see each other we'll get your dad to take videos of us," Gabriela put in. "In the meantime if he meets any movie people he can show them the videos and see if they want us to be in movies. Give them Jennifer and Allen's phone number if they do."

GÖTTERDÄMMERUNG,
IN WHICH NORA JANE
AND FREDDY HARWOOD
CONFRONT EVIL
IN A WORLD THEY NEVER MADE

I

NEW YORK CITY, NEW YORK, September 13, 2000. The inhabitants of a building on the upper left-hand corner of 92nd Street and Park Avenue were experiencing a disturbance of the first order. Music had begun blaring out of an apartment on the fifth floor at all hours of the night and day. Loud, crazy music played on Mittenwald zithers, or worse, Wagner: Brunhilde, the Valkyries, Siegfried, Götterdämmerung. The music was coming from the opened windows of the largest apartment in the building. The apartment had been empty for many months. It had belonged once to Emily Post, then to Alice Walton, then to a diplomat from Jamaica, and finally, mistakenly it was turning out, to a couple from London no one had ever seen. The couple's résumé had seemed perfect. He was a London stockbroker, she was a photographer. They had no children, no dogs, and the real estate agent told the condominium association the couple only planned to use the apartment a few months each year. There were recommendations from people members of the association knew, if not well, at least well enough to speak to at cocktail parties. Because the résumé had seemed so stellar, the association voted to allow the sale without a personal interview. The buyers were in London, the association was told, and didn't plan on coming to New York for many months.

There were three empty apartments in the building and several more for sale. Four occupants were in arrears in their condo fees. It was not a year in which 92nd and Park could afford to turn down a cash sale that included a year's condo fees paid in advance.

The sale went through, a yellow van came and stripped the apartment of the Jamaican's possessions, painters arrived and painted the rooms, a flooring company came in and pulled out the carpets and installed oak floors, mirrored walls were dismantled and replaced with wallpaper. Then, nothing for six months. Before the first year was up, a check arrived to cover the condo fees for the second year. "Apartment 17, the cash cow," became a joke at association meetings. "Let's get some more London brokers here. What a deal."

Then, suddenly, in late July of 2000, several tall, unpleasant-looking Middle Eastern men began to leave and enter the apartment at all hours of the day and night and the music began to blare out of the open windows. *The Ring of the Nibelung,* and, even louder and worse, music played on zithers.

This activity would go on for several days, then nothing, then begin again.

A retired orthopedic surgeon named Carlton Rivers was the new president of the condominium association. He thought it was just his luck that this situation should develop the month he took office. He had run for the unpaid job because he had it in for the building supervisor and was planning on firing him soon. Instead, this blaring music, coupled with the sleazy-looking Middle Eastern men. Carlton wasn't Jewish but his college girlfriend had been, and he felt a deep empathy and connection with Israel, to which she had disappeared the day after their college graduation. Her name was Judith and she had given

Carlton the greatest sexual experiences of his life. He had let her go, thinking he could reproduce those experiences elsewhere in the world. It had not proved to be true. It had been his initiation into sex and it had proved unbeatable. For years after she was gone he would drift off in the middle of an operation and remember her teeth or mouth or hair and sigh deeply for the paradise he had lost.

When he began to make money, his main charity was a research hospital in Haifa. He thought of going there to find her but he never did. He was busy in medical school, then as an intern, then establishing a practice. Finally he married a dark-haired nurse who gave great blow jobs and went on with his life. There were no children of this union and Carlton was secretly glad of that. He was not a man who could tolerate much disorder.

His wife died the year after he retired. When he recovered he threw himself into campaigning to become president of the condominium association. He had barely had time to enjoy his success and begin his campaign to rejuvenate the place when the goddamn Arabs started coming into the building and blaring out Wagner at all hours of the day and night.

He called the condominium lawyers and they wrote letters to the owners in London. There were no answers to the letters. Phone calls were made to the phone numbers in the records of the condominium association and those at the real estate firm which had handled the two-million-dollar sale. A call was placed to the brokerage firm the owner was supposedly associated with. All these telephone calls were answered by machines. Mr. and Mrs. Alterman were out of the country and could not be reached was the information supplied by the machines.

Carlton was going ballistic when, as suddenly as it began, the music stopped and did not start up again. No one entered or left the apartment. There was no mail. The apartment phones rang but were not even answered by machines.

Three weeks of silence went by. Then, on September 13, there was a meeting of the association and the first order of business was what was going on in 17 and what should they do about it, if anything.

"Apartment seventeen," Carlton began. "We allowed the sale to a couple we had never met. That's done. They never set foot in the building. Nothing wrong there. Wealthy people buy things they never use. Then, suddenly, there are Middle Easterners coming and going at all hours and music waking up eighteen, nineteen, twenty, fifteen, and the people on the fifth floor of 988. Our lawyers write the owners and get no reply. We call all the numbers left by the owners with us, the Realtor who sold the place and the brokerage firm where he supposedly worked at the time of the purchase, but they say he is no longer with them. So what are we to make of this? And what should we do?"

"Nothing," Mrs. Bloodworth answered. She was the vice president of the association and still had her nose out of joint because Carlton had been chosen over her for first in command. She was a stout matron with iron gray hair who wore old-fashioned suits made by a tailor on the Upper West Side. She had taught chemistry at Harvard and never let anyone forget it. "We called this meeting to talk about raising the condo fee three hundred dollars a month to make up for the shortfall of unpaid dues on empty apartments. That, coupled with the seven-hundred-dollar raise in insurance premiums, has put many owners in distress. The last thing we want to do at this point is create a problem with seventeen. Seventeen is paid in advance for the next fourteen months. The problem has ceased. We should forget it and get on with the business of finding someone to work on the eaves and roof."

"You're prejudiced against Middle Easterners, Carlton," a man named Herman put in. "You wouldn't vote for that nice Saudi woman two years ago. She was an internist."

"With a degree from a medical school in Guadalajara, Herman.

Don't talk about things you don't understand. It was on the basis of her so-called education that I voted against her."

"And now that apartment's empty too. You can afford to pay these ever-higher fees but some of us can't. . . ."

"Please, ladies and gentlemen." Mrs. Bloodworth stood up. "Please. Order in the room. Order."

"They were advance men for a decorating firm," Herman said. "One of them told the supervisor that. I don't understand this constant prejudice we encounter in this group at every step."

"Bleeding hearts," Carlton snapped. "I'd have an easier time believing they were making a nuclear device. The music was to cover up conversation. That's what people do when they don't want to take a chance on being taped. High decibels render even very sophisticated listening devices mute. I saw that on 20/20 last year."

"Oh, please," Mrs. Bloodworth said. "Let's move on, may we?"

The meeting broke up after a vote on raising the condo fees to cover the cost of the roofing problems, and everyone went back to their apartments muttering about ineptness and the cost of life in the city.

That night Carlton decided to take matters into his own hands. He had a key to the back door of 17 that one of the former tenants had left in his care. He could have used the keys the maintenance crew kept in the basement, but those had to be checked out. After dinner he drank a couple of brandies, found a flashlight, and went up the back stairs to 17. The key worked. No one had bothered to change that lock. He let himself in and, using only his flashlight, began to search.

After an hour of poking around in empty drawers and closets he found the first piece of handwriting he had come across in the whole apartment. It was in the drawer of a bedside table near a phone. It was a list of names.

Frederick Sydney Harwood, Berkeley, California
Joseph Leister, Madison, Wisconsin
Holly Knight, Eureka Springs, Arkansas

Carlton copied down the names and carefully replaced the paper in the drawer. He wrote down the serial numbers of the expensive Bose CD player and the television set. Then he left and went back down to his apartment and called a private detective he knew named Lynn Fadiman and asked to have someone come and get fingerprints from the doorknobs and glass surfaces. "Possible," his friend answered. "But very expensive."

"I'm rich," Carlton said. "Do it tomorrow night. In the meantime, if I give you the names of three people can you get dossiers on them and tell me what they have in common?"

"You could probably do it on the Internet. Have you tried?"

"I don't have a computer. I'm a Luddite."

"Okay. Tell them to me."

Fifteen minutes later Lynn Fadiman called Carlton back. "I've got data on all three. Easy. You do have a fax machine, don't you?"

"No. But there's one at the all-night drugstore down the street. Here's the number. 212-555-2345. You got it?"

"They're booksellers."

"What?"

"The three names. They sell books. All three of them are big shots in the Independent Booksellers Association."

"My God!"

"Maybe your music man was a budding author."

"I don't think so. Can you get the prints tomorrow night?"

"I told you I would. You're sure I won't be caught?"

"I'll go down and talk to the night watchman while you're in there. He loves to talk. I'll pretend I'm having a fight with one of the tenants. I am having a fight with one. I'll stay with him. He's the only person who might go in."

At nine the next morning Lynn called Carlton on his cell phone. "Go to a pay phone and call me now. I don't like this. Call me now."

Carlton put on a coat and shoes and went out of the building and over to the drugstore where he had collected the facsimiles the night before. He called Lynn Fadiman. The phone rang once.

"Holly Knight died last night in an accident on a remote highway. She was alone in a car and the car went off the road and into a lake. She was a fifty-seven-year-old woman who never went anywhere at night and at eleven at night she drove a Pontiac off a bridge into Beaver Lake near Rogers, Arkansas. It's a hit list, Carlton, and it's time to take this to the police."

I I

A FIVE POINT TWO AT TEN A.M. in the locker room. Nora Jane Harwood was in the ladies' locker room of the Berkeley Athletic Club trying to get Little Freddy to put on his new swimming trunks when the earthquake moved beneath San Francisco. It began in the sea and roiled its way inland, moving and shaking and being mean. Moved by forces beyond our control, Freddy Harwood was always saying for a joke and it sure fit earthquakes. If the metaphor fits, wear it, was a private joke between his twin daughters.

"He's going metaphor," Tammili would say.

"He's close. He's almost there," Lydia would answer.

"It itches me," Little Freddy was complaining as Nora Jane tried to get him to put his fat legs into the denim bathing suit Lydia had ordered him from Lands' End. Little Freddy wanted to wear his old red trunks with the torn inner lining and the small, thick elephant sewn on the side. He was immune to arguments that the red trunks were too small. He wanted to take the elephant into the water, where it wanted to be. He was fascinated by two things in the waning months of his third year on the planet Earth. Elephants and *The Wizard of Oz. Elephants of the World* was his favorite book. *Horton Hears a Who!* and *Horton Hatches the Egg* were his second favorite books, and his favorite garment was his red bathing suit with the elephant on the side and he wanted to take it into the water and let it swim. Besides, it kept him from getting drowned.

Little Freddy hated his swimming class and the big, bossy girl who was always making him put his head under the water or wait his turn to practice on the kickboard. The longer he put off stepping into the new denim trunks the longer it was going to be before Nora Jane took him out to the pool.

"If you just wear it this one time we'll go out to the mall and get you another one like the red one," she was saying. "The red one is too tight for you. It pinches your little tally-wacker."

"Tally-wacker," Little Freddy replied, moving away from her and climbing up on a bench where a woman the age of his grandmother was putting on her running shoes. "Me don't have any tally-wacker." He paused, while his mother recovered and the older woman began to giggle. "If you gimme that PowerBar, I'll put them on."

The older woman was really laughing now. Her name was Sylvia Kullman and she was in charge of fund-raising for Marin County Planned Parenthood. Nora Jane had seen her on television and admired her brilliance in debate and her fabulous designer clothes. All the famous designers liked to dress Sylvia for her debates. She was always at the athletic club. She worked out four days a week and it showed. She was past seventy years old and still as trim and supple as a girl.

Little Freddy eyed Nora Jane while she considered his offer. "Okay," she said at last. "You can have part of the PowerBar but not all of it. You can have one third of it now and the rest when you finish your class." She pulled the PowerBar out of her bag and showed him how much she would break off if he agreed to the deal. He climbed down from the bench and went to her and began to step into the denim trunks. Sylvia finished tying her shoes, still laughing and smiling at Nora Jane.

"Enjoy them while you can," she said. "They grow up so fast. Then they're gone and you have to pretend you don't miss them."

Then Berkeley moved. Not just the concrete slab that held the athletic club but the whole town moved, slanting to the east, and then it moved again and then it stopped. Nora Jane grabbed Little Freddy and pulled him to the floor. Sylvia dove beneath a sink. The other women in the dressing room began to moan. A group of three women beside the private lockers were moaning as a group.

"That's a big one," Little Freddy said. "I want my PowerBar. You said I could have it. It's bad to break your promise."

Nora Jane sat up and handed him the bar. "Are you all right?" she asked Sylvia.

"I'm okay. Should we stay here or go out in the main area? I mean, aftershocks."

"There're no windows in here. Not much to fall."

"But the lockers," a woman called out. "Could they fall?"

"They didn't," Nora Jane answered.

"It was built to specs," Sylvia said. She stood up and began to take charge. "We're okay. That wasn't a big one. We're all right here. Let's just stay here a few minutes and not panic. Does anyone have a phone?"

Nora Jane got one out of her bag. "Let me call my husband, then I'll give it to you. I have two girls at school. Surely they're okay." She pushed a button and Freddy Harwood answered at the bookstore. "I'm okay here," she said. "I'm at the club. Call about the girls. I need to let other people use the phone. Call me back when you can."

"What are you doing?"

"I'm in the locker room. We're going to stay here for a while. I won't leave."

She handed the phone to Sylvia, who called her husband, then handed the phone to the other ladies and they made calls but none of their calls went through. The lines were getting jammed.

Little Freddy was sitting on the floor eating the PowerBar. Nora Jane got another one out of her bag and offered it to Sylvia.

"Half," Sylvia said. "He's making me hungry. What's his name?"

"Frederick Sydney Harwood. I'm Nora Jane. We own Clara Books. On Telegraph Avenue."

"I go there all the time. Sylvia Kullman. I'm glad to know you. I see you working out although why you bother with your body, I don't know."

"To be healthy," Nora Jane replied. "I like to do it. It feels good. I think about all the carpenters and cowboys and people who do real work and how fine and strong their bodies always are, compared to people who sit at desks all day and screw up their minds with thinking and selling things."

"I'm afraid it's vanity with me," Sylvia replied. "My mother was injured in a face-lift situation so I won't do any surgery. I have to do it with exercise and so I do. Sometimes I like it but I think it's mostly vanity."

One of the three moaning women had gone around the corner to the sofas where the young women nursed their babies and had opened the door to the main room of the club. A woman was screaming in a distant room. Screaming her head off. Screaming like there was no tomorrow.

Then the second shock shook the building and the woman began to scream even louder.

"A hysteric," Sylvia said. "It doesn't sound like pain."

"We should go home now," Little Freddy said. "I want to go to my own house."

"Let's get on your shoes," Nora Jane answered. "There could be broken glass anywhere. You have to wear your shoes."

"Let's make our way to the lobby," Sylvia suggested. "At least let's move to the nursing sofas and get near the door to the lobby. There's nothing in that area to fall, is there?"

"The glass table with the flower arrangement."

"Let's move it." Sylvia led the way around the corner to the nursing alcove, which was near the door to the main lobby. The others followed. There was a glass-topped table on a thick pedestal near the door. Nora Jane and Sylvia moved the flower arrangement, then picked up the glass top and set it on the floor. "Upper-body strength," Sylvia said. "I told my husband it would come in handy. He thinks I'm nuts to work out all the time. He's jealous." They shoved the beveled glass tabletop underneath the coatracks, and Nora Jane dumped a basket of wet towels on top of it. They moved past the nursing sofas and pushed open the door to the lobby. It adjoined the racquetball courts and the basketball court and the aerobics and yoga rooms. Men and women were herded into small groups in the lobby. The glass walls of the racquetball courts were intact, and two of the trainers were passing out bottles of Gatorade and trays of health food snacks, Luna Bars, PowerBars, peanut butter bars, and homemade raisin cakes. People were talking on cell phones and looking subdued. Two young women were nursing babies on a large flowered sofa. Little Freddy made a beeline for that activity. "Titties," he whispered to Nora Jane. "Titty babies. Them not big like me." He burrowed his head in her legs and she sat down and took him into her arms. Weaning had been very hard on Little Freddy. Just the thought of titties drove him wild with deprivation. There was nothing on earth he liked as much as sinking his mouth onto his mother's sweet, milk-filled teats. His lost paradise, his Shangri-la.

"You're a big boy now," Nora Jane told him. "You have chocolate milk in a paper carton with a straw."

"Yes," he said mournfully. "That's what I do."

A young trainer, one of the fifteen or sixteen men at the club who was in love with Nora Jane, that is, deeply smitten, not just in constant appreciation of her startling, luminous beauty, stopped beside the sofa to ask if she was all right.

"Who was that screaming?" Nora Jane asked. "Was someone hurt?"

"A woman fell on one of the treadmills. She skinned her knee. Jay Holland, the eye doctor, was up there and took care of her. He's got her in Beau's office. There were three doctors on the machines, a radiologist, an eye surgeon, and an internist. I guess this is the place to be if an earthquake hits. The little guy seems happy. He didn't cry?"

"He was eating a PowerBar. He loves to eat."

"Did you see that demonstration at the Democratic convention? With those nuts protesting breast-feeding? They said it caused unhealthy oral fixations. I thought it was a joke, but then the cops arrested some of them."

"I didn't see it. I guess we have enough crazies in California now. I guess we've reached our limit."

"There is no limit. They keep coming. Anyway, I thought of you when I saw that on television. I thought you'd get a kick out of it."

The owner of the club had come out into the center of the lobby and was holding up his hands. "There could be other aftershocks. The police have asked us to stay here for another hour or so. Traffic is going to be horrific everywhere anyway. You can take mats into the aerobics or yoga rooms and do stretches, none of you stretch enough, admit it, or you can use the basketball court but we don't want anyone upstairs near the machines. Snacks and drinks are on the house. Jeff will get a television going in the snack bar if you want to see it on television. We think there are forty-six people in the club and fourteen three- to four-year-olds. If your children are okay, take them into the playrooms and let them play together. No one was in the pool. There was only one injury and it's being treated. Let the trainers know if you need help. It's ten forty-five. Let's shoot for staying in the building another hour."

People began to wander off into various activities. Sylvia invited

Nora Jane to stretch with her in the yoga room and Little Freddy agreed to go into the nursery to play with the other children.

The third shock hit just as Little Freddy was settling down with a Lego game. His friend Arthur was sitting beside him. When they felt the floor and table move they started laughing so hard they couldn't stop. "It's a big one," Little Freddy yelled. "Get on the floor."

"Titty babies," he whispered to Arthur to make him even more hysterical with laughter. "Them are titty babies."

Nora Jane and Sylvia had just unrolled their mats when they felt the third shock and they felt it roll and took it. Then they got up and went to the nursery to see if Little Freddy was all right. He and Arthur were still sitting at the table laughing their heads off.

"We could learn from that," Sylvia said.

"I do," Nora Jane replied. "It's a new world. I never had a boy."

"You sing opera, don't you?" Sylvia asked. It was an hour later. People were beginning to fan out into the parking lot to find their cars. "I know Anna Hilman, the director at San Francisco Place. She told me about your voice. She heard you sing last year at the benefit. She said it was divine. I wish I'd been there. The reason I'm bringing it up is that we are having a fund-raiser in December and I wondered if we might persuade you to sing for us. It's national. I mean, you'd have to go to New York. It's going to be in the Metropolitan Opera House. We want to take San Francisco talent with us so it won't be all East Coast. Would you even consider doing it? We'd pay your expenses, with your husband, of course. I have a house on Park Avenue, actually. You could stay with us if you don't have a hotel you like."

Nora Jane wasn't answering, so Sylvia went on. "I don't mean to ask you on a day like this but I thought you might want to do it. It will be on C-Span. I don't even know if you are interested in Planned Parenthood."

"Of course I am. I just never sing in public. It just isn't something I enjoy doing. I've done it five or six times in the last few years, but proving I can do it doesn't make me like it. My grandmother was a diva. She taught me, years ago in New Orleans. Somehow it has always been part of my love for her, not something I want the world to hear."

"Anna said you sing like an angel. She said you had a really astounding range."

"I do. It's a gift. I've almost never studied or used it. I took from Delaney Hawk for two years. Sometimes I go over and sing with her for a month or two, but that's about it. I like being a housewife and a mother."

"That's lovely, Nora Jane. Commendable in this day and age. Well, think about my offer. I might even be able to get an honorarium. If you get interested, call me." Sylvia handed her a card and smiled and left and Nora Jane took Little Freddy by the hand and walked out to her Volvo and put him in the back in his car seat and got into the driver's seat and started driving. She had been in a fine mood, glad the earthquake was a small one, glad to spend time with a star like Sylvia, feeling good, and now she was feeling bad. The world was always reaching out and wanting things from her that she didn't want to give.

There had been no home for Nora Jane when she was young. Her father was dead and her mother drank. Only when she was at her grandmother Lydia's house was life beautiful and quiet. All Nora Jane wanted in the world was to keep the world quiet and good for her children. She didn't want fame, she didn't want applause, she didn't want half the money Freddy gave her and put in her name and put in bonds and stocks and accounts for her. All she wanted was for the days to pass in peace and the people she loved to be safe.

Is there no way they'll let me alone? she thought. All I ever wanted was to keep this one thing to myself, this music Lydia gave to me, the Bach and Scarlatti and, oh, the Puccini. She began to sing an aria from *Tosca* and Little Freddy raised his voice and sang with her, screaming at the top of his lungs to match her high notes and beating his legs on the car seat with power and joy.

Five days went by and Nora Jane avoided the weight room at the club because she didn't want to run into Sylvia. Once or twice she brought up the subject of the offer to her husband, Freddy, or her daughters, but they were busy with their own thoughts and didn't seem to want to discuss her quandary at any length.

"It's up to you," Freddy kept saying. "If you want to do it, I'll go with you and support you in any way I can. If you don't want to, just tell her so."

Then a letter came in the mail from the national office of Planned Parenthood inviting her formally to participate in the program and offering her five thousand dollars and her expenses and a dress designed especially for her by Geoffrey Beene. He would send someone to take measurements and consult with her about her taste in color and fabric.

"I'm going to do it," Nora Jane declared and put the letter in front of Freddy at the breakfast table. "I am doing it for Planned Parenthood and for the dress. I'll give back all the money I don't spend. I might have to spend some on lessons with Delaney for a few months. I want to work something up. A tenor from the Met will be there and they think Christopher Parkening. I have to do this, Freddy. I can't turn this down. This fell in my lap. Grandmother would want me to do this. She would want me to sing at Lincoln Center."

"Are you sure? Absolutely sure?"

"Yes, I think I am." She stood in the light from the windows, with her beautiful face screwed up into a terrible imitation of courage and Freddy loved her so much he could not breathe.

"Then say yes. When is the performance?"

"On December the eleventh."

"We'll take the kids and spend a week and do Christmas things."

III

IN 1996 THE GROUP LED BY ABU SAAD had killed a writer named Adrien Searle as part of the cleansing that surrounded the Salman Rushdie shame. Now more killing must be done. Blood revenge, blood for blood, life for life. If blood doesn't flow, men never learn.

The new cleansing was supposed to take place on the three days covering the anniversary of the day the three men who killed Adrien Searle were locked away in a prison that was worse than death.

September 13, Holly Knight. September 14, Freddy Harwood. September 15, Joseph Leister. The paladins would move from Arkansas to California, then to Wisconsin.

It would be a full moon, the brightest moon of the year, a lunar shadow, three victims, three assassins, a car wreck, a throat slit, a fire, and they were done and the message was delivered that Fire From Heaven takes vengeance on the ones who helped the one who broke the sacred vows that knit the souls of the faithful together for all time. Amen.

But no one could have predicted an earthquake that would not let the 747 land in San Francisco and took the protectors of the faith to Las Vegas, Nevada, instead, into a hell of iniquity and disgust, unclean past all imagining.

They spread out to stay in three different hotels. They waited for orders but none came. Nothing could be depended upon for several days.

"Allah is good. Blessed be his name," Abu said. "Order things from room service. Maintain yourselves in patience. We have to wait until he returns to his routine. It won't be long."

"Then we go to Wisconsin and do the third act."

"No, it must be in sequence. The president, the vice president, the secretary-treasurer of their organization, this bookseller's group. His holiness wants it that way. Do not question things, Davi. Say your prayers, eat food, rest, amuse yourself. In good time."

Abu hung up the phone and settled himself on the bed to study his French grammar. He was no longer a young man with fire in his blood and was glad that he was not. Every year his study and learning made him a more valuable man to the God he worshiped, and in that knowledge lay all his happiness. He had learned four languages in ten years. French would be his fifth. He needed no praise for his work. He was his own praise. He thought of his father in heaven thinking of him and his begetting and he was glad.

Nora Jane dropped Little Freddy at his play school and started off for Delaney Hawk's studio on Euclid Street. When the Presidio became the place to be, Delaney had sold her house in Marin and moved back into town. It was a typical Delaney move. A sixty-four-year-old woman selling her house and all her furniture and starting over in a Bauhaus world of bleached wood floors, stark white walls, uncurtained windows, and Pensi and Mies van der Rohe copies. The piano had a room to itself. The only other furniture was three Wassily chairs and an Axis table.

Nora Jane had not seen Delancy since the move, and it added to the strangeness of her decision to sing in New York to have to seek out and find her teacher in a neighborhood she knew nothing about.

Delaney was waiting on the front sidewalk, watching for her. It might be a new neighborhood but it was the same old Delaney, dressed in a long skirt, an orange linen blouse, and a gray cashmere sweater that had belonged to Nabokov when she had known him in London. She always wore the sweater around her shoulders. She wore it summer and winter. The sight of it reminded Nora Jane of whom she was dealing with and made her humble. Delaney Hawk had walked with gods and she did not forget.

Delaney tied the arms of the sweater into a knot and began to direct Nora Jane to a parking place in what anyone would have thought was the front yard. When Nora Jane had turned off the motor, Delaney came around to the driver's side and opened the door and held it for her while she got out. Delaney was smiling her professional, no-nonsense smile. It was her main smile at this time in her life.

"I'm glad you want to get back to work," she said. "I need money to get a driveway poured and tear off this porch. Come on in. See the new place." She led the way to the fated porch and up the stairs and opened the front door and held it while Nora Jane moved into the living room. Four Mies chairs sat in a square around a marble table holding a vase of yellow tulips.

"It makes me want to sing right now." Nora Jane was laughing. "My God, I bet the acoustics are wonderful."

"You bet they are. The floors are synthetic wood, they're made of oil, they contain liquid, not that everything doesn't although we forget that. Well, let's get started. What do you want to sing?"

"The *Ave Maria* by Schubert. Handel, *Let the Bright Seraphim.* And a modern piece. The girls want me to sing *O Holy Night.*"

"Oh, God. The Schubert's tricky. If you have the slightest cold, anything can ruin it. Well, we can do it. This is some turn you've taken. What are they paying you?"

"Geoffrey Beene's designing the dress. I get to keep it. Oh, it isn't that. It's for my grandmother Lydia. I might sing Puccini. We'll see."

"Which Puccini?"

"*Vissi d'arte.*"

"I see." Delaney went to the piano bench and sat down on it facing the piano. She played several notes of the Puccini. "Well, why not. You can do it."

"It was what Lydia was listening to when she died. When she sang it she wore a blue velvet dress and that is what I'm going to ask Mr. Beene to make for me. I have never sung it out loud since she died. Only in my heart, but I know it better than I know any music in the world." Nora Jane was crying. Standing in the beautiful, pristine room crying without moving or making a sound. "This is for her. She was the most important person in my life and I have to quit being in denial about what her death did to me and celebrate what I knew."

"Oh, God." Delaney was crying also. She had not sung and taught grand opera all her life to back away from the heart and breath of life.

"Then let's begin," Delaney said. "There's water in the pitcher on the table. Have a sip. Come over here. Maybe I'll go to New York with you if you do this thing. My sister lives there, on the Upper West Side. Yes, if you do this, I'll go with you. I haven't been in several years. It's time to go."

"Yes," Nora Jane answered. "Yes, yes, yes."

She went to the table and poured the water and drank a small amount and walked over to the piano and waited while Delaney looked for the music in a Treviso bookshelf filled with scores and sheet music.

"Do scales," Delaney ordered. "Start warming up." She moved back to the piano and struck one note, a C, and Nora Jane picked it up and began to move her voice up and down her incredible range. Delaney shivered, then straightened her shoulders and went back to the bookshelf and began to take out music.

I didn't forget how, Nora Jane would decide later. You don't forget. It's like skating or skiing, balance sports. No, it's like looking at my children, like love, because it is love and I have not forgotten. My body can still do this thing I love so much, this clear happiness my grandmother gave to me so long ago when there was nothing else I had but this and her and it was enough and I survived and lived to find Freddy and have Lydia and Tammili and Little Freddy and become a person who is going to sing Puccini at the Metropolitan Opera and not be afraid.

That coming weekend, Nora Jane's twin daughters, Lydia and Tammili, were planning on being gone for two nights to a Girl Scout retreat that included a tour of the California Academy of Sciences in Golden Gate Park.

"Let's take Little Freddy and go up to Willits," Freddy suggested. "I have a huge desire to get out of town. Please say yes. You can rest and I'll take care of him. I want to take him. He never gets to be there alone."

"If you're absolutely sure the power is going to be high enough to pump water."

"The cells are full. No one's been in months. I'll call and have Deesha go out and clean it up and check. Then you'll go Friday afternoon, as soon as the girls leave?"

"Okay. I'll go. I love the house at Willits. I just like to think I can take a bath if I want to. Yes, yes, I'll go."

"You're in a good mood lately. I would have hired Geoffrey Beene myself if I'd known that's what you wanted."

"It isn't that. And it isn't about singing either. It's about my grandmother. I haven't finished figuring it out yet. It's about who she was and being part of that. She used to polish my shoes twice a day when I stayed with her. It's about having had her and remembering it and being grateful."

Little Freddy pushed open the door and came into the room. He had his hands folded across his chest as if to begin complaining about something.

Freddy picked him up and carried him to the bed and sat him on his knee. "We're going to see a mountain lion, son of mine. We're on our way to Willits to feed the lion."

"That is not the way to get me to Willits."

"I'm teasing. I'll let him look through the binoculars. I won't take him where there's any danger. You know that. I wouldn't take him down to the woods unless I knew it was safe for him to go."

"He doesn't need to see a mountain lion. He's only three years old. He can look at pictures of wild animals or see them at the zoo."

*   *   *

Abu, Davi, and Petraea moved into a suite at the Sands on the third day of waiting. On the fourth day a message was delivered by a room service waiter. It was in a dialect only Abu read, so he interpreted it for the others.

"On Saturday we go to Berkeley and wait until he closes the store. He is having a book signing for a famous person from New Orleans. He must be there. He parks his car a block from the store beside a shoe store called Intelligent Feet. We can follow him home or we can take him on the street. We will have to use a sedating shot because of the public place. Everything cannot be perfect now. We will leave him in the alleyway between the shoe shop and a ladies' clothing store. Then we go to the airport, give the car to a messenger who will meet us, board airplanes, and go to Wisconsin by three different routes. All luggage will be checked. Anything we need for the work will be supplied when we get there. Leave only clothes in the suitcases. Nothing else of any kind. The messenger will try to return your things later."

"It has been a long wait," Davi said. "Allah be praised."

"Amen," Petraea added.

It was Thursday afternoon when Freddy remembered that the Neville Brothers were going to sign their book in the shop on Saturday night. "There's nothing I can do about it now," he told his secretary, Francis. "Tell them I got sick. No, just say I'm sorry. They don't know me. They aren't going to get their feelings hurt."

"Okay. Okay. We can handle it. I just wish you wouldn't schedule these things if you aren't going to be here to help. We could have two thousand people, for God's sake. I'll be awake for nights thinking about it. They'll tear up the store."

"We can straighten the store. We sell books for a living, Francis. We can't afford to sell only ones we wish people will read. Don't be a snob."

"I like their music, some of it."

"Well, there you are. I'm taking Little Freddy to Willits, Francis.

He never gets to go without the girls so he never gets to be there in peace and quiet."

"He's three years old. Three-year-olds don't want peace and quiet."

"He might if he ever knew what it was like."

In New York City Carlton Rivers was arguing with Lynn Fadiman. They were in a bar on Third Avenue drinking martinis. It was past two o'clock in the afternoon and they had been arguing for two hours. "Don't drink any more of that," Lynn said. "We've got to be sober when we talk to the police."

"We're going to drag the condominium into this before it's over. I know we will. It will get out, Lynn. It will be in the papers."

"What about me? I've been snooping through someone's apartment. But I'm taking my chances. This is duty, plain and simple. That's it. Let's eat something and go on over there and tell them what we know."

Carlton got up from the bar stool and left his third martini untouched on the bar. They walked off to a table a waiter had ready for them. Carlton went back to the bar and retrieved the martini just before the waiter wasted it. "I'm drinking this," he told Lynn. "Goddammit, Lynn, I'm not a lush. You're right, civic duty is the price we pay and I was raised to honor that. We're going. Order something fast. Let's get a steak. Let's have some ballast. They could keep us there all afternoon."

An hour and a half later they were in the office of an assistant district attorney for upper Manhattan talking to a man who was listening very carefully. He was not acting like they were crazy. He was not interested in why they took prints or anything else. As soon as he saw Freddy Harwood's name on the list he began to fit the pieces into place. He had been part of the team that tracked down the writer Adrien Searle's killers. They had killed her by mistake while trying to get to Salman

Rushdie's American publisher. The district attorney even recognized the date of Holly Knight's accident in Arkansas as the date when the murderers were finally locked away in a maximum-security prison.

"I'm sending a team over to dust this apartment seventeen," he told Carlton. "I don't want any fuss. The quieter the better. Can you trust the doormen? The supervisor? How long have you known them? We'll have to do background checks on them, but until we do I don't want them to know anything. Can you get my men in without anyone knowing they're there?"

"Sure," Carlton said. "When do you want to leave?"

"We have to hope they'll come back. You understand that. That's why the secrecy."

"What about the owners? Can you find out who they are?" While Carlton was speaking, a secretary came in and handed the assistant district attorney a note.

"They don't exist," he said to Carlton. "You guys were had. They aren't there. Just the money, being paid from Swiss accounts. By next month it will be gone, like smoke, no more condo fees, I'm afraid."

"Mr. Rivers's sister is married to an Arab," Lynn put in. "You'll come across that. She married a wealthy Saudi and they raise Thoroughbred horses in Virginia, when they're in the United States. We discussed it coming over here and decided we'd better tell you about that."

"Is this relevant?"

"They don't speak to each other. Mr. Rivers tried to prevent the marriage. The sister's fifteen years younger. He was trustee of her estate. If this concerns Saudi Arabians, he thinks he might also be a target. It's just an idea."

"This has nothing to do with Saudi Arabia. This is about Iran. It's part of an ongoing problem. Maybe a group called Medina or Fire From Heaven. They're enforcers. They killed a woman writer four years ago, by mistake. Got the wrong target. They were after the man who published Salman Rushdie in the United States and killed his girlfriend instead. We caught those bastards, some of them, and threw their butts in a federal prison. I can't believe we couldn't get a death sentence. Chickenshit judges, covering their asses. People are afraid of these guys, Lynn, and with good cause. Here's the other thing. One of the people on the list you found is the owner of the bookstore that the publisher and the writer they killed, this Adrien Searle, had just been visiting. He had just had dinner with them. The bookstore owner, Freddy Harwood, is an heir to the Sears Roebuck fortune. He had his store bombed when *Satanic Verses* was published and the death decree went down. So he's been in this all along. He's always been a target. This is a list of the officers of the Independent Booksellers Association. They've already killed one of them, Holly Knight, the president of the group. Well, they won't kill the others. Okay, let's get cracking. How can you get two or three men inside the apartment in the quietest way?"

"Have them come to my apartment as electricians, workers, and we'll go up the back stairs. I have a key an ex-owner gave me. The locks haven't been changed on the back."

"What about the hit list?" Lynn asked. "Are you going to talk to the other two people on the list?"

"The CIA and FBI are already on it. It's the first thing I did. You both are considered sworn to secrecy. Don't tell this at a cocktail party tonight."

The FBI put four men on Freddy Harwood and even considered warning him, but decided against it. If they could catch the killers trying to make the hit it would be better. Warning people did no good. They always tipped off the assassins. No one can act normally when they think they've been targeted.

The helicopter that passed over the house at Willits and scared away the wildlife was not looking for marijuana.

*   *   *

Saturday, September 23, dawned clear and cold all across the American West. In Las Vegas the men who had set out to kill Freddy were in a happier frame of mind. They had been taken by limousine to a ranch sixty miles from town and were being treated as honored guests by a Medina sympathizer and former Olympic boxer who had retired to raise cutting horses in the desert. Their host was an elegant, vicious man who had seen to it that everything they wanted was within their reach, including several young blond girls who were working their way through modeling school in Vegas. Davi and Petraea took advantage of these gifts, but Abu asked only to go riding in the desert. He woke before the sun rose and said his prayers and went to the stables where a groom was waiting with a big, gray stallion. By the time he was in the saddle, the owner rode up to join him. The groom ran ahead opening the gates, and they rode out into the beautiful morning.

"You are sad that it could not be on the perfect day, but Allah knows what he is doing, Abu. Your prey is waiting. It will not be taken from you. Blessed be the name of Allah. Allah be praised."

"What time does our plane leave this afternoon?"

"At two. We'll get you there. When we return we will eat and then leave. I wish I could go with you. I would like to be the one to draw the knife across his throat. This one is the Jew?"

"We hack away at the legs while the true infidel sits in splendor in London being idolized by dogs."

"Come, let's ride down into the arroyo. This is beautiful country, Abu. I am honored to show it to you."

In Berkeley, Nora Jane and Freddy were putting Tammili and Lydia's gear into the Volvo while Little Freddy sat in the car seat complaining.

"I'm hot," he kept saying. "Where them going to?"

"We're going to a Girl Scout Jamboree because we are junior counselors. We help the little girls learn things they have to know."

Tammili climbed in the backseat beside him and gave him a big kiss on the cheek. "You have to do without us for two days."

"You all don't have to take us," Lydia said. "We aren't going very far. Why are all three of you taking us to Golden Gate Park?"

"Because we're going on to Willits. We've got our gear in the back."

Freddy locked the front door and got into the driver's seat and started down the driveway. "I forgot the stuff in the refrigerator," Nora Jane said. Freddy stopped the car and waited while she ran back into the house and got the milk and lunch she had packed. He was so accustomed to waiting on women he didn't even sigh. He looked out across the street and examined the neighbors' yards. He was learning patience. If there was a heaven he was a shoo-in, he was always telling his best friend, Nieman. A man who lives with three women is a humble man.

So he was watching as the BMW 750 came down the street going ten miles an hour and turned into the Musselmans' driveway and stopped. Since the Musselmans were in Europe for the fall, Freddy thought that was out of whack and picked up the phone and called the Neighborhood Watch and reported it. He picked out the first three numbers of the license plate as he drove by a few minutes later and called that in also. There were three men in the car. Just sitting in the driveway. Not good, Freddy decided. Doesn't make sense.

Information was going everywhere. The Neighborhood Watch alerted the police who told the FBI within minutes. The men in the BMW called Abu while they were waiting for Freddy to leave his driveway.

The Harwood family drove off in the beautiful morning light. Little Freddy had figured out that Lydia and Tammili were leaving him and he was in a bad mood about that. Lydia slipped him a handful of Teddy Grahams and that cheered him up some but not completely. They always went off and left him. He couldn't figure out what he was doing wrong.

"Would you make me a baby coffee?" he asked in a pitiful little voice. Baby coffee was his name for chocolate milk in a baby bottle.

"Not now, sweetie pie," Lydia said. "We're going to Jamboree. Can I make baby coffee in the car? Think about it. Do you see a refrigerator in here?"

"Momma has some. She's got some."

"He needs to stop drinking so much chocolate milk," Tammili declared. "He's getting too fat. He's outgrown all his clothes. We need to start giving him juices and water. He never drinks water."

When Abu and the owner got back to the ranch, the plans had been changed. "They're sending a plane to take you sooner," the owner told Abu after he read a long e-mail. "You need to get ready. The Jew has left town. They are following him. Wake the others and tell them to get packed."

Many things were happening in and around the house in Willits. The ground was still shifting due to the five point two that had rocked San Francisco the week before. Because of that, the doors and windows in the house were getting out of alignment. Not badly, just enough so it was difficult to raise and lower the screens or to lock the sliding glass doors.

In a ravine a mile from the house an FBI truck was setting up for business. In nearby Fort Bragg, California, two helicopters and their crews were on standby. A third helicopter was already taking reconnaissance photographs.

A satellite was also filming the area.

Seven men were now in charge of Freddy's safety. Three were watching the house at Willits and the remaining four were following him in two vehicles. One vehicle was staying within sight of Freddy and his family. The other was three miles ahead.

★   ★   ★

Abu and Davi and Petraea were in a Ford Explorer driving behind the FBI men but they did not know that was what they were doing. They thought they were alternately following and being followed by a group of gay men and it enraged Davi, who was driving, to have to keep changing lanes with the Chevrolet carrying the FBI people. The FBI men had taken off their coats and loosened their ties in order to seem inconspicuous. Something about the closeness and quietness of the men drove Davi to decide they were gay. He was still in a heightened sexual state due to his days on the ranch. He had also caught a sexually transmitted disease but he wouldn't know that for several weeks. "I can't stand to see them," he told Petraea. "This country is so foul. All foul things are here and nothing is done to stop them."

"How long have you been here now?" Petraea asked.

"Fifteen years. Only twice did I go home and see my family. Allah is great. He has given me this to do in his service. I do not complain about my exile."

"Do not look at them," Abu said from the backseat. "It looks suspicious to stare at other motorists. The police will stop us thinking we are in road rage. And don't break the speed limit. There are weapons with us now."

Davi slowed down and let the FBI get ahead. "But they will get ahead and we can't find them."

"Sensors are on the car. I can pick them up. Besides, we know where they are going. The man has a shack up in the hills where he goes sometimes on weekends. We are sure that's their destination. We have a man up there watching for us."

The fourth Iranian was parked at a small filling station and grocery store at the turn-off from the highway up into the sandy dirt roads that led to Freddy's house. He had already been waiting long enough to read three newspapers and begin on a magazine. He had told the store owner he had to wait until his engine cooled down. But this was taking too long. He read two articles in the magazine, went in and thanked the owner and bought some potato chips and went back to his car and began to drive slowly up the dirt road. When he was half a mile from the FBI truck he pulled the car behind a large outcrop and turned off the motor and went to sleep. He set an alarm on his watch for twenty minutes. He was very tired. He had not slept the night before. It was difficult work and he did not like not knowing what it was about.

Freddy speeded up to seventy and reached across and patted Nora Jane on the knee. Little Freddy was asleep in the backseat. They were on a two-lane highway that Freddy loved to drive. It had curves and wonderful cuts through the mountains and you could see the history of the land laid bare. He knew it bored Nora Jane to be lectured on geology so he spared her that and told the story to himself. When it was my best friend, Nieman, and myself, we could stop and look at rocks, he thought, but those days are gone. We are married men with lives. He sighed, remembering the year when they built the house, driving up from Berkeley on the weekends in a pickup truck, sleeping in a tent, building fires, seeing stars, studying rocks.

The FBI men had dropped way back. The helicopter had them now and the point man was in place. They could take their time.

In the Explorer Abu was going over their plans. "I want to make sure of the destination," he said. "Although it could be no place else now that he's on this road. He's a creature of habit. Then we will circle around on a connecting road that leads to the house. Then we wait until dark. We go in after midnight and take him without hurting the others. All communication lines will be cut and the car disabled. We leave him in the meadow below the house and walk back to the car and drive to an airport near Fort Bragg. A plane is there already on the ground, waiting. It will take us to catch the planes to Wisconsin."

"Allah calls for blood," Davi muttered. "Allah is thirsty for the blood of infidels."

"Don't preach, Davi," Abu answered. "We have not become Baptists yet. You should not watch those preachers on television so much or listen to them on the radio stations. I have been meaning to talk to you about that. You must keep your mind clean to do your work. Also, it is bad for your English and makes you say strange things. It is not good to call attention to yourself. They do not like us here."

Freddy turned onto the gravel and dirt road that led to his house. The bumping woke Little Freddy and Nora Jane gave him his bottle of baby coffee to get him back to sleep.

When they arrived at the house, they began to unpack the car. The helicopter had its camera trained on them and missed the two minutes it took Davi, Petraea, and Abu to get out of their car and start on foot down into a dry riverbed and begin to walk the back way to Freddy's house. There was still foliage on the trees near the dry river. It had been a wet summer and the river had been full for months. The trees had had a banner year. Now they waved their leaves above the assassins and hid them from every camera.

"We've lost the ragheads," the FBI agent in charge yelled. "Speed it up. They're gone. The goddamn sand niggers have fucking disappeared. Let's go. Let's get to the house."

By the time Freddy and Nora Jane had unpacked the car and opened the house and turned on the solar fans and started running water to clear the pipes there were men hidden all around them. Abu, Davi, and Petraea were in a stand of Douglas fir and madrone trees below the house. They were only thirty feet from the mountain lion's den but they did not know that. The lion had been gone all day foraging near the falls to the west of the riverbed.

The FBI men were out of their car and spread out in a fan along the front of the house. The FBI helicopter was frantically trying to find the men it had lost but was only coming up with the man asleep in his car.

The satellite picked up the lion and got some really good footage of him crossing a sump below the falls, heading for home.

Little Freddy was playing on the back stairs while Freddy watched. Nora Jane was putting groceries away and wondering how the girls were getting along at the science museum.

At five o'clock the sun was still high in the sky and people were getting sleepy. Everyone was getting sleepy except Little Freddy, who had slept so long in the car there was no hope of him taking a nap.

"We'll spell each other," Freddy said. "You nap first and then I'll nap. I want to take him down to the edge of the woods and leave some food for Alabama. You don't mind if I take him that far, do you?"

"Take the gun then, will you? Wear the holster and cover it up. I don't want him to see it but I want you to take it."

"I don't know about that. What's the big secret? If you have a gun you explain it to them."

"All right. I'm going up and sleep in the loft."

Freddy got the .38 revolver out of the glove compartment of the car and checked to make sure it had shells. He had never owned a gun until Adrien Searle was killed in a hotel in Berkeley after reading at Clara Books. Adrien's death had wiped out a lot of Berkeley liberal bullshit. He had bought a gun, and both he and Nora Jane had learned to use it.

Freddy put on the shoulder holster, put the gun in the holster, and then opened the trunk and got out an old photojournalist's vest to use to cover it. He zipped up the vest and walked to where Little Freddy was arranging rocks on the bottom steps of the stairway.

*   *   *

From the stairs there was a wonderful view of the woods with the sky stretching out beyond them. There were always clouds in this vista, because of its nearness to the sea. It was a landscape that changed its colors all day long. In the center of the view was a rock outcrop where the old mountain lion Freddy called Alabama loved to come and sun himself. It was there that Freddy had first seen him. For fifteen years since that time he and Nieman had left treats on the rocks when they were there. It was a ritual.

Freddy had been an overprotected child who had not had a father to teach him to be brave. He had had to figure it out for himself or with Nieman's help. They figured it out intellectually as they did most things in their lives. If there was a wild animal who had the potential to be dangerous, they studied it and were cautious in their dealings with it.

Still, Freddy liked to walk down to the outcrop and leave dog treats on the rocks. He liked thinking of the old lion's pleasure when he came upon these windfalls. Also, he liked to believe that the lion could smell his hands on the treats and would know they were gifts from a friendly member of another species. Usually he carried a heavy walking stick and a can of Mace on these excursions. Now, rather than argue with Nora Jane, he had added the gun.

"Would you like to walk with me down to where the old lion lives?" Freddy asked his son. "We can take him some dog treats and leave them on his rock and then we can sit on the balcony and watch to see if he comes to get them."

"Like dog food?" Little Freddy asked, looking up from his rock work. He had lined up ten rocks to make a rock family.

"Better than dog food. These are dog treats, very special. To animals these are like candy. See, they come in different colors, like the cereal Grandmother Annie gives you when our backs are turned."

Little Freddy studied the box of dog treats. If there was one thing he really liked to do it was get his grandmother's poodle's dog food and go behind the sofa and eat it. If his grandmother or her maid caught him they went crazy. They ran around and yelled and held their hands up in the air. Dog food was good! It was hard, like eating salty rocks, and you could keep it in your mouth a long time, like the gum the baby-sitter gave him once. Like those round chewing gums they never let him get out of machines, only once that baby-sitter had gotten him some, and he had never forgotten it.

"You remember that baby-sitter that time that give me that gum?" he asked his father.

"Well, these aren't for you to eat, son. These are for our friend, Alabama. He isn't our friend really. He's a wild creature and we have to be careful, but we can go and leave him treats. He doesn't care about us one way or the other. He hunts for a living."

"Well, okay. If you let me carry the box."

"Okay. Let's go." Freddy held out his hand.

"Wait a minute. I got to put the daddy rock on the top." Little Freddy picked up the largest rock in his collection and put it on the highest step he could reach from the ground. Then he stepped back to look at his creation.

"What are they doing?" Freddy asked.

"Them are watching *The Wizard of Oz.*"

"Who all is there?"

"Momma rock, daddy rock, sister rocks, these ones are friend rocks that came over to play, this one is the baby-sitter rock." He held up a pretty granite formation split to show pink inside. His favorite baby-sitter wore pink all the time. It was her signature color. Freddy shook his head in wonder.

"Okay," Little Freddy said. "Let's go down there then."

They started down the long sloping hill to the woods, thick stands of Douglas fir and cedar and madrone trees. They were the pride of the property and the reason Freddy and Nieman had chosen this piece of land on which to build their house. It was virgin woods, sprung up when the cataclysms that built Northern California had stopped long enough for plants to begin to grow. "Birds brought these seeds," Nieman loved to say. "Or they were carried on the hides of animals or blew in with the wind. It is dazzling to imagine how it came here."

"Uncle Nieman says birds brought the seeds that made those trees grow here," Freddy began. "We should get some of the seedlings and plant them in town. Would you like to do that with me?"

"Is the lion going to eat this whole box of treats?" Little Freddy asked. "Every one of them?"

"Well, he's a pretty big lion, for mountain lions. He's old. He probably isn't a very good hunter anymore. He's probably hungry a lot of the time and he needs a treat. I have some treats for you at the house. When we get back we'll have them."

"What treats do you have for me?" He was hoping it was gum but he knew it would not be.

"Well, some oatmeal cookies for one thing, with raisins in them. And some graham crackers for another."

Davi saw them coming. "Allah brings the man to us," he said. "Now it is revealed." And he thought suddenly that his whole life had been lived for this moment, when he, Davi, who had been sent from his mother at the age of seven to live in the hard camp and learn a warrior's ways, who had been beaten and despised and risen up from his despair and become so good at his work that he was chosen to go to the United States to do Allah's work on earth and earn his way to heaven, he, Davi, now stood moments away from that reward. Allah is good, he knew. And he rewards the faithful.

"Abu, can we take him with the child watching, or must we wait?"

Abu bowed his head. He was quiet for a long moment while he sought help in prayer. "Now," he said finally. "Allah guides us. We will follow. You, Petraea. Take him quick. I will get the child out of the way."

The old lion moved back toward his den smelling the sack of treats that was moving his way. Nieman and Freddy had been leaving them for fifteen years. Occasionally, he walked out of the woods and sunned himself on the rock outcrop visible from the house. That was the whole encounter for all those years. A bowl of dog treats on a vertical uplift near an old madrone. A lion walking out and sunning himself within smell of men.

But these smells were confused. The good smell of the treats and the familiar smell of Freddy's photojournalist vest, then another smell, of fear and musk and oiled guns. The lion knew that smell and knew its danger.

The lion moved through the high grass and out onto the glade until he was about twenty feet from Davi and Petraea.

He stopped and waited.

Freddy was almost to the outcrop where he always left the treats. It was a group of three large rocks with an opening in the center. On top was a large flat rock with an indentation like a bowl in the middle.

Petraea moved a few feet. The lion moved with him.

Freddy sat Little Freddy on a flat rock and let him fill the stone bowl with the treats. Little Freddy filled the bowl half full, then took a blue treat and raised it to his mouth, watching his father as he did it.

"You know better than that," Freddy said. "Those treats are for animals. We have human treats at home for boys."

Little Freddy held the blue treat up into the air, then dropped it into the bowl and continued very slowly filling the bowl from the sack.

Petraea moved several feet, then stepped out in view of the rocks and raised the rifle. Little Freddy saw the lion before he saw Petraea. He saw both of them before Freddy did. He was looking right at Petraea when the lion leaped on the man and began to mangle him.

Freddy threw himself on top of Little Freddy and pushed the child down into the crevice between the rocks. He took out the revolver and stood up and raised it. He did not want to shoot a man or a lion or anything that lived, but he shot. He shot at the lion's flank and then the field was full of men. Two men were on top of him and talking.

"FBI," one of them said. "We are here to help you. Don't move. Where's the child?"

Behind them two other men were running into the woods. The old lion was heading down a path to the river, disappearing like a streak of sunlight.

"Did I hit Alabama?" Freddy asked. "God, I hope I didn't hit the lion."

"He ran off all right," the agent said. "I don't think you could have hurt him much."

Little Freddy was still in the crevice. It was a nice, roomy place. He had brought the sack with the remaining treats with him and was lining some of them up on a ledge in front of him. He put two on the ledge and then he started eating some. He was eating a blue one and a reddish one. They were good. He liked them almost as much as he liked his grandmother's dog food that she kept in the closet in her big house with the big pool.

Nora Jane heard the shots and came running out onto the balcony. She stopped and looked and then ran down the stairs and then down the pasture as fast as she could run.

"Let me go," Freddy said. "She'll be hurt." But an FBI man got to her first and took her arm and began to explain what had happened. "Your husband and child are all right, Mrs. Harwood," he said. "Everything is under control. Let me take you back to the house."

"I want my child," she said. "I'm going to my child."

*　　　*　　　*

By the time she got to the outcrop Little Freddy had his mouth full of dog treats. "What are you eating?" she said. "Oh, my God, what do you have in your mouth?"

"Sometimes when they eat things like that you need to get their sodium and potassium checked," the young officer began. "We had a problem with one of ours eating dirt after it rained. It turned out he was low on sodium because of some allergy medication we were giving him."

Petraea had been mauled but not badly. His left cheek was cut and there was a long tear on his upper arm and he had sprained an ankle. The medevac crew decided to helicopter him to Fort Bragg before they stitched up the wounds. "I don't want to go sewing that up until we culture some of the saliva," the young M.D. decided. "We'll clean it and wrap it and take him on in."

"His blood pressure's very low," a male nurse insisted. "I think he's in shock. How are we going to sedate him? I think we should get the truck and do it here."

"Well, it's not your call," the M.D. said. "Goddammit to hell, I'm the doctor here."

It took several hours for the National Guard and the FBI to find Davi. The Guard brought in German shepherds and they tracked him to a madrone tree. He was covered with insect bites by the time they got him down. He was armed with a Ruger and an old Ortigies caliber 7.65 but he did not shoot when the tree was surrounded. It seemed somehow not to be worth the trouble and besides he was tired and very hungry.

Abu had been harder to take. In the struggle he had wounded a young guardsman from Petaluma. The young man would never throw a football again or hold a woman against his chest without pain. He would try playing soccer with a group of wealthy men in Marin but it would never be the same. Still, he would have five hundred thousand dollars in corporate bonds with which to build a great house with a recreation room in which to watch other men play sports, and that was something. Fortunately, both his children were girls. It's not as if he had a son he could have taught to be a quarterback.

They had surrounded Abu in a grove of young trees. The dogs had him. There had been no need for the young man to go in but Abu had shot a dog and the young man had gone crazy and charged. He shot Abu in the leg before Abu got off the shot that ruined his arm. After he was down one of the big dogs came over and lay down beside him and whimpered like a child. It had been the young man's job to care for the dogs and he was fond of them and they of him.

"Is this ever going to end?" Nora Jane asked. It was several days later. They were at home in Berkeley, in their own home, in their bedroom. "If it isn't we have to go somewhere and change our names. I can't live like this, Freddy. I want you to take Salman's books out of the store and put an ad in all the papers saying you won't carry them. If you don't do that I will take the children and go away. I will not be part of this. I am not a revolutionary or a political person."

"The death decree was lifted. This sect is a bunch of crazies. They have to have enemies to exist. I was just in the line of fire."

"They killed Holly Knight. We had dinner with her in Portland last summer at the Association meeting. Adrien Searle, then Holly Knight, that's two people that we *knew*. And Little Freddy was there when armed men came running out from all directions. I think he'll remember that. Plus, the girls know everything because it was in the papers. God knows what it will do to them to know their parents were almost killed in a Holy War."

"I'll sell the store, Nora Jane, if that's what you want. I'll call a broker and put Clara Books on the market. Say the word. If you want me to, I will."

"I don't know. Let me think about it."

"Are we going to New York still?"

"Yes. I think we are. I have a lesson with Delaney this afternoon. She's been calling every day. She thinks you should give in and take the books out of the store. It's not as if they were asking you to quit selling Shakespeare."

"It's the principle. I'll sell the store but I won't refuse to stock books because of terrorist threats."

"Then sell it. Principles are abstractions. I'm talking about live children, live lives."

"Then I'll sell it."

"Then I want you to."

They were in their bedroom. The drapes were drawn back. A cool blue sky was visible through the windows. It was eleven o'clock in the morning.

"Arabs and Palestinians have their side to things," Nora Jane said. "They have families. They eat and sleep and need houses and security, they need part of that goddamn sand the Jews were crazy to want in the first place. Peace is never going to happen over there until the Israelis give back some of the sand. But I live here, in Northern California, in the richest country in the world and I won't be involved in that mess. I have one political idea. To protect my children. You can help me with that or I'll go away and do it by myself."

"I'll do whatever you want me to do."

"This is it, Freddy. This is how the world works." She opened the sliding glass doors that opened onto her walled garden, which was modeled on the Japanese garden at the Metropolitan Museum of Art. She went out and sat upon a bench and looked at the designs in the windows of the wall and she thought about the carpenter who had made them for her and she thought about design and patterns and how space was bent into time and the heart of matter and the universe of stars and all the work there was to do to get ready to go to New York and the reality of evil and how it never leaves the world, never, never, never goes away. Greed, envy, cruelty, hunger, disease, and death.

And in the face of that, beauty, "the frail, the solitary lance." I will sing my heart out for that audience, Nora Jane decided. I will walk out on the stage in my blue velvet dress and for a moment beauty will win and I will be its helper.

The old lion could still smell the dog treats on the stone. The two pieces Little Freddy had left in the crevice were still on the ledge where he put them. The lion had bloodied his paw trying to get them a few days before so now he just climbed up on the flattest stone and rested in the smell and the warmth from the sun. He had eaten well the night before, a snake he caught by the falls and a crippled rabbit he found in the woods. Hunger was leaving him alone on this fine September day and he fell into a light sleep. A memory of spring came to him, waking up and moving out into a field deep with grass. The smell of flowers and a den high on a bluff.

It was some days later. Nora Jane was in her house being talked to by a man in a suit who had once been the star of a college track team. It was very hard to be in Nora Jane's presence without being distracted, but the man was trying. "You are being guarded twenty-four hours a day by the best and most highly trained men and women in the world," the man was saying.

They were in the sunken living room with the pianos. There was a tray with tea and cookies. There was a pitcher of lemonade and tall frosted glasses and a plate of lime and lemon slices. Nora Jane was wearing a yellow play dress and her hair was pulled back into a bun like a dancer's. A yellow flower was in the bun.

Tammili and Lydia were listening from the upstairs balcony, sitting very quietly on the floor, not hiding, just being quiet.

"You are being guarded as if you were the president of the United States," the man continued. "This is the treatment we give federal judges when they are threatened. We don't think there is a threat to you. We think we have most of the group. The one named Davi is talking his head off. An Afro-American preacher got to him on a television show. We've been letting him watch television as long as he keeps on cooperating. I don't think he's playing us. We think he's spilling his guts. It's a huge windfall. It's what we wait for. We've got this shrink talking to him. Davi's telling him about the camps where he was raised. He's crying all the time. Everything he's told us so far checks out. The position of the camps, the number of personnel, everything. We think we have rounded up the entire group in the United States. I don't think you have anything to worry about, Mrs. Harwood. We think we can keep you safe."

"If we go to New York?"

"You'll be safe there. We'll have personnel in the hotel. We will stay on this. We have orders to stay on it."

"Please have lemonade. I made it an hour ago. It's very good, I think. Please let me pour you some."

"There's one other thing." The agent took the lemonade and sipped it. "The man in New York City who found the list is a retired surgeon. He knows about your concert. He asked if he could meet you when you're there, after your concert, of course. It's unprofessional of me to give you this message but he's been hounding us to get in touch with you. He's from New Orleans originally. He knew your father or something."

"My father died in the Vietnam War."

"We know about that. Well, I just wanted to give you his name if you ever want to call him."

"Okay. Give it here." She waited, here it was, the part she hated about performing. But this man had been instrumental in saving Freddy's life. And he had known her father. It might be all right to talk to someone about that at last.

"His name is Dr. Rivers. I'll write it down for you." The agent took a pad and pencil from his pocket and wrote down a name and address and handed it to her.

"I'll write to him," Nora Jane said. "Thank you for giving this to me."

"This lemonade is fine. I haven't had a lemonade in many years. It's good. It's really good."

"Let me pour you some more." Nora Jane leaned over and poured the lemonade. She was so near the agent that for a moment he thought that he might faint. It was all right for someone to be that beautiful, he decided, but it takes some getting used to for a working man.

"We're going to New York," Tammili declared. "She's going to do it."

"I knew she would. She's brave, Tammili. She only worries because of us."

"Let's call Grandmother Ann and get her to take us shopping. She's the only one who's going to let us buy something we really like to wear up there."

"She's the best one to shop with."

"Let's call her now."

"Okay."

FAULT LINES

A NOVELLA

1

NORA JANE was swooping around the room picking up coats and gloves and hats, pushing pillows back into place, scowling so deeply she wasn't even pretty anymore, much less one of the most beautiful women most of the people in the world had ever seen.

"Slow down, Momma," Tammili said. "Go out in the kitchen and find us something for lunch. We can't cure Daddy's cancer this morning. We can't do anything now but wait."

"Right," Lydia agreed. She always agreed with her twin sister about how to handle their mother. "Little Freddy's coming home at noon today. We've got to get our act together before he gets here. He'll go crazy if he thinks we're worried."

"He knows we're worried." Nora Jane put down the pillow she was holding and sat down on a sofa beside her daughters. It had been an hour since they had returned from the internist's office with the really bad news that the white-cell problem Freddy Harwood had been fighting for twenty months was now officially and finally leukemia, and it was time for chemotherapy and radiation and the search for a bone marrow donor.

"Donor, dolor, as in grief and sorrow," Tammili had said on the drive home. Tammili was deep into a poetry-writing mode and was learning words by the hundreds. The problem with learning them was finding ways to use them in conversation. "Little Freddy knows we were going to Danen's office this morning because he answered the phone when the nurse called. He wanted to stay home from school because he said we didn't look 'wite.' "

"He has to stop doing that or he has to go to speech therapy. You and Daddy are indulging him by laughing at it," Lydia said. Lydia considered herself in charge of her five-year-old brother. She thought she was the only person in the family who took Little Freddy's future seriously. Actually it was her own future she was really worried about, due to a very poor showing on a PSAT test she had taken in the spring. Lydia thought she was dumb. Compared to her fraternal twin, Tammili, she was dumb, but compared to the rest of the sixteen-year-old people in the world, she was way up there in the ninetieth percentile for verbal skills and the eighty-fourth for math and science.

"I'm going to make some tuna-fish salad and some slice-and-bake cookies," Nora Jane said. "Who wants to help?"

"I will," Tammili said. "Lydia needs to do her homework. We have to go back for fourth period. We shouldn't cut geology and history."

"Come on, then." Nora Jane got up. Tammili stood up beside her and took her arm and they walked into the kitchen. Lydia sighed deeply and went into her room to study plate tectonics. It was really pretty interesting given the fact that they lived right on top of the most active fault line in the United States, maybe the world. Their neighborhood in Berkeley was so exactly on the fault line it was almost a joke.

"It's live or die time," Freddy Harwood's best friend, Nieman, was saying. He and Freddy were on the balcony outside Freddy's study. Nora Jane had called Nieman from the doctor's office and he was waiting when they got home. Nieman was teaching at Berkeley now, but he had canceled his day's classes and walked out without remembering to tell his wife, Stella. She had found out he was gone and canceled his class cancellations and was teaching them herself. She hadn't called

Nieman to find out the details. She already knew. She had known for five months that Freddy's "problem" was going to end up being called cancer, but she had kept her mouth shut about it except for one night when she was drinking wine. "That's leukemia you're describing," she had said to Nieman.

"No, it is not!" Nieman said. "My God, Stella, don't even say that."

"Okay," she said. "All right, whatever you say. I'm sorry. What do I know? I'm not a medical doctor."

"You're the best biochemist on the West Coast," Nieman said. "But he doesn't have leukemia, Stella. It's a blood disorder and they'll fix it with cortisone. He eats health food, for God's sake. He works out."

Stella had let it go at that. She wasn't taking a chance on harming her marriage to Nieman by being the harbinger of this bad news.

"Denial's not going to work on this one, is it?" Freddy was saying. "It's trenching time, old buddy. Dig deep, and all that. I don't think I'm going to die. I can't imagine dying, never have been able to, never have believed anyone's dead—Shakespeare, Leonardo, Daddy, your dad—anyone who was really here. I'm not making much sense yet."

"Tons of sense."

"So it's definitely live. I wonder who they'll find for a donor. It's painful. Imagine anyone doing that for a stranger."

"What if it's one of the girls?"

"It won't be. Danen's ruled them out."

"It might be me. Our ancestors came from the same part of France. I'm sure everyone at Touro Synagogue will try out."

"It's not a play, Nieman."

"Don't be so sure. It might turn out to be. What if it's someone we don't like, Joe Diel or old Leo Thalberg? That would be a nice turn."

"How did you get away on a Wednesday, Nieman? Don't you have classes?"

"I canceled them. I'm staying for lunch. Come on, let's go join Nora Jane. Don't have that look. I haven't missed a class since I started teaching at Berkeley. I have so much accumulated leave I could go to the Galápagos for a vacation, something we should think about doing very soon."

Freddy touched his best friend's arm, not much, and not for long, just a touch, then he held the door and let Nieman precede him through the two-million-dollar architectural dream in which he and Nora Jane lived their perfect life with their good children. "Live," he kept saying under his breath. It was going to be the mantra. He had tried "Om Mani Padme Hum" all the way home in the car and it had held up, but he thought maybe now he'd just get something quicker. Breathe? Live? Please?

"What Salinger book has that Jesus prayer that Franny Glass kept using?" he asked. "You know, where she's having the nervous breakdown on the sofa while the painters are painting the apartment?"

"*Franny and Zooey*," Nieman answered. "Remember when Janie Gugleman was writing that paper on Salinger and she got obsessed with counting the times characters lit cigarettes in the book? She's president of a women's college in Georgia now. Can you believe that? She sends me the alumnae magazine. She's always on the cover looking beautiful beside some visiting dignitary."

Freddy was quiet, watching Nieman spin out anything he could find to fill the awful reality of the day. "We've had enormous lives," he said, looking at Nieman without hiding anything he was feeling. "We've had the best lives anyone could imagine and we're going to have plenty more. I'm not going to die, Nieman. They're letting me do the chemotherapy as an outpatient. If it was really acute they'd put me in the hospital right away. So stop worrying and let's go cheer up those women."

*   *   *

They went into the kitchen and pretended not to notice the scared faces trying to pretend they were normal people putting together a lunch, and then Freddy's mother's chauffeur, Big Judy, came in the back door with Little Freddy. It was two weeks before his sixth birthday. He had curly blond hair and deep blue eyes and a kind and serious demeanor. "He takes dominion everywhere," Nieman was fond of saying of Little Freddy. "He's a force of nature," his grandmother said.

"He can sing," a teacher told them. "You should train that voice."

"Why is everybody here?" Little Freddy asked. He walked straight to his father and put his hands on his father's knees. "What did they do to you at the doctor's office?"

"Gave me some bad news," his father said. "They said I have to have a lot of shots. I have to have about two hundred shots and the shots will make me well, but first they'll make me so sick I'll have to go to the hospital where Andean and Sivagamu work—and get this, I can't even have visitors for a while. I'll have to talk to people on the phone and look out the window at you. Bummer." He smiled widely as if he had just told Little Freddy the funniest joke he knew, then took the child into his arms. "You know what the worst thing is? The thing that's making me sick is the part of our blood that keeps us well. My blood is such a good fighter it has outdone itself, made itself too full of white-cell fighters and not enough good old red cells that run around carrying oxygen to our muscles. So, what can we do? We're all here to talk about how we'll keep the bookstore running and boss you kids around while I'm sick."

"I'm going to be the boss," Tammili said. "Because I'm the oldest."

"No one knows you're the oldest," Lydia said. "It was dark in the cabin and only Dad was there. He could barely keep everyone alive. It's a wonder we didn't all die and Momma isn't sure which one of us came first, so quit saying you are the oldest."

"She probably is the oldest," Nora Jane put in. "I thought you said you were going back to school after lunch."

"We are," Lydia said. "Come on, Tammy, we need to get going."

"We don't need a boss," Little Freddy said.

"I do," Nieman put in. "I need one every day. Or else I forget to give hugs to my uncles when they are right in the room." Little Freddy gave his father's cheek a kiss, then walked over to Nieman and moved into his embrace.

"Please eat lunch," Nora Jane said. "We have to vow to all be the healthiest people in the world so we can take care of Freddy while he fights this thing. We have to break any bad habits we have and start concentrating on the main important things in life."

"What are they?" Tammili couldn't stop herself from asking.

"Physical health, concentration, meditation, love, philosophy, poetry, literature, music, living in the moment," Freddy said.

"Breathing exercises," Nieman added. "Knowledge, learning, geology, astrophysics, medicine, caring, thinking, sleeping, children, anthropology, history, archaeology, history — I already said history, didn't I?"

"We have to get going," Tammili said. The twins kissed their parents and gathered up the small lightweight backpacks Nieman and Stella had given them for their sixteenth birthdays and went to the garage and got into their old Mercedes station wagon and drove off to return to school.

"Where are they going to put the shots?" Little Freddy asked.

"I don't know," Freddy answered. "I guess just in my arm but some people get shots in their hips, you know, and they say you can't even feel it if you get them there because the hips are so fat and strong."

"Let's go see about the hot-tub project, Little Freddy," Nieman said. "You can tell me if you're learning anything in kindergarten. I still think you ought to quit that school and just go to work at the lab with Stella and me. You're wasting too much time at that school."

Nieman and Little Freddy finished their tuna salad and rye bread and took their cookies and went off to look at the construction of the new hot tub on the stone porch overlooking the bay. The wide vista out across the water and into the Pacific Ocean was interrupted by the great red bridge and made especially beautiful today by a long string of cirrus clouds, so perfectly designed and moving so slowly in the balmy October air they seemed painted on the sky.

Two Hispanic men were at work setting beautiful smooth stones into the walls of the tub, which was so large it could hardly be called a hot tub anymore and should be called a hot pool. It was going to be fed by an underground spring the plumbers had found by accident while investigating what they thought was a leak. Nora Jane had had the idea of building a hot tub on top of the spring, which had led to a seven-month project that still was not finished.

"*Hola,*" Little Freddy said. "*¿Qué pasa, mis amigos?*"

"Come and look," they said in English, and Little Freddy and Nieman climbed down into the pool and inspected the stones.

"Carlito not coming today," the older man said. "He have to take his wife to the dentist for her teeth."

"Has to take," Little Freddy said, seriously. "He has to take."

"Has to take," the man repeated.

"*Bueno,*" Little Freddy said.

Nieman and Little Freddy took a seat beside the pool and watched the men working. They never talked much when they were together. Nieman had watched Little Freddy being born. They were deeply bonded.

In the kitchen, Nora Jane and Freddy were alone for the first time since the bad news had enveloped them like a cloud. They looked at each other for a long minute, then Nora Jane went to him and took his hands and held them against her chest. "It's live or die time," Freddy said. "I'm not going to lose my life, N.J. I don't feel that I'm going to. It's just going to be a long hell of a fight and we have to make it. I'll be out of it; you're the one who has to be strong. You may get mad at me for being sick. I think that's normal. We just have to live each day and see what happens. We have today. We have, for God's sake, this house, these children, this tuna salad, we have Nieman Gluuk, we have doctors, medicine, miracles. Ninety-nine percent of what we have is good and then we have this other thing with my white cells but that's not the main thing in our lives. It's just the battle we have to fight this winter and maybe this spring. Maybe summer."

Nieman came back into the kitchen. "I've got it," he said. "We need to call in Henry Wilkins. I mean it. We need some meditation updating. We can do it on Sunday nights, like we did in the seventies. I'm going to call Henry this afternoon."

"We're reverting to hippie bullshit?" Freddy started laughing. "We're calling in the gurus?"

"Meditation works," Nieman said. "It heals. It helps. We need all the help we can get."

Before he became a biochemist, Nieman Gluuk had been a film critic for the *San Francisco Chronicle*. He had spent ten years seeing every film ever made in the world plus all the ones that were being made. His ability to read body language was like radar, and what his radar told him now was that Nora Jane and Freddy wanted to be alone.

"I want to take Little Freddy down to the labs for an hour," he said. "Stella will still be there. I promise not to let him look through the electron microscope again. I'm really sorry about that. I never dreamed he'd take it so to heart."

"He scrubbed himself to death." Nora Jane giggled. "Then he forgot about it, I guess."

"Well, I'll be more careful. I'll have him back by five. Is it all right if he goes?"

"Sure. It will be good for him to get out of here until we get used to this."

Nieman took his leave, went to the balcony, retrieved the child, and hurried toward his automobile.

"So why were you correcting Diego's English?" Nieman asked. "I'm not fussing. I'm just asking."

"He told me to do it. He's trying to get good in English so he can run his business better. He told me he'd tell me Spanish and I could tell him if he says the wrong words."

"So what Spanish has he taught you so far?"

"A lot. He told me a bad word to call Charlie Isaacs if he's mean to me again. You want to hear it?"

"Sure."

"*Sirveengweeen sa.* It means something really bad. If you say it to someone in Mexico they have to kill you for saying it."

"I wouldn't say it at school if I were you. A lot of those teachers are bilingual."

"I might say it to Charlie though. If he hits me or something."

"If he hits you, you tell me and I'll tell his daddy. His daddy was a mean kid too. His daddy used to be mean to me." Nieman reached behind him and gave Little Freddy the high sign as well as he could from the front seat. "You're the best kid I've ever known, Freddy. If anyone is mean to you, you just call me up and I'll fix it."

"It's okay. Are we going to that smoothie place when we get done at your office? I really liked that smoothie you and Stella got me last time."

"We can get anything you want this week, old buddy. This week we do anything we think up to do." Nieman parked in the parking lot behind his office and got out and unbuckled Freddy and hand in hand they went into the building.

In the kitchen, Nora Jane moved into Freddy's arms and they held each other for a long time without speaking. She took one of his hands and moved it down her dress to her hips and then she began to make love to him.

"I don't know if this will work," he said.

"It might," she answered. "Let's go to bed."

He took her hand and led her to the fabulously beautiful bedroom they shared. They pushed all the clothes and toys off their bed and got into the bed and took off their clothes and moved their bodies until every inch of their skin touched. "Don't do anything," she said. "Just hold onto me." She was trying not to cry. She was trying as hard as she could try.

"Imagine Nieman bringing Henry over here," Freddy said. "Can you just see Stella's face when she finds out he's going hippie bullshit on us? No kidding, N.J., Henry's just the tip of the iceberg. There will be Buddhist monks and those nuns in Ohio he paid to pray for Leta when she got sick. I'd rein him in, but, Christ God, I have to go to the hospital on Monday. There may not be time."

"Leta got well. I saw her last week at a shop on College Avenue. She had a good-looking man carrying the bundles and she was just exactly like she used to be. She told me she was glad she got cancer because it made her appreciate her money."

"Don't move away. I want all of that arm just where I had it. I love your skin so much. If you knew. If you only knew."

"Be inside me, then," she said. "And don't worry about whether it's going to work. It feels like it's working to me."

Stella had dismissed Nieman's class early and gone back to her lab to check some messes she had going in a set of petri dishes. It was an antiviral she'd been playing around with for two years. She never talked about it and hadn't published any of the data. She was taking her time, playing with it in her spare time, watching it mutate, testing it against different cold and herpes strains.

It was her secret project, and even though several people in the department, and Nieman, knew what she was doing, they never asked her about it. Stella was their intuitive genius and people left her alone.

She was chewing a number-two lead pencil and staring at the dishes when Nieman and Little Freddy came into the room.

"Put gloves on him," she said when she turned around. "You too. Never mind, let's go in the office." She led the way out of the lab and down the hall and into her office. There was a jar of Hershey's candy on the desk, and Little Freddy went and stood beside it. "Have some," she said. "What's going on?"

"Poppa has to have a hundred shots," Little Freddy said. "He's going to put them in his hips so they won't hurt." He opened the top of the candy jar and took out one and then two and then three of the miniature candy bars. "Is this okay?"

Stella melted into love. She could stare at Little Freddy's head all day. It was a braincase she recognized.

"He's going in on Monday to begin chemotherapy," Nieman added. "We have to find a donor. I called Rabbi Felton. I'm sure the whole congregation will turn out. And of course they're searching the donor banks. It's just more likely to be someone with French Jewish ancestors."

"Not necessarily. You'd be surprised at how it's dispersed. It's genetic but it's also hugely random. There are nine common ancestors for eighty-seven percent of white male Europeans."

"I sort of half believe that."

Little Freddy had finished two of the pieces of candy and had started on the third. "I want to see the bugs on my skin again," he said.

"No!" Nieman and Stella both screamed. Then Stella said, "Have two more pieces of candy. You can't see the bugs again because they made you think your skin was dirty. It isn't dirty. It's inhabited by nice tiny little creatures that help keep you clean. Besides, we have to go to our house and see Scarlett. She's all by herself with the baby-sitter and she wants to see you. She likes you so much. She thinks you're the best boy in California. Get your candy and let's go."

Stella took off her lab coat and put on her suit jacket and Nieman took Freddy's hand and they started out of the room.

"So have you called the nuns yet?" Stella asked.

"No."

"Who have you called except the rabbi?"

"I called Henry. We're going to meditate on Sunday night. I have to do something, Stella. I can't just sit by and not do everything I can think of to do."

"I'm with you," she said. "I'll call the nuns myself. I'll call them tonight." She kissed her husband and took his other hand and they marched down to the car like a brigade.

Stella knew things about Nieman that she never talked about. She knew he had mystical, intuitive capabilities beyond those of anyone she had ever known, and she had studied with Freeman Dyson and worked for Crick at the labs in England.

She knew that some change had come over Nieman right around the time she met him that had profoundly altered his life. Everyone knew he had given up money and fame as the leading film critic on the West Coast and gone back to Berkeley to earn doctorates in bio-chemistry and physics in half the time it takes younger students. Everyone knew he had a photographic memory, but only Stella and Freddy Harwood had ever been privileged to watch him read when he decided to read really fast.

She knew his devotion to his friends and family. She knew he would kill or die for her or for their child and she knew that when he wanted to find something out he found it out that afternoon, or, at the latest, the next day.

So when they got to the house she paid the sitter and then left her three-year-old daughter with Little Freddy and Nieman and went into her office and sent a check for five hundred dollars to a group of Episcopal nuns in Ohio, who pray for cancer patients in their spare time. In their regular time they run a home for the children of AIDS victims and drug addicts. Even if the prayers didn't work, the money would not be wasted.

When she finished that letter, she e-mailed a young monk she knew at the San Francisco Buddhist Center and asked him to get her an appointment with Lama Doge as soon as possible. She liked Nieman's friend Henry Wilkins, but if they were going to call in Buddhists she thought they ought to find one from Tibet.

Stella went back to the room where Nieman was playing with the children.

"You don't think he could have touched anything in my lab, do you? I don't mean to guilt you about not gloving him. I just mean, I ought to go wipe things down if he could have left anything in there."

"We just came in the door. We didn't go near the tables. Listen, Scarlett's hungry and so is Little Freddy and so am I. Let's go to Chez Panisse and get some fish and vegetables. It's a good time of day. No one will be there."

"Okay. Let's go. What are they doing over there?"

"He's playing cards with her. She turns one over and he keeps saying, 'You win!' She's crazy about it." Nieman went across the room and picked up his little girl and told Little Freddy to bring the cards. "Hurry up, before Stella changes her mind and wants to use the money to pay someone's tuition. She's letting us go to Chez Panisse."

*　　*　　*

Freddy woke before Nora Jane and lay on his side looking at the cascade of black curls that fell across her shoulders and down her back. N.J.'s hair had always seemed to him like a dream that had somehow managed to invade his consciousness so he would believe in beauty.

He rose up enough to see the clock and slipped out of the bed and put on his clothes and shoes and went into the kitchen to wait for Tammili and Lydia to come home from school. It was past five o'clock. This was the day they stayed late for choir practice.

I can eat and I can make love and I can see and smell and hear and touch and think, he told himself. I can read and I can add and subtract and multiply and divide. Ninety-nine percent of me is just fine. All I have to do is help them kill a bunch of white blood cells that have gone terrorist on me, in me. I never had to go to a war and now I am one. That's it. I won't obsess about this. This can't have my whole life.

Why hasn't Nieman come back with Little Freddy?

There was a light blinking on the answering machine and he pushed a button and listened to four messages from Nieman, telling him they had gone to Chez Panisse because they were hungry. "Stella wrote the nuns and the monks," the last message said. "Then she set up a meeting with Lama Doge. This is not a joke. Call when you get this."

Freddy pushed the button to hear the message again. He felt a great rush of energy and hope fill his body. You bet I'm not going to die, he decided, and got up and walked across the room and started making a pot of coffee. I'm not going to die and I'm going to have a cup of coffee in the afternoon.

He left the coffee to brew and went out into the side yard to wait for the girls to come home. I think I'll get them a new car tomorrow, he decided. I like to buy cars for people. It's my vice and I like it. I think I'll buy Little Freddy one of those new three-wheeled scooters while I'm at it. I don't know why I didn't buy one the first time we saw them at that toy store. So what in a finite world? It's time to mix it up around here. It's time to start making every minute count.

Nora Jane woke up and put on a robe and went out to see if the girls had come back yet. She leaned out the front door and looked down the driveway and saw Freddy standing by the flower beds with his hands in his pockets, looking absolutely normal and absolutely well, and then she went into the kitchen and saw the pot of coffee and then she went back into her bedroom and put on her new red velvet pants and boots and a white shirt with raglan sleeves. And an embroidered vest and long silver earrings. I'm making cheese grits and an omelet for dinner, she decided. I am really, really tired of healthy food. I am from New Orleans, Louisiana, and I happen to think fat is good for you if you don't eat it all the time.

It was a warm spell in October in central Ohio. Blue skies and brilliant fall trees rose above the long hill of crosses where Sister Anne Aurora went each day at noon to spend an hour after lunch in prayer. At the school the teaching nuns could also help with the prayers if they found time to do it, but it was not compulsory or even, during school months, expected.

The reason Sister Anne Aurora spent her noon hour at prayer was partly because she was trying to stay thin in case she decided to go back to secular life. Also, she had always loved to pray. She loved to be down on her knees at the edge of the graves of the departed nuns. She loved to stand at the very top of the hill and pray while walking in the small circle that had been worn down by many other praying or mourning feet. She loved to watch the seasons and the weather. She loved to be alone and wonder if her thoughts could really travel across space and time and somehow add to goodness or to healing.

If I quit teaching it will only be for a while, she told herself today. I must go back to college. I need to know more. My chemistry is old now. So much is happening. I must go where I can find out all I don't know. It isn't vanity to wish for knowledge. The world needs leaders. I can't be a leader unless I know what's going on, can I?

The order of Episcopal nuns to which Sister Anne Aurora belonged was seventy years old. It had been started in Cleveland, Ohio, and then moved to the small town of Wheeler. There were forty-six sisters in the order. They ran a school and home for orphans and children of many kinds from many places. Sister Anne Aurora taught science to grades seven through twelve. So when the letter from Stella came in the mail, Mother Grace took it in hand and walked over to the school and put it into Sister Anne's hand. "This is a biochemist in Berkeley, California, asking us to pray for a Jewish bookstore owner there. I thought it was right up your alley."

Sister Anne Aurora took the letter and put it into the pocket of the long blue overall that was the usual costume of the teachers. Not all the sisters wore uniforms. The Order of Saint Jennifer was not strict about such things. Women came and went, women wore what they chose to wear, women smoked and sometimes drank wine — the work they did was not "insulted" by rules, they loved to say.

In 2001 they had collected and raised $4,207,000 for their work. In 2002 they had raised $6,510,000. The money was invested and cared for by a redheaded stockbroker in Fort Smith, Arkansas, who had been raised by the nuns and now had six children of her own and was the highest-ranking Merrill Lynch broker in the state of Arkansas.

It was counted and audited by the only woman member of the best CPA firm in Jackson, Mississippi, whose husband was an alumnus of the school.

The teachers could save or spend their small salaries. As long as they were at the school they had no need for money except for personal things. Sister Anne Aurora had been saving hers for nine years.

It had grown to almost $300,000 under the care of the redheaded stockbroker.

When the nuns took on one of the prayer missions, they were paid extra money, as the prayers cost ninety dollars an hour.

Sister Anne Aurora picked out a place near the top of the hill of crosses and decided to kneel on the cold ground for a while to see if she could feel the underground river a geologist told her was in this part of Ohio. "It's as wide as the Ohio, but deep under the ground," he told her. "I don't know why no one ever wants to talk about it."

Sister Anne Aurora opened the letter from Stella and began to read it. "We do not know why people who are prayed for seem to heal better but there is documented evidence that it is so. EVEN WHEN THEY DON'T KNOW THEY ARE BEING PRAYED FOR THEY HEAL FASTER. I have been interested in this for several years. Doctor Andrew Weil is also open-minded about this possibility, and since, as a scientist, I believe that staying open-minded is the single most important thing a researcher has to strive for, because it is often the most difficult, I am asking you with an open mind and an open heart to pray for the recovery of our dear friend Freddy Harwood, of Berkeley, California, from acute myelogenous leukemia. Yours most sincerely, Stella Light-Gluuk, Professor, University of California at Berkeley."

The letterhead was from the Department of Biochemistry.

Sister Anne Aurora folded the letter and put it into a shirt pocket near her heart and began to pray. She used prayers she had memorized as a child, parts of poems she loved, thoughts of the seasons and the rivers and the plant life of southeastern Ohio, the names of people she had known and loved, the names of children she was teaching, bits of Buddhist and Hindu lore she had picked up here and there, but mostly she talked to the white cells in Freddy Harwood's bone marrow and blood. She directed the red blood cells to seek out and destroy the malignant cells; she told the malignant cells to give up and change into more useful proteins and amino acids; she worked her way from the chambers of Freddy's heart to the arteries and capillaries, and then she decided just to concentrate on the marrow. I need to know about the chemotherapy, she decided. I need to know what they are giving him. I need more language.

She cut the hour short and hurried back to her office and dashed off an e-mail to Stella before hurrying off to her ninth-grade biology class.

"Dear Doctor Light-Gluuk . . . I am the science teacher at the school here and have been assigned the prayers for your friend, Freddy Harwood. I need more information. Please send me any medical records you think appropriate, especially the names — and, if possible, natural or man-made sources — of all drugs currently being used to treat Mr. Harwood. I am bending every effort to add my prayers to those of everyone who loves him. I need data, if you think it is appropriate to trust it to me. Yours most sincerely, Sister Anne Aurora. (My secular name is Janet McElroy. I have a degree in chemistry from the University of Arkansas at Fayetteville, Arkansas. I am planning on going back to get a doctorate soon. I study all the time. I study everything I can get my hands on about chemistry and biochemistry.)"

Freddy was scheduled to go to the hospital on Monday morning to begin the chemotherapy that would lead to a bone marrow transplant.

On Sunday night the Buddhist monk Henry Wilkins, from Greenville, Mississippi, came over to the Harwoods' house and set up meditation cushions in the living room. At six o'clock Freddy and Nora Jane and Nieman and Stella sat down upon the cushions and began to try to concentrate on the breath going in and out of their bodies. Once or twice Little Freddy got away from his sisters and came into the room and tried to talk to them, but sharp looks from Henry dissuaded him, and his sisters were able to drag him back into their bedroom by promising to let him watch a video about the animals of the Serengeti.

When the meditation hour was over, Nora Jane served salmon croquettes and green peas and carrots and homemade bread to the guests, and after dinner they all went out on the balcony and looked at stars and sat around the edge of the almost-finished hot tub.

"I got an e-mail the other day I want to show you," Stella told Freddy. "Nieman said I should just keep this to myself, but I don't do anything behind people's backs if I can help it. You want to come in your office a minute and look at this?"

"Sure," Freddy said. He stood up and extended his hand to Nieman's wife, and the two of them walked into his office, where she handed him a copy of the e-mail from Sister Anne Aurora.

"Don't get mad," she said. "Nieman's suffering. I have to indulge him. He's suffering as much as you are, you know, feeling helpless."

"This is great," Freddy said. "I like her style. Are these the nuns that prayed for Leta Giles?"

"It's the nun who prayed for her. After I got the e-mail I called the mother superior and asked about this young science teacher and she told me—I had to dig it out of her—that this is the same nun who did most of Leta's prayers. After I got her going—" Stella stopped, then kept on telling the whole truth. "Well, I told her I wanted to send more money, as a donation for the school they run. So then she said she didn't want to be mystical—imagine a nun saying that—but this Sister Anne Aurora has some sort of gift for prayer that they all take seriously."

"They're not Roman Catholics, Stella. These are a kind of free-form nuns, I think. I've heard about them for years."

Freddy looked down at his hands. He had always been in awe of Stella Light. She was an awe-inspiring woman. "Send her anything you want. I don't know what they are going to give me. I'll find out tomorrow from Herbert Rosenstein." He started giggling, then really laughing. "I'll tell Herbert he needs to send the information to Ohio so in case he doesn't save my life we can get some nuns to rev up the process. Can't you just imagine him trying to be nice about it?"

Nieman was in the door of the room. "What's going on?" he asked.

"Freddy's in," Stella said. "Well, is Henry still here? I guess we need to go entertain him, don't we?"

"Just because meditation doesn't seem to be doing any good doesn't mean it wasn't good," Nieman said. "Sometimes you just have to waste some time on it."

"We're going to ask Herbert to e-mail data on the chemotherapy to the nuns," Freddy said. He was still laughing. "Why should this go through Stella? We'll just have Herbert put Sister Anne in the pipeline. Maybe I'll suggest he confer with her."

"Could we possibly call this something other than chemotherapy?" Nieman asked. "In the first place it's a misnomer."

"Hopefully cancer-killing chemicals hopefully administered slowly enough to save the patient unbearable discomfort?" Freddy offered. "How about holding action until gene therapy is perfected."

"It will be perfected," Stella said.

"Meanwhile, human prayer." Nora Jane had come in and was standing in the doorway. "Father Donovan is coming to dinner Thursday night, Freddy. He just happened to call this afternoon. He said he'd had us on his mind."

"The more the merrier." Freddy went to his wife and slipped his arm around her waist. "Where is Henry? You didn't leave him alone?"

"He went to tell the children good night. He's worried about them. He said we have to pay more attention to them. He said just because they seem to be dealing with this, don't bet on it."

"Good thinking," Stella said. "I'm going to see them too. Then we have to leave. One of my lab assistants is with Scarlett. I have to let her go home."

The party was breaking up. Henry emerged from the children's rooms with Little Freddy by his side. Stella went to the girls' rooms to talk to them. Nieman took Freddy's arm and asked to walk outside with him. Nora Jane stood on the front porch watching people leave.

Then it was ten o'clock and Freddy and Nora Jane began to close up the house for the night. They locked the doors and turned off the lights and went to tuck their children into their beds and sat beside them while they fell asleep. Then they went into their own bedroom and got into bed without brushing their teeth and lay in the dark trying not to let each other be afraid. "We've been through worse things," Freddy said.

"No, we haven't," Nora Jane replied. "We just haven't been through this, so we don't know how bad it will be."

"It isn't bad tonight. Let's go to sleep."

"I hope you don't mind Father Donny coming over."

"I like Donny. He's your cousin. How could I not like him?"

"I told him. He said he knew something was going on because he hadn't heard from me."

"I bet I go to sleep first. Watch me." Freddy pretended to be sleeping, an old trick he used to play when Nora Jane would be anxious over something about the children.

She snuggled down into his scrawny, sweet arms and fell asleep because he wanted her to.

Need her, he was thinking. Have her here, and then he went to sleep also. Good old brain, always trying to help out in emergencies.

At nine the next morning they got into Freddy's Volvo and started off for the hospital. "I don't want you coming in," Freddy said. "I forbid it. It's going to be a roomful of cancer patients reading magazines and waiting to be poisoned. I'm going to sit there and read the new Tony Hillerman. He's coming to do a signing at the store next week. So just let me off and I'll call you on the cell when I'm ready to leave. I mean it, N.J. I do not want you in the waiting room. What's going on this morning doesn't change anything. I have leukemia. Hopefully this therapy is going to cure that. If you want to do me a real favor, go spend some money on clothes or buy the girls something or go check out the new Barnes and Noble and let me know what they're up to. Please let me have my way in this." He stopped the car by the emergency entrance of the great teaching hospital associated with the University of California at San Francisco Medical School. "This is a safe place where several thousand of our fellow human beings are trying to achieve miracles and save lives. I'm not going anywhere bad."

"Then why can't I go in?"

"Because I don't want you to. I love you. I don't want you in a roomful of cancer patients. I don't want you to think of me as one."

"That is ridiculous. I don't want to shop while they put chemicals into your body."

"Please. I'll call if I get scared. Let me be a hero here, okay? Or go over to the bookstore and talk to Francis. Go calm her down."

"All right. I'll leave. I'm coming back at eleven. I'll be in the front of the building in the parking lot by then."

"Good idea. Go on. Go buy something yellow to cheer me up. I want everyone in yellow for dinner tonight."

"I don't know if I can do that in two hours."

"Okay, I'm gone." He kissed her on the cheek and got out of the car. "And don't wreck my Volvo," he added. "Be careful." He turned away. Nora Jane watched him disappear into the double doors of the emergency room.

She got into the driver's seat of the Volvo and put on her seat belt and started doing breathing exercises. She drove very carefully down ten blocks to a parking garage and gave the car to the attendant and started walking in the direction of a new Saks Fifth Avenue that had opened some months before. She went in the front doors and walked back to the juniors' department and kept on walking and went up the escalator to women's sportswear and picked out a bright yellow sweater set and bought it without trying it on and then she went to the shoe department and bought some yellow Capezio sandals, and then went back down to the juniors' department and bought several skirts and a yellow-and-white-striped shirt and a blue-and-white-striped shirt and then she left the store and went back to the parking garage and got into the car and drove back to the hospital and sat in the car in the parking lot. It was eleven o'clock. At eleven twenty her cell phone rang and she answered it.

"I'm still alive," he said. "Come get me."

"I'm here. Come out the front door."

He got into the car looking all right. "I'm supposed to go home and go to bed," he said. "If it gets bad it won't happen for a few hours. Did you go shopping?"

"I spent five hundred dollars. Are you happy?"

"I'm elated. You drive. They said not to drive myself."

"Don't act like nothing's wrong."

"It's all right. It wasn't bad. I met a couple of nice people. They're on my schedule. I'll get to see them twice a week. Okay, I'm going to sleep." He reclined the seat and lay back in it and closed his eyes. "Keep breathing," he said. "Don't worry, N.J. They don't give you much the first time."

"Nieman said he's sending us some movies in case you need them."

"I need the wisdom of the gods, the patience of a saint, and you driving me home from battle," he said, but he was fading now. He was starting to feel the effects of the chemicals. "You know what I really want at this exact moment? I want not to throw up until I get home, so speed it up, would you?"

"I don't think I'm going to take you to the hospital anymore. You're too demanding."

"I don't want you to. I don't want anyone I know to do it. I just want a driver and to get to know my fellow sufferers in the poisoning room."

2

MITZI OZBURT had been cutting Tammili's and Lydia's hair since they were ten years old. Not that either of them had ever let her do anything but trim the ends. At first she had cut their hair at the shop, but after she and Nora Jane became friends she just stopped by in the afternoon and had a glass of wine and cut it in the back hall. She had planned on coming by on Thursday afternoon anyway, but after she heard about Freddy's diagnosis from someone at the shop, she took off early and went by St. Anthony's to light a candle. She ran into Father Donovan on the stairs and stopped to talk to him.

"I was on my way to Freddy and Nora Jane's to cut the girls' hair," she began. "I just heard the news. So I stopped here."

"I'm on my way there too," he said. "I'll wait for you."

They entered the church together and knelt near the altar and got out their rosaries and began to add their love to the store of love both in Berkeley, California, and anywhere in the universe where it might be needed at four o'clock on this Thursday afternoon in October of two thousand and three. Mitzi smelled of roses and Cape Jasmine. The silk jacket she was wearing made a sound as she moved her fingers, and Father Donovan, who was only thirty-six years old, had to add a few extra Hail Marys for the way human love sometimes turns into desire.

*   *   *

"I could drive you there so you wouldn't have to fight the traffic alone," he said, later, when they were back on the steps leading to the sidewalk where their cars were parked.

"Thanks," she said. "I hate driving on the bridge this time of day. But don't talk about Freddy. I can't stand to think about it anymore."

"We'll talk about a project I'm starting," he said. "A rape crisis center at the church. I really need volunteers for the late evenings. If you could give me two days a month it would help. Stars in your crown."

"I might. I don't know if I'd be any good. I might get too depressed."

They got into Father Donovan's minivan and started out down the narrow winding street. Mitzi put on her seat belt and tried not to look at the good-looking, redheaded priest who was driving her. I've already been in love with a priest, she lectured herself. I am not going to start that again.

"I don't know what I can do to help Freddy and N.J.," she said. "It's terrible not to be able to think of anything to do."

"Just keep on being their friend," he answered. "Just do exactly what you were doing. When people get sick they don't want other people to start acting like they are more important than they were. I've had many people tell me that the worst thing was being the center of attention."

"Right," Mitzi said, and swore she would not think about how strong and fine his hands looked on the wheel. This goddamned church will never change, she decided. Excuse me, God, but you just make it too hard for normal people, and you know, damn well, I mean, you know you do. I can't help it if I curse. My father cursed like a sailor and I learned it from him. "We learn everything we know from our parents, don't we," she said out loud. "I was thinking about that the other day, because this lady I was doing an oil pack on said she was reading this book about how everything we do is already decided when we are two years old because of who our parents are. Do you believe that?"

"There's a long-standing argument about how much is learned and how much is hereditary," he answered. "I've always thought they never take luck into account. So much is luck, coincidence, being in the right place at the right time, having parents who protect you, or ones who don't."

The sun was moving down the sky. It made the skies above the city into a panorama of color and design. I'll just look at the skies and not look at his hands, Mitzi decided. I'm not getting into another of those things with a priest and then he'll have me down at the crisis center listening to rape stories and not getting any sleep worrying about them.

"So where did you learn to cut hair?" Father Donovan asked. "Did you go to school out here?"

"Mitzi's coming over in a while," Nora Jane was telling the twins. She was sitting on Tammili's bed watching them do their geometry homework. Ever since Henry's pep talk on Sunday, she had been hovering.

"Why don't you go see about Little Freddy," Lydia suggested. "I can't concentrate with you sitting here."

"Okay." Nora Jane watched them for a minute, then got up and went in the kitchen to finish fixing dinner. Freddy had gone to the bookstore to help Francis set up for a book signing. He had insisted he felt well enough to go.

"I'll be back by nine," he said. "Tell Mitzi and Donny I'm sorry I missed them. We aren't going to let this disrupt our lives, Nora Jane. I refuse to let leukemia become my life. Okay, I'm leaving. I'll call when I leave the store. About nine, or ten." He was wearing an old tweed jacket with pencils in his breast pocket and he looked nineteen and not a day older. He was her Freddy, pure, original, never to be replaced.

"All right," she said. "Go on then."

He started out of the room, then came back in and took her in his arms and squeezed her until the pencils cut into her chest. She pushed

him away and took the pencils and laid them on the table and hugged
him again. "I'm not talking," she said. "I'm not nagging. I'm not giving advice. It's your leukemia. You run it."

"It's a mistake the system's making. And the technicians will fix it
or they won't and the universe will still be so huge we can't begin to
imagine it. One hundred billion light-years filled with galaxies and
planets. I am not thinking about dying until they get a new telescope
up there, at least one more before I leave." He stopped hugging her
and put his pencils back in his pocket.

"What are you cooking?" he asked.

"Baked chicken and mashed potatoes. I wanted to make crawfish
bisque but I couldn't find any crawfish, even frozen."

"Okay. I'm leaving. I'll call you by ten." He walked across the
room and out the door. John Wayne, he was thinking. Do the Duke
for this one, and for God's sake don't forget to breathe.

It was sundown in Ohio and Sister Anne Aurora was doing a special
walk around her prayer circle. She didn't do it every day. Just when the
spirit moved her. She would try to recite the names of all the people
she was praying for in one very slow revolution, then say them one at
a time for twelve revolutions apiece. Frederick Sydney Harwood of
Berkeley, California, I send you my energy and love, I send you
strength and wisdom. In the midst of your fear I know joy can grow
and flourish. Joy can rise up from fear and overcome it. Joy is in every
atom of creation. It is life. It is wisdom. Let it in. It wants to be with
you. Strength guards you. Strength heals you. You are not alone. You
are going to make it.

I might start writing down some of my prayers, Sister Anne decided, stopping at the top of the prayer circle to look down at the row of
crosses, then up into the beautiful skies of sundown. Some of these
prayers are pretty good.

*   *   *

Father Donovan and Mitzi came in the side door and Mitzi went to Nora Jane and hugged her, then began to look at the ends of her hair. "I'm trimming this while I'm here," she declared. "This is out of hand."

"Hello, cousin," Father Donovan said. "I was in New Orleans last week for a conference at Loyola. Everyone sends their love."

"I'm going crazy," Nora Jane said. "I can't pretend I'm not, but my main thing is to keep the children well. It's what Freddy wants me to do."

"Then let's feed them and cut their hair and see if they want to talk to us," Mitzi said. "I'll go round them up. What are you cooking for dinner?"

"Baked chicken and mashed potatoes. I've reverted to comfort foods for the duration."

"I'll finish those potatoes," Father Donovan said. "I know how to do it." He moved to the sink and took the pan of boiled potatoes Nora Jane had been mashing and began to expertly mash them. "I use lots of butter," he said. "I hope you don't mind."

"Take off your jacket and let me give you an apron." Nora Jane helped him with the jacket and then opened a pantry and brought out an apron that one of Freddy's salesmen had given him for Christmas. "Life is the urge to ecstasy," it said in Old English script.

"Oh my," Father Donovan said, and reversed it so the writing didn't show.

Don't take his coat off, Mitzi was thinking. If I look at his arms I can't stand it. "Well, I'll go set up in the hall by the breakfast nook," she said. "Bring on the victims."

Mitzi set up her scissors and capes and brushes and combs on a side table, and Little Freddy appeared and allowed her to trim the back and sides of his hair without complaining. He liked Mitzi and thought she was interesting. Also, he didn't like it when he had to waste time combing his hair, and right after it was cut he could always get away with not combing it, sometimes for weeks. Mitzi finished with Freddy and then trimmed Lydia's bangs and clipped the ends off her curly black hair.

Dinner was ready before she could get to Tammili. They all sat together at the dining room table and held hands and said grace and then ate the chicken and mashed potatoes and green peas and carrots and French bread.

After dinner Tammili got in the chair and asked Mitzi to cut four inches off her hair so she would have a short bob like one she had seen in a magazine.

Then Nora Jane had a trim and then Father Donovan got into the chair and Mitzi cut his soft red curls. She was praying the whole time he was in the chair. You did this to me, she prayed, and for that I forgive you, so forgive me. Why did you make half the good-looking men in the world into priests when there aren't enough men to go around? I am only twenty-six years old and I want to get married and have children, but, oh no, you just keep throwing priests at me instead.

It was nine o'clock when Mitzi put all her supplies into her bag and received her thanks and the check Nora Jane always made her take whether she wanted it or not. "Give it to the poor if you don't want it," Nora Jane said. "I won't let you do this unless you let me pay you."

"You are so nice to do that for them," Father Donovan said when they were driving back to where she had left her automobile. "It's very kind of you."

"Nora Jane got me back into the business," Mitzi answered. "I was a waitress in an all-night bar when I met her and she found out I had a degree from a beauty school. She saved my life. I owe her a lot."

"How did you meet her?"

"I was down at the bookstore trying to find a book about how to stop drinking and she waited on me. After that we got to be friends.

I'm from Louisiana too. I didn't tell you that, did I? I'm from Alexandria, and New Orleans."

"Here's your car," he said. He came to a stop on the deserted street. "I'll watch until you get on the way. Think about coming to help me at the crisis center. I could really use someone like you."

Mitzi didn't answer for a minute. She went over her options. They all seemed equally bad. "I'll think about it," she said. "I'm pretty busy. I might just work extra and give you some money. I don't like to hear people's troubles. I have to do that all day."

"I guess you do," he answered. He got a whiff of gardenia perfume that was coming from the hand cream Mitzi had applied after she finished cutting everyone's hair. "Thank you so much for cutting my hair. That was nice."

"You're nice," she said, and got out of the car and got into her own and started the motor and did not look his way again. Been there, done that, she kept repeating. Devil, get out of my way. Devil, devil, devil.

3

IT WAS FRIDAY MORNING. "We have to tell
Mother," Freddy said. He was sitting on the edge of the bed putting
on his socks. "I guess I'll go by there on the way to the hospital and
just tell her something."

"If she doesn't already know. Her canasta game was yesterday.
What do you think the chances are it isn't all over the Jewish community by now?"

"If she knew she would have called."

"It's seven in the morning."

"That's never stopped her yet." He finished the socks and pushed
his feet into his leather shoes and stood up and started buttoning the
Brooks Brothers shirt that was his uniform for the store. Old tweed
jackets, button-down Oxford cloth shirts, leather shoes. Freddy's daytime attire had not changed in years. He got up, he got dressed. Short-
sleeved shirts in summer, long-sleeved shirts in winter. That was it. He
was dressed for Boston, New York City, Chicago, Seattle, or San
Francisco. Once or twice it had occurred to Nora Jane to ask him to
change, but she had never gone through with her plan.

The phone started ringing just as Freddy buttoned the last button
on his shirt and started tying his red-and-blue-striped tie. "I know,
Momma," he said into the receiver. "I was on my way over there
just now. Fix me some breakfast. Nora Jane too. She might come

along . . . I know . . . I am going to tell you. It's not as bad as you think it is. It's just something we have to fix. Danen's taking care of me. Well, and some other doctors who are friends of his . . . What? One of them is Jewish. I don't know about the rest. One is Indian, I think. From India, not Arizona. Look, make some real coffee, would you? I'll be there in twenty minutes."

"Do you want me to go?" Nora Jane asked.

"Bring Little Freddy with you. As soon as you get him ready. Follow me in your car."

"Okay." She moved across the room and took her husband in her arms and held him close, close, close, for a long minute.

"Let's go," he said. "Let's get this show on the road."

Freddy had a complicated relationship with his mother. He had a complicated relationship with being Jewish because of having been sent off to school for three years when he was a teenager. He had been thrown into a world where being Jewish was a handicap and he had acted accordingly. He stopped going to temple, he never talked about being Jewish, and he spent most of his time with Episcopalians. He dated girls who weren't Jewish and from that he learned that you didn't have to let women boss you around. By the time he came back to San Francisco, he was a changed person. He slipped back into the Jewish world into which he was born, but he never went back to Jewish women. Also, he was wary of his mother and her guilt-trips and hovering instincts. He loved her and honored her and secretly adored her, but he didn't tell her what was going on until she asked and not always then. Nieman was his confidant and compadre in all things concerning mothers, since Nieman had a mother even more controlling than Mrs. Harwood would have been if she had been given the chance. "Like a war between magicians," Nieman was always quoting Tom Robbins. "It can last a long time and even then the outcome may not be what it appears to be.

"They're always waiting to pounce," he added. "You can never let your guard down and for God's sake never admit that anything is wrong."

It had been a mistake not to tell his mother about the cancer sooner. Freddy knew it was a mistake but he had gone on doing it. He could face the chemotherapy but not the moment when he looked at his mother and watched her get ready to make leukemia his fault, or worse, if she found out it was a genetic defect, her fault, or his dead father's family's fault. It could go any way. He had to be ready, and pretending to be John Wayne wasn't going to work on his mother. So, so, so, so, so, he thought. The hour has come. "There is more stuff than is dreamed of in your philosophy, Horatio. There is Oedipus and Jocasta, and of course there is Stuart. I'm sure she has called him by now." Stuart was Freddy's older brother, a son his parents had adopted when they thought Mrs. Harwood would never be able to carry a child of their own. Stuart was a tall, powerful Eastern European orphan the Harwoods had found in New York City when he was two years old, *or so Freddy had been told and had always believed.* Stuart had been a perfect son, graduated from Harvard and Harvard Medical School, and then went off to South Africa to run a clinic financed by Harvard. He was a surgeon and an AIDS activist. He never came home. He called his mother every Friday afternoon and talked to her for an hour. He wrote her letters and had his secretaries send her articles about himself and his work. He never married. He and Freddy had never gotten along very well. He was humorless and driven. He thought Freddy was a dilettante.

"I guess it was the money that made Stuart angry," Freddy said out loud as he pulled into his mother's driveway. "It would have made me mad, I guess." Their father's estate had been divided fairly, although most of it was still in their mother's control, but their wealthy paternal grandmother had left all her money to Freddy. Soon after that Stuart had left San Francisco and gone to Africa for good.

Freddy parked next to his mother's Lexus and went in the back door past the cook and the chauffeur and the laundry woman who were gathered around the big kitchen table having breakfast. All three of them were as old as his mother and all of them still came to work because they liked to be there. They had rooms in the house besides their own homes and came and went in a haphazard fashion. Freddy paid their salaries and the household bills.

"She's waiting for you," the chauffeur, Big Judy, said. "She's in the dining room. You want me to bring your breakfast in?"

"Yes. Please. How is she?"

"She's pretty mad."

"Okay." He heaved a sigh and went on through the doors to where his mother waited. "I was going to tell you sooner, but I forgot about it, to tell the truth," he began. "We've been busy getting things settled at the store."

"What's the prognosis?"

"I won't really know for another week. I have to have chemotherapy, Mother. I already had one round—it wasn't bad. They have better drugs now. They tailor them to your blood. I'm going into the hospital for a few days soon. They keep testing everything. It's really high-tech. They know what they're doing. Then, when they finish killing the cancer, they may do a bone marrow transplant like the one they did on Steven Arthurs last year. Look at him, he's doing great."

"He's nineteen years old. You are fifty-four."

"That's a nice thing to say." He took a seat by his mother's right hand and leaned near and gave her a kiss. She was dressed in a tweed suit, with her hair back in a bun. She had on makeup and earrings. As always she was perfect, perfectly behaved, perfectly in charge, perfectly dressed, ready.

"I'm going to the hospital with you," she said.

"No. Don't do that. No one's going to be there. Danen won't be there. There's nothing going on. I'm just going in for tests. Wait until something important happens."

"I can't believe you didn't tell me this."

"I am telling you. I'm telling you right now." Big Judy had put on a white coat. He came into the room carrying a plate of eggs and bacon. Celeste followed with a coffee cup and a basket of toasted biscuits. Freddy began to eat. "I'm going to be all right, Mother. This is just a problem to be solved. It isn't as bad as you think it is."

Mrs. Harwood took one of the biscuits and put it on her bread plate and broke it in two and used her butter knife to put a small amount of apricot jelly on the biscuit. She took a small bite and chewed it and swallowed it before she spoke again.

"What can I do to help you, son?"

"Nieman and Stella are sending money to some nuns at a school for orphans in Ohio. They're buying prayers for me. Why don't you send my Christmas money to those people? That would be nice."

Mrs. Harwood always gave Freddy a thousand-dollar donation to a charity of his choice for his Christmas present. His father had started the gifts, and since his death Mrs. Harwood continued them.

"All right. If that's what you want."

"Don't look like that. They are Episcopalian nuns who take care of children. It's making Nieman feel better, so I'm going along with it. Listen, Momma, he's got Stella e-mailing the nuns about the chemotherapy. Isn't that hilarious?"

He was trying to get his mother in a good mood. Usually anything to do with Stella made his mother happy. She approved of Stella and of Nieman Gluuk's settling down to have a family. Before Stella, she had always thought Nieman was a bad influence on Freddy.

"If it's so hilarious, why do you want me to join in?"

"Because I like the idea. I think it's helping me. I believe in these nuns. I have decided to believe in them. Nieman and Stella and I are believing in them."

"I wish you wouldn't make a joke out of everything in the world, Freddy. I can't see the humor in any of this. Leave the address of the nuns. I'll have someone take care of it." She was very quiet, eating a small bite of scrambled eggs without looking at him. He forgot to be wary, eating the heavily buttered toast and thinking that in a few minutes he'd be able to make an excuse and leave.

"What about Stuart?" she said. "I wrote him a letter but I haven't sent it yet. Have you consulted him at all? I think he will be hurt if you don't ask for his help."

"My God. I knew you'd bring that up. Stuart is in South Africa running a clinic for the United Nations and the Centers for Disease Control. He's looking for a Nobel Prize, Mother. He doesn't have time to worry about a simple leukemia problem they can take care of right here. The University of California at San Francisco is one of the best in the world. They don't need any advice from a surgeon."

"He's not a surgeon only, Freddy. He's a very important and hard-working man. I don't understand why you don't love your only brother."

"He is not my brother. He's your adopted child. I can't believe you want me to get Stuart in on this. I've got this taken care of, Mother. I'm being treated by the best doctors in the United States. For God's sake, this is why I didn't tell you sooner."

Mrs. Harwood closed her lips into a thin, hard line. Her eyes didn't leave his.

Blessedly Nora Jane and Little Freddy came in through the door from the kitchen, and Little Freddy went to his grandmother and began to do his magic on her.

*　　　*　　　*

Fifteen blocks away, Nieman was getting into his small, energy-efficient automobile and setting out for his laboratory. Stella had already left to take Scarlett to the university day-care center. Stella was on the board of the center. She had hired the woman who ran it and was on the hiring committees for most of the other employees. She never minded leaving Scarlett there and Scarlett never minded going. Scarlett thought she helped run the place because that is what Stella and Nieman always told her. They told her it was her duty to help with the other children, and she believed it.

Nieman turned on his meditation tape as soon as he moved out into the morning traffic and tried to concentrate on driving. Mindfulness, the tape was saying. Paying attention, in the moment, right now, the only time there is.

"Drive the car," Nieman said out loud. "Pay attention to what you're doing."

On the ramp at Geary Boulevard, there was a wreck with three ambulances and at least three wrecked cars. Nieman tried not to look for injured people. It was no way to start a day that was already shadowed by Freddy's problem.

It was the seventeenth of October and already some radio station was playing a Christmas song. Perhaps that is why Nieman's mind wandered away from Zen meditation and he began to make up new words to the song. Five golden rings, four nuns praying, three Buddhist monks, two Jewish physicians. One Hindu oncologist, six worried friends, the synnnagoooogue. Ten movie stars, ninety hungry writers, everyone we know. My secretary, his secretary, our certified public accountant. Our Merrill Lynch broker, his old mother . . . and so on, he decided. We are down to praying, that's for sure. He turned onto a side street and decided to weave his way around to the Berkeley campus. Okay, then. The double-blind study at Caltech proved to the satisfaction of everyone who read it that the patients who were prayed for got well four times faster than the ones who were not prayed for. They only stopped the study because people at the churches they were using insisted on adding the other people to the prayer list. It is of no importance that we don't understand why prayer works. It's all electricity and chemical transfer, and you don't have to believe in magic to know that thought has an effect on matter. Duh.

The traffic began to move and Nieman continued the song he was making up. "Everyone we know, everyone we love, one glorious nun . . . give us this day a bone marrow donor," he prayed. "We really need one, Sir or Madam. It's not that I don't believe in you, it's just always been hard for me to put a human face on something so huge and amazing. I do believe in you. Now I do."

He pulled off the highway onto the campus and began to search for a parking place nearer than the parking garage, but of course he couldn't find one because it was nine o'clock and he was late.

Sister Anne Aurora had gone out at dawn in the crisp, clear, bitingly cold air to climb the hill and put in another thirty minutes on Frederick Harwood of Berkeley, California. Stella had wired five thousand dollars to the school and sent a list of the probable drugs that would be used and everything she could find about the sources for the ingredients in the drugs and their places of manufacture. Plus some diagrams of the molecular structure of anything relevant.

Sister Anne Aurora had the papers in her inside coat pocket. She knelt by the grave of Sister Margaret Hoy Biggs, who had been one of the founders of the order, and began to pray. We ask your mercy and goodness to descend on Freddy Harwood as his ordeal continues, she prayed, and on all who suffer anywhere in the world. Let energy and power and goodness cover the world. Keep illness and evil at bay this morning for the whole world and especially for this good man and for his friend, Stella Light-Gluuk, and let your light so shine upon them that no harm can come to them this day . . .

*   *   *

Stella's monthly egg was taking on a sperm as Sister Anne Aurora prayed. As an unintended side effect of Sister Anne Aurora's prayers, little Scarlett's deep desire for a baby brother was beginning to come true. "We could have a baby here," she had been telling her parents for several months. "They have a bunch of them at my day care. We could take one home with us and I would talk to him if he was crying."

4

THE NIGHT AFTER Freddy's second round of chemotherapy, Nora Jane was awake all night. She was having dreams of wandering around the parking lot of the hospital trying to find the door to go in. The second time she had the dream, she slipped out of the bed and went into the bathroom and took a sleeping pill, something she hadn't done in months.

The next morning she was groggy and scared. "You were having bad dreams?" Freddy asked. He was feeling all right. Not half as bad as he had expected to feel. "Tell me, Nora Jane. Tell me the truth."

"I dreamed I couldn't find a way to get into the hospital. It's all right. Dreams are clues, I know. But this one was pretty clear. It's because you wouldn't let me go inside."

"Next time you aren't going at all. I'll take a taxi or have Nieman drive me or Big Judy. I am not going to have you get sick too. I need you to be healthy while I'm doing this." He got up from the bed and went to stand by the dresser where she was combing her hair. "It's my leukemia, N.J. Just let me run it."

"All right." She turned around and looked at him. He was wearing a pair of striped Brooks Brothers pajamas and his hair was curled all over his head like a child's. "You can run your leukemia, but if you don't let Mitzi cut your hair you can't sleep with me. How do you feel?"

"I feel all right. I could eat some eggs and toast. I'm going to go to the kitchen and see if the girls are up."

"I'll fix your breakfast. I love you, do you know that?"

"Then cook the eggs, woman."

"I'm going to. When do you have to go back and do it again?"

"On Monday. Until then we are going to ignore and forget this damned leukemia. I am sick of leukemia. I don't want to hear a word about it. I ignore leukemia, by Jove. Leukemia is dead for me." He strode out of the bedroom trying to look like Paul Newman, an actor his mother had always thought he resembled.

"Paul Newman," Nora Jane said out loud. She stuck two thick brown barrettes into her hair above her ears and gave up trying to do anything about the way she looked. Not that it was possible for Nora Jane Whittington Harwood to look bad. She looked beautiful on the worst day of her life. "And the sleeping pill will wear off and that's the last one I'll ever take," she added. "Leukemia will not drive me to sleeping pills. Leukemia can suck hind teat." She liked having said that, since she never cursed in any way. "Hind teat," she repeated and stalked out after Freddy to get breakfast ready for her family.

"The dread, that's the worst thing about any medical procedure," Freddy was saying. "So just watch where you're going and remind me of something nice." Nieman was driving Freddy to his third round of chemotherapy.

"It was nice while you were starting the bookstore. Nineteen seventy-five it was. And you had all the catalogs of books and we were making lists and the boxes started coming while the shelves were still being built. I had to wear a dust mask to come watch. Remember that carpenter from Baton Rouge, Louisiana, who was making the trim on the shelves? He was a good man. I wonder what became of him."

"He went home. He writes to me occasionally. He married a

woman he met out here and took her home with him. Jake Farley is his name. Turn over there, let me go in the emergency-room exit. It's a shortcut I found. You just come pick me up at eleven fifteen. I'll call if it will be sooner."

"I'll go to the medical-school library and hang out or maybe go walk on the labyrinth. I haven't been in this part of town in a while."

"Okay. Stop here. It doesn't hurt, Nieman. It's just a drip and I have some friends that come here when I do. A nice girl who's going to law school."

"Are you all right?" Nieman stopped the car and turned off the motor. He turned around. "I can go in with you. It won't bother me."

"Yes it will. You'll have nightmares." Freddy closed the car door and walked off. He was trying to walk forcibly and keep his shoulders back. Dread, he kept repeating. Dread is the normal emotion under these circumstances. I will experience it but not let it take me. I will make a mental list of all the books I ordered for the store in the months before it opened. Eight hundred dollars for the Karsh book. Another six hundred for the Hemingway with the Karsh print. The Faber and Faber books I got from that guy in Canada. That was probably against the law, but he said they were secondhand and some of them weren't available in the United States. Freddy stopped at the desk. "Hello, Lucy. Hello, Maria. How's it going today? Is everyone showing up? Who's calling in with lame excuses?"

"We very busy today, Mr. Harwood, but we'll be on time. You wait in waiting room, okay?"

"Okay. Can't wait until my turn. Get it over with and stop thinking about it, right?"

"Right."

Freddy settled into one of the pink leather chairs by the magazine stand. He pulled a paperback edition of Rilke out of his suit pocket and started to read "The Panther."

"I'm staying," Nieman said, coming up beside him. "I'm not going roaming around uptown San Francisco while you're sitting here. What are you reading?"

Freddy held out the book.

"Okay. That's good and depressing."

"It is not depressing. If you didn't know Rilke's biography you wouldn't think it was depressing. You have a bad habit of getting the author confused with the book, Nieman. There are moments of great joy and happiness in this book and that is what I'm reading it for."

"'The Panther'?"

"It's a beautiful poem."

"Mr. Harwood." Maria had come to get him.

"That's me. Don't wait here, Nieman. Go find something to do."

"I'm doing something. I'm waiting here for you." Freddy stood up and Nieman stood up beside him and took his arms with both his hands and held them tight. Then he sat back down and Freddy followed the nurse back to the room with the poison.

At eleven fifteen he came back out into the waiting room looking sick. "I guess it's working," he said. "Take me home."

Nieman took his arm and they walked out of the hospital and found the car and Nieman drove without talking.

"Say something," Freddy finally said. "Say I hope you don't throw up. Say leukemia sucks a big one and I hate leukemia's guts. Feel free to talk."

"I kept thinking about all the books we had when you first opened the store. I never would have read Freeman Dyson or those Einstein essays. Remember that book by the French anthropologist who got into the South African veld after the Boer War and made those first studies of primates in the wild? The same guy wrote *The Soul of the White Ant*. I ought to go around my house and make a shelf of the books we read because of the store. That was a real contribution to the world, starting Clara Books. Are you okay?"

"No. Just drive. You don't need to talk anymore. Yeah. Eugène

Marais, *The Soul of the White Ant*. And *The Soul of Something Else*. What was it?"

"*The Soul of the Ape*. Eugène Marais. The soul of the cancer cell. We could write that now, I guess."

"Oh no, we won't. If this stuff makes me sick it's working. I have to remember that."

"You surely do."

"God knows what else it's killing except cancer cells. I should have put some sperm in a bank before I did this. I think it's killing the lining of my stomach at the moment."

"That's sixty percent of your immune system. It's just reacting. It's supposed to react."

"Tell your buddies in the labs to hurry up and find something better than this crap, okay? Will you tell them that? But not Stella. She might think I don't appreciate this crap, which is better than nothing, which we used to have." Freddy was rolling down into the seat. He was rolling down into a ball. "Hurry up and get me home."

"I am hurrying. And so is medical science, Freddy. Thousands of people work every day all day for every miracle. You know that. Try to stop thinking. This is not thinking time."

Nieman leaned down on the wheel of the car and started taking chances.

Three weeks into the chemotherapy, Freddy's doctors had a meeting and decided to put him in the hospital for a while. They didn't like the results they were getting from the tests. The chemotherapy wasn't doing what they had hoped it would.

"We need to get him ready for a transplant," his oncologist said. "If we can't find a match, then we'll have to use stem cells. We have to make a move here. I don't think we can wait much longer."

"How close a match will work?"

"Whatever we can get at this point. I'm going to tell him this afternoon. If any of you have objections, state them now."

"Go on," Freddy's internist, Danen Marcus, said. "Do what you have to do. What have you already tried?"

"Everything I have. We need to give him blood. I can't wait any longer on that."

"Go on."

"Good."

Nora Jane had always liked to be alone. Ever since she was a child she had needed long spaces of time when she sat and daydreamed or did ordinary things without talking to anyone while she did them. She liked to be alone cleaning up the house or grocery shopping or moving the cleaning equipment in the swimming pool. She liked to lie in bed and read in the afternoons while she waited for the children to come home from school.

Now, with Freddy's illness, she found she needed company constantly. Even with the children all around her, she wanted other people in the house. She stayed at the hospital as much as Freddy would let her stay there, but it bothered him if she stayed all the time. "This isn't Schweitzer's hospital in Africa," he kept telling her. "We don't need the family moving into the tent. Go on home and call me every hour. There's nothing to do here but worry about catching something. I'm more worried about staph infections than I am leukemia. They're fixing it, N.J. It just takes time."

Father Donovan and Mitzi were frequent guests at Nora Jane's, and Stella came by with Scarlett when she had a few minutes. It consoled Nora Jane to talk to Stella, since Stella used the Latinate names of the drugs and acted like she understood what was going on. Father Donovan and Mitzi were helping Nora Jane as an antidote to the thing that was going on between them that neither of them had any intention of stopping. Also, it gave them a place to be together.

"I have ended up alone all my life," Nora Jane told them one night. "I do not think I could take care of the children without him. I can't live without him now that I have had him here so long. I don't know what to do. I don't know how to wait and see what happens."

"He isn't going to die," Mitzi said. "He isn't the type to die. They'll find a bone marrow donor and he'll get better."

"They might not find one."

"Then they'll do the stem cell thing." Father Donovan went near to her and took her arm. "You must be strong, Nora Jane. You have no choice because of the children."

"I'm trying," she answered. "I am trying as hard as I can."

Three weeks went by and it was the twelfth day of December in the year of our Lord two thousand and three. Because it was Friday, Tammili and Lydia had rode their bicycles to school. Little Freddy was mad because he was too young to ride his, so he sulked in the back of his grandmother's limousine and only stopped sulking when Big Judy's girlfriend, Lenora, started talking about her psychic.

"It doesn't hurt to let her try," Lenora said. "She told me the spirits are with her so much now they talk to her all the time, trying to get out their messages to the right people."

"Witch talk," Big Judy replied. "The last thing we need now is some dead people in on this. Freddy's not going to die, Leeno. Don't go telling a psychic our names. I don't want her knowing anything about me and I can tell you right now if Mrs. Harwood found out you were telling her business to some fortune-teller she'd never hire you to work at another party."

"It doesn't hurt to let spiritual people see what they can do. I didn't tell her anyone's names yet. I just asked her if there was any way she could make some gris-gris to help us out."

"You ought to quit going out every night and seeing all those good-for-nothing people that hang out in the bars. It's starting to make you look old, you know that."

Little Freddy had loosened his seat belt and was almost in the front seat now. He was fascinated by Big Judy's friend Lenora and always loved it when she came along to take him to school. In the first place she had beads braided into her hair and in the second place Big Judy argued with her and that was fun to hear. It took thirty minutes to get from the Harwoods' house to Little Freddy's school and it was usually pretty boring, but when Lenora came along something always started up.

"You just promise me right now that you won't talk anymore to this psychic about any of my business or the Harwoods' business," Big Judy was saying. "You just give me your promise, Leeno, or we're finished."

"I was only trying to help. I want to do something to help. I can't help wanting to help." She sat up and looked straight ahead.

"Yeah," Little Freddy put in. "She just wants to help Daddy get well so he won't have to stay in the hospital. We're tired of him being there. It's no fun when he's gone."

"Look at what you did now," Big Judy said. "I'll be damned, Leeno. He's going to tell them."

"No, I won't. I won't tell them anything you said."

"All I did was tell this very nice lady who is able to talk to spirits that I wanted her to be praying for your daddy to get out of that hospital soon," Lenora said. "There is more to life than a lot of people think there is. There are certain people that can find out things the rest of us can't, and all I was trying to do was to help."

"What is 'gris-gris'?" Little Freddy asked. "Like you said maybe she could get some gris-gris."

Big Judy stopped the car in the parking lot behind the school and turned around in the seat to talk to Little Freddy.

"Don't go telling this to your momma, honey. We got to be careful what we say to all of them while your daddy's sick. Leeno is not going to have any more truck with that lady she was talking about, and gris-gris is what some dumb people call luck. It's like when people tell you a fairy is going to come get your old teeth out from underneath your pillow and put some money there. It's just a bunch of superstition from a long time ago when people didn't know anything and had to make stuff up."

"Yeah," Little Freddy said. "I know all about that. Nieman got me a book about superstitions and how magic used to be science before they had the labs at Berkeley. And the scanning electron microscopes or the telescopes at Mount Palomar."

"That was the easy part and now we're going to start the hard part." Freddy was lying in the hospital bed with Nora Jane beside him. She had on a cap and gown and mask and gloves but she was still able to touch him. In another day she would not be able to come into the room.

"I'm not going to come in after they start the new drug. I talked to Stella about it. She said isolation means isolation and that Nieman was fixing a phone you can use by remote control."

"If Danen lets me have it. They took my cell away because they can't sterilize it. Can we talk about something else? Tell me what's going on at the store."

"Christmas sales. Francis said they were doing better than they did last year."

"What else is happening?" He pulled her closer to him but not so close that she would know how scared he was. He was trying very hard not to let her know that he was scared.

"Big Judy's girlfriend went to a psychic to see if she could get some gris-gris for you. What else? Mitzi has a crush on Father Donovan. He brought her over one night because he was leaving St. Anthony's the same time she was starting over to cut the girls' hair. She's praying for you every morning now." She started giggling. "Oh yeah, Nieman's writing a song to the tune of 'The Twelve Days of Christmas,' about everything everyone's doing to help you get well. 'Five golden rings,' " she sang. "One nun praying, three rabbis too."

"How about a bone marrow donor. A perfect one."

"We'll find one," Nora Jane said. "I know they'll find one."

Then Nora Jane was gone and Freddy was left alone to examine the room, wish he had his cell phone back, and generally begin to slump into a decidedly pessimistic mood. In another day the room would become a real isolation ward, a prison. I will become Rilke's panther, Freddy decided. No phone, no books, thank God for the poetry I memorized with my fantastic memory, which these drugs, God knows, may be scouring clean for all I know. How does it begin?

THE PANTHER

IN THE JARDIN DES PLANTES, PARIS

His vision, from the constantly passing bars,
has grown so weary that it cannot hold
anything else. It seems to him there are
a thousand bars; and behind the bars, no world.

As he paces in cramped circles, over and over,
the movement of his powerful soft strides
is like a ritual dance around a center
in which a mighty will stands paralyzed.

Only at times, the curtain of the pupils
lifts, quietly—. An image enters in,
rushes down through the tensed, arrested muscles,
plunges into the heart and is gone.

Freddy remembered the whole poem and that made him feel better. He lifted his eyes and looked toward the large window to the hall. Outside it stood his brother.

Stuart waved and opened his hands as if to ask a question.

"Come in!" Freddy yelled. "My God," he said, when Stuart was in the door. "You didn't fly all the way here for this, did you? Tell me she didn't make you do that."

"She doesn't even know I'm coming. I wanted to be here. I talked to Danen a few days ago. It sounds pretty good, Freddy. They seem to know what they're doing. How are you feeling? How are you holding up?" He came nearer to the bed. He looked good. Older, thinner, but still outrageously healthy and strong. "May I sit down?"

"Sure. I'm glad to see you. You better call her and tell her you're here. She'll go crazy if she finds out from someone else. I tried that with this mess but her canasta network found out and told her."

"I didn't come to see Mother, Freddy. I came to see you. I want to tell you something you have a right to know. I haven't told you sooner because Father didn't want me to, but now I think it's time. You need to know and I need for you to know. It may mean something to you, especially now."

"Tell me then." Freddy sat up in the bed. He wanted to reach out and touch Stuart's hand but kept himself from doing it. "Go on. Say it. What is it?"

"I'm not exactly an adopted child, Freddy. I am Father's child. My mother was a Polish actress. He met her on a business trip. It went on for several years. When I was two years old she gave me to him and went back to Poland to marry a man she knew there. I have always thought I can remember that, but, of course, I can't. Father told me the day I graduated from medical school. He was crying. Mother doesn't know. She thinks my parents died. No one knows. Now you know. Please don't ever tell Mother or anyone until she dies. That's all I ask. Anyway, for one thing I came to be tested as a donor."

"I should have given you part of Grandmother's money. That was selfish of me. I'm sorry I didn't do it. I was just always so jealous of you, Stuart. You're taller than I am, better looking, you went to Harvard. It just kept piling up. I'll give you the money now. I'll have to figure out how to divide it. It was three million dollars when she died fifteen years ago."

"I don't need any money, Freddy. Father left me plenty. I just want you to know that I'm your brother. That's what I came here for."

"What is your blood type, Stuart?"

"AB positive, same as you, so there's a chance I'll match. I hope I do."

"You being my blood brother, that's too sweet to believe. Come here, give me a hug if you can find a place around the paraphernalia. I'm being a great patient, Stuart. You wouldn't believe my patience and my real thankfulness to the medical profession and all these wild protocols they pursue like the philosopher's stone. Well, I think it's going to work. So does Nora Jane. Come over here." He held out both his hands.

Stuart leaned down and put his hands in Freddy's. "I have always loved you," he said. "Since the day you were born. You fascinate me, Freddy. You're a very special man. An unusual man."

The next day they moved Freddy out into the hall while the cleaning crew came in and coated the room with antibacterial and antiviral bleaches and cleaners. Then a new bed and new machinery were brought in and a remote telephone and plastic curtains. Then his body was scrubbed with an iodine solution and they settled him back in the bed and no one, not a soul except the doctors, was allowed to enter the room as they systematically began to destroy the marrow in his bones. If no donor showed up they were going to use marrow that had been grown from stem cells.

Stuart's marrow didn't match, but on December 18 a donor was found. His name was Larry Binghamton and he had gone to school with Freddy and Nieman from first grade until junior high, when his parents put him in a private academy in San Rafael. The family still belonged to Freddy's synagogue and that is how Larry happened to be one of the volunteers who signed up to have his marrow tested. Larry ran a computer firm. He was still the quiet, solemn man he had been as a boy. Now he had volunteered to undergo the painful process of donating marrow out of his left hip to save the life of a man who had not even been very nice to him as a boy.

"I feel guilty," Freddy said when his physician, Danen Marcus, told him the next day about the lucky match. "Should I call him, write him, send him presents? I don't know what to think, Danen."

"I'll tell him. He's glad to be able to help. I think he's proud that he can do it." Danen was standing by the bed with his big, fine hands clasped at his waist. He was a tall man, lanky and serious. "We're lucky, Freddy. I can't tell you how lucky it is to find someone this soon. And right here, in town. It's going to be good. I feel good about it. It's as close a match as I've seen. Better than some siblings."

"Call Nora Jane, will you, Danen? Oh, and call Nieman. Never mind, she'll call him."

"I'll call them. As soon as I leave here. Do you want anything? Are they taking care of you all right?"

"What else could I want? Thank you. Thank you so much. And thank him for me."

"Okay. I will. I'll be back this evening, after rounds. Try to get some rest."

Danen left the room and Freddy lay back in the hard white comfort of the sheets and pillows and looked at the light pouring in the windows onto the pale walls and the hospital bed with all its strange wires and machines — the light pouring into the room from all over a world full of nuns and priests and hairdressers and polluted air and oceans and microorganisms and genius. So much genius, and so much left to find out and sing and buy books about. And children everywhere and joy and sorrow and work to do and causes to espouse and time to do it after all—he was going to have some time, except, of course, time is only energy caught in fields, if you believe that theory.

I think I do, Freddy decided. As a hypothesis it's working for me. Manifestations, fantasy, whatever it is I'll take all of it that I can get or that darling old Larry Binghamton will give me, but even if it was the nun, how did that make Little Larry's marrow match mine? The match was made when our parents were screwing, long before we started this. Wait a minute, wasn't Larry's birthday always in the summer, like mine? I remember going to a pool party at their house when they got the first aboveground pool any of us had ever seen and Mary Anne Axelrod fell off the stairs and had to go to the emergency room. We're almost astral twins. Isn't that what the astrological people used to call people born on the same day, same year?

But, even if the match was made when our parents screwed, it doesn't matter, because, if the physicists are right, time isn't going in one direction. There isn't any time—it's only matter and energy, as if anyone is prepared to believe that, which we're not, thank goodness. We're all crazy enough without that kind of knowledge.

I love Little Larry with all my heart. I love the bloody angel.

Freddy was frantically trying to find the button he pushed so that the nurse would dial the phone for him, but it had slipped down in the sheets. Finally he found it and he gave her Nieman's number.

It was several minutes before the connection was made because of the high volume of calls on this Friday morning in the Bay Area.

"It's Larry Binghamton's marrow," he said, when Nieman answered. "Little Larry, Nieman. There is a God, old buddy, and he's right here, in this town, today. What should I do? I want to call and thank him. I don't know what to do."

"Be grateful," Nieman answered. "You want me to come up there while you call him? I can get there in ten minutes."

"Find the number. Call me back."

Nieman grabbed his laptop computer and headed out the door. He called the rabbi while he was pulling out of the parking lot. By the time he got to the hospital he had Larry's number. He parked in the visitor's lot and ran into the hospital and only slowed down when he got to the elevator. On Freddy's floor the nurse recognized Nieman and ushered him down to the window looking into Freddy's room. He scribbled the phone number on the signboard, although Freddy could hear him as soon as the nurse turned on the speaker. "I'm here," Nieman said. "Make the call."

Freddy held the phone while the nurse made the call. Larry's secretary put him through. "It's Freddy Harwood," Freddy said, when Larry answered. "What can I say, Larry? How can I thank you for doing this?"

"Get well," Larry said. "My cousin, Allie, died of this four years ago because they couldn't find a match. I'm proud I match, Freddy. I have admired you all my life. I can't imagine not being happy I can do this. I'm happy about it. I really am."

"It's painful, Larry. They're going to take the marrow out of your hip."

"I've been in pain. I can stand some pain. Nell and I are divorcing. Did you hear about that? She's trying to take my boys to live in France, but Jay David and Harold Levi are representing me. I don't think she's going to get to do it. Right now she can't even take them out of the county. So this is good for me. I know Danen. He won't let me have any problem. I talked to him yesterday. Did he tell you that?"

"All he told me was that you are going to save my life. I don't know what to say, Larry. Nieman's here. He's standing outside this room. I'm in an isolation room. You want to talk to Nieman?"

"Sure I do."

Freddy flipped the switch and said in a loud voice, "He wants to talk to you too. Say something."

"Hello!" Nieman yelled into the speaker. "Hey, Larry, let's have lunch tomorrow. Could you do that?"

"Sure," Larry said on the phone to Freddy. "Tell him I would like that."

Two nurses were standing by the window watching and listening. One of them was almost in tears. She was young and had not been on the oncology ward long enough to get tough.

"Tell him Maggie Bee's at twelve. I'll come get him," Nieman said into the speaker.

"He said can you make Maggie Bee's at twelve. He'll come get you at your office."

"It's Friday," Larry said. "I'll call him after I talk to you and make plans."

"He'll call you," Freddy said into the speaker. "Tomorrow's Saturday."

"Larry." He had turned back to the phone. "Look, I don't want to take up your whole morning. I just want you to know that I can't think of anything to say to thank you except, I don't know, thank you. Look, is there anything you need? Is there any way I can help you with the divorce?"

"Just pray she doesn't find a way to get them to France. I'd never get them back. Her mother has dinner with Jacques Chirac."

"I can get the prayers," Freddy said. "I learned how to do that this year. Okay. Hey, what is your birthday?"

"July tenth, nineteen fifty."

"Mine's July the fifteenth. I guess our mothers were in the hospital together. I'll ask mine."

"I'll ask mine too. Maybe that's how the match got made."

"Ask Nieman. He'll do research." They both started laughing at that and then they hung up and suddenly Freddy was so tired he almost fell asleep with the phone in his hand. The two nurses looked at each other. The younger one was really crying now.

"You have to learn to control that," the older woman said. "I applaud your humanity and so forth, but don't let patients see you cry."

"I know, but no one is looking at me, are they?"

Danen Marcus called Nora Jane and then Nieman called her. "I was getting dressed to go down there," she answered. "I don't know what to think, Nieman. What if it doesn't work?"

"It will work. It has to work."

"Okay. Maybe. The Binghamtons are in the middle of a terrible divorce. Did you know that?"

"No."

"His French wife is making a lot of trouble. She's saying bad things about him all over town."

"That will stop," Nieman said. "I'll put a stop to that."

"Danen said they might do it as soon as next week."

"Okay."

"Well, I'd better finish getting dressed. I like to be there by noon."

"Hold on, N.J. We have a chance now. A real chance. Be grateful if you can."

"I know. I will." She put down the phone and went over to her bedside table and turned on the CD player with the meditation tape by Jon Kabat-Zinn and listened to it as she dressed. She pulled on a pair of Gap jeans, then took them off and put on panty hose and a silk dress. I have to get dressed as though every day were the main one we'll ever have. I will not start looking like someone who needs sympathy. Every thought counts. So does every minute. She put on a pair of two-inch heels that matched the brown in the print dress and then she put on a string of pearls and went into the bathroom and pulled her mass of curly black hair back into a ponytail and clasped it with a silver clasp she and Freddy had bought the first time he took her to New York City. She pushed it firmly into place and went into the bathroom and put on foundation and powder and eye shadow and mascara and rouge and lipstick, then took a towel and wiped part of it off. She went back into the bedroom and removed the CD from the CD player and went out the side door to the garage and opened the trunk of the car and put the CD in the player and got in and listened to it all the way to the hospital. "No matter what is wrong with you," Dr. Zinn was saying, "even if you have the worst kind of cancer, there is still more right with you than wrong with you." There is still more right with him than wrong with him, there is still more right with him than wrong with him, Nora Jane kept repeating. Such a world to give us doctors and medicines and Larry Binghamton. I'll go see his wife in a few days and tell her what he's doing and that she ought to quit running him down at cocktail parties because all it does is make people think she's mean.

The transplant was set for December 23. As the day drew near everyone drew together into a tight circle. Nieman and Stella were coming to Nora Jane's for dinner every night. Little Freddy was teaching Scarlett some new card games based on old maid. Tammili and Lydia had started sleeping together in Lydia's bed. Freddy's mother was calling every morning and coming by in the afternoons. She and Big Judy would come sit in the kitchen and talk to the girls when they came home from school or give them clothes she ordered for them from her cousin's shop in New Rochelle, New York. "Just pretend to like them," Nora Jane said. "You can give a few things back but keep some of them."

"Do I have to wear them?" Lydia asked.

"You don't like that mauve sweater set? I'll take it if you don't want it," Tammili said.

"I like the sweaters. I just don't like the plaid skirts."

"Then give her back the skirts," Nora Jane said. "But keep some of the things and wear them when we go over on Friday night. Think of what pleasure it gave her to have them sent from New Rochelle."

"Grandmother has to have something to do," Lydia said. "Days pass slowly when you are in extreme anxiety."

"All right," Tammili agreed. "I'll wear the blue sweaters and I'll wear those mauve ones if you change your mind."

Big Judy had convinced Lenora that plain old prayer was better than psychic intervention, and she had started going with him on Saturday to sing at his church in Marin City. She had really started liking her evenings there. She'd forgotten how nice it was to be with sober people who had jobs. Lenora was having a real makeover in the spiritual and lifestyle departments.

Mitzi had turned her prayers into confessions and promises and deals. If you will let Freddy Harwood get well, then I will not entertain sexual thoughts about your priests and servants. I will mind my own business and do a good job helping people look better so they'll be in a better mood and I will not keep going to church if I can't keep unclean thoughts out of my head about Father Donovan, for Christ's sake. Hail Mary, Full of Grace, blessed art thou among women and blessed is the fruit of thy womb, Jesus. Holy Mary, Mother of God, pray for us sinners now and at the hour of our death, amen . . ."

At seven o'clock in the morning on the twenty-third of December, they rolled Freddy Harwood into an operating room and put Larry Binghamton's bone marrow into his body and waited to see if it would take.

Long, long ago in a small town in France the match had been made when their common great-great-great-great-great-great-grandmother gave birth to twin boys and both of them lived, a rarity in the seventeen hundreds. Now the DNA met again and was not surprised, was even pleased, very pleased, in some smooth chemical version of that emotion we don't know how to talk about in words but can imagine if we watch a tree put out its leaves, or cherries ripen, or our own hands when they are at work.

"He keeps quoting Rilke," Nora Jane was telling Nieman. "He's quoting it a lot."

"It's the hospital," Nieman answered. "He doesn't like to be confined and he's a control freak. I've never been in a hospital to stay. I know it would drive me crazy. Some of the aids seem, well, less than competent. I'm not sure I'd trust half those people to touch me."

They were waiting while the transplant was taking place. It was Mrs. Harwood, Big Judy, Nora Jane, Lydia, Tammili, and Nieman. Stella had Little Freddy at her house with Scarlett.

Lydia and Tammili were sitting very close together on a sofa. They were reading books from school. Tammili was reading *The Return of the King* for the fifth time. Lydia was reading a biography of Eleanor Roosevelt for a paper she was writing for American history. They were snuggled down very close to each other.

"I heard Stuart went back to South Africa," Nieman said to Mrs. Harwood. "It must have meant a lot to you to have him here."

"He is good to have around," she answered. "What time is it, Nieman? How long have they been in there?"

"They took him in at seven. So it's been fifty-six minutes. I think it takes a while. They have to wait and watch it. Well, I made that up. I'm sorry."

"Are you enjoying being at the university?"

"He loves it," Nora Jane answered. "He is a different man. Can't you tell, Miss Ann?"

"How long do you think it will take?" she asked.

"I'll go ask." Nora Jane got up and left the waiting room and walked down to a nurse's station. She wasn't really going to bother a nurse with a question like that, but she thought it might make Mrs. Harwood feel better if she believed information was forthcoming.

Nora Jane spoke to the nurses at the station, thanking them for working so hard to help people. Then she went back to the visitor's waiting room and told Mrs. Harwood it would not be too much longer.

Twenty minutes later a doctor came to the room and spoke with them. "It went well," he said. "He'll be in a recovery room for the rest of the day. You might as well go home and rest. Tonight or tomorrow morning we'll move him back to an isolation room. You can see him then. If you'll give me a telephone number, someone will call when he's back in a room."

Mrs. Harwood stood up. Nora Jane stood up beside her. They gave him both their numbers. Then everyone began to gather his or her things and move out into the hall and down the hall to an elevator and down the elevator to the lobby and out the doors to the steps and the parking lot. Nora Jane was crying. Tammili and Lydia were beside her. Big Judy had Mrs. Harwood's arm.

"I'd better get back to the lab," Nieman said. "Call me there if you hear anything."

They went their separate ways. "But this," Nieman was quoting from Rilke as he drove, "that one can contain death, the whole of death, even before life has begun, can hold it to one's heart gently, and not refuse to go on living, is inexpressible."

Nora Jane was also thinking of Rilke, but she was thinking of something Freddy had written down for her that was nicer to think about.

> Earth, my dearest, I will. O believe me, you no longer
> Need your springtimes to win me over—one of them,
> Ah, even one, is already too much for my blood. . . .

Lydia was driving the car. "I don't know what this means," she said, after they had gone twenty blocks and were stopped at a stop sign. "Is Daddy going to live?"

"It means the transplant was successful and the leukemia won't have a place to be. Yes, it does mean he is going to live." Nora Jane realized as she was talking that she didn't understand what was going on any better than Lydia did.

"Forever? He's going to live forever?"

"No one does," Tammili answered. "He'll live as long as normal, I guess."

"The next few weeks will be scary," Nora Jane said. "But we have to have faith in the doctors and what they are doing. These are miracles that are occurring. We are the beneficiaries of the work of thousands of people over hundreds of years."

"Yeah, science," Tammili added. "We live in a world made out of other people's dreams. That's what Mrs. Harley told us in chemistry lab. That's why we have to study it even if it's hard to do."

"Yeah," Lydia added, choosing to ignore her abysmal grades in science. "I may take some science courses in summer school this summer."

"That would be wonderful, Lydia," Nora Jane said. "That is a very mature decision."

"I didn't say I'd do it. I said I might do it."

"Oh, right," Tammili couldn't keep herself from adding. "I'm waiting for that day to come."

Lydia reached across the seat and pinched her sister on the leg. Not much of a pinch. Such a small pinch it would have been difficult to prove it wasn't a pat or touch.

"I saw that," Nora Jane said. "Go over to Stella's and get Little Freddy. And please don't fight today. Please. Just for me and just for the sake of goodness, mercy, and love."

"Don't start crying again, Mother. Please don't cry when we should be happy."

"We won't fight," they both said, and Nora Jane decided to believe it.

*　　　*　　　*

It was two days later when Nora Jane was allowed to enter Freddy's room. Gowned and masked, she was allowed to talk to him for five minutes. "That's over," he said, when she took his hand. "Would you tell Danen I'm ready to go home? And what happened to the twins' birthday? We didn't even have a party? Have you registered Lydia for the Kaplan course?"

"I thought you wanted her to do Princeton Review?"

"She might need both. Tammili still doesn't want to do it?"

"She doesn't need to do it. Are you all right? Do you feel all right?"

"I feel like a different man. I think I have taken on some of Larry's characteristics. I'm serious, N.J. Yesterday I found myself being profoundly, even mysteriously, patient."

"That would be interesting."

"Is Mother out there?"

"No, she's coming this afternoon at five. It's Christmas, Freddy. Do you know that?"

"Of course I know it. Good that Mother's coming."

"All right. I have to leave." She stood up beside the bed. "Did I tell you Little Freddy was picked to sing 'The Star-Spangled Banner' when school starts in January? So we have to practice. If you can't make it I'll videotape it for you."

"I'll be there. Are you kidding? This is over now, N.J. . . . I am done with this mess."

She stopped at the door. "I think you are. You know what, Freddy? We're lucky. I have this huge feeling of being grateful and feeling lucky."

"You bet we are," he said. "You bet I know that."

5

MITZI OZBURT MAY HAVE SWORN OFF
lusting after Father Donovan, but that didn't mean Father Donovan
wasn't still getting a hard-on every time she showed up to work at the
Crisis Center in her little matching pants and shoes, with her low-cut
blouses and her long arms sticking out all the way down to her pale
pink fingernails with a star on top of one of the index fingers so that
all he could think about in the long January nights was what would
happen if those fingers slid along the curve of his ribs and down onto
the rest of him.

"To hell with it," he said. He got out the vacuum sweeper and
hooked the hose onto the rod and began to vacuum the floor of the
room where the volunteers met once a month to workshop their
cases and, sometimes, as tonight, be lectured to by various profes-
sionals in the field.

"I cannot keep on if I don't believe it's right," he said out loud,
turning on the vacuum and beginning to push the brush into the corners. "Everything is sexual, everything is blossom and seed and pod.
In every niche in nature only one thing is going on. For all we know
the stars are fucking. The church is wrong to ask this of us. It is wrong
and it is evil and it creates evil. When women died in childbirth,
chastity was an act of mercy. When priests had to minister to starving
people, there was no time for them to become husbands, fathers,

lovers. If I were in Africa it would be different, but I am in San Francisco, California. I am a good man. I am a priest, but I love this woman, I covet her, I lust for her, I want to live with her in a house with a real kitchen and see her grow big with child. I want a little boy like Little Freddy to hold my hand and tell me things." He stopped talking and began to pray. He prayed as he vacuumed the room and continued to pray as he pushed the tables back into place and set out the coffeepot and platters for cookies and put away the vacuum. He left the recreation hall and walked across the playground to the church and went into his office and called his cousin, Nora Jane.

"I'm having a crisis," he said when she answered. "But first, how is Freddy? Is it still going well?"

"He says he likes the way he feels. He says he is a quieter and more patient person now that he has Larry Binghamton's DNA. He says he is becoming wise and solemn. We hope he can go home soon. What's going on with you?"

"I want to leave the church. I want to do the work but I can't do the rest anymore. I want to be a normal man, Nora Jane. I'm lonely here. If it wasn't for you . . . I shouldn't tell you this but you're the only person who knows who I was before this. Sometimes I can barely remember myself. Will you have lunch with me tomorrow? Anywhere. We could meet at the hospital if that's where you'll be."

"Okay. Meet me at the front entrance at noon. There's a little French place in the neighborhood that Nieman discovered. I wondered when we'd have this conversation, Donny. I've been waiting for it."

Father Donovan put down the phone and changed into his running shoes and told the secretary he was going for a run. "In those clothes?" she asked.

"The volunteers will be here in an hour and a half. I won't have time to change."

"Okay." She looked worried, so Father Donovan went back into his office and took off his coat and collar and put on a sweatshirt and sweatpants and his running shoes and left by the back door and began to run. He ran all the way to the children's park and began to circumnavigate it. His heart was heavy. He could not concentrate. He could not pray. I am a man, he kept thinking whether he wanted to think it or not. I was a man for twenty-three years before I went to Texas and signed those papers and drove to Saint Louis and entered the seminary and began this long, long lie.

He lost track of time. When he remembered, he turned and ran back to the church as fast as he could and hurried into the recreation hall. Most of the volunteers were already there, filling cups with coffee, eating sweet rolls and cookies, waiting for him. The speaker, Sally Monroe from Los Angeles, was moving among the volunteers talking to them.

"Please forgive me," he told the ladies. "I forgot the time. I am so sorry. I'll change and be right back. Never mind, I'll introduce Miss Monroe and let her begin her talk. I don't know what happened to me . . ." Then Mitzi was there, wearing something made of silk. It was yellow or gold or the color of marigolds or sunlight and it fell around her arms and the sleeves went down to those fingers and that star, but he couldn't look at it. He looked at her face, which was quiet and still. The light was missing from Mitzi's face tonight. She was solemn, as Nora Jane said Freddy Harwood had become. Maybe the world has grown solemn the last few years, Father Donovan decided.

"Hello," he said. "How are you?"

"I'm good," she answered. "I'm glad you were running." He was sweating and the old sweatshirt from Tulane University was sticking to his chest. He wanted to touch her more than he had ever wanted anything in his life, even God, even salvation, even hope.

"I better get this started," he said. He reached out and touched her arm through the silk and walked to the podium to thank the volunteers for coming. He said a prayer for the whole state of Christ's church and then he turned the meeting over to Sally Monroe and left the room. He ran to his office and put on his pants and shirt and collar and coat and leather shoes and ran back to the recreation building and stood at the back of the room, looking at Mitzi's soft golden hair and thinking of the night he drove her to Nora Jane's house and she had cut his hair. Her fingers had brushed against his forehead and God had drained out of his brain into her hands and it was over now.

"The main thing you must do is be a coach," Sally Monroe was saying. "You must always stay positive about the future. This was a terrible and life-changing thing that happened to these women, but it was ONLY ONE THING. Yes, it will take them a long time, for some of them years, to understand and lessen the fear. The fear is real for them now in a way none of us can understand, unless it happened to us also." She stopped and looked down a moment.

"Where am I? It is a process. You will be better with some victims than others. If you are feeling like you can't help a woman, call for help from Father Donovan or one of your team captains. Never keep trying to do it alone if your lady isn't getting better. You are only one person doing what you can. Don't get frustrated. We need you. You are true angels to do this work. We love you for it. I love you for it.

"I was a victim. I know what it means to have been raped. But more importantly, I know what it means to be helped."

She bowed her head and folded her hands in prayer at her chest. The volunteers clapped and cheered.

Father Donovan went to the podium. "Let's take a break for fifteen minutes. Then we'll have questions for Miss Monroe and I'll read you some letters we received last week from women we have helped."

Mitzi was not moving toward him. She was talking to another woman, but when he looked at her she turned and looked back at him and it was a caress and they both knew it.

When the meeting was over, Father Donovan was busy taking

care of Sally Monroe, thanking her for coming and attempting to give her the small check that most of the speakers either refused or sent back as a contribution to the center. Mitzi was glad he was busy. She left as quickly as she could after the final prayers were said. Pray for grace, she told herself. Pray for something.

She went home and watched HBO for a while, then got in bed and tried to read a book of poems Freddy had lent her months before, but they were all about love and that was the last thing she needed now.

> I walk down the garden paths,
> And all the daffodils
> Are blowing, and the bright blue squills.
> I walk down the patterned garden paths
> In my stiff, brocaded gown.
> With my powdered hair and jeweled fan,
> I too am a rare
> Pattern. As I wander down
> The garden paths . . .

But this poet lost her lover in a war, Mitzi decided. I lose mine to God. Or am I just a bad girl, and always love the wrong people, like my cousin James in Baton Rouge. That was worse than this, I guess, because we just did it to be mean. We weren't in love. We were just young and mean.

Oh God, I ought to stop these patterns. They are killing me.

Mitzi got up and went into the kitchen and made some Sleepytime Tea with lots of Splenda and went back into her bedroom and snuggled down into the blue comforter she had had in her bed in her mother's house and thought about calling her mother, but her mother was the last person on earth to talk to about this.

She turned on her meditation tape and began to pretend she was on a lake looking at the water and the lake birds and all the stuff growing all around it like that lake they have near Las Vegas that is so beautiful — no, that was Reno, Nevada, when she went there with Charles Cortwright before he left her for a sorority girl he knew at LSU.

In the morning, Father Donovan went to the record store on Telegraph Avenue to walk about among normal people and try to imagine himself becoming one again. He bought an expensive double album by Bob Dylan, then went to a coffee shop down the street from Freddy's bookstore that Nora Jane and Freddy had taken him to one night when he first got to town. He ordered coffee and a croissant and sat down at a table near the sidewalk. He found a newspaper on a chair and opened it to the sports pages, then put it aside and sipped his coffee. He had not eaten since half a sweet roll at the meeting the night before.

He broke off a piece of the croissant and ate it slowly, trying to remember what it was like to hold a woman in his arms and be a man. Then Mitzi was there, standing beside the table with a plate and a cup. "What are you doing here?" she asked. "I'm glad. I want to ask you about that talk last night, what she said about not getting worried."

He stood up and took her cup and plate and put it on the table next to his. "Please sit down. Stay with me." She sat down across from him and he took her hand in his.

"There aren't any accidents," he said. "We don't run into people we like by accident. No, look at me. Please look at me. I'm falling in love with you, Mitzi, and you know it and you feel it too. I am going to leave the priesthood. It's decided. I'm going to call my spiritual adviser this afternoon and tell him that."

"You would be sorry," she answered. She was not amazed, not frightened, not surprised.

"I'm not and I won't be. I was old before I went to seminary. I was a normal person for twenty-three years before this began."

"How old are you now?"

"Thirty-seven years old on the twentieth of the month."

"I'm twenty-six," she said. "Nora Jane says it's the best age there is."

"Eat your breakfast," he suggested. "Stay here with me."

"I was going to the bookstore," she said. "I canceled my appointments this morning. I wanted to find another book to read. I had this book of poems Freddy gave me but I couldn't read it. It was all about the sadness of love. I wanted a book about Iraq or something for the real world."

She had not moved her hand and now she turned it over so their palms were touching.

"What are we doing?" she asked.

"What men and women do," he answered. "Eat your scone."

She took back her hand and picked up a fork and used it to cut off a piece of scone and put it into her mouth. She began to chew, very elegantly, deliberately, beautifully.

The sun, which all morning had been behind a thick line of clouds, broke out above them and shone down on San Francisco with the full force of a solar storm that had begun many years ago but only now was hitting Northern California on its way to Nevada and New Orleans and Mississippi. It burned down upon the Bay Area as if to touch and warm every atom in all the animate and inanimate matter known to man or God or the idea of God or order or memory or dream. It is the sun, and anyone with any sense would worship it, Mitzi was thinking, because, for goodness sake, it isn't always asking hard things in return and just lets people soak it up and be. Amen.

6

"I KNOW ALL OF MITZI'S COUSINS," Nora Jane was saying. "They're an old German family, except Mitzi's mom is Irish. Mitzi knows all those Irish dances that are the fad now. I want her to start teaching a class but she's too busy. Mitzi's somebody, Freddy. Wait a minute." Nora Jane was using the speakerphone outside the isolation room. She would be able to go in soon, but for now the doctors "just wanted to be sure the marrow is everywhere we need it."

"Just to be extra careful. It's been so nice so far," the Indian oncologist had said, so the Harwoods had taken that to heart and become the model recovery patient and family.

"This speakerphone is getting bad," Nora Jane said. "Don't you think so? It's worn out from everyone yelling in it."

"We won't need it soon. Okay, go on. So, in other words, she's worthy of him and he can just dump the priesthood like he did coaching and what else, oh yes, writing. I like your cousin Donny, Nora Jane. I just mean this is his pattern, you know. So don't be surprised."

"I am not surprised. I begged him not to go to that seminary. I told him it wouldn't work. When Mitzi was in New Orleans she worked for the John Jay Salon. She quits things too. If it wasn't for me she wouldn't have gone back to hairdressing. She gets burned-out easily."

"All the young people are like that now." He sat up in the bed and pushed both machines away and thought about unhooking one, then thought better of it. "I am tired of you seeing me like this. Do you still love me, Nora Jane? I wouldn't blame you if you didn't."

"Don't talk like that. I'll show you when you get home if I love you or not. Can anyone but us hear this? I'm sorry. Go on."

"I was going to say no one wants to work. Well, my people do. Maybe the only people who still like to work are people who love books. Anal-retentive book lovers."

"It's because they work for you, you and Francis take care of them. Anyway, don't worry about Donny and Mitzi . . . although . . ." She started giggling. "I guess it's your fault they both came over on the same night. I blame it on that automobile ride together."

"N.J., may I buy the girls a new car, well, two cars? I want to so much. It will get me through this last week if I could only get Steve Hart to come up here and tell me about the BMWs. I'll get them secondhand. I can take them off my income tax if the girls work in the store this summer."

"I give up. Okay. But they have to be completely safe, Freddy. I mean it. No convertibles and that's final."

"You better go on. Donny will be waiting."

"I love you."

"I love you too. Tell Donny I'm behind him. He can work at the bookstore if he needs a job."

He waited until she was down the hall, then called the BMW dealership in Walnut Creek and told his friend Steve to hurry up. "Bring everything you have," he said. "Bring a laptop in case we have to look at other stores."

"I'm on my way." The good-looking blond man gathered his notes and laptop and ran out of the dealership and got into a new 740i lender and headed off for the hospital. He and Freddy had been plotting to buy the twins new cars for months. Today was the day.

*　　　*　　　*

Father Donovan was waiting in the hospital lobby. He took Nora Jane's arm and they walked two blocks to the French café Nieman and Stella had found while Freddy was undergoing the transplant. It was small and clean and smelled like wine and garlic and hot bread. Nora Jane ordered asparagus and trout almondine and Donny told the waiter to bring him the same.

"So it's over," Nora Jane said.

"It won't be all that easy. You can't just walk out. I'll volunteer to stay until someone else gets here and gets settled. I have the Crisis Center running. I think I can get a lady we had speak the other night to be the director for a while."

"I don't know why everything about the church is so sexy," Nora Jane said. "Well, it is. The mass is sexy. It is, Donny, you have to admit it."

"Vacuum sweepers and vacuum-sweeper bags are sexy to me this year," he answered. "Don't you want wine?"

"No, I quit. Too much sugar." She took his hand and held it on the table. "I was thinking this morning about when I used to come watch you play rugby on Sunday afternoons and you would be so beautiful. You're too handsome to be a priest. I knew it was the wrong thing for you to do."

"It wasn't wrong. I had to try it. I've paid the Jesuits back for what they gave me."

"The Jesuits?"

"It's the Jesuits at Loyola who put this idea in my head. I just went with the Dominicans because they could take me in a hurry."

"The next thing you do for a living, decide on it over a long time, okay? I mean, don't just go jump into anything. Freddy said to tell you that you have a job with him anytime you want or need it."

"How nice. How good of him."

They were quiet. The waiter brought French bread and butter and they broke the bread and ate it. "So is Mitzi in this too?" Nora Jane asked. "Have you told her?"

"I ran into her this morning. There are no accidents, Nora Jane. We ran into each other at that coffee shop near the bookstore. I took it as a sign. I told her that I love her. I'm going to call her this afternoon and ask her to have dinner with me."

"Oh God, this is deep, Donny. This is deeper than the mass. This is going to be all anybody talks about for weeks."

"I can get a job in social work. I'm not worried about working. I have money in the bank. I never touched the money Mother gave me. I should have given it to the church but I never did. So see, I knew I was going to do this. I've known for a year, ever since Mother died."

"I knew it from the time you thought it up."

"Maybe we can go home some weekend," he said. "Go visit Grandmother's grave, see people. I miss New Orleans, don't you?"

"No. I don't have good memories of being there, except for Grandmother. I just remember Momma being drunk."

"I'm sorry, dearest cousin."

"'The past is a swamp, where we wander at our peril.' It's a new year, Donny, and it's going to be a good one for all of us. A year to remember."

"I believe that. Let's have dessert? Let's have crème brûlée?"

"Yes, oh, yes, yes, yes, yes, like Molly Bloom, yes, like Grandmother singing Puccini, yes. Like here and now and this golden, golden day."

She began to hum "Vissi d'arte," which their grandmother had sung in *Madame Butterfly* at the Metropolitan Opera when she was twenty-six years old, and later that same year in Paris and Milan. Donny's eyes filled with tears and Nora Jane moved her hand from his hand to his arm and held it as if to save him from all harm, as her grandmother would have done if she were there. She moved her chair nearer to her cousin and kept holding his arm and the waiter came and took the dessert order and returned with crème brûlée on beautiful lavender-and-blue plates. Nora Jane picked up Father Donovan's spoon and handed it to him and he brushed the tears from his face and she said, "Go ahead, you go first."

"No, ladies first as long as I live, especially if we're going to call in Grandmother's ghost."

"Okay. God, I love this stuff." She took her spoon and broke the golden baked sugar and dug down into the lovely egg-and-milk center and took a bite. "Perfection," she said.

Father Donovan, soon to be Donovan Michael James Whittington the Fourth again, aimed his spoon at the exact center of the custard and broke it cleanly. The cream poured up around the spoon and of course that took his breath away. If it hadn't been for Nora Jane being there, he would have just looked at it and not even eaten it.

"Proving my point," he said in a low voice.

"What?" she answered, because she was thinking about where it would be good for him to get a job in the Bay Area so he wouldn't move back to New Orleans and take her good friend Mitzi with him. Nora Jane didn't like losing people that she loved. She liked to keep them near.

That night Mitzi Ozburt dressed in her most conservative navy blue pleated skirt and a blue cashmere sweater with a white collar and cuffs. She looked like a Catholic schoolgirl when Donovan came to pick her up. She had intended to show him what a good girl she was, but of course the sexiest thing in the world to a Catholic man is a woman dressed in something that looks like a school uniform. If her slip had been showing a little bit or she had worn saddle oxfords, it might have taken less than an hour for them to get into Mitzi's cherry four-poster bed, but as it was they had a glass of wine and talked about feeling guilty for a while before they made love, and vowed devotion, and said will you marry me, and this is crazy, no it's not, you're right, it's not, and do you want some babies, I do, I do too.

"God forgives everything and we are not sinners," Mitzi said. "Those old guys who want to keep people from being happy are the sinners."

"We will live lives that are good," he said.

"And live right now," she answered. "My client, Sui Wong, is a physicist and she says living in the present is the most spiritual and Zen thing anyone can do. It teaches other people to do the same, and if you could teach that to suicide bombers they wouldn't blow themselves up."

"Amen to that."

"I am really hungry," Mitzi said. "I'd really like to go somewhere and get something to eat, and I mean fast. I haven't eaten in days, it seems like. Could we just go to a fast-food place and get something, if you don't mind?"

"We can do whatever you want to do."

"Come on. Get dressed. I'll show you the real me."

On their way out of the house, Mitzi stopped and picked up a handful of crackers and ate them on the way to the car. Fifteen minutes later they were at an Arby's Drive-Thru window collecting roast beef sandwiches and Jamocha milkshakes. They sat in the car in the parking lot and ate their dinners, and Donovan decided it was like coming back from a trip to Antarctica and finding himself in heaven instead.

When Nora Jane got back to the hospital, Nieman was in the hall by the speakerphone and Freddy's room was full of nurses and technicians unplugging machines and getting ready to transfer him to a private room. He was sitting on the edge of the bed arguing about getting into a wheelchair. He was really angry, he wasn't pretending or joking. "I can walk, for God's sake," he was saying. "I have been patient, as in *the patient,* for several months now and I'm tired of this. I want to walk down the hall to the room. Get me a longer robe." He turned to the window where Nieman was looking into the room. "Go get me my robe!" he yelled.

"Okay," Nieman signed, and moved back from the window and pulled Nora Jane back to the nurse's stand. "Don't let him see you. He doesn't want you to see him in a wheelchair. I surmise that's the problem here."

"Larry's DNA is fading," she answered. "I think the Harwood genes are reemerging."

"The Rosenstein side," Nieman added. "It's his mother's side that have the tempers. Well, where have you been?"

"To Le Comte, the food was really good. My cousin Donovan is leaving the church. That's the latest news. He's in love with Mitzi Ozburt."

"You're kidding."

"I am not. He's leaving the church for her."

"Stella had a breakthrough this morning, with some antiviral she's been nursing. I came down here to tell Freddy but when I got here this had started."

They moved out into the hall so they could see the door to his room. As they watched he came walking out the door with a white cotton blanket wrapped around his shoulders like an old Navajo chief. He was wearing hospital slippers and his skinny legs were sticking out beneath the hospital gown and they were as white as snow except for the veins and scars from high school soccer. He was smiling and he was triumphant and he came toward his wife and best friend with two nurses and three attendants trailing behind him, plus a fat man pushing the empty wheelchair.

"*Hola, amigos,*" he said, in a perfect imitation of the Spanish Little Freddy was learning from Diego Martinez, the contractor who was building the hot tub on the Harwoods' stone patio. "*Qué pasa* in *los realidad* worlds? Freed any priests today? Invented any miracle drugs? Started any student protests? Saved anybody from their darker selves?

Enrolled my daughter in the Princeton Review course like I told you to do six weeks ago and no one has done it yet?"

He stopped and kissed his wife and took Nieman's arm. "Wait until you see the cars Steve is bringing to the parking lot this afternoon. I'm going to make them let me go down and look at them. One is red and one is blue and the girls can draw lots for them."

"They had better not be convertibles," Nora Jane said. "And they better be secondhand."

The nurses looked at each other and then took back their territory. "Please come on, Mr. Harwood. We have other patients. We need to get you settled."

"*Vaya con Dios hasta todos* meet anon," Freddy said, and moved on down the hall with the nurses.

"I love the world," Nieman said. He took Nora Jane's arm and steered her to the elevator. "Let's go downstairs and get some coffee or watch people smoking on the corner by the benches. Let's have some fun."

7

DANEN MARCUS, MD, had Stella Light-Gluuk pressed into a corner of a hall leading to the Harwoods' living room. It was a champagne party from three to seven on a Sunday afternoon, and everyone understood it was supposed to start late and end on time. Freddy was dressed and in the living room when everyone arrived. He had disappeared around six and the party was winding down.

"The most useful ideas often come from research that doesn't seem scientifically challenging," Stella was saying. "A woman at Technion in Tel Aviv is way ahead of me in this. She's already isolated a protein and it's destroying cancer cells like crazy in the dishes."

"I wanted to go into research," Danen said. "Robert Gallo is my idol. I saw him on C-Span the other night and it all came back to me. He's so healthy and strong, still such a presence."

"Why didn't you do it?"

"Dad wanted me to practice with him. You know. So I did internal medicine. Sometimes I wonder if it was the right choice."

"Why?"

"Oh hell, treating colds. Telling fat people to lose weight, watching them die when they don't. I lost three patients from October to Christmas. You know who they were. You went to the funerals."

"You saved Freddy. You diagnosed it."

"Not soon enough. I believed the lab work."

"You did what anyone would have done."

"I hope so. So tell me what you're doing?"

"I'm breeding a cold virus I had a couple of years ago. It was a bad one. It took three rounds of Levaquin to get it. So I cultured it a few times and I kept noticing it had extra spikes so I started messing with the proteins. It's killing one of the herpes viruses in the dishes. I need to try it with the monkeys, but I hate to start that unless I'm sure I have something worth the money and bad karma."

"Karma?" He started giggling. "Sorry," he added. "The champagne."

"I'm open to those ideas. My parents were old hippies, Danen. How do you think I got named Stella? For all I know they got me stoned when I was young. They deny it but I have my doubts. Look, anyway, it's good to talk to you, Danen. We appreciate all you did for Freddy."

"I didn't do much. I was just standing by. Is it true you had nuns praying for him?"

"I'll tell you about that one day." She touched his arm. "There's a lot going on in the universe, Danen. Stay open to it."

"I do. Well, tell them to keep praying. We're not out of the woods yet. I would have kept him in the hospital if it were me. His immune system's so compromised. I'd have him where I could watch him. Don't tell anyone I said that. That's just between you and me."

"Quality of life and all that notwithstanding."

"Graft-versus-host disease can develop very slowly. I'd be testing constantly if it were me. It's not me."

"We're watching," Stella said. "Everyone knows what's going on. Well, I better go find Nieman. It's good to talk to you, Danen. Come visit the labs sometime. We'll hit you up for a contribution. Just kidding." She gave him one of her best smiles, touched him on the sleeve again, and made an escape. GVHD, there's a happy thought for a party, she decided. God, Danen's really burned-out. We use people up too fast in this culture. We eat them up.

When they got home from the party, Stella sent an e-mail to Sister Anne Aurora. "Keep praying for Frederick Harwood. The enemies now are anemia and GVHD (graft-versus-host disease). It's a sneaky demon. Can't see it coming. It can happen in days and become acute. Also, check arriving by mail to buy two hours of prayer for the International AIDS Vaccine Initiative. Also, one hour for the Primate Center at Louisiana State University in Baton Rouge, Louisiana. Plus an hour for the Centers for Disease Control in Atlanta. And half an hour for Danen Marcus, MD, San Francisco, for peace of mind, gratitude, and to make him believe in his work. I guess it would be too much to ask for his patients to stop killing themselves with food and cigarettes.

"I ordered a weekly journal called *Science News* for you. Thought you might like it. Just a late Christmas present.

Love, Stella."

When she finished the e-mail Stella went into the kitchen where Nieman was feeding Scarlett baked chicken and vegetables for dinner.

"Here's a weird bit of data," she said, standing by the microwave oven and watching Scarlett boss her father around about *exactly* how many vegetables could go on the fork he was holding. "I'm four days late. I just realized it. Isn't it the sixteenth? I missed a few pills."

Nieman turned his face to hers. Scarlett reached up her left hand and delicately removed a green pea and a carrot slice from the fork, leaving only one pea and one square of potato. She was eating the vegetables to get to the dish of chocolate pudding waiting by the fruit bowl and she was getting sick of this stupid game and counting all these forkfuls of peas and carrots.

Nieman did not notice that she had moved the pea and the slice of carrot. He was looking at Stella.

"You stopped the pills?"

"I didn't have any last month for about a week. It was while Seth Rosen was in town and Freddy was still in crisis . . . priorities . . . the day-care center had that chicken pox case so I had to take Scarlett to get a booster. I think it was about a week, ten days maybe, that I didn't have any."

"You could have had them delivered from Mallison's."

"They charge too much. I wanted to get them at a Walgreens."

"Stella!" He put the fork down for Scarlett to use herself, then took the pudding and put it before her and handed her a spoon. "Go on, honey, eat the pudding if you want it." He walked around the table to his wife. "Do you think it could be — tell me what you think."

"I think we made ourselves another child, is what I think, and if it's true it means you will have to take over my project because I'm not going to play with viruses while I'm pregnant."

"Preeegnant," Scarlett said. "Preeegnant." She tore into the pudding, eating it so fast a weaker child would have choked to death. "Can I have another one when this is threeew?" she asked, pausing near the end of the dish. "Can I have just one more pudding?"

"May," Stella said to her. "And yes. Just this once you may have two."

Nieman was crying. Not weeping and not looking sad and not really even understanding what he was feeling. He was just looking at Stella and tears were falling down his face.

"I think I deserve to cry," he said at last. "I didn't cry the whole time I thought Freddy might die and now I'm crying over this and we don't even know if it's true."

"It's probably true," Stella said. She opened the refrigerator and got out a second chocolate pudding and pulled off the top and put the dish in front of Scarlett. "The simplest explanation is the best. Plus, the conscious mind is the size of a screw in the door frame of the mansion of the unconscious. So I guess we wanted this." She was laughing and extremely pleased with herself and absolutely delighted that Nieman was crying. One thing about Nieman Gluuk, like all true intellectuals he was a sucker for his emotions.

Danen Marcus drove home from the Harwoods' party the long way that had less traffic. He was listening to an old Gato Barbieri tape called *Viva Emiliano Zapata* and thinking about his wife, Donna Marie, how she'd played it all the time when he met her and how excited it made him when he'd walk into her hot little house on Cafino Drive. She'd tell him about her day in the shop and he could never trust it that she loved him. He was so jealous of her he couldn't stand it until after their third child was born and he finally settled down and believed she was going to stay.

I have wandered away from Donna, he decided. I shouldn't have been holding on to Stella Gluuk's arm so long. My goodness, was she telling me she cultured her own cold virus? I would never think to do that, but how can I think? I have three times too many patients and most of them are either related to me or knew my father or my grandparents. This town has gotten too small for me and I need another doctor in the office and I need one now.

His buzzer was going off and he let it ring for two blocks before he picked it up and listened to the answering service and turned off the music and started back toward the hospital. Shit, he decided. Goddamn it to hell. I am not behaving well lately and I need a vacation in the islands or at least in Cabo, or anywhere. Antarctica will do.

He pushed a button and Donna's voice answered the ring. "You aren't going to be here for dinner," she said.

"I have to go see about Buddy Caison, because it looks like his aorta burst. Could you come and meet me at the hospital later and have dinner somewhere? It's just a thought. I know—"

"What time?"

"An hour. He's in MRI. He was drinking again, I suppose."

"I'll be there."

"No underpants."

"Bad man."

Danen pushed the button to end the call and went into emergency mode. He turned on the blinkers, called to notify the police, pulled into the center lane, and started making time. Buddy Caison, who had gone to high school with him and who had been in his office two weeks ago and told for the tenth time to start walking and stop eating and smoking. Now he was maybe an hour away from being dead, if not dead already, and he was a really wonderful man with a wife and two children and a couple of million, if not ten million, dollars. At least thirty movie stars would be at the funeral and that would be another day on which he would not get any work done — no wonder he didn't have time to culture a virus or fuck or even think.

Danen pushed the button to talk to Donna, and the first thing she said was, "I'm not coming to meet you if you don't slow down. How fast are you going?"

"Seventy-five, sixty-five, sixty. Are you getting dressed?"

"Yes."

"Put on that red silk suit you wore at Christmas when we went to Momma's house, with that little blouse with the swirly things on it."

"Are you okay?"

"I'm tired, Donna. What are the boys doing?"

"Teddy's doing homework in the kitchen. Al's watching a football game, and Arthur's in his room, probably masturbating. I think that's all he does half the time now. Don't talk while you're driving."

"Okay. Hanging up. Ten-four."

I'm not just going to tell them anymore, Danen vowed as he left the highway and started the half mile to the hospital on the side road. *I'll give* them a printout. I'll tell them if they don't lose weight I won't treat them. I'll tell them I don't think it's funny. I'll tell them to grow up. I'll quit, is what I'm going to do. And then I'll go back to Berkeley like Nieman Gluuk did and do what I really want to do. Is there anything I want to think about tonight? Freddy Harwood, that's a light in the tunnel. I can't believe it was Larry Binghamton and that it worked. I don't think we're completely out of the woods, but it's the best match I've seen since I was part of this.

He got out of the car at the emergency exit and gave the keys to the attendant and hurried into the hall and took the elevator and went down the hall to find out if there was anything that could be done to save a life, although the answer was already there.

Fucking cigarettes, he thought. Don't be negative, he lectured himself. Slow down, take some breaths. Donna's on her way. I'll get to go home. I'll get to sleep in my bed. Grow up. The hell with it anyway.

It was Sunday night. Freddy Harwood was in his bed, wearing a pair of paisley pajamas Lydia and Tammili had picked out for him while he was in the hospital but which he had not taken out of the box until tonight. They were made of artificial silk and looked like one of his favorite ties.

The twins were sitting side by side on the edge of the bed, and Little Freddy was cuddled up beside him trying not to fall asleep.

"So did you like the party?" Lydia was asking.

"Yes, I did. I liked it as much as I like any party, which is not much, but don't tell your mother. Where is she?"

"Paying the caterers. They left all sorts of food. We have to take part of it to the neighbors tomorrow. I don't want all those petits fours left around here if nobody minds." Tammili turned and patted her father's leg. "I'm quitting dance. I can't stand having that bitch yell at me anymore. I mean it."

"We told you you could quit if you wanted to. It's given your mother a lot of pleasure, but you don't have to do it."

"I want to take a geology class at the university. They let people from our school take night classes there if they get recommended. So can I do that?"

"Drive at night?"

"I'll carpool."

"My daddy was right. You should put bricks on children's heads the day they are thirteen. Who did you torture when I wasn't here?"

"No one," Lydia put in. "We saved it for you. Oh yeah. I'm quitting too, but I'm not going to take anything else. I have too much to do, that's why I didn't do well on the PSAT." Lydia lay back across the bed with her black hair spread out on the covers exactly like her mother's always was and Tammili just kept touching Freddy's leg and Little Freddy gave up trying to keep his eyes from closing and let them close, saying in his small voice as he did, "I'm awake."

"As soon as I'm well we're all going up to Willits and start figuring out how to build some more rooms on the house," Freddy said. "Nieman wants to do it too."

"Did you know that nun is coming here to visit?" Tammili asked. "She wants to visit the labs at Berkeley and see the scanning electron microscopes and all the stuff. She wants to see the first reactor and all the things you and Nieman used to show us all the time."

Nora Jane came into the room and stood looking down at the tableau, her husband and her children, all there ever is, the blessed moment, life and peace. Today. Tonight. Forever.

"Let's go to bed now," she said. "Lydia, can you move Freddy?"

"Let him stay," his daddy said. "I like him there. I like to listen to him breathe."

8

MITZI OZBURT'S MOTHER had got wind of what was going on in California and she was headed that way in a Lincoln Continental Town Car with her boyfriend, DeLesseps Johnston, to stop it.

Mitzi never did find out how her mother knew, but she blamed the Dominicans, since who else would have told except Nora Jane and she didn't, and, besides, never would.

"It's happened before," Carla Ozburt was saying. She and DeLesseps had spent the night near the Petrified Forest in Arizona, but Carla barely glanced at the scenery when they passed it right after dawn. "When she was sixteen she fell in love with a priest at St. Mark's and I had to change churches and go to the cathedral for a year. I had her in Sacred Heart for a year, but she wouldn't kneel in the gravel by the statue and she wouldn't learn anything she wasn't interested in, so then we put her in a school out in Metairie where they mostly teach art, but she didn't like that either. Then she started staying at her daddy's half the time and I totally lost control. *A hairdresser.* I can't believe I clawed and fought my way out of Boutte to end up with a hairdresser atheist as a child."

"Mitzi's not an atheist, Carla. How would she meet a priest if she were an atheist? You are exaggerating this, and she wasn't just a hairdresser. She worked at the John Jay Salon. My mother goes to John Jay. She'd miss my funeral not to break an appointment with that man."

"You can't know. You don't have any children."

"That's a mean thing to say. I'd like to go back by that Petrified Forest. I wish we'd had time to look at that." DeLesseps was a small, pretty man who had been spoiled rotten by his mother and his aunts. He worked halfheartedly in the mayor's office in New Orleans, a job one of his uncles had arranged for him. Before that he had been in the admissions office at UNO but got fired for not showing up. He was forty-eight years old and had not really found himself until he met Carla and signed on to be her slave and driver and sometime lover. "I carry the bags," he told his friends. "I like to watch her operate. She's a piece of work."

"We need to find a place to stay in some good part of San Francisco and go there and change and then just go find her. There's no reason to call her anymore. She's not going to return the calls."

"We don't even know for sure she's in San Francisco. They may have run off somewhere."

"No. He's still at his church. I checked on that."

"I think we should have flown. This is going to take another day and part of one after that. We can't make it tonight, Carla. It's too far. We could stop in Las Vegas. Look on that map. It couldn't be that much out of the way."

"When I get my hands on her, I promise you this time it is going to be real. If she does this she is out of the will."

DeLesseps kept his thoughts to himself. There was no point in talking to Carla when she was on the crazies over Mitzi. The worst thing was that they were exactly alike. They looked alike, they dressed alike, they were the same size. Mitzi was softer and sweeter and more reasonable, but she was more determined also. DeLesseps had known her since she was eighteen and just out of high school. He had never known Carla to win a battle with Mitzi yet.

They were in a desert now. After about fifteen miles DeLesseps had to speak. Carla had been on the phone with her travel agent in New Orleans, finding a hotel in Sacramento for the night and one in Berkeley for the following week. He waited until she settled down from that and then he made his pitch. "Maybe this guy wasn't really cut out to be a priest and he was going to leave the church anyway and Mitzi was just in the right place at the right time. You don't know what's going on, Carla. Reserve part of your judgment until we get there. Remember when you thought she was into drugs and it was just some loose face powder you found? You could have had a heart attack while we waited for those tests."

"He is an ordained priest in the Holy Roman Catholic Church. He is a servant of God and my daughter has played his Abishag."

"His who?"

"King David's whore. In the Old Testament. Don't Episcopalians read the Bible? I thought you all read the Bible."

"No, that's Methodists, I think. Listen, Carla, is this heat gauge always like this? I don't remember this being way over here."

"Let me see." Carla leaned over him to look at the instrument panel. She didn't know anything about machines but she always pretended that she did. DeLesseps certainly didn't know anything. He could hardly change a lightbulb from being the great-grandson of a famous Louisiana politician and spoiled rotten from being the only male in his branch, not to mention being raised in a house with two older sisters and more servants than there were family members and then having the family lose all the money and being thrown out to try to make it in a real world, where people worked and had to fix things that were broken.

So there was no one in the car who understood what was happening as the motor heated up and the power-steering hose began to split. Carla hadn't had the car serviced for forty thousand miles, because she was too involved in the Race for the Cure luncheon she was cochairman of that year.

The car really began to heat up about ten miles out of Weggins, Arizona, a small town near Death Valley National Park. By the time they limped into Weggins, the Lincoln was going to need a major overhaul before anyone was going to drive it to San Francisco. There was no one in Weggins to fix it, and the truck to haul it to Bishop couldn't get there until afternoon, so Carla and DeLesseps paid the service-station owner to drive them to a motel and got a room with a hot tub that didn't work and a television with fifty channels and settled down to wait it out.

DeLesseps had his laptop computer and Carla had her cell phone and that was going to be about that until late the next day.

"We just have to make the best of things," DeLesseps volunteered. "We could make love. We haven't done it in a long time."

"Are you kidding? My only child is on her way to eternal damnation and you expect me to want to fornicate. I hope you aren't serious, DeLesseps. I hope you didn't mean that."

"Then could we find somewhere to eat? I'm starving, to tell the truth."

"Okay." They left their bags unpacked and went to the dining room and looked at the wilted lettuce in the salad bar and decided to see what else was available.

"There's the Four Steers Steakhouse two blocks down the road," the man at the desk told them. "It's nice. I eat there myself."

"Just down the highway?"

"Yes. Just keep on the side so you don't get run over." The man put down his newspaper and handed them a card with the name of the restaurant on it. "Tell them Will Maynes sent you. It will help me out."

They left the motel and began to walk along the highway past a junk-yard and some small businesses and an optometrist's office. Carla wasn't talking. She had put on her tennis shoes and she was feeling her age for the first time since the last time she was stupid enough to leave New Orleans and go wandering around the world. She was in such a bad mood that she had forgotten why she was in Arizona on the first day of March, two thousand and four, only five days past her sixty-fourth birthday and what seemed like a million days since the last time she was comfortable or happy.

"I give up," she said in a quiet voice, just loud enough for DeLesseps to hear but not loud enough so he had to hear it unless he wanted to.

"Don't do that. I can see the sign. It's right up there. We'll have lunch and then call and see if there's an Enterprise rental that will bring us a car."

At the Morning Glory Motel the man who was living off of the Mexican girl who cleaned the rooms had taken her keys and was in the room Carla and DeLesseps had rented. Going through the bags, he found the case with Carla's jewelry and opened it and thought maybe he would cry with joy. He took the case and the laptop and the leather holder for the cellular phone and three of DeLesseps's shirts and a suit and sweater from Rubenstein Brothers and a pair of running shoes from Fleet Feet of Boston and stuffed it all into a laundry bag and got into his truck and took off for Mexico. He was leaving Maria Elena behind without a word of farewell. He didn't even have the courtesy to stop off and give her back the keys he had taken while she was napping in their room.

He threw the keys away in the desert near the Arizona border. He traded in the car in Nogales and crossed the border into Sonora, where the spoils of his evil would make him a wealthy man for many months before his karma caught up with him.

Carla dug into her steak and baked potato, forgetting her low-fat, low-carb life and concentrating on saving room for apple pie and ice cream.

DeLesseps was almost as indulgent. At least it was a break from sitting at a desk at the mayor's office being a flak-catcher for every out-of-work voter in the parish. "My great-grandfather was the governor of Louisiana," he reminded Carla. "And I have to work for that asshole and he didn't even give me a raise this year. I think I'll stay out here in California and start over again."

"What? What are you talking about?" She looked across the expanse of the tabletop, with its cheap paper place mats and dirty salt and pepper containers, and past the tables to the dusty windows with the plastic curtains and tried not to think of what would happen if she caught giardia as she had one time in Colorado.

"Never mind. Just go on thinking about yourself. I'm going outside to smoke. Order me some dessert. Just pick out anything." He got up and left the table. He almost never got mad at Carla, but this trip and this day were too much. He walked outside and lit a cigarette and watched as the pickup truck carrying his laptop computer and half his clothes sailed by on the dusty four-lane highway.

After they finished lunch Carla called New Orleans and had her travel agent search the area for a car rental place that would deliver. In fifteen minutes the agent called back to say there was a place in Reno, Nevada, that could have them a car by ten that night. Five hundred dollars' delivery and fifty a day. "We'll take it," Carla said. "Charge it to my card."

Carla called the service station to check on the Lincoln. The attendant said the tow truck still hadn't come to take it to the dealer-

ship in Bishop. She gave him her cell phone number and told him she
would pay him to call her when it came.

"Would you take fifty dollars to drive me back to the motel?" she
asked the cashier at the restaurant.

"Sure," he said. "But you have to wait until the lunch crowd
clears out."

"We'll wait." Carla went back to the table where the remains of
their lunch had not been cleared away. The pie plate was covered with
flies. She sat down at a clean table and DeLesseps joined her and they
sat like that for a long time, talking about times they had been in
California with different people they had been married to or sleeping
with. By the time the cashier came and found them and said he could
drive them back, they had become friends again, full of each other's
stories and jealous of everyone each of them had ever known.

The cashier's name was Frank Donald. He was twenty-six years old,
had been an Orkin field man for a while in Los Angeles and returned
to Weggins to decide what to do next. He was a stepson to Will
Maynes, the clerk at their motel. Frank said he wanted to go to the
motel anyway to borrow a shovel for digging up a broken sewer line
in his mother's yard.

"So that's about it for my story up to now," he said, turning into
the parking lot at the motel. "What room are you guys in?"

"Three one three," DeLesseps answered. "You can just let us out."

"I'll be up at the office if you want to go anywhere else." Frank
took the fifty-dollar bill Carla gave him and looked embarrassed.
"This is way too much money. I'll take you someplace else if you like.
We have a movie house in town, where you rent movies for the VCR
on your TV. You may have some time to kill. Or I could just drive you
around and show you the town and where folks live. We have a Hopi
ruin about ten miles from here where some professors from the uni-

versity are digging. You can see part of the main kiva, that's where they did their religious ceremonies. It's pretty cool really. We used to hang out there after dances when I was in school. I know all about it. You have to walk to get there. You got any good boots with you?"

He was still talking while DeLesseps was opening the door and still there when DeLesseps discovered what had happened. "We've been robbed," DeLesseps said. "Goddamn it all to hell. What next? Is there anything else that can go wrong this week?"

"What?" Carla said. "What, what, what?"

Thirty minutes later both of the policemen in Weggins were there and ten minutes after that the sheriff and the sheriff's deputies. Carla and DeLesseps were ordered to stay out of the room while the deputies dusted it for fingerprints.

Carla called her insurance agent in New Orleans, then called her lawyer, then called her travel agent, then tried to call Mitzi for the fifteenth time that week. Then the rented car arrived from Las Vegas with a second car following to take the driver back to Las Vegas. It was a Dodge Intrepid. It was not the Mercedes Carla had ordered, but she took it nonetheless. Frank suggested they go into town to the sports bar to get a drink while they waited for the fingerprint experts to arrive from Holcomb and do their work. Carla stormed into the motel room and demanded her cosmetic kit and when they refused she screamed until they took the things she wanted out of the kit and put them in a paper bag and handed them to her. Holding the bag, she stalked back to the Dodge Intrepid and got in behind the wheel. DeLesseps got in the passenger seat and Frank got in the back.

"We're going to Willy B's to have a drink," Frank told the sheriff. "These visitors have had enough for one day."

"Go on," the sheriff said. "Get them out of here."

*　　　*　　　*

Carla Ozburt and DeLesseps Johnston and their new best friend, Frank Donald, were settled down in a booth at Willy B's, a sports bar on the main street that was the meeting place for everyone who was anyone in Weggins. Willy B's had been the local drugstore when Frank's father was a boy, then a restaurant, and, finally, when a man who had been in the Korean War and played football for his regiment there came home to stay, had turned into a bar with three large television sets, "no smoking" signs everywhere, and a bartender who kept the place as clean as a barracks and allowed no bad behavior. There were always flowers on the tables because the bartender's girlfriend owned and ran the local flower shop.

"What time is it?" Carla asked. "I feel like I don't know where I am anymore."

"It's four o'clock in the afternoon," DeLesseps said. "We ought to call the service station again and see what's happened with the Lincoln."

He took Carla's cell phone and called and the owner said the tow truck had just pulled in. The tow truck driver got on the phone and assured DeLesseps that the Lincoln would be at the dealership in Bishop before it closed at six.

"We're moving across the desert leaving things behind like the early settlers did," DeLesseps said. "I'm starting to feel light."

"There's no point in hoping you're going to get that stuff back from the motel," Frank put in. "If I was you I'd just get a night's sleep and then drive that Intrepid on wherever you are going. You said you'd called the insurance people and it all was covered, didn't you?"

"Yes." Carla sipped her Diet Coke. She had stopped drinking twenty-six years ago when she was pregnant with Mitzi and had never started again. She didn't go to bars. Willy B's was the first bar she had agreed to enter in years. "I'm sorry about your clothes, DeLesseps. I know how much you liked that jacket."

"It's okay." He was sipping a light beer and feeling better. He had expected Carla to go into one of her moods, but she was acting nice. You never could tell with Carla what she might decide to do.

"So where are you folks heading?" Frank asked.

"We are going to San Francisco to see about my daughter, Mitzi," Carla said. "She is in love with a priest. You can see why I'm in a hurry."

"So how does that play out?" Frank asked. "I was raised a Methodist. I don't know what Catholics do. We have problems with our preachers sometimes, that way, you know." He put his hands around his beer bottle and tried to get the feel of the problem.

"It doesn't play out," Carla said. "I'm going there to talk her out of it or bring her home to Louisiana."

"What does she say about it?"

"She won't talk to me. I have called her sixteen times and left her messages and she doesn't return my calls."

"Far out. How old is she?"

"Twenty-six years old. She's my only child."

"Well, I guess you better drive on up there and see about it. Just drive the rental car and come back through Bishop and pick up your Lincoln on your way home."

"That's what we're going to do," DeLesseps put in. "That's our only option, don't you think?"

"There's another hour of sunlight," Frank suggested. "We could go out and see the Hopi ruin. It's not far from here. I think you'd be glad you saw it. It's about the most interesting thing around Weggins."

"Let's go." Carla pushed her Diet Coke to the middle of the table and the men left their beers and followed her to the Intrepid and she handed Frank the keys. "Take us to this Indian place."

"It's on a mesa," Frank told them as he drove down the two-lane high-way going east. "The land flattens out at Weggins, but there are still mesas out here. This kiva is the last one. They told us in school it was the last one ever found this far west of the Painted Desert. They don't know much about those Hopis. They died out, but when they were here they must have been real smart because they built these cliff dwellings just like the way the earth throws up mesas. And some of them have lasted so long now. They had a real civilization and they were peaceful people too. We had a family of Hopis in Weggins when I was a kid but they moved away one summer. They were nice people. There was a boy a year younger than me who was a good athlete. We hated to see him go. Look out there, you can see the land starting to go up. See the mesa."

Ten minutes later they had parked the car by the side of the road and were walking across flat, scrub-covered, hard-packed red soil toward a hill with structures that looked like they had been designed by Frank Lloyd Wright. Around the base of the mesa were sawhorses and bright orange tape held down by steel spikes. A pickup truck was parked beside a pile of stones. A young woman wearing khaki pants and a pale blue jacket was sitting on one of the stones, writing on a legal pad.

"Nellie Anding," she said, getting up and holding out a hand. "I'm a geologist from the University of Nevada. We're excavating here, as you can see."

"Frank Donald," the driver said. "I live in Weggins. I've been coming out here since I could drive. You don't mind if I show my visitors the kiva, do you? I mean, you aren't keeping people out, are you?"

"No. I hope you won't move any of our markers, of course, but I won't be territorial. We have a permit to dig, of course, but not to tell anyone they can't be here. Would you like me to give you a tour? Everyone else is gone. I'm just cleaning up some paperwork." She smiled and put her notebook and pen down on the ground beside a backpack.

She was about five-seven, wiry and athletic, with dark hair pulled back into ponytails. She was wearing a large man's watch with a compass. In her ears were long silver earrings, very shiny and simple against her small, pretty face. "It gets lonely out here in the afternoons. It's a holy place and you feel it when the sun starts going down. I'm glad to have company."

"Where are your headquarters?" Frank asked, moving in. "Where are you guys staying?"

"We were camping for a couple of weeks, but now we're at the Best Western in Weggins," she said. "You live there? We're trying to hire some local people to help with the sorting. You might put me on to someone. It's not hard work, just tedious."

"I might do it," he said. "What can you pay?"

"Ten dollars an hour, as of yesterday. We just got our funds renewed by the university. We're celebrating that." She smiled again, the same beautiful, wide, intelligent smile that had greeted them when they came walking up. Then she turned her attention to Carla and DeLesseps. "I don't know how much you know about Hopi culture," she began. "Come on, walk this way. You're lucky to see the kiva in this light. It gets really spooky when the sun starts moving down those mountains over there. That little range." She pointed due west.

"I don't know much," Carla said. "But I had a book of photographs by Edward Curtis with Hopis in it. The best photograph in the book was a group of Hopi women. I copied it. I traced it and drew it and colored it. I used to paint when I was younger."

"These ruins might make you paint again," Nellie said. "Follow me."

They climbed the mesa to a set of small steps that led up to the flat-topped ruin. Very carefully, one at a time, they climbed to the top and then went down into the kiva and stood there with the red and purple and orange light of the setting sun lighting up the stone- and mud-daubed walls, and it was very, very holy. It was a long time before

Carla remembered what she was doing there and thought to say a prayer for Mitzi. "Guide her to the right way," Carla prayed. "Take over, God, because I'm about to give up."

She climbed out of the kiva and sat down upon a stone outcrop and put her head into her hands and began to cry. DeLesseps followed her and sat beside her, patting her on the back. "I'm sorry about the jewelry," he said.

"It doesn't matter," Carla said. "I hate all that old heavy stuff anyway."

Frank and Nellie stayed in the kiva being quiet, then they moved up the small stairs and walked around Carla and DeLesseps and began to climb down to where there was a smaller room on the far side of the mesa. "We think this is an apartment where people lived," Nellie was saying. "We have excavated this for weeks and can't find a thing but one comb that isn't Hopi."

Carla reached into her pocket for a small gold rosary she had brought along for emergencies. As she touched it her cellular phone started ringing. She glanced at the number and then answered it.

"I'm really sorry, Momma," Mitzi started saying. "I know you're mad at me for not calling you and you should be mad but something's going on that I just had to . . . well, not talk about just yet. What do you know?"

"That you are living with an ordained priest and that's what I expected to happen when you went to California."

"Momma, listen. You don't know the rest. If you'd let me explain you'd feel better." There was static on the line. Carla stood up and walked down to a cleared place on the mesa and tried again.

"Can you hear me?" Mitzi said.

"Yes. I am in Arizona, Mitzi. I am on top of a mesa at a kiva of the Hopi Indian Nation. The air is very clear up here. I haven't had to take an antihistamine all day. I am coming there."

"Coming where?"

"To San Francisco or Berkeley or wherever it is that you have chosen to lose your mind in. I'll be there tomorrow. The Lincoln broke down. I'm driving a Dodge."

"Oh, Momma."

"DeLesseps is with me. He has been very kind. We are with thoughtful people who are caring for us and tomorrow morning we will drive on to where you are. I don't know how long it will take in the Intrepid."

"Momma, I wish you weren't doing this but I want to see you. I love you, Momma. I miss you very much and I love you."

"You had better and you should. Tell me how to get there after we get into town."

"It's complicated. It depends on how you come. What road will you be on?"

"How would I know? You stay there at your house so I can call you."

"I have to go to work. Do you have that number?"

"I supposed you'd quit since they said you hadn't been there for a week."

"Who told you this? How did you find out?"

"I won't talk about that now. I'll call you tomorrow. I have to hang up now. We are on a mesa as I told you. I love you, Mitzi. Do not do anything you will regret until I get there."

Carla turned off the cell phone and put it in her pocket. She turned to DeLesseps. "Well, she called. That's a beginning, I suppose." She took his hand and they began to walk hand in hand down the mesa. At the steps he kept his hand on her sleeve as she descended the steep, narrow little stairs. To the west the sun was all the way down to the horizon. Only the brilliant red and purple and lavender and golden plumes were left to light the desert. "There will be splendid stars tonight," Nellie told them, when they had come to where

Nellie and Frank were waiting. "There are stars out here some nights that are all the philosophy a man or woman could ever need. Be sure and get out of town and look at them. You won't see this in many places."

They decided to eat dinner at a place Frank knew about that was near-by and then drive back to the kiva to see the stars. "Come with us," Carla said to Nellie. "We're stuck in transit. We'd like the company."

"All right," Nellie said. "I'll go with you. If there's a restaurant near here I should find out about it for my helpers."

"It's not a restaurant," Frank added. "It just has hamburgers and shakes and sometimes a few other things. It's part of a country store." He paused. "They have pickled eggs and cheese and crackers."

The store was not a disappointment. It sold turquoise and silver jewelry, and Carla couldn't resist buying two bracelets and a belt buckle. All four of the travelers splurged on chocolate milk shakes with their burgers. "I guess I've only gained five pounds." Carla laughed. "I don't think I've gained ten."

"You haven't gained an ounce," DeLesseps insisted. "You're as thin as a rose."

They went back to the mesa at dark. The stars were out in full battal-ions, millions upon millions of stars and galaxies and shooting stars, and around and behind the stars the blackness of eternity moving past infinity into concepts no human mind can grasp.

"Maybe there are reasons," Carla said to DeLesseps. "Maybe he wasn't really a priest. Maybe he was still thinking about whether to be ordained."

"We'll find out soon," DeLesseps said. "Look up there where the Big Dipper is near those Seven Sisters. Look at that bunch of them down near the end of that. Good grief, Carla. How did we get here?"

"How does anyone get anywhere?" she answered.

9

MITZI AND NORA JANE were sitting on stools in the kitchen. Nora Jane was drinking grapefruit juice. Mitzi was drinking a glass of white wine. It was seven o'clock in the evening. Father Donovan was holding an Alcoholics Anonymous meeting at the church. Freddy was at the bookstore. The children were in their rooms.

"They'll be here tomorrow night," Mitzi said. "God knows what they'll do."

"Don't care what she does. Just tell her what you are doing. If she doesn't like Donny, then that's that. Tell her to go away."

"You don't know Momma. She's going to start making everyone cry."

"Maybe not. Well, don't suffer it now and tomorrow night too. How are things going with his negotiations with the church?"

"They're acting pretty nice. What with all the stuff that's been going on this year, the church can't afford any bad publicity. They want him to keep running the Crisis Center and doing the AA meetings. He isn't officially out until we marry. It's weird, they just keep stalling, hoping he'll change his mind, I guess."

"He won't."

"Well, he sure isn't celibate anymore. I'll tell you that."

"You can have the wedding here if they won't do it in the church.

We had Nieman and Stella's wedding. Stella's pregnant, did you know that?"

"I know. I think it's great. Donny and I want a lot of kids. As many as we can afford." Mitzi looked scared somehow and Nora Jane reached across the table and took her hand.

"It's all good, honey, and it's going to be all right. I think we're in for some good luck this year. I feel it in my bones. Your mother will love Donovan. He's a charming man."

"We'll see. We'll see what happens."

"I want you to bring them over here next week as soon as you can. We'll just overwhelm and dazzle them."

"All right. That's good. I will."

Freddy came in the back door. He was thin and he definitely looked like he'd been sick, but there was an air about him of power also, like a runner nearing the end of a desperate race — an air of being, by God, unbeatable. He came into the room and kissed his wife and turned to Mitzi as though she were the only person in the world. "How's it going, Jezebel? You holding up in your love affair?"

"My momma's on her way." Mitzi laughed. "It's weird the way they keep after you, no matter how old you get or where you go. She's a devout Catholic. She probably thinks I've burned my bridges with God and Jesus."

"So much is happening." Freddy laughed and leaned nearer to Mitzi. "But things keep working out. Don't worry, Mitzi. Let her come. You can't keep mothers away if they think you're in danger."

"They're stuck in the desert with a broken car," Mitzi added, "and they went to see some Hopi ruins and Mother thinks she's on a holy quest."

"We'll holy quest her then," Freddy said. "Look, is there anything to eat around here? I'm starving."

"We had meat loaf and wild rice and it's in the oven," Nora Jane said. "Sit down and I'll fix you some."

"What's her name?" Freddy asked. "Your sainted mother."

"Carla," Mitzi said. "Wait until you meet her. She'll fit right into California. My worst fear is that she'll like it here."

"We're going to get to meet her," Nora Jane said. She put a place mat and napkin on the table and then a plate of beautiful, fragrant meat loaf with wild rice and asparagus. "Mitzi's going to bring them over one evening."

"I can't wait," Freddy said and dug into the meat loaf with his fork. "I mean it. I am looking forward to watching Mitzi wrangle with her mother. I may write a book about mothers. Nieman's going to help me. It's going to be a primer for people who never got to be in psychotherapy."

10

THE FOLLOWING SATURDAY MORNING
Nieman and Freddy were sitting on chairs on the patio watching the
workmen put the finishing touches on the hot tub. It was a cold clear
day, one of those days in early spring in Berkeley that drive visitors to
dream of buying houses in the hills and never leaving the lovely place.
"The Dominicans are a strange bunch," Nieman was saying. "Just like
them to take this in their stride."

"They offered Donny a post at the library of their college or to
administrate the antipoverty programs," said Freddy. "And he'll be
able to keep on working with the outreach programs—Alcoholics
Anonymous and the Crisis Center. What the hell, he fell in love and
wanted to get laid. Those guys had better start knowing how to deal
with that or they are through."

"Not in our lifetimes, old buddy. The contemplative life is too
seductive. The whole thing's seductive. Praying, living on the high
moral ground, the whole mystical range—all we don't, can't, know.
We're blaming Stella's pregnancy on the nun's prayers, by the way."

"It wasn't just your nun." Freddy laughed. "Donovan had the
Maryknoll nuns praying for me too. The way we found out was they
sent us a card. Wait a minute. You need to see this." Freddy got up and
went into his study and Nieman watched him walk away. He was as
thin as he had been when he was a boy but his hair was full and strong

and his color was good. He was clear-eyed, a phenomenon Nieman had noticed before in cancer survivors. Maybe it was all that rest. My best friend, Nieman thought, and we talk about anything except what's happening. It's the razor's edge, waiting to see if old Larry's DNA can make it. But Freddy doesn't want to think he's waiting. He and Nora Jane are acting like it's over.

"We are going to work on the house in Willits next week," the Mexican supervisor said. "Freddy said you helped build it. Is very good work. You must have been strong man back then."

"Thanks, Fernando. I was strong. I may come up and help you guys this spring. Get my muscles back in shape."

"We will be living up there for two months. Freddy said there is a mountain lion there we must see. You have seen it also?"

"Many times. I don't like the lion as much as he does. I think wild animals are dangerous."

Freddy returned from his bedroom carrying a small, pale blue envelope containing a square of colored paper printed with the seal and order of the Sisters of Maryknoll and informing him that in his name fifty masses had been said around the world. Nieman held it and then passed it to Fernando. "Have you seen one of these?"

"Oh, yes," he answered. "They make money from this. My wife say they don't remember the names even, just put with so many other people. They cost much money. Was it a gift from friend?"

"Yes." Freddy laughed and took the card back and put it in his pocket. "I can't afford to be cynical about anything these days, Fernando."

"Nieman is going to come help on house when we get started there. You should come too. Help build you back up from time in bed." Fernando moved near to Freddy and put his hand on his arm. "You need to eat more. Build up your body." Freddy put his arms around the man and gave him a mighty hug. Then he stood back and flexed his muscles.

"Nieman's wife is going to have another baby," he told Fernando. "She may not let him go to Willits and help pour concrete. He may be here babysitting until we're sixty years old."

"You must not let the women tell you what to do." Fernando looked serious. "They will take *cajones* away. They are always looking for way to do that to you. Do not allow it in your house. It is not good."

The three men walked over to the edge of the patio and looked out across the waters of San Francisco Bay. They looked toward the ocean, where men could live without women if they wanted to. "My sister's boyfriend cut his face in two on surfboard yesterday," Fernando offered. "See, if you let them have your, how you call it, balls, they will drive you to ride on waves to get away from them and then you cut your face open in the sport. It is very sad. She will leave him now. She only like him because he was pretty. It is going to be very sad. I blame it on men losing *cajones* and not running their homes."

"They used to go into monasteries and be monks," Freddy said. "Maybe surfing is the modern equivalent of that."

"This conversation has wandered too far afield," Nieman said. "I came over here to take you for a health walk. Are we going or not?"

"Okay," Freddy said. They said good-bye to Fernando and walked down the long winding hill to Levittson Street, where they could cut over to the running track behind Arthur Goldwyn Magnet School, which specialized in getting twelve- to fifteen-year-old students into the movie industry.

"The Dominicans were in charge of the Inquisition," Nieman said. They had started up a long hill and he wanted to keep Freddy's mind off the pain. "Remind Donovan of that if he needs it."

"He doesn't seem to be needing anything. Mitzi Ozburt's mother is in town, staying at the Richelieu Guest House in Berkeley and buying them a house. She told Nora Jane she thought it was a great investment."

"Buying them a house. That's manipulative."

"I'm sure it is. I have to have dinner with all of them tonight. I know, we should welcome life in all its forms and embrace people's craziness."

"Where did you get that idea? Not from me, old friend."

"Someone told me that recently. I thought it was you. I have a lot of confused memories from the hospital. I wish I knew what they were giving me."

"Sister Anne Aurora knows," Nieman said. "She was praying to the molecular systems of the drugs, talking to them in the abstract and universal. She's coming out to visit in May. Hey, maybe we can take her up to Willits to see the foundation being poured."

"When is this baby due?"

"August. Maybe for our birthdays."

"That would be cute."

"Shut up or I'm going to stop babying you on this hill." Nieman increased his pace and Freddy struggled along behind him. As they turned the corner to go across the street to the Berkeley campus, Freddy saw his mother's Lexus coming down the street from the other direction. Big Judy was driving, dressed in his gray uniform and wide cap. Mrs. Harwood was riding shotgun. Big Judy stopped the car and Mrs. Harwood rolled down the window.

"What are you doing out here?" she asked. "I don't think they want you out exercising this soon."

"Sure they do, Momma." Freddy leaned in the window and gave her a peck on the cheek, not enough to ruin her makeup, just enough to make her worry that he had ruined it.

"Did you know Stella and Nieman are going to have another baby?" Freddy asked, to keep the spotlight off himself. "Tell Nieman you're happy. We were on our way to pick out flowers for Stella at Kelli's."

"How long have you been out here walking?" she asked.

"Not long," Freddy answered. In his life he had managed almost never to give his mother any data he could protect. "Where are you taking her, Judy?"

"My canasta game," Mrs. Harwood said. "It's at Marilyn Phillips's house this week. Well, don't stay out long without a hat."

"I won't. We have to go now, Momma." Freddy moved back onto the sidewalk and waited while his mother congratulated Nieman and he bent to receive a kiss on the cheek and a message to tell to Stella.

"Well, it's now all over Northern California," Freddy said as Big Judy drove off and Nieman rejoined him. "AMBER ALERT, STELLA'S PREGNANT. POOR STELLA, MARRIED TO NIEMAN GLUUK."

"We really ought to send Stella some flowers," Nieman said. "That's a fine idea. Let's send some to Nora Jane and maybe some to Mitzi Ozburt's mother and anyone else we can think of to send some to."

They continued to walk toward the campus, then cut off on a side street and found a little flower shop that was owned by one of Nieman's old confederates at the *Chronicle,* a Marxist who'd been fired for writing book reviews that panned everything that didn't suit her politics. She had sued the paper, then taken the settlement, married her girlfriend in a wedding ceremony that included part of *A Midsummer Night's Dream* performed by actors from Spoken Word Theater, and opened a flower shop. She made sixty or seventy thousand dollars a year for doing six hours' work Monday through Friday and was a happy woman, content to watch the United States spend itself into trillion-dollar debt, believing her ideas would triumph if she waited.

★   ★   ★

Freddy and Nieman wandered around the shop, examining the flowers, then walked over to the cash register and spoke to Kelli, who was reading a book by the Italian Marxist Antonio Gramsci. "Listen to this," she said. "'The crisis consists precisely in the fact that the old is dying and the new cannot be born; in this interregnum a great variety of morbid symptoms appears. . . . '"

"Wow," Freddy said. "Listen, can we get some of those yellow roses delivered today to several different places?"

"Twenty dollars a dozen, just for you. They're not that fresh, but I won't have any more for a few days."

"They're okay." Freddy started writing down the names and addresses of the recipients of the roses. Nieman stood beside him holding a potted gardenia he had picked up from a table in the back of the shop. "So when is Mitzi coming over with her mother?" he asked.

"Tonight. God forbid. They're all Catholics. Not a freethinker among them, unless the mother's boyfriend turns out to be one."

"Send the mother some roses too," Nieman said. "Soften her up. I'll pay for them. I'm in an expansive mood, Freddy."

"I'll split the bill with you. Maybe I'll send Francis some too. She's run the store the whole time without me and didn't even call me and complain."

"Send this gardenia plant to someone. I really like these things and they last a long time." He looked at the price tag. "Let's send this to your mother." Freddy turned around and examined the gardenia plant, then took it from Nieman and put it on the desk by the cash register.

"Are you guys feeling guilty about something?" Kelli asked. She was tall and skinny and rakishly dressed for a Marxist. She had been a dancer until she was converted in the sixties and she did not forget her dancing roots. "Why are you sending all these flowers all of a sudden?"

"A friend of ours got a priest to quit the church," Nieman said. "Don't you think that rates a few flowers?"

"I think it rates a discount. How about twenty percent for the lot?"

"Thanks, Kelli. But you don't have to do that."

"I want to do it. So write down the addresses and stop pretending to examine the flowers. You don't know a damn thing about flowers, Nieman."

"I might. Don't be too sure of that. My wife's pregnant with our second child, Kelli. Would you have thought that of me?"

"Of course. You have a bourgeois soul, Nieman. I always knew you'd revert to type."

She reached behind herself and picked a pale pink daisy and reached over and stuck it into Nieman's buttonhole. "No offense intended," she said and smiled at him.

Freddy and Nieman left the store and decided to walk back to Freddy's house the way that they had come. "I can't do five miles yet," Freddy said. "I'm feeling normal half the time, but the energy hasn't come back."

"Do you want to talk about it or do you want to forget it? I'd be glad to talk about it if you want to."

"I want to blot it. I want to go back to being someone who isn't a cancer survivor or victim or subject. I just want it to be done."

"Good. Let's do that. Walk faster. You won't get the hemoglobin back until you force it. Let's try to double-time that hill. After that it's downhill all the way."

"Okay. Let's go." They trudged off together, past the lovely gardens of a row of restored houses and up a long hill to where the street parted and moved down into Freddy's neighborhood. "Breathe," Nieman kept saying. "Watch out where you're going."

11

LITTLE FREDDY WAS IN HIS ROOM, drawing a floor plan for the addition they were going to build at Willits. At Nieman's suggestion he had made a scale model of the existing house. He had it on a card table beside his computer, which used to be Tammili's computer. Because the scale model and the computer took up so much room, Little Freddy had had to spend two afternoons changing everything in his room. He had put all his toys and sports equipment under one of his twin beds. He had taken most of the clothes out of his closet and folded them and put them in stacks underneath the second bed. He had painted his closet brick red with some paint he found in the storage shed and nailed a lot of nails on the walls so he could hang more things there. This arrangement left room along a wall for two card tables. One held the scale model that Lydia had helped him make out of cardboard. The second held the computer. He was sitting at it now, drawing the addition he thought they should build. The problem was that there were too many people now. If they all came to Willits at the same time there would never be enough rooms, because the place where the house was built wasn't wide enough to make many rooms. "I'll make the kitchen all by itself like another house," he decided. He was pondering that idea when his sister came and got him to come meet the visitors from New Orleans.

"Who is it?" he asked. "Why do I have to meet everyone?"

"It's Mitzi's mother and her boyfriend. Come on. You know you have to. It won't take long. What have you done in here? My God, what have you done to your closet? Has Mother seen this?"

"I'm making an office for my work," he said. "Get out. It's not your room."

"Where are your clothes?"

"Under the bed. I folded them. Lydia, come look at this picture. See if you like this."

"You are going to be in big trouble for doing this to your closet . . . Well, never mind. Come on. They're waiting for you." She dragged him off his chair and out the door to the hallway and down the hallway to the living room.

Carla Ozburt was sitting on the sunken sofa, telling everyone about the Hopi ruin outside Weggins, Arizona. She had brought a book about the Hopi dwellings and was showing it to Nora Jane.

Little Freddy walked up and was introduced and began to look at the book.

"This gives me an idea," he said. "This is it, Daddy. This is the way we can fix the house at Willits. Look at this."

His father looked his way. "I'll be there in a minute, son. Mr. DeLesseps Johnston was telling me about their trip. This is Mitzi's mother, Freddy. And Mr. Johnston is her friend and they have driven all the way out here from New Orleans, where your mother lived when she was a little girl."

"But look at this," Little Freddy said. He was holding the book now. They weren't listening. They never listened if company was there.

"It's a mysterious and holy place," Carla said, pointing to the book. She moved nearer to him. Ever since she arrived in the Bay Area she had been searching for someone she could talk to without feeling she had to gauge every word to see if it was correct. The aggrieved look on Little Freddy's face made her think she had found a friend at last. "What are you building that this gives you an idea for?"

"We're making some more rooms for our house in Willits. It's far away from town with twees all over the place. Trreees, I mean." He looked at Lydia, who was listening. It was Lydia who kept threatening him with speech therapy, so he tried to pronounce words when she was around. He turned back to Carla.

"You want to see it? I have a model me and Lydia made and I'm dwawing, I'm drrrawing the plan. See, first you dwaw something if you want to build it. If you dwaw it first you know what to do. You want to see?"

"I'd love to see your drawing." Carla turned to Nora Jane to see if that was all right. Nora Jane was beaming. Nora Jane's favorite people in the world were people who liked Little Freddy as much as she liked him.

"Go with him," Nora Jane said. "Go see what he's doing."

Carla stood up. She was wearing a pink silk pantsuit with a matching lisle sweater and in the moist air her hair was curling around her face in little ringlets. She looked very pretty this afternoon and much younger than her sixty-four years. She liked little boys, because she liked and understood ego and the will to power.

"You won't believe what he's done to his room," Lydia said, moving over to take Carla's place beside her mother. "But we'll go into that later. I don't want to bring it up when we have guests."

"What?" Nora Jane asked. "Tell me now."

Little Freddy made his escape with his new friend, Mrs. Ozburt. "Call me Carla," she said. "My young friends always call me Carla."

"What kind of house do you live in?" Freddy asked.

"An old house that is a hundred years old. It is very tall and has a lot of rooms I don't use. It has flowers all around it. It's in a place called the Garden District, where all the houses are very old. Maybe you will come to New Orleans and see it someday."

"We forgot the book," Little Freddy said. "I'll get it."

Carla waited while he ran back to the living room and got the book of photographs of Hopi ruins. He put the book on the table by the scale model of the house in Willits.

"See this house?" he said. "It's too little for all of us. Dad and Nieman built it when they were at Berkeley to prove you could make things work with just power from the sun. See these things? They are panels that collect power from the sun and it goes into this wire and then the tank over there, and when you need it it can make cold water hot and turn on lights but they don't get very bright so sometimes we have to use flashlights or go to bed when it gets dark, or have candles.

"We like to go there and there's not room for everyone, so our friends that built the hot tub, Carlito and Fernando and their dad, Diego, are going to help us build more rooms but first we have to draw them so they know what to do. They have to know what to bring up there, how many boards and nails and windows." He paused and checked to make sure Carla was really listening. "Me and Nieman are drawing it because my dad was sick and he is just taking it easy now. Okay." He waited while Carla inspected the model of the tall square house with long wide windows on one side. "The reason I like this book is our house is on a sandy hill just like these Hopi dwellings are."

"Mesas," Carla said. "They call those kinds of hills mesas."

"We could make our kitchen and our dining room on one of those hills and not have it in the house where everyone is sleeping, and then if Dad got up early to do his work he could go over there and not wake everyone up making coffee. See?"

"What a wonderful idea, Freddy. I mean it, that's a really good idea."

"See these steps they got here. We could make steps up the side like that." Freddy was drawing on white paper to show Carla what he had in mind. Carla bent over his plans thinking, suddenly, that if Mitzi got married and settled down maybe she, Carla, would have a grand-child and it might be a little boy like this with intent blue eyes and small fragrant hands, moving a pencil across a piece of paper as if to invent the world all over again with every stroke.

Nora Jane and Lydia and Mitzi had come to stand in the door to Little Freddy's room. Freddy and DeLesseps and Tammili had gone out to the yard to see the apple trees Freddy had planted the week before.

It was six o'clock in the afternoon on the tenth of March in the only world there is, on top of one of the most active coastal plates in North America, with a rainstorm coming in over the Pacific Ocean, but not due to arrive until midnight, with babies in the wombs of women and colts in horses and puppies in dogs and kittens in cats, not to mention deer and mountain lions and antelope and moose and squirrels and robins.

Danen Marcus, MD, was watching his wife make pasta. He was madly in love with her again and planning on taking her to France to buy a house in Provence. Sister Anne Aurora was praying for a man in Ocean Springs, Mississippi, who was recovering from surgery; Larry Binghamton was at his ex-wife's house fixing to make the mistake of his life by attempting a reconciliation; and the babies in Stella Light-Gluuk's womb (the fetus had split and become two) were settling down to grow thinking apparatuses at the ends of their spinal columns.

"What happened with this closet?" Nora Jane was asking.

"I fixed it," her son answered. "Carlito gave me the paint."

"Where are your clothes, if I may ask?"

"Under the bed," Carla answered.

"Where are the paintbrushes?" Lydia asked.

"With the paint, out by Carlito's tools in the shed. Come and look at how we could make a kitchen like these Hopi Indians had theirs. Come look, Lydia, don't worry about my room. It's not your room. Don't worry about it."

They all gathered around Little Freddy's drawings. Carla got up and went to her daughter and put her arm around her waist and was content for the first time in months. All of a sudden she just decided to be content.

"There is food in the dining room," Nora Jane said. "I wish some of you would get something to eat."

12

THE NEXT MORNING Carla and Mitzi were in Mitzi's kitchen making coffee in an old-fashioned coffeepot. It was chicory coffee that Carla had brought from New Orleans and it had to be brewed in a percolator, unless you had time to cold drip it, which Mitzi certainly did not, not with all that was going on, planning a wedding; finding a way to sleep with Donovan when her mother wouldn't have to know about it; worrying about Nora Jane and Freddy; working at the shop so she wouldn't get fired; looking for a house for her mother to buy for her; mopping up rainwater every time it rained and water came in the bathroom wall of her rented condominium; trying to find time to get in a few Pilates classes, etcetera.

Her mother was being a doll. She was buying Mitzi a house and talking about buying her a new car.

Mitzi poured the coffee into small blue cups and added boiled milk and sugar. She handed one cup to her mother and took the other one herself. They sat down at a small wooden table painted with flowers. Mitzi had painted it herself one night when she was lonely, before she met Donovan and her life started up again.

"Nora Jane said we could get married in her garden if the church isn't nice about marrying us. Or in that front room with all the pianos and the harpsichord. You saw that room, didn't you?"

"They had better be nice. There's no question of them marrying you, is there?"

"It might take more time than we want to wait. We want to go on and get married, Momma. I mean, right away."

"Before we buy the house?"

"Before I end up pregnant. Donny doesn't like the idea of birth control."

"I see. All right then. Set a date and tell me where there's a florist so I can order flowers."

"I think next Saturday then. A week from tomorrow."

"Who will marry you if not a priest?"

"Nora Jane and Freddy know a federal judge who does it for friends of theirs. He's this very good-looking man who was in a John Grisham movie, that one about the runaway jury. He played himself. It was a real role. All right then. I'll call Nora Jane and see if the judge is free a week from Saturday and we're all set. You're an angel, Momma, to be so nice about everything and buy us a house."

"It's an investment. I'm just letting you live in it. We need to start shopping for clothes. I'm not going to my daughter's wedding in some old dress I find in a mall. Call and find out where the good shops are. I want to go this afternoon."

That was Friday morning. By Saturday afternoon the plans were laid. The ceremony would be at eleven in the morning in Nora Jane and Freddy Harwood's living room. A cake and petits fours were being made at Fantastic Foods in Oakland. Flowers were being delivered from Nieman's Marxist friend's shop; Tammili and Lydia would be bridesmaids in dresses they had worn in the spring for a dance recital. The dresses were long and soft and white. In their hair would be barrettes decorated with cymbidium orchids. Mitzi was wearing an off-white ankle-length cocktail dress and Manolo Blahnik shoes in pale blue. Carla was wearing a pale gray suit with a fitted jacket and shoes to match. Little Freddy had agreed to wear his suit. No one was coming except the Harwoods, the Gluuks, three of Mitzi's friends from the salon, the judge and his wife, and a few other assorted friends.

There would be cake and champagne, and then Mitzi and Donovan were going to a spa near Las Vegas to spend four days being pampered and taking walks in the desert.

"It's so Hollywood," Carla told DeLesseps. "You just pick up a phone and get a wedding going. This would take months to arrange in New Orleans."

"This wedding stuff makes me feel left out," DeLesseps said. "Not that it matters, but I'd like to get married too, as I've told you a dozen times. I'll have more money than you do when my grandmother dies. But I guess you won't marry me until then, will you?"

"No, I won't. But I love you asking." She went to him and let him caress her breasts.

"I love your breasts," he said. "They are as soft as silk."

"They're in my way," she answered. "They ruin the way my blouses fit, so I'm glad someone is getting some use of them."

The wedding went off without a hitch. Things went so well that Carla kept wanting to throw a pinch of salt over her left shoulder to ward off feeling cocky and setting them all up for disaster.

DeLesseps said later he thought the affair was a triumph of specialists being too busy to get in each other's way. Father Donovan reached down into the two years he spent trying to be a writer and wrote a really beautiful ceremony that ended up owing more to Shakespeare than to Saint Paul. Judge Hancock Mayes had most of the good lines and he delivered them in his best and most lyrical voice. Nora Jane found a pianist and sang an *Ave Maria* by Handel. Little Freddy arranged the chairs for the service; Carla concentrated on flower arrangements; Freddy spent a morning at May's Wine Cellar choosing the wines; and Mitzi did everyone's hair, declaring that not only would it keep her from getting nervous but she couldn't bear to see hairdos she didn't like. "Everyone always goes crazy doing hair for weddings," she said. "Too much pouf, too much mousse, too much spray. I'm doing this myself."

Scarlett had an especially fine time, because her parents were busy talking to people and didn't notice how many petits fours and mints she ate and collected in the pockets of the white organdy-and-lace dress Carla had delivered to Nieman's house on the Friday before the wedding. "I had to have it," Carla apologized to Stella. "Please accept it as a gift and let me have my fun."

"We'll let her wear it," Stella said. "Then we'll have to frame it."

13

SPRING MOVED ON INTO SUMMER. Freddy
Harwood continued to grow stronger and was able to take fewer drugs
and get more exercise. At the Gluuks' house, Little Scarlett had a new
outlet for her obsessive-compulsive nature and her organizational
skills. She was collecting toys in a box in her room. She was studying
catalogs of baby clothes and equipment. She was deciding where to
put the cribs. Her first choice would be her room, but she realized that
wasn't going to happen. Stella had bought her a video, *Your Baby Is on
Its Way,* and she loved to watch it. Every month another segment was
added. She got to see the developing fetus, and she understood that her
mother had two babies growing in her womb, so, once again, she
knew that she, Scarlett Jane Gluuk, was blessed and had to work harder
than other people to pay the world back for its largesse.

Stella was also working harder than she had ever worked in her life,
trying to set things up so her lab would run smoothly while she was
gone. "There aren't enough lab technicians in the world for the work
we need done," she said ten times a day, to anyone who would listen.
"We need more students, we need more scholarships. We need more
money. We need high school teachers who can teach science so it is
interesting to students. We need, for God's sake, less football and
more biology. It makes me so mad."

"You can't get mad," Nieman said. "You're incubating twice the human capacity and you can't get mad. I'll get mad for you and I'll go raise money. How much do you need?"

"Billions. Trillions. Never mind. We live in the present moment. We do the work before us. I can work at home if you do the lab work. Aventis Pasteur wants us in on the pandemic vaccines. We have to inoculate the Asian farmers. The World Health Organization is going to run that out of Zurich. You'll have to go to the meetings . . ." Stella lay back on the sofa. Scarlett was across the room playing with a set of small people that belonged in her dollhouse but that she kept in her pockets most of the time. She would only wear clothes with pockets, so Stella sewed pockets onto any clothing that didn't come with them.

"Why does she have to carry everything around with her?" Nieman asked.

"Why does everything have to be lined up? She has a rage for order."

"We shouldn't worry about it?"

"No. Not unless you want to do a gene transplant. Come here, you are so sexy when you worry. There's nothing to worry about. We just have work to do. We need to talk to the dean about more assistants. We need to do that right away, so if you want to worry, work on that."

"Let's go see him then. How about tomorrow?"

"Call him. Start sucking up. Remember when he wanted you to read his film script? Tell him you'll read it."

"All right. I'll call now." Nieman leaned down and kissed his wife on the cheek, then the mouth, then the stomach, twice. He left the room and made the call.

He returned in five minutes. "He'll see us at four. I told him I wanted to see his script. He almost went crazy. Okay. Well, hell, maybe I'll rewrite it for him. I haven't touched one in so long it might be fun. What else can I do for you today?" He knelt beside his wife, his goddess, his angel, his dream come true, his Stella, Stella, Stella.

"I am going to shut down the mess in my laboratory," she said. "It's just ego. I've found two other cold viruses with at least as many similar spikes. It was all just to keep me going while I waited for something to sink my teeth into. I need you to destroy the petri dishes. Put them in the burner. The office should be sterilized and sealed for a while. I may have to use it for the Pasteur work . . . don't look like that. I know when I've hit a dead end. Can you do it today?"

"Of course. I'll ask Elise to help me. We were only doing some cleanup work on the transfer sequences."

An hour later Nieman was in full protection gear, transferring two years of Stella's work into a container for the incinerator. It took less than an hour to remove every trace of two years' work. He checked to make sure all the paperwork was on a computer disk, then called the cleanup crew in to sterilize the lab.

"Do you want it painted?" he asked Stella on his cellular phone.

"Yes. Ivory will do. Like the big labs. And the paint sealed, of course. I talked to Sister Anne Aurora. She wants to come help with the Pasteur work. I told her she was hired."

"The dean will be glad to hear that."

"It's done. He won't complain. How many acts is his script?"

"He said two hundred and five pages."

"I'll hire someone else too."

"Go home and take a nap after lunch. I'll meet you at his office at four."

"Love you."

"Love you too."

Scarlett walked around the dean's office looking at things while the grown people talked. She was wearing a plaid skirt, navy blue tights, and a navy blue sweater with a white collar and cuffs. She was such a perfect little four-year-old girl that the dean hardly noticed when Stella told him she had hired an assistant from Ohio and was planning on hiring two more. "Aventis Pasteur is going to pay the university millions, and it's going to last for several years. So we need a lot of help. The problem is getting anyone who will come."

"Of course. I can find you the money for three positions, I'm sure." The dean was waiting for Nieman to ask for the manuscript, which he had on his desk in a black folder.

Scarlett walked toward him, looking him in the eye. "You have a nice room," she told him. "Your room is bootiful."

"Oh, thank you, Scarlett," he said. "I'm delighted that you like it."

"When can I see the manuscript?" Nieman asked. "I haven't read one in a while. It will be a nice change."

"It's right here." The dean handed it across the desk. Nieman took it. Stella stood up. "Three assistants for next semester, or as soon as I can find them, then? Thanks, Carl, you are the best. The other thing is the outreach program for high school seniors and the programs for high school teachers. We need to talk about that soon. It's never been more critical."

"Everything is critical. You wouldn't believe, you don't want to know, what's happening in this university."

"Complexity is part of life." Stella stood up and looked at him with kindness and real sympathy. "Be strong, Carl. We're lucky to get to do this work."

"I know. I forget. Don't worry about the manuscript, Nieman. I'm honored you would read it. I appreciate it so much."

"I'll get to it right away. You won't mind if I mark it up."

"Heavens no. I hope you do. I know it's silly to dream of writing a film, but it is the main way we influence the public now. Books are preaching to the choir, I'm afraid."

"Then we'll get you a film." As he said it Nieman decided he meant it. "I'll be glad to help."

*　　　*　　　*

So began the impetus that led to the inception that led to the rewriting and making of the Oscar-winning *The Nun's Discovery*, about a nun from Ohio who came to San Francisco to work as a secretary, then as lab assistant to a scientist who was dying of leukemia. She not only healed the scientist with prayer but discovered the vaccine for the bird-flu virus that was killing thousands all over Asia.

The film starred Stockard Channing as the scientist and Dakota Johnson, daughter of Melanie Griffith and Don Johnson, as the nun, with Brad Pitt as the young researcher who falls in love with the nun and agrees to take the vaccine because the nun can't allow it to be tried on primates.

Brad lives, the nun gets laid, the vaccine works, and the labs at Berkeley made fourteen million dollars in royalties the first year and continued to make money for the next ten.

It was July. Tammili and Lydia were in the pool house going over a study book for the SAT. Lydia had given up and started sunbathing. "You can't use Daddy's illness as an excuse to quit trying," Tammili was saying. "He is getting well. He is not going to die."

"You all keep saying that, but he isn't getting well very fast or he wouldn't have to keep going to the doctor and he wouldn't be so tired all the time. I hate the SAT. I'm going to acting school or to art school. I don't want to go to Stanford. Go to Stanford if you want to and I'll come and visit you."

"I'm going to Harvard, Lydia. I'm only going to Stanford if I can't get into Harvard."

"Then go on. I don't care." Lydia got into the swimming pool and swam long, slow laps. Her tears were mixing with the water and she felt her heart beating against her bathing suit. She was tired of trying to be things she didn't want to be.

She pulled herself up at the deep end. Tammili was squatting by the edge, waiting for her to stop. "You are almost there, Lydia," she said. "You had good scores on the practice tests. Just study one more hour and then we'll quit for the day. You don't have to go to college but you need to get in so you can say you quit because you wanted to."

Lydia pulled herself out of the pool and sat beside her sister. "I'm sad," she said. "Too much is changing."

"Life is change. Think how bored we'd be if everything stayed the same."

"All right. Ask me questions."

"How large is the universe?"

"We don't know."

"Right. What makes people happy?"

"Work and love. Money. Money makes them really happy."

"What does money represent?"

"Power. Get in the pool. It's July, Tammili. Those questions are not on the SAT."

Nora Jane was spending the summer doing Pilates and yoga. She was making desserts from a fabulous Italian cookbook Carla Ozburt had given her as a gift for having Mitzi's wedding. She was trying not to worry about the future or Freddy's health. She was making lists and writing in a journal. "Ninety-nine percent of what we have is good," she had written that morning. "And some of it is not so good and scary. He's probably going to be all right. Graft-versus-host disease is not going to do us in, and if it starts there are plenty of things they can do for that. Don't start thinking negative thoughts when we have just been the recipients of a miracle made for sure by human hands and maybe also by love and prayer."

To do today:

1. Stop worrying.
2. Practice scales for an hour or do breathing exercises.
3. Stay home and don't drive the car unless you have to.
4. Be here now. That really is a good idea even if it seems stupid the first few times you hear it.

In the spirit of carpe diem and let the good times roll and trust your instincts, especially after the near death drumroll, Freddy and Nieman were hatching a plan to spring their innocent and still trusting younger children, Scarlett and Little Freddy, from the clutches of their mothers and their mothers' surrogates in the private-school system of Berkeley, California. It had begun as a plot to homeschool them, then, more realistically, turned into a plan to keep them home one day a week and take them to learn things they would never learn in school. This latter plan was posited on the hope that Nora Jane would not refuse Freddy anything after his scary drumroll, and Stella would have to go along or be thought a spoilsport.

"Stella was homeschooled herself," Nieman said. "She studied in the back of a station wagon while her parents drove around California being hippies. When it was cold they would spend whole days in libraries or art museums. She was twelve years old before they put her in a regular school. Of course she doesn't look on that as the boon you or I would have thought it was, given our proscribed little lives."

"We will start with the Palomar telescope and astronomy," Freddy said. "Then move to the microscopes. Then move back and forth between the infinite and the microscopic, with stops at painting and sculpture and canyons and dinosaur digs. If we take them out on Fridays we will have entire weekends. Maybe Tammili and Lydia will come along for some outings."

"We better not broach it until the babies come," Nieman said, pursing his lips and starting to get nervous. He and Freddy were at Bread and Chocolates, indulging in caffe latte and croissants and dark chocolate bars from the Netherlands. It had been their favorite meeting place for years.

"There's no hurry," Freddy said. "I just want to get it in the planning stage. Francis is getting me the stats on homeschooled children and their achievements. Nora Jane doesn't like data as much as Stella does, but she does sometimes believe it."

"Good always comes from bad," Nieman mused. "Like when you had to move out of your house for a year and had time to spend at the beach."

"Don't remind me of that year. Okay, so we're set. You'll definitely do it if I will."

"Sworn. Progress is being made. We had to be brainwashed and bored five days a week. Our children will suffer for four. Perhaps their children will only have to go Mondays, Wednesdays, and Fridays."

"Eat your croissant. They're really fine today. I heard they had a new chef. Someone Augustine brought in from Quebec."

Nieman broke off a piece of croissant, put it into his mouth, lifted his eyebrows in delight, and began to chew. A wide shaft of sunlight came down through the clear glass windows and cut a line across the marble table.

"It's all good," Freddy said.

"You bet it is," Nieman answered. "You bet your life it is."

A Reading Group Guide

NORA JANE

A LIFE IN STORIES

ELLEN GILCHRIST

A conversation with
Ellen Gilchrist

Your first book wasn't published until you were in your forties. How and when did you decide to become a writer?

I always thought I was a writer. I didn't begin to write seriously and professionally until I was in my forties because I was busy being alive.

Your novels and stories are largely populated by an ongoing cast of characters—individuals and families whose lives intersect and occasionally collide. Is this something you've planned?

I have planned my oeuvre the same way I have planned my life. On a day-by-day and obsession-by-obsession basis.

What writers have influenced you the most over the years? What writers working today do you admire?

My strongest influences are the British and American poets of the last four hundred years and the Greek poets and playwrights and all the British and American literature that I have devoured over the years. It is all a jumble. I adore William Shakespeare and William Faulkner and anyone who writes beautifully about anything they know well and feel passionately about. There are many writers mentioned in my books, here and there, scattered about. I put them there as homage. I am still being influenced every day by everything I read. Freeman Dyson is a favorite and John Fowles and many more too numerous to mention.

Nora Jane suffers—and also benefits—from her passionate nature. Do you think that passion is the overwhelming force that drives people to their destinies?

No. People are driven by two emotions: fear and excitement. If you aren't paralyzed by fear, you run toward excitement. Nora Jane had a chaotic childhood. What she wants is an ordered life and things she can depend upon. So I gave her the most wonderful and dependable man I could create, and she is wise enough to love him. All young people are driven by passionate desires, but Nora Jane outgrew that insanity more quickly than most young women do.

How do food and literature provide comfort to Nora Jane and company?

The same way they provide comfort to all people everywhere. Cave dwellers sitting around a fire eating scorched meat and telling stories are no different from Nieman Gluuk reading Rilke and taking children to a four-star restaurant.

Most of your fiction has a southern setting. Nora Jane, however, takes place primarily in Northern California. How does setting affect your writing?

I set the Nora Jane stories in Northern California because at the time I was writing many of them I was visiting a friend in San Francisco for long periods of time and had become fascinated with that world, its bridges and earthquakes and Asian peoples and food and ideas. I would stand for long minutes reading the posters tacked up to telephone poles in Berkeley, dazzled by the range of ideas that were floating around and being taken seriously by many people.

Your first story about Nora Jane was published in 1981. Fault Lines was written more than twenty years later. What special qualities does Nora Jane have that compelled you to return to her and her family over the years?

I always keep wondering where my characters are and what they are doing. I never get finished with wanting to know what happened next, so I keep on writing about them to find out. I am not only interested in Nora Jane. I'm interested in Freddy and Tammili and Lydia and Little Freddy and Nieman and Stella and Scarlett, and now I'm wondering what Donovan and Mitzi will be up to next. By the time this book is published, the Gluuk twins will be a year old. I hope Nieman isn't trying to teach them Latin yet.

Questions and topics for discussion

1. Ellen Gilchrist has said that books by Freeman Dyson, a physicist and writer, have influenced her. How is Gilchrist's interest in the scientific world reflected in her fiction?

2. When we first meet Nora Jane, she is smart, headstrong, and willful, with a keen instinct for survival. She doesn't have much money, but her circumstances are altered when she marries Freddy Harwood. Does having money change Nora Jane?

3. Freddy and Nieman have been friends for life, through thick and thin. What do you think draws them together?

4. Many of the romantic relationships in *Nora Jane* have unlikely or challenging beginnings. Discuss.

5. Although Freddy Harwood's family and friends are not devout in a religious sense, they turn to an Episcopalian nun, a Buddhist monk, and Freddy's Jewish community for help when he is diagnosed with cancer. How do prayer and meditation help him and his family? Do you believe that seeking spiritual connection can be helpful in times of need?

6. By the end of *Nora Jane,* Tammili and Lydia are unaware that their father could be someone other than Freddy. Do you think they should be told as teenagers or should have known earlier, or do you think it's acceptable for Nora Jane and Freddy to withhold that information from them indefinitely? Why or why not?

7. Many different mother-child relationships are depicted in *Nora Jane.* Discuss the differences in the relationships between Nora Jane and her mother, Freddy and Mrs. Harwood, and Mitzi and Carla Ozburt. Which relationship most closely mirrors the relationship between you and your mother? Does Nora Jane have any weaknesses as a mother?

8. Stella Light-Gluuk and Nora Jane have very different lives: Stella is a working mother with a brilliant future in science, and Nora Jane has chosen to stay at home with her children. Are they content with the choices they've made? Why or why not?

9. How do you think hopes and dreams shape or define the characters of *Nora Jane?*

Ellen Gilchrist's suggestions for further reading

Great and startling books have taught and changed me, have made me wish for nobility and dream of changing the world. They have solaced me when I was young and in love, made me laugh at myself for needing solace, and helped me grow old without noticing I had. To choose eleven out of the hundreds of books that have had their way with me is difficult, but I will try. To be on the list, the book will have to be one that shook me awake and taught me something I would not have learned in any other way, or else a book so beautiful and seductive that when I finished it I immediately went back to page one and started reading it again. I read the first two books on this list at least three times before I moved on to other fields.

The World As I See It by Albert Einstein
A collection of brilliant, gentle essays by one of the great minds of the past century. The writing is so perfect one can only quote it: "A hundred times every day I remind myself that my inner and outer life depend on the labors of other men, living and dead, and that I must exert myself in order to give in the same measure as I have received and am still receiving."

One Hundred Years of Solitude by Gabriel García Márquez
I began reading this book on a sailboat in the British Virgin Islands. A fellow poet had given it to me, saying it was poetry made into prose, the thing Ernest Hemingway felt we should strive to create. William Faulkner also made poetry into prose, and later I would discover that Márquez had studied Faulkner when the former was learning to write. The opening line is famous among writers. We all wish we could write one this good: "Many years later, as he faced the firing squad, Colonel Aureliano Buendía was to remember that distant afternoon when his father took him to discover ice."

The Territorial Imperative by Robert Ardrey
First published in 1966, this dazzling book about the science of anthropology taught me my place in the universe. On the same boat where I discovered Márquez, a friend handed me this book and changed the way I understood the world. It was full of humbling, exciting ideas. "We may prefer to think of ourselves as fallen angels but in reality we are risen apes," as Ardrey's contemporary Desmond Morris would later put it. Risen apes who could create written language and walk on the moon and transplant hearts and write the Constitution of the United States of America.

The Curve of Binding Energy by John McPhee
I had tried for years to comprehend nuclear power, and finally McPhee, by his magical ability to make the complex understandable, taught it to me. Still, I have to learn it over and over again. The knowledge is too terrible to carry in the front of my brain. People are in denial about the radioactive materials we've created and can't get rid of. If you read only one of the books on this list, let it be this one.

The Riverside Shakespeare

These thirty-nine plays have been my most important writing teachers. They remind me that the greatest author who ever lived wrote bad plays to begin with and then got better and better until he wrote *Hamlet* and *Macbeth* and *King Lear* and *Romeo and Juliet.* For eighteen years, a group of friends have come over on Sunday afternoons to read the plays aloud. No matter how many times we read one of the great plays, I always feel I have never understood it before. There is no way to grasp the genius of Shakespeare. I am content that it exists in the world and that I have copies of the plays and friends to share them with.

North Toward Home by Willie Morris

This is the story of Morris's rise to power as the youngest editor of *Harper's* magazine and of how he left the South behind and shook off the racism he had learned as a child. There is no bitterness in Morris's writing. His book was very important to young people in the South when it was published in 1967. It taught me that it was all right to be a traitor to my family and my culture and to go out on the street and march for civil rights. It was a terrifying adventure, and Morris's book was the bible I carried with me as I marched.

Collected Poems by Edna St. Vincent Millay

Since I was thirteen years old and was taught a poem called "God's World," I have read and loved Millay's poetry. She was a devotee of Shakespeare, and his influence is everywhere in her work. I know all her sonnets by heart, since I read them so assiduously when I was young and always in love with whoever wouldn't love me back. Now that I am older and have read Shakespeare, I hear the echoes between his poetry and lines I loved in Millay. She didn't copy him. She was deeply influenced by him, which is a glorious thing for a reader to discover, like knowing that two friends knew each other in another world.

The Hamlet, The Town, and *The Mansion* (called the Snopes trilogy), and *Go Down, Moses,* a book of stories, by William Faulkner
I think these four books are the heart of Faulkner's work. Eudora Welty told me to read these books. It was the best advice she ever gave me.

ALSO BY

ELLEN GILCHRIST

The Cabal
and Other Stories

"Difficult to resist. . . . It's a comedy of manners, tarted up for the twenty-first century. . . . For entertainment with a bite, you can't go wrong with *The Cabal*."
— Vicky Uhland, *Rocky Mountain News*

Flights of Angels
Stories

"Readers will find the penetrating intellect, deep compassion, and dark sense of humor that mark Gilchrist's best work and place it among the best writing coming out of the South — or anywhere else, for that matter — today."
— Ron Carter, *Richmond Times-Dispatch*

I, Rhoda Manning, Go Hunting with My Daddy
and Other Stories

"Gilchrist levels her keen gaze and wickedly funny wisdom on the relationships we all stumble through — with parents and children, friends and lovers, strangers and those we hold most dear. Her insights will, at times, move you deeply."
— Polly Paddock, *Charlotte Observer*

BACK BAY BOOKS

Available in paperback wherever books are sold

ABOUT THE AUTHOR

Ellen Gilchrist is the author of many books of fiction, including the National Book Award–winner *Victory Over Japan*. In 2004 she received the fifth annual Thomas Wolfe Prize from the University of North Carolina. She lives in Ocean Springs, Mississippi, and in Fayetteville, Arkansas, where she teaches at the University of Arkansas.